CW00459194

AMANDA BECKER

THIS BOND BETWEEN US

A NOVEL

Bibliographic information of the German National Library: The German National Library lists this publication in the German National Bibliography; detailed bibliographic data is available on the Internet at dnb.d-nb.de

TWENTYSIX
A brand of Books on Demand GmbH

© 2022 Amanda Becker

Title of the original edition "Dieses band zwischen uns"
© 2021 Amanda Becker

Contact: AmandaBecker_Autorin@web.de

Production and publisher: BoD - Books on Demand, Norderstedt

Graphics: Nadia Grapes/ Volha Khamitsevich/ Shutterstock.com

ISBN: 978-3-7407-8777-6

For my husband.

Thank you for believing in me and for your support
in making my dreams come true.

Every word of love is for you

Chapter 1

Sophia was annoyed. She had dressed up, was wearing a sexy outfit and her face had been given a frightening makeover. She found her image in the mirror so disgusting that she could no longer look at it. It looked really bad, with the gaping wound on her cheek and forehead, the blood that seemed to run from her eyes. The most violent thing, however, was the contact lens that made her left eye look blind. The creepy make-up had taken her friend Céline two hours. The longest time had been spent on the scars on her face and neck. The swollen scars on her thighs and arm were simply glued on. Céline loved such things. If it had been up to her, she would have been a make-up artist for horror films. If it had been up to her, she would have been a make-up artist for horror films. Instead, she had to work in the family business and keep her love of make-up a hobby. Regardless, she was very well equipped to make all her friends look super creepy tonight.

Ina had searched all her friends' wardrobes for clothes and even bought a few wigs and was happy Sophia had agreed to dress up as a sexy blonde without any protest on her part and highlight all her curves. Sophia had lost a bet and only agreed to being "hot" for one night, if they deformed her face so that no one would recognise her. Because being wild and sexy wasn't her thing. Usually. Of course, she could be wild, but she didn't like her lush curves or, as her friends said, she couldn't really handle them.

Nevertheless, she was looking forward to going out with her

girls and having fun in the bar around the corner. She even decided not to be the sensible one for once and look out for the others, but to relax completely. Maybe even flirt with someone and maybe even let someone kiss her. Well, maybe she would think about that again, but she was in such a good mood that it spoiled her mood extremely when everything went down the drain. Not only had Viviana come from work very exhausted after visiting a client who had to go to prison, but she had also seen Ina's boyfriend on her way to Sophia's, which in itself wouldn't have been a big deal, but Ina broke down and told her that they had only broken up two days ago. Viviana cried with her, because her fiancé Jérôme was still not back from his last trip abroad and would probably be gone for at least another ten days. She missed him very much and wanted to talk to him about the wedding, but it seemed he didn't have the time. Céline could no longer bear to live under the same roof as her stepbrother, because he was constantly making advances toward her. Her mother and his father did not see the point and forced them to be like sister and brother, although it was obvious that he had no brotherly interest in her at all.

All three toasted Sophia and were happy for her, as she had been single for ages, although it had only been two years. Or was it three? Her last relationship had only lasted a few weeks and was barely memorable. They acted as if she had done everything right and had been lucky, but that was exactly the opposite of how Sophia felt. But that wasn't why she was angry. It annoyed her that every three minutes some child from the neighbourhood rang the doorbell and shouted "Trick or Treat!" in the shrillest voice. It was up to her to answer the door all the time, which made her only hear half of her friends' conversation. Every time she came back, it made her feel left out and as if she knew nothing about her friends or their problems.

Speaking of problems, lately it seemed to Sophia that they talked about problems as much as her grandmother and her friends talked about their minor and major health complaints. Instead of talking about hip pain, diabetes or high blood pressure, her friends mainly talked about men, of course. In the past, her friends from school at least talked about different topics, such as grades, pimples and mostly imaginary fat pads, which unfortunately was and still is quite normal among a group of young girls. But when the four of them met, seven years ago when Sophia came to Hamburg at nineteen to work in a gallery and was looking for a room in a shared flat, it was all about the future. Ina and Viviana were already living together and were looking for a new flatmate and had called for an audition. That's how it seemed to Sophia at the time, when she realised that Céline was only there to assess the potential new flatmate and didn't live there herself. She had asked completely different questions than the two she would be sharing the apartment with. Céline literally grilled her about her hobbies and views, started discussions about films and books. When she was asked to wait in the hall for the three of them to discuss, Sophia heard with relief when Céline advised the other two to choose her.

"She's a great match for us. And it doesn't hurt that she already earns money, so you can be sure that the rent will always be paid on time."

It had been a great time, they had spent great days and evenings together, often enough Céline had slept at their place. They had gone on holidays together, even though it was usually a shorter trip for Sophia, as she only got two weeks leave at the most, while the others could extend their holidays for weeks since they were students. That had changed, of course, since they also had to fill out all the applications for leave. It had also generally become more difficult to find a common travel time for a longer holiday, with work commitments and their respective relationships. They did,

9

however, stick to a wellness weekend that they enjoyed once a year, ever since the first of them, Ina, had moved in with her boyfriend.

Sophia was the last to move out of the shared apartment after the landlord had announced personal need. However, she assumed it was due to the wild parties that her new flatmates hosted almost every day.

Sophia missed the times of the shared flat, even though she loved her small flat very much and, to be honest, also enjoyed being alone. She missed the stimulating and horizon-expanding discussions about books, French films and art, but not the constant sitting together, nothing could be done alone back then. The conversations were sometimes about the best low-fat recipes or remedies for skin blemishes after a diet - which, to be honest, none of the four had ever needed. Their families. Of course, there were times when they talked about boys, but not to the extent they did now. Sometimes it seemed to Sophia that her three best friends only defined themselves by the number of their suitors or how many one-night stands they had had. Even though Viviana was already engaged, she still stressed the fact that she had been with many men and would comment on men that she still was rejecting.

On the other hand, it was somehow understandable, Sophia thought. After all, all four of them had got their pimples under control, had more or less come to terms with their bodies and grades or good degrees no longer mattered, now that they all had a job. More or less happy.

Nevertheless, Sophia couldn't quite shake off the feeling that she was somehow left out. The others didn't repeat what they had said when Sophia would re-enter the room and when she asked why she didn't know about one problem or another, they just shrugged.

"I didn't tell you since you're not exactly the relationship expert." Usually, this statement would be followed by a chuckle.

They hadn't seen a man at Sophia's side for a long time and assumed she didn't want one. The comments they would make, were like: "Oh, you don't know these problems."

Made Sophia feel like a stupid, ignorant child. Like she didn't know how hard it was to bear lovesickness or how much you suffered when your heart had been left bleeding. It was sad that her friends couldn't see how she really felt, how her heart ached with pain and longing, but maybe it was her own fault. Apparently, she was just too good at hiding it. The only statement from her girls that she agreed with without hesitation was: "Oh, you weren't there to notice, you were working, you just work too much."

Yes, that was true, but she loved her job at the photographer's agency and since there wasn't much else in her life, she didn't mind the amount of work. But of course, it made her sad, because she also had problems and heartbreak, well, or something like that, but she didn't deal with her feelings as openly as others. Besides, if they knew, they would probably scold her about how stupid she was, or make fun of her about what a cliché it was to fall in love with the boss. And that the way he behaved towards her, he hardly deserved to get anything from her. Except cheeky answers. And of course, they would tell her to ignore him. As if you could choose how love works or who you fall in love with.

However, in order to somehow keep up the mood, she said nothing in response, entertained her friends and ran to the door to hand out sweets every time the doorbell rang. Always anxious to put on the *Hello Kitty* mask that a little girl had lost after being so frightened at the sight of Sophia that she had run away crying. After this little girl's mother complained that she couldn't answer the door looking like that, Sophia felt so bad that she almost cried. She hated making mistakes that hurt others in some way. Being yelled at wasn't okay either, but most of the time she could understand it, even though she tended to keep her frustration and grief to herself rather than shout it out. It would take a lot for her to scream. It took a while for her to be pushed to giving a snippy or sassy response, but lately it was happening more often, mostly at work. Her friends didn't know about this change in attitude and would just dismiss it to stress or being overworked.

They didn't really ask Sophia how she was doing simply assuming that everything was fine with her, just because she didn't give too much room for her problems and didn't talk about them much or at all. Besides, the relationship problems or the frustrating jobs of her friends gave much more material to talk about. Sometimes Sophia had the feeling that her friends were annoyed when she talked enthusiastically about her job or how she had solved a problem at short notice. To them, it might look like everything always went smoothly for her, which of course wasn't the case, but she didn't complain so much and if she did, one of her friends would come up with a better story. It also seemed to Sophia that they could only suffer with each other instead of being happy for or proud of each other. She tried to cheer her friends up, to encourage and comfort them. But also, to praise and be happy for them when they told of a good thing. This was gratefully accepted and celebrated, even though she often had the feeling that this applied to everyone but her.

Secretly, Sophia thought that the others were envious. Maybe it was because no matter how frustrating and exhausting her job was at times, she could always take something positive from it. For her, the glass was always half full, not half empty. Well, except when it came to her love life. In that case, the glass was dried out inside, had a few cracks, or it was just in the back of the cupboard. Dusty and forgotten.

After the doorbell rang for the third time, Sophia pulled open the door to find *Elsa* and *Anna* from *Frozen* and a little skeleton standing in front of her, chanting in unison, "Trick or Treat!"

For a brief moment Sophia had to laugh since the three of them looked so cute, but immediately became serious as the three of them opened their mouths to reveal vampire fangs and tried to make creepy noises. Sophia pulled the basket of sweets towards her, looked inside and then answered them.

"Unfortunately, I only have the sour stuff."

There was a general groan in response, and the skeleton moaned: "Kitty is really mean."

One of the girls shouted: "No, Kitty is cute!"

"She's very mean!"

"No!"

The children were screaming and arguing, Sophia tried to calm them down, but somehow it didn't work very well until a dark voice helped her.

"Don't fight about it. I think..."

Sophia felt the warmth rise to her cheeks under the paper mask, for the voice had the effect of a touch. She also felt the gaze of the man behind the Dracula mask slowly wandering down her bare legs, where it stopped at her feet, which were in fluffy bunny slippers. Then his eyes slid back up and he explained:

"*Kitty* isn't mean, she's very sexy.... erm cute."

Suddenly, Sophia feared that she might have forgotten to put on the jeans shorts and looked down at her. The tight, light blue, worn piece only barely covered her butt. Although she had felt quite uncomfortable in the outfit before, she suddenly felt incredibly sexy under his gaze. Their eyes met and Sophia wanted to know what he looked like without the mask.

"What's that?", *Elsa* asked, drawing attention back to her. The girl pointed to one of the bright green lollipops in the basket in Sophia's hand and she bent down slightly to the girl. The feeling of the man staring at her cleavage, which was impossible to miss in the skin-tight flannel shirt (from which Ina had quickly cut off the top buttons so that Sophia could no longer button it), made her feel quite warm and she straightened up again and leaned towards him a little.

"I'm not cute at all." Her voice was darker and more threatening than she had planned, but the guy just chuckled and then cheekily returned.

"You have to show me."

It was strange, but that voice made her swallow. Goosebumps ran down her body and Sophia really didn't know what to think. Although she was a little shocked that this man, in fact obviously the father of these children, seemed to be flirting with her, she nodded. She was ready to show him how she felt about such men and gave another sour lollipop to the children, who took it and ran down the stairs screaming joyfully.

"Wait at the door!", Dracula called after them.

Sophia put her hand on her waist and arched her back on purpose. Knowing from her friends that this would show off her curves even more, she waited until he turned back to her. Only then did she rip off her mask and he groaned in shock. She was very glad that the guy was quite taken aback and slammed into the wall as he took a step back. Yes, she knew her face looked as bad as if not only a murderer or a truck had rolled over her, but also a bus with sharp wheels. But her joy lasted only about seven seconds, the time it took him to recover.

"Neuhaus!", he shouted, slightly out of breath, and pushed his Dracula mask into his hair.

Sophia suddenly felt cold. Surely this couldn't be true! Oh, crap!

14

Of all the men in the world, it had to be *him*? Finally, someone who made her feel sexy, and then of all men, it had to be *him*? Him? The universe hated her. At that moment, she was quite sure. Well, she was also sure he wasn't a father of three, but that was the only good thing.

She no longer felt desirable under his gaze, but somehow naked, and her body and her imaginative mind argued about whether that was good or bad.

She had to hold on to the door frame. A thousand questions were buzzing around in her head. What should she do now? Why had he recognised her at all? When she had hardly recognised herself in the mirror. Not only did she have this dead face, but she also had a blonde wig on. How could that be? She should say something, but what? *What*? Her heart pounded in her chest and from afar she heard her own voice saying his name.

Chapter 2

That can't be true! A shiver ran down Nick's back. How horrible the idea that something so terrible could happen to her that made her look like that! He wanted to rip off the blonde wig and scrape all the scars from her body. He really couldn't believe it. Sophia.

"Neuhaus!", he moaned and lifted his mask, wanting to look at her properly. She looked at him with her mouth open and held on to the door frame.

"Mr Falkner?" Her voice was only a hint of a whisper. And once again a shiver ran over him.

He swallowed, for he was not quite sure whether this breathless question, which almost was like a sigh, was good or bad for him. On the one hand, it gave him that certain feeling he always got when she addressed him. Quiet and reserved, as if she didn't want to disturb him. She was the only woman who didn't ask questions whose answers they should all know by now. She only came to his office to get a signature or to tell him something important that could not be clarified by e-mail. On the other hand, her wide eyes and slightly open mouth told him that she was not only surprised to see him here, but shocked. Was it really so shocking that he was celebrating Halloween with his nieces and nephews? Was he not allowed to have fun once in a while? Or was it his words that had shocked her? Who wouldn't think she was incredibly sexy? Surely, he couldn't know that of all people, it was *her*!

As he thought about it, he wanted the ground to open up and

swallow him. He hadn't used such a lame pick-up line in years, and then it had to be *her* of all people! He should explain to her that he had drunk a little too much of Tea's wine. He didn't really care, but he just didn't want Sophia to think he was a sexist or a creep who talked to women like that. His mind had just been preoccupied with other things, which were also the reason for all the wine from his sister-in-law. Once again, he had thought of ... *someone* and had been annoyed with his brother Ruben.

She, or rather her appearance, had been such a pleasant distraction that he talked before he thought, although he normally thought twice before opening his mouth. But somehow, he had forgotten that since ... since *she* had stumbled into his life. He smiled and tilted his head.

"Nick."

Sophia looked at him in disbelief, he surely didn't expect she would address him by his first name! Never, ever! Something she had to say, but surely not his name, she would probably say it so carefully as if it could break and he would think she was completely nuts, which he probably already did anyway. As often as something unpleasant happened around him and she hardly spoke to him.

"How did you recognise me?", she asked instead, biting her lip.

Laughing, he let out his breath. Was she really serious? He would recognise that face anywhere, even if she wore a sack over it ... well, maybe not that, but honestly, her beauty was second to none! He hadn't been able to get that face out of his mind since they first met. Which was only due to its symmetry, of course! Both halves of the face could be placed exactly on top of each other and they would be exactly the same. He had tried it out when he had edited the photos for the company's website. He had simply noticed the symmetry. And the perfect little straight nose, the luscious lips and the little dimple on the chin. The round forehead and the high

17

cheekbones that had dipped a little lately. Maybe she was on some stupid diet? Or maybe she had problems? His heart clenched a little at the thought ... or worries? Her eyes looked even bigger. Those impressive, wide, moss-green eyes, even if one of them currently had a horrible white lens in it. That face, with all those little freckles scattered like they were everywhere, she had covered them with white make-up now, but ... yes, even those looked perfectly arranged, and the slightly larger beauty marks. On her left cheek, on her right shoulder. He wondered where Sophia had hidden more. But he could hardly tell her all that. She looked at him and crossed her arms in front of her stomach as if she were cold. Maybe she was, in that outfit. *My goodness, her legs!* He really should get a grip! Now he was staring at her bunny slippers and saying to them rather than to her.

"I never forget a face."

Sophia exhaled loudly and her eyes met his. It was disturbing that one eye was so white.

"I thought I had scared you so much, Mr Falkner." She smiled impishly. "I thought I looked awful."

"You do."

She looked up at him. There was an awkward little pause, for she was well aware that they were normally on a first-name basis and that she had addressed him as if they didn't already know each other.

Nick was also searching for words. The embarrassing silence dragged on like chewing gum. Yet, Sophia pointed down the stairs, slightly confused, and magically found her voice again.

"Are these Ruben's children?"

"Hmm?" Nick was distracted for a moment, as he couldn't look into just one eye, he had dropped his gaze and yes ... she seemed to hide everything else very well, because he would never have guessed

18

what she was hiding under her loose jumpers and blouses.

He looked back into her face again and nodded.

"Yes, they are. I'm sorry, but looking at your face is really... difficult."

And that was the first time he could say *that*, even if this time it was because of the sight of the scars and the blind eye. Not due to her almost hurtful beauty. He had had it on his lips a few times before, but had kept silent. It was hard to tell someone that one could not bear the sight of her simply as she was too beautiful.

Although Sophia laughed and kept her bad eye closed, his words somehow hurt. It was completely stupid, but she felt rejected. Maybe it was just for the fact that he had said it a bit too harshly, though. It probably annoyed him to meet her here when all he wanted to do was have a bit of fun with his brother's children. Again, there was a small pause in which the two did not look at each other but at their hands and the wall next to the door.

"Shall we bring them back in?", Sophia asked. It felt like the three children had been gone for ages and it was cold outside.

"Oh, erm. Nope, thanks, we'd better go."

"Ok."

Nick nodded and opened his mouth as if to say something more, but remained silent. He turned to the stairs and then said over his shoulder: "You also seem to have other plans."

In the half-light of the stairwell lights, Sophia thought she saw him clench his jaw, which he always did when he needed to control his temper. Sometimes she imagined he only did it around her, but that wasn't true. Mainly he did it when he came out of a conversation with his brother, or when one was standing at the door to his office shortly afterwards, indicating that there was a problem or a question.

It was clear that he wanted to leave quickly, not only for the sake of the children, but also to get away from her. Everyone knew that the two of them didn't really get along. Or, well, they didn't have many interactions and when they did, it was always short and to the point. Without small talk or a little joke. He was rarely there and then he was usually annoyed, stressed and quickly gone again. The two of them had never talked as much as they did today. That's why she hadn't recognised his voice.

The fact that she went out on the streets or even into a bar with that outfit annoyed him, for no reason at all. It was really none of his business. They didn't know each other and he didn't care about her anyway. He shook his head at that lie. She was an adult and would know what she was doing. Although she seemed to have no idea what she was doing. To him.

"Well, at least that's what we had in mind.", Sophia replied absent-mindedly and looked into her flat.

Oh, well, in there probably sat her boyfriend, who she would go out with, yes of course. He would take care of her. Nick didn't really know why his bad mood came back, but suddenly he wished he was still sitting in Tea's kitchen drowning his bad mood in wine instead of making a fool of himself here with this silly costume.

"Well then...", he pressed through his teeth and then walked down the stairs with quick steps.

"See you Monday." Sophia murmured, although she knew of course that it was only a wish that he would somehow greet her in a different way on Monday because of today's encounter. Not that he wouldn't greet her, but a generally muttered "Good day!", was of course not a personal greeting.

While she was closing the door, she dreamed about it in her silly head. Well, she dreamt of more, but that wasn't silly, that was absurd, stupid and simply unimaginable. That's what her friends would tell her if she told them about it. Just the thought that they wouldn't take her seriously or would laugh at her, kept her from telling them even the slightest thing. She groaned. Maybe today was the famous hint of fate? That chance encounter that was destined to happen? Yes! Sophia nodded. She would tell her friends the whole dilemma today and see what they had to say.

The children started to groan when their uncle told them they were going home, but as it was already after nine, he managed to convince them. They left the street where Sophia lived and turned right, but at this late hour they did not take the shortcut through the park, but walked up the street and then turned into the villa district. Only when they were in their street and the house was visible did Nick let the three children run home. He had two minutes to think about his meeting with Sophia. He was still quite agitated and couldn't quite hide it from his sister-in-law when he entered the hallway.

"Are you okay?" she asked.

"Yes, sure."

"You don't look like it."

"Everything is fine, Tea", he briefly squeezed his sister-in law's arm.

"I thought running around with the kids would do you good, but you look exactly the same as before."

"Tea ..." Nick rolled his eyes.

"Something is bothering you and I just want to help you."

"You can't."

And it was true. No one could.

"I can't take it anymore!", Ina shouted. Laughter. Or rather loud snorts. Including a splash of champagne, which Céline was about to drink.

Sophia was deeply hurt. She wished she had followed her gut a few minutes ago and not told them anything. Her three best friends were sitting on her sofa, knotted up and laughing their heads off. At her *clichéd, stupid, girly crush* on one of her bosses. When the three of them laughed hysterically and didn't look at her, Sophia quickly wiped away the tear that threatened to roll out of her eye. Forcing herself to grin, making sure not to show them how much their words had hurt her. Her mother's words rang in her ears.

Be strong! Don't show any weakness!

Well, her *silly girl crush* as Céline had so aptly called it and Viviana had made an abbreviation of it, which she kept shouting out loud, was just not as interesting as her friends' love stories. And it wasn't a dramatic on-off relationship like Viviana's either. Who had often enough called her at night, crying so that Sophia jumped out of the bed at every hour and rushed on her bicycle through the city for twenty minutes, still in her pyjamas, just to comfort her. It wasn't even worth taking a walk to the next pub, as with Céline's problem. After all, she always had to reassure herself that she was attractive and desirable to other men too, not just her completely crazy stepbrother. These evenings were used not only to gossip nastily about the ladies' present - the competition - but also about the men who queued up to buy her a drink and flirt with her.

And this little *silly girl crush* was nowhere near as fascinating as the many little affairs Ina had going on. No, it was a simple crush, for the distant, almost never-present third brother of the bosses, who was incredibly attractive but just not in Sophia's league. After all, stupid as she was, she had told them that he mainly dated long-legged, beautiful, fairylike models. At least, if the gossip of the other women in the company was to be believed. Sophia was probably just projecting one of her heroes from her books onto him, who always had a soft heart despite his rough manner. That had been Viviana's explanation and the reason for another collective laughter.

Nick sat on the rooftop terrace in his usual place and stared up at the cool night sky. Strangely, he had always been looking in that direction. Towards the east. To where the sun rose and, as he now knew, Sophia Neuhaus lived.

Smiling, he shook his head. He had apparently drunk even more than he had admitted, for a small voice told him that this was not an oddity, but rather a sign. That's nonsense! What kind of sign anyway? He groaned in annoyance at the fact that this was one of his favourite places. Emphasis on *was*. Now it was just another place where he would think of her. Constantly.

"Shit!"

Although Sophia was a master at hiding her true emotions and hurt feelings, she managed to do so only with great difficulty and mainly because of her disgusting looks. She had let the others have fun at her expense and seemingly endured it stoically, even though she was bubbling over with pain.

Luckily, Jérôme had then called and Viviana had argued with him loudly, forcing everyone else to stop laughing due to the change in mood. After that, they had decided to go to the bar. Even though Sophia would have preferred to stay at home and cry in peace, she had said nothing of the sort. She knew her friends only too well and knew that they would then tease her as a party pooper and make her heartbreak even worse if they accused her of making a mountain out of a mole-hill. And yes, of course it wasn't bad at all, and certainly not as bad as all the problems the girls had or thought they had. So, Sophia gritted her teeth, put on a hoodie and joined her friends in the bar. As always, she stood a little apart and took in the situation.

To distract herself from her grief and disappointment, she made a bet with herself as to who would become the object of desire for Ina and which man would be allowed to buy Céline a drink. At some point Viviana pulled her onto the small dance floor and although Sophia had neither the desire nor the strength, she danced with her. Fortunately, she was one of those people who, whether they danced for joy or with little enthusiasm, always hit the right rhythm. Every movement fit, and usually the joy of dancing came back after the third song at the latest, and the two young women whirled around each other, bringing a smile to the face of one or the other observer in the crowd. Their dance seemed like pure liberation.

Only later, when Sophia had taken off her make-up and was finally alone, did she walk through her flat and clear away the empty bottles and the half-full glasses. She wiped down the table and the bowls where unhealthy snacks like chips and pretzels had been in a few hours ago. At first the girls had looked at her as if she had served fried spider legs, but after one had started there was suddenly no stopping them.

Sophia knew exactly what she was doing. She tried to avoid being alone with her thoughts. Knowing that she couldn't think about *him* without thinking about what her friends had said and how they had hurt her with their words. As clearly as she had won all the bets, she had made with herself in the bar, she knew she had to analyse the whole thing. Her friends and her relationship with them.

Half an hour later, as she lay exhausted in her bed, she stared at the ceiling and tried to suppress the pain of having made a fool of herself. Probably she wasn't worth it to the others to take her heartbreak seriously. Her friends thought her crush was ridiculous. But it wasn't. Neither ridiculous, nor just a crush. Sophia knew her feelings were more than that. That's why it hurt so much. Not just the words of her girls. Also, the knowledge that she would never have a chance.

She knew it was unthinkable, but she also knew she was in love with him. Otherwise, she would hardly remember every moment she had experienced with Nick Falkner. There weren't many, and she couldn't remember the exact dates, but she knew what job she had been in charge of at that moment, what photo shoot she had organized. Partly even how she was dressed. But that was not important.

She saw him right in front of her, every gesture, every clenching of the jaw or rolling of the eyes. Those beautiful, dark blue but somehow sad eyes, with shamelessly long lashes that cast a shadow on his cheeks depending on the light. His slightly amused wry smile, which he desperately tried to suppress. The short chuckle that usually died away immediately when he saw her, followed by a twitch of the jaw. Those huge but warm hands with long fingers that she had only touched once, and that by mistake, but she could trace their shape exactly. Which she had already done. And above all, she could remember the feeling he had triggered in her every time she had met him.

Unfortunately, he had only ever exchanged one or two words with her, or even less. A murmured "morning!", or an almost growled "Hmm" is hardly a conversation. Not like before in the stairwell. Sophia closed her eyes for a moment. His voice was as soft as velvet. And somehow sensual like dark chocolate or a song by Barry White.

And if she had known that less than a mile away someone else was lying awake thinking about exactly the same things, she might not have shed a tear or two.

Chapter 3

Nick closed his eyes. He saw Sophia before him again, as he used to see her at the office. Concentrated at her desk, bent over calculations. In the completely useless conference room where she was rearranging photographers' portfolios for special requests from clients instead of just sending a sample of the artist's work. Laughing with her colleagues.

Then images of her from last night kept creeping into his head. Those legs! For being so small, they were amazingly long and well formed. And yes, everything else was also really ... well formed. Nick cleared his throat. He wasn't allowed to see her like that! After all, she worked for him, and that was never good. It only caused problems. Besides, she would only take advantage of him one day and steal data to sell it to a rival and then marry him. No, that would never happen to him again! Apart from the fact that Sophia didn't seem to like him very much. They had never spoken to each other as much as they had the night before, and well, it had been more than embarrassing.

But what could he do? The images of her flooded his mind and there was nothing he could do about it. A shy smile there, a ducking of the head here, a look that was impossible to interpret. Followed by a very clear look, as if she wanted to lecture him. He put away that thought and forced to think of something else instead, but already she came running into his office, cheeks slightly flushed, to put something on his desk and leave immediately. But at some point, he could no longer keep the memories at bay and gave in. The memory of their first encounter, when she had not only stumbled into him without warning, but had also made him feel something inside again.

He could even remember the smell of her hair. Apple.

Sophia could remember everything as if she were looking at a photograph, or rather as if she were watching a film she knew by heart.

It had been hazy and cold when she boarded the train at four twenty in the morning and drove to the shooting location. She didn't want to do anything wrong and certainly didn't want to be late. Exactly one hour later, she had an appointment with the caretaker of the cement factory that was to be used as a location for an advertising shoot that day. Even though regular business had to continue as much as possible. She had known that she would arrive much too early, but she wanted to get an impression of the surroundings on the way there. Her boss Ruben Falkner was personally in charge of this client and wanted her to be there that day to learn how a photo shoot worked on location. He had told her only the night before that she should replace the *runner*, because that was how she would learn best.

Sophia had no idea what a runner did exactly. She wasn't afraid, though, because her boss would explain it to her then. But Ruben had simply not come. He hadn't been available by phone either and Sophia had to jump into the deep end and swim as best she could. She remembered that everything had been easy at the beginning, the model was super-friendly and the photographer was enthusiastic, reminding her of Ruben with his almost unbearable, completely exaggerated enthusiasm. Everyone seemed to be happy, though. But then everything went down the drain. Suddenly, the doors of the main house were locked and no one could go to the toilet. The caretaker had turned off his phone and the nice and friendly staff had suddenly disappeared for lunch break. The coolers with the drinks were no longer cooling, the pizza delivery boy couldn't find them and Sophia had to run to the main entrance to get 13 boxes of pizza. Not only did she burn herself in the process, her jeans were also stained with the mixture of oil and tomato sauce. Although everyone was eating their pizza between shots and Sophia was glad that the model wasn't just living of water and air, she suddenly had the strange feeling that she was under observation. A tingle ran up her neck. This handsome man came closer and even though she had seen the Polaroids of the male models and did not recognise him, she asked him his name. Before he could answer, the photographer called out:

"Hey, Falkner! I thought Ruben would come." And pulled him away from her.

Their glances had met for a tiny moment. The feeling in her stomach was not the shame of not having recognised him. No. She knew that tingling feeling that lifted her stomach, like sitting on a roller coaster and being in free fall for a tenth of a second before gravity brought her back to reality.

Oh.

Despite laughing and chatting with the photographer and making small talk with the rest of the crew, he didn't say a word to her, just looked at her with a piercing gaze and narrowed eyebrows. A nod. A clenching of the jaw. Nothing more. Not even when she handed him the list for the coffee order. He just looked at her in astonishment, but turned his back on her so quickly that she could barely hear his muttering.

"Where will she find it anyway?"

Since he confused her with his unreadable expression, and of course with his incredibly good looks, and the fact that he was one of her bosses, she was so anxious not to do anything wrong, but of course that's exactly what happened. She stumbled around him and spilled not only two of the coffees she had picked up in the third round, but of course also the one that had been meant for him. The fact that some of it spilled on his shoes didn't make it any better, although he kindly didn't say anything about it, just cursed softly as he pushed her away from him.

Sophia had feared she had burned him by the way he had pulled his hand away so quickly. Except that hadn't been the case.

At that moment, she had been just a small step away from tears, because honestly, everything had been going great until he had shown up. The day was far from over after that and she had been glad that no further disaster had occurred and she could relax again. But that could have been because Nick Falkner had faded into the background and was on the phone for the rest of the day.

After 17 hours on her feet and the excitement of the day, she was so awake that she had not been able to sleep even after a relaxing bath. Her brain was processing what she had experienced. But not the work, the fresh impressions and new insights. No, just every expression on Nick Falkner's face, every look and gesture. And when she finally fell into a restless dream, she dreamt of him.

And every night since then.

Nick stared at the ceiling, but not annoyed, rather because the first time he met her, almost exactly a year ago, was replaying in his mind's eye like an entertainingly edited music video.

First there was the call from Ruben, who was totally stressed out since he had agreed to several appointments at once and had forgotten that he had promised the client to meet him on location, at the photoshoot. Of course, he was completely indifferent to the fact that Nick had only returned from Barcelona the night before and, as always, he appealed to Nick's good nature by making him feel guilty if he didn't help him.

Upon arriving at the location, Nick could neither see that the client was there at all, nor that the new colleague was overwhelmed or stressed. He relaxed immediately when he saw how she seemed to have everything under control. Even Rafael, the photographer, who with his completely inappropriate attitude was one of the more difficult people to work with, laughed, and that was a great art, after all he saw himself as a serious artist, and always had plenty to complain about.

As Nick walked closer, he noticed several things at once. The new colleague was a lively young woman, wearing old Chucks and an absolutely ugly waist bag in which she obviously kept the cash and which constantly slipped off her narrow hips. She was wearing a light grey sweatshirt that was far too big. And her first words made him smile, since he had forgotten what they sounded like.

"Can I help you?"

She had only looked at him briefly and was already looking for his name on the call sheet. She probably thought he was one of the male models, which usually annoyed the hell out of him, since most women said that to flatter him. But not Sophia. Sophia wasn't trying to hit on him or flirt. She was just so focused on her work that she didn't even look at him properly. He smiled as he thought of her adorable rosy cheeks when she realised, he was one of her bosses after Rafael had greeted him and dragged him away from her. He still had his words in his ears.

"Where did you find this golden treasure?" Golden treasure. A treasure of gold. Yes, she was.

In the afternoon, Sophia had sweet-talked the grumpy-looking guy at the coffee stall for the construction workers on the street into selling her coffee as well. Even if she spilled some when she stumbled into his arms, he simply admired the way she managed everything and never once asked him for help.

The tender warmth emanating from her as he stopped her from falling was uncomfortable in an almost intimate way. And the sight of her at that moment had burnt into his brain. The witty comment he was about to say stuck in his throat as the tree they were standing under shed its leaves at that moment. The red and gold leaves floated around them as if in slow motion. That moment stretched, though it was over faster than the blink of an eye. It hit him like a slap in the face. Completely unexpected and it annoyed him immensely.

Those eyes, wide and kind, an irresistible smile on her lips. He stared at her and her smile faded. But it was too late. At that moment, it had already happened. Boom. Everything was silent. All sounds faded into the background. Only the leaves rustled as they fell on her and to the ground. Time and space no longer existed. Except for her face. She got under his skin, in that one brief moment. His heart lifted for that one millisecond. And he understood everything at once. Her bright red and tempting lips were slightly parted. He thought he saw the same questions mirrored in her mountain lake green eyes. The cream-coloured woollen cap sat askew on her head. There was a small orange spot on her sweatshirt. Freckles, but symmetrically arranged around her eyes and on her nose. His fingers, wrapped around her wrist, felt hot, as if he had burned them. What was going on here? Of course, he knew what was going on, but he didn't like it at all and quickly pushed her away. Damn it!

Although the whole situation had felt like an out-of-body experience and he couldn't help shaking for a moment, he was immediately back in the here and now. He didn't dare look in her direction again, but he did so anyway, as if he had nothing to say.

Sophia stood with the others and handed out the coffees. She did her work with flushed cheeks and occasionally cast a shy glance in his direction. He heard her laugh and it shook him how warm and genuine it was. It was so beautiful it almost hurt. Nick was furious and tried with all his might to fight it. But he was powerless. He was aware that Sophia would not see him as a nice person, because he hardly spoke to her and avoided all eye contact after the thing with the leaves. He pulled back a little and pretended to be working and talking on the phone. Instead, though, he watched her. How she continued to take care of everything and everyone. She had worked hard to make everyone happy.

Groaning, he now sat up in his bed. It had to stop! He knew she was special, but he would never try to let anyone in again. And it was absolutely clear to him that she didn't like him at all. She avoided him as much as she could. Maybe she saw him as the arrogant snob he was to everyone else. It was also her fault how he lived his life. Why he didn't move back completely, but kept all the acquisition appointments and accompanied the photo shoots around the world. Why he was everywhere and yet nowhere really at home. And yet couldn't stay away either. He couldn't bear to see her every day if she wasn't meant for him. And if she was interested at all, what good would that do?

In the end, she would break his heart, as well.

Sophia had the feeling of suffocating. Not only due to the grief her friends had caused but rather for the truth behind their words. Nick was unreachable. He would probably laugh at her too if he knew about her feelings. She closed her eyes and took a deep breath. Luckily it was Sunday and she could take her time to think about how she would behave at the office the next day. Only two more days until he had to go for another trip. She could deal with that. Still, at that moment she couldn't bear the confinement of her flat and took her jacket as she left it. She wandered around without a goal until she found herself in the park. With happy children running across the grass and playing with leaves. Couples in love sat on the benches, friends talked. She found a place to sit down and tried to read her book. Contrary to what her friends suspected, she hadn't read romance novels for a long time since they all had happy endings and only dragged her down more in her heartbreak. She had now switched to challenging thrillers to distract her brain and prevent her from dreaming about Nick.

However, luck was really not on her side this weekend.

After a silent breakfast, Tea had persuaded her husband and his brother to go to the park with the children. The girls were rollerblading and Henrik was riding his new bike, which he had got for his birthday last month. Ruben and Nick tried to make conversation. But the success and expansion of the Falkner Production Company was Ruben's only topic. Nick was lost in his own thoughts about who he could call to distract himself instead of just thinking about Sophia Neuhaus, who was just ignoring him away.

His brain felt like it was about to burst. Which wasn't necessarily her fault, but rather the amount of wine and whiskey he'd downed last night to forget her. He didn't usually drink this much, but lately it was getting worse. Even though he was at the company as rarely as possible, they were in constant contact. She took care of his former photographers and every now and then they just had to talk to each other. Which they only did by e-mail. He wondered if Sophia disliked him so much or if she was just too shy to talk to him on the phone. After all, he wasn't the easiest guy. Especially not with her. Then again, she just never left him alone! If he didn't think about her for a few minutes, an email would come from her, or she would come running into his office and hand him some papers, gifts or a photo portfolio of a new potential talent. It was like an invisible bond between them. That always drew him back to her. Even when he was with incredibly beautiful women, he thought of Sophia and felt guilty as soon as he even tried to flirt with another.

Groaning, he slid further down the bench and looked up at the sky.

"What's wrong, Nick?"

"Nothing, Ruben."

"I know you're stressed, but we'll soon have the office in New York and then you can finally settle down there. January or February is the time."

Nick looked at his brother and was still searching for words to address the delicate subject that he would actually prefer to stay here. He had no desire to travel around the world like a homeless vagabond or to eke out an existence abroad. Actually, it would be quite simple. Nick also had a solution as to who could take over the New York office instead. Their younger siblings had to finally take flight instead of hiding in the office. Ruben, however, at forty-three the oldest of the four and the self-confessed head of the family - and the company - saw things quite differently.

Before Nick could form the words, however, they heard Anneke cry out. They both jumped up and he could only shake his head. For who was there crouching on the ground with his niece, helping her up?

Sophia.

Before she saw him, Sophia sensed his presence and turned in his direction. Tears sprang to her eyes. Why was fate being so mean to her and not letting her get away from him? She took a deep breath and was glad that Ruben came running towards her alone, eyes only for his daughter, while Nick went to get the other two children. This gave her two minutes to collect herself.

"Great to meet you here", Ruben exclaimed enthusiastically and wiped Anneke's bloody knee with a handkerchief.

"Do you live around here?"

Surprised that his brother had said nothing about their meeting yesterday, she only replied: "Yes. On the other side of the crossroad."

"Hey Nick!", Ruben called out to his brother as he came closer. "Sophia also lives around here."

"Ahh." Nick looked in her direction and tried to interpret the expression on her face. She was probably wondering why he hadn't talked about their meeting and he was wondering the same thing.

"I think we'll go home", Ruben said to Anneke and then said to Nick: "you're free to stay here with the others."

"Yeah, sure."

"Well, I'll be off then. Bye.", Sophia replied and smiled at Ruben and the children, but again avoided looking at Nick. He was busy with Henrik's shoelaces while he looked after her and noticed how quickly she wanted to get away from him. She didn't even go back to the bench where she had apparently sat earlier and obviously left her book. Without really thinking, he got up, grabbed it and ran after her.

"Sophia!"

Immediately she turned around. Lacking words, he simply handed her the book, and only when she smiled a little, did he manage to relax. Which was strange, since he was usually completely confused around her.

"Thank you, Mr Falkner."

"Nick." Was the only thing he could say, and slowly he felt stupid, as even though she was already holding the book in her hand, he didn't want to let go of it. He was too captivated by her eyes. Which had changed so much in that one year. Still deep and beautiful, but they seemed somehow ... sad.

Sophia didn't answer, just nodded.

"I didn't tell him because... I don't really know why." He admitted and curled his beautiful mouth into a wry smile, which in turn made Sophia take a deep breath.

"That's ok."

Their gazes remained glued to each other and they both knew they were thinking about last night.

"I didn't mean to sound so stupid. I'd had a bit too much to drink and ... well." His gaze dripped down her legs, which were now in normal length jeans.

"Neither of us expected it." She shrugged and he finally let go of the book. Again, this silence arose between them, only this time it was not awkward, but somehow pleasant.

"Uncle Nick!", Jule called out and he turned to his niece and gave her a quick wave. "I'll be right there!"

Nick turned back to Sophia.

"Well, I just..." Sophia pointed behind her, she wanted to go, should go, but she would rather stay. And as if he knew what was on her mind at that moment, he interrupted her.

"Just stay a little longer."

Chapter 4

Neither of them could quite believe what he had just said. Nick wondered why he had dared and was convinced she wouldn't stay when that little crease between her eyebrows deepened. She looked at him doubtfully. Heavens, what did she have to think of him?

He hardly spoke a word to her and then suddenly he invited her to stay with him in the park. Well, not to stay there with him, just in general. The children were there too, and about a hundred other people, so she was hardly there just with him. And why should she do that? He was her boss, he wasn't nice, she didn't like him ... or did she like him? No, she never asked questions. Maybe she didn't ask because she didn't have any questions? But why would she stay, after his behaviour the night before? Would she stay to wait and see if he would flirt with her so she could tell her colleagues? No, she wouldn't, she wasn't that kind of girl, he was sure of it. Maybe she would make an excuse and turn to leave.

Nick braced himself for the rejection. It wouldn't be a real rejection anyway, just a co-worker who didn't like hanging out in the park with one of her bosses. Ok, he admitted to himself, they wouldn't really hang out, more like sit next to each other and he knew there were a few female colleagues who would love to sit with him in the park on a strangely sunny November day. Maybe not just sit, he knew the rumours but didn't pay that much attention to them. It didn't matter anyway. Sophia was the only one he wanted to sit next to in the park. Oh, had he just thought that? But he didn't want to get involved with her, and neither did she, she didn't like him, he was sure of that, and that would be the reason for her rejection. So, he searched her face for an answer.

"Okay."

Had she actually lost her mind? Why had she said that? Sophia asked herself. She couldn't stay here with *him*! Then she would probably have to talk to him, and how would that work? She would just stare at him and forget how to use her mother tongue. It would be so embarrassing. The thought that she would be sitting next to him on the park bench, gawping and stuttering, made her smile, but she sat down anyway.

As she got used to the fact that she was sitting far too close to him and was more near him than she had been in months, she listened inside herself. Her heart was racing as her whole right side tingled. The silence stretched again, uncomfortably. Sophia cursed herself for her stupidity and believed her friends were right. It wasn't that her feelings were nothing more than a little crush, but that it was childish, she was acting like a teenager. She could feel her cheeks glowing and whenever she got nervous, her hands went cold. She couldn't think straight, except that up close he looked even more handsome and smelled even better than she remembered. Sophia closed her eyes and breathed in his scent. Shocked at what she was doing, she opened them again and dared to look at him.

He held his handsome face up to the cold autumn sun, and her fingers twitched at the thought that she would like to touch the stubble on his jaw. How would it feel? Would he like it? Oh, crap! She really should control herself! He was one of her bosses. This man didn't like her. She didn't mean anything to him. Why had he asked her to stay? Was he just being polite, or did he want her to stay, and if so, why? She should ask him that or say something. But what? What could she possibly say?

Nick cleared his throat. Oh man, this was even worse than he had imagined! Sophia obviously felt so uncomfortable being here, sitting next to her boss, and yet he wondered why she had agreed in the first place. Maybe she had only stayed for lack of a balcony and to enjoy the sun? Or maybe she was so annoyed with her boyfriend that she just didn't want to go home. But did she have one? And if so, why did he even care? Of course, he knew why, but it wouldn't do any good to know, and maybe it would only hurt more. Damn it! He ran his hand over his face. And watched the children.

"So... did you scare a lot of people yesterday?" His mouth asked it as if of its own accord. Nick wasn't sure who had formed that question for him, he couldn't remember thinking it.

"Oh yes, a few."

Sophia was amazed that she could talk to him without stuttering and exhaled with laughter for a brief moment. For him, the sound was so enchanting that he dared to look at her and only then noticed how close she was sitting. She was not even an arm's length away of him. Now he knew why he had felt so warm. Their eyes met briefly and he noticed how her cheeks regained that rosy tone and he too had to smile.

"My girls and I looked really bad. I'm not just saying that, I was really the most harmless of them all!"

She meant it in more than one way, but of course he couldn't know that. She pulled a face and shook at the memory of the way Céline had appeared. She even had a plastic eye hanging out of her eye.

"That was so gross."

With a lot of facial expression, she told him about Céline's appearance and fascinated, he listened to her beautiful voice.

40

"I wish I could have seen her." Nick said casually, smiling that smile that usually made Sophia sigh, but just like in the stairwell, the tiny pain of being rejected stung her.

Of course, he would have liked to see Céline, she was beautiful. He couldn't know that, of course Sophia knew that, and yet she felt that way. So, her friends were right once again. She was behaving ridiculously. But she tried to keep talking.

"One guy compared us to a bunch of battered girls in that movie .... erm..."

Trying to keep the conversation going, she closed her eyes briefly to remember the title of the movie, but of course she couldn't remember it, it had been too long since she had last seen it. The director's name was on the tip of her tongue, but then her brain shut down completely when she looked over at Nick and saw him clenching his jaw. If that wasn't one of the hottest things in the world, she didn't know anything. How many times had she dreamed of touching his jaw and feeling that strong muscle under his skin.

"Ahh Tarantino!", Nick called, and then looked at her. His eyes were so ... dark and had such a sparkle in them. "Do you like him?", he asked.

"Hmm?" Sophia had forgotten for a moment what he had said before, since he had leaned a little in her direction and she was really having trouble concentrating. And breathing. The length of his eyelashes was downright outrageous and an insult to all women. She shook her head at her stupid thought, but he understood it as a response.

"Well, as long as you and your girls had fun."

She nodded, although she was reluctant to think how hard she had tried, and was still trying, to overlook their nasty remarks.

"Uncle Nick, just look!!" Jule shouted very aloud, even though she was standing only three or four steps away. The two turned to the girl. "You listen worse than Daddy", she pouted, and Nick stood up and sauntered over to his little niece.

"I'm looking."

"You've been looking at her the whole time..."

Nick felt a cold and warm shiver run down his spine. Jule hadn't screamed so loudly that Sophia had heard it, had she? He glanced over his shoulder to check if she had heard, but it seemed she had not, because she had opened her book to read. So, she hadn't seen Jule pointing her finger at her, either.

"Sorry, I'm all yours now." he said, but he could hardly take his eyes off Sophia.

How she sat there. Cross-legged, her book lying on her lap. The cool autumn sun shone on her face and cast a silvery-yellow light on her. A strand of her chestnut hair was blown into her face by the already wintery cold wind. Lost in thought, her fingers reached for it and pushed it behind her ear. There dangled a small silver earring she often wore, obviously something that had a special meaning for her.

Again, the strand flew into her eyes and she pushed it back again and held it there. How he would love to do that. Every time he saw that one unruly strand fall forward, he wanted to brush it out of her face. And that happened often. When they were in a meeting with the whole company, or looking at a photographer's portfolio, or sometimes when she had lunch at her desk. And he imagined pushing her hair back over her shoulder, and then his hand would linger on the back of her neck and he would lightly touch her cheek. Her warm, tender skin under his fingers, and then he would lean in closer and...

"Is she your girlfriend?" Jule asked with a slightly jealous undertone in her voice.

"No!" He grimaced, why did children or his nieces always have to ask these embarrassing questions? Did they know he would be uncomfortable?

"But you want her to be."

He widened his eyes and mouth in disbelief, but fortunately his niece did not wait for an answer to this guess, but drove quickly to her waiting brother. The little boy then rode off on his bike as fast as he could until his sister caught up with him and held onto his luggage rack. She then lifted one leg upwards and Nick exclaimed enthusiastically how great she had done it. Jule let go of her brother, turned around a bit shakily and then came back at full speed. She threw herself into Nick's arms, and since he had been expecting it and luckily hadn't looked over at Sophia again, he spun her around and threw her up. They both laughed.

"Oh no!" Sighed Sophia, fortunately only in a whisper. This couldn't be true! Frustrated, she shook her head. Was he good with children as well, now? Why did he have to be so damn perfect? Now she would add these images to her collection of nightly dreams. Nick, laughing and having fun with his niece. And she would also add to her dreams that little bit of skin that cheekily caught her eye as he tossed his niece up and his pullover slid up. Were those side abs? Holy shit! Sophia tried not to stare at him and forced herself to look down at her book, but she couldn't read a word. His laugh caught her off guard, and it was a beautiful sound that made the strings of her heart quiver. It was full of joy and deep and ... she could find no other word than sensual.

Sophia groaned again and looked up at the bright sky. She tried not to let her frustration show, how much this sight before her warmed her inside and made her want to cry in the same moment. He would never see her the way she saw him, her friends had told her that, and she knew it too. She was out of his league.

The little boy, Henrik, sped past her on his bike and snapped

43

her out of her thoughts. When the children did their trick again, Nick went back to Sophia and sat down. They both watched the children and he tried to engage her in conversation to learn a little more about her than he already knew.

"What are you reading?"

She put the bookmark to the place she had just tried to read, closed the book and handed it to him. He read the cover text and then remarked dryly: "Matches your outfit from yesterday."

They both remembered what he had said before he knew it was her, and Sophia blushed at the thought that he had found her sexy, even though he didn't like her as Sophia.

"I mean the bloodthirst.", explained Nick further, but his smile disappeared when he remembered how she had stood long-legged in front of him and how incredibly sexy she had looked with those extremely tiny jeans shorts and that tight flannel shirt. He cleared his throat again.

"Sorry for... yesterday", he then said, "I don't usually say stupid things like that."

Sophia nodded and took the book back from him. She should leave. It wasn't easy sitting here with him, but the fact that he had just taken back his compliment made it even more unbearable. She felt the tears prickling behind her eyes. She squeezed them shut and tried to avoid his gaze. The hairs on the back of her neck stood up as he continued in a slightly husky voice.

"Not that I didn't mean what I said, but you know...."

Oh.

"Usually I'm more subtle."

Nick ran his hands through his hair, he knew now it was sticking up from his head, and he noticed Sophia's gaze lingering on him.

He smiled that smile again and Sophia couldn't help noticing a few things at once. His lips looked like they would feel really good on hers, and yes ... he didn't take the compliment back.

44

That was ... she had no words for it and closed her eyes for a moment to suppress the smile that wanted to appear on her face. He shouldn't know what his words meant to her. Perhaps he would know anyway, for she felt her cheeks glowing again and her heart pounding. He must really think she was a pubescent teenager. She gathered all her courage and nodded in understanding.

Then they talked about safer topics. About work. About the upcoming shootings and his acquisition trip on Wednesday and the few ideas Yvonne and Jörn, the younger siblings and junior bosses, had gathered for the Christmas party.

"Yvonne thinks it would be a good idea to involve all colleagues a bit more this time.", Nick said.

"To strengthen team spirit.", nodded Sophia, glad that they could talk in such an unaffected way.

"Yes", he said, pleased that Sophia was so enthusiastic about the ideas and was on board. "How about we go over this again so I can take some notes?" Dared he to ask, taking a deep breath as he realized at that moment how pleased he would be if she would say yes.

"Yvonne already knows, we had a meeting last week about it."

"Oh, really?" Nick looked disappointed and Sophia saw him clench his jaw again. It had to be frustrating for him to be absent from so many meetings as he was the only one travelling.

"She said the final decision would be made this week." Sophia would have liked to squeeze his hand, which of course she didn't dare to do, but she thought he would be happy to be there after all.

"They'll do it without me again anyway."

Yes, the fact that he was often left out annoyed him, even if he often did more for the company than the others. He groaned and sank even lower onto the bench. In this movement, he accidentally brushed Sophia's arm. Despite the thick jacket she was wearing, she felt the goosebumps this little touch caused.

"It's scheduled for Tuesday so you can be there too."

His head snapped to her, and though he didn't ask for it, he knew he owed it to her. For she moved her beautiful mouth into a small encouraging smile, her eyes sank and her cheeks looked as if they had become a shade warmer.

"Thank you."

She didn't answer, just looked shyly into his face, and at that moment the children came back and moaned that they were *so* hungry and wanted to go home. Nick pursed his pretty mouth again, for he would rather stay here with her.

Sophia, however, was ready to go home, looking forward to dreaming about this encounter more than once and analysing everything he had said and done. She felt as if there was something between them, even if he didn't feel the same. Maybe he knew she could be something like a friend.

"Well then ..." She made an effort to leave as the children's shouting got worse and stood up.

"Ok." Nick also stood up. And he felt that this was the beginning of something, even if he was in danger of falling even more in love with her. She was so lovely and he never wanted to not talk to her ever again. Maybe one day she would shed her shyness, stop being so inhibited, and see more in him than just her boss. He thought he had shown her that he was not as intimidating as he pretended to be.

"Have a good day."

"You too."

It almost seemed as if neither of them wanted to leave, but the children ran ahead and they smiled mischievously at each other for a final goodbye. Both were engrossed in their own thoughts and feelings that were running through their heads. They turned around a few more times though, wondering if the other would turn around too. But they didn't want to be caught doing so. So, Sophia forced

46

herself not to look over her shoulder again, and so she missed his gaze resting on her until large trees blocked his view.

Nevertheless, Sophia felt more light-hearted and carefree than she had in a long time. When she arrived home, she threw herself on the bed and conjured up every second of their meeting to lock it in the memory box in her heart. She was happy and the pain her friends had caused her had faded almost invisibly into the background. But of course, the voice of reason also spoke. *Be careful!* But Sophia shook her head. It was too late to be careful or change anything anyway. She was hopelessly in love with him. After that day even more than the day before. And now she had to live with the consequences.

Nick also thought about the consequences of the encounter in the park. Groaning, he closed his eyes, sat down on his favourite spot on the terrace and looked in the direction of her home. He knew it was dangerous. She was dangerous. She could destroy everything he had built up over the years. The protective wall around him. Sophia touched something in him like no one had done in a long time, maybe never. His heart was frozen as if in several miles thick ice. For years he had only functioned, even if he had ended up in bed with a woman once, it had meant nothing. It had been a long time since he had felt so ... understood and somehow free. As if anything was possible. And that after only a few hours with her! He knew he had to be on his guard, but he also liked the sound of his heart beating a different rhythm every time he thought of her. And it was as if he could hear the sound of ice cracking around his heart. It scared him, yet that voice inside him told him to dare. To try. Try to let her in.

If only she would let him enter her heart too.

Chapter 5

When Sophia was a little late for work the next morning, no one noticed because everyone else was even later. She had needed a little longer than usual in the morning. Not only had she lain in her bed with her eyes closed and let the dreams linger for a moment longer, it also took longer to take a shower as she kept thinking about him. And what he would look like in the morning. Would his hair be as dishevelled as when he had run his hand through it the day before? Then she imagined how it would feel to run her fingers through his curls. And when she finally banished that thought from her mind, she couldn't find anything to wear. Sophia changed her clothes several times. Although she usually didn't find it difficult, that morning she just couldn't find anything that seemed to fit her. Until she realised that she had put so much thought into her outfit because Nick Falkner had more or less told her that he thought she looked sexy, or, well, her Halloween looks. She scolded herself that she would make a complete fool of herself if she suddenly changed her appearance, and so she dressed as usual.

Her friends would say *her uniform*, and in a way it was. Casually cut jumpers or shirts and comfortable jeans. And that wasn't just due to the fact that her friends always accused her of trying to hide her curves, but also because it was so much more comfortable. She felt nothing worse than sitting at a desk for ten hours or more in clothes that were too tight. It was enough for her to dress up for the important appointments. Otherwise, she reserved it for theatre visits or parties.

Later, as she sat at her desk going over the calculations for a fashion shoot, a certain feeling made her look towards the door.

"Good morning."

Even though it had only taken two milliseconds longer than his usual impersonal greeting, she knew that Nick Falkner had just stood outside her office door to greet her. Just her. And foolish as she was, she was pleased about it, and not even embarrassed as she smiled at him. He tilted his head as he turned, but she caught a glimpse of his smile and her heart tingled.

The morning was busy and the whole day kind of flew by, and every time she leaned a little closer to the computer screen, she dared to look out of her office door and her view of him was only blocked by a stunted green plant standing in the hallway. Sophia could only see his left arm anyway, but when he sat in his office all day, mostly discussing on the phone, he eventually rolled up his sleeves and his forearms were as beautiful as the rest of him. A few times he would pace the room, putting said arm on his hip or gesturing annoyed or even angry. When he was almost standing at the wall, she could see the drumming of his fingers on his hips or even his familiar eye roll. And when, as at that moment, he leaned his back against the wall, kneaded a relaxation ball with his big hand and dropped his head against the wall to look up at the ceiling, his Adam's apple was clearly visible and Sophia had to swallow.

She blushed, even though she was alone in her office. Ashamed, she promised herself she wouldn't do it again and watch him from a distance like a creepy stalker, but she just couldn't help it and dared one last glance in his direction. He had never caught her watching before. Until now. Oh, how embarrassing! But unlike what she had expected, he held her gaze, raised his coffee mug and offered her a small nod. She couldn't help smirking and also lifted her cup, which hadn't seen coffee since this morning. So, she decided to get a fresh one and walked out of her office, which she normally shared with two other colleagues, but they were in a team-building seminar all day with Yvonne, the most harmony-seeking fourth part of the executive team.

Although everyone on the executive floor, except Ruben, sat here on the same floor as everyone else and integrated themselves like all the other employees, Yvonne also flattered this aura of the unapproachable boss, although she, just like two of her brothers, did not seem nearly as enraptured as Ruben.

When Sophia was on her way back from the coffee kitchen, which was also on the first floor, Ruben gestured her to come into his office, whose walls and door were made of glass. Like a glass cube that was only tidied up on important occasions or when star photographers visited, and everything in it was then draped like an exhibit to make an impression. Yes, that was Ruben, and although everyone despaired of his chaotic and unstructured manner, he was as likeable as an absent-minded professor. Or at least that's how people were supposed to see him. Yet Sophia and other staff had often overheard the siblings arguing or him shouting at people on the phone. She kind of liked him and actually got along well with him, but he could also be quite a troublemaker, especially when he messed something up. To save face, he often just blamed someone else.

Now they were talking about a few things that were coming up and that he was looking forward to meeting the whole team tomorrow to talk about the Christmas event. Sophia wondered why *event* seemed too big a word for a small office Christmas party, but before she could ask or say anything, she felt a certain someone standing behind her. A shiver ran down her spine as if a shower of water had been poured over her that was too hot.

"Nick!" Shouted Ruben, as if he hadn't seen his brother for years, and got up to get some papers from one of the cupboards. Sophia thought she should leave and when she turned around, her eyes lingered on Nick's and the hot shiver ran all the way back. He was standing in the doorway. His broad shoulders looked like they were pressing against the frame of the door left and right, and he only stepped aside when she almost touched him.

Nick was almost unable to step aside as she passed. He couldn't take his eyes off her for he had a silly feeling that there was something in the air between them. A little flicker in her eyes, and he hoped so much that maybe it had something to do with him and their encounter in the park. He wished it was still Sunday afternoon and he was still sitting there with her. Talking about books and listening to her soft voice and her stunning laughter instead of here in this glass cube that showcased all the madness of his brother and the chaos of his work.

He took a deep breath and closed his eyes for a moment before closing the door behind her, catching a glimpse of her face turning towards the stairs and imagining that she had looked back at him but couldn't say for sure. Distracted for a moment, he tried to remember why he was standing there in his brother's office. He would much rather have gone back with her than discuss some accounting discrepancies with his brother. He knew they had to talk to the other two about it too, but first he had to discuss with Ruben the last phone call he had made a few minutes ago. The only thing that helped him stay calm was the scent of green apples lingering in the room. Her scent.

As Nick forced himself to focus on the problem with Ruben and sat down, he realised he was still smiling and he had to shake his head a few times to get her out of his head. At least for the next twenty minutes.

Sophia's heart was still beating wildly and his aftershave still hung in her nose as she caught herself grinning at the brief encounter in Ruben's office. She had so much energy and so the almost two hours she had to wait until Nick was back in his office passed so quickly that she hardly noticed how much work she had done in that time. After seeing him sitting at his desk again, she went over to get some signatures. As always, she stood at his always open office door and let him know that she needed his signature. And as always, he nodded at her and with a motion of his hand instructed her to come in. As always, she stopped in front of his desk. But something had changed. He smiled at her. But he had done that the day before too. Then she noticed that he ended the phone call. He had never done that before. Because of her? That fluttery feeling inside her was back and her heart pumped faster. Did it mean something, or did he just want to talk about the photo productions? Nick took the papers from her as he stood up and skimmed them. Sophia felt her knees go weak as he leaned in, seemingly unintentionally, and mumbled something about the upcoming shoot. Her skin prickled and she felt warm even before he leaned down to the table to sign the papers. She stared at his muscular neck and spotted a small birthmark at the bottom of his hair, and felt caught again when he handed her back the papers.

"Shall I take you home later?" Nick asked unexpectedly, as Sophia had already turned to leave, and she looked at him in surprise, too puzzled to find an answer.

"I know you always come by bike, but ... well, it's a long way and I thought..."

That was not good! He had just revealed to her that he wanted to take her home, not *take her home* .... take her home, but yes, and she probably knew now that he knew something about her, that others wouldn't find out in years, like his brother. Besides, it wasn't a good idea anyway. He would probably cause an accident because her proximity would keep him from paying attention to the traffic. Why hadn't he thought about this before? Why couldn't he think twice before opening his mouth when he was near her? Why did she erase all his superiority and just let him react all the time? Evasion and ignoring worked much better than this! Whatever that was.

"That's very nice of you," Sophia replied, squinted her eyes at the word *nice*. "Just that I'll meet my friends later."

Never had she regretted the Monday meetings with her girls as much as she did at that moment and she thought about how she could show him that she would gladly accept the offer if she could. Surely, she would pass out in his car or make such a fool of herself that he would regret it, but that didn't matter. What did it mean that he had offered it to her? Was it really just in the sense that she lived nearby, or did he want to be alone with her? Sophia reminded herself to stop thinking such things, she was already drifting off into her ridiculous dreams.

"Viviana lives just two streets from here ..." she explained lamely.

"Yeah, sure, no problem. I just wanted to ..." Nick thought he was talking his head off and wished someone would call to get him out of this situation. As this didn't happen, he just nodded to her and sat down at his desk. Sophia paused for another moment, but he pretended to look through a stack of papers.

"Maybe Friday?" asked Sophia hesitantly, and her voice had taken on a strangely high tone, hopefully he hadn't noticed! She tried to swallow and jutted her chin to get the lump out of her throat.

Nick looked at her with this expression she could hardly interpret. Was he upset or even angry, or had he just forgotten that they had an invitation to the exhibition from one of their photographer teams Keith and July? Then his expression softened and his eyes - oh heavens, those eyes took on an expression she had never seen before. Sophia lowered her gaze to the floor for a moment, trying to remain calm. She knew that if she wasn't already in love with him, that look would have made her.

"Yeah, sure." His brain repeatedly screamed *Friday, Friday!* But at the same moment he asked himself, why not tomorrow? And as if she could read his mind, she reminded him of his meeting with a production company from South Africa the next evening.

"Yes, yes, I know." And before he could say anything more, his phone rang and Sophia left his office.

Nick shook his head, sure she thought he was completely clueless about his own schedule. But it wasn't his fault he forgot almost everything when she looked like that. Adorable. A little blush on her cheeks. The nibbling of her lower lip. Then, she was wearing the pullover from their first meeting, as if it was a secret sign that only he understood. Even though he knew it was work on display, he had a tiny tingle in his chest, like it was a real date. He shook his head and scolded himself to get a grip. If he wanted a real date with her, he should ask her.

But first of course, he should make sure she would say yes...

After this encounter with the new Nick Falkner, as Sophia secretly called him in her head, she was sure that even the remarks of her friends would not hurt her. And since the three of them probably didn't feel like teasing her, or maybe even had a guilty conscience, they didn't make any sort of comment, or Sophia didn't notice because she didn't pay much attention to their conversations.

Her thoughts were with Nick. She was not only thinking about his change in behaviour, but also that she was worried about him. With all his travelling around the world to the different locations of the photo shoots and meeting so many different companies and potential clients, he had lost track of what was going on. She had an idea how he could change that, feeling that he was not as happy as he seemed to be a year ago. But who was she to tell her bosses what to do? Anyway, this charming encounter and the fact that he hadn't taken back his compliment gave Sophia a bit more confidence. And instead of always encouraging her friends in their actions and opinions, she became a little braver.

So, when Viviana complained about how neglected she felt by Jérôme as usual and how mean he was for travelling the world instead of talking about the wedding, Sophia told her what she normally kept to herself out of respect for her friend.

"Ana" only Sophia was allowed to call Viviana that, since that was the nickname, her mother had given her, and Viviana knew Sophia only used it when she had something special to say, and looked at her in surprise. "I really don't know what your problem is." And yes, it annoyed Sophia that they only ever talked about problems.

"I realise that ...", but before Viviana could finish the sentence with the usual words: *You're not an expert on relationships*. Sophia interrupted her.

"No, I know," she held up her hands and continued quietly. "But it was your idea for him to join the medical charity."

Silence.

"Yes, that's right." Céline pointed out and Ina went one step further, reminding everyone what Viviana had said to her fiancé at the time.

"I think you put quite a bit of pressure on him," laughed Céline, nudging her friend happily.

"I'd say it was definitely blackmail." Cried Ina with a smile and the women laughed at the memory of how intimidating Viviana could be at times.

"So, you think it's my own fault?" Viviana asked and the others laughed, but not Sophia, who had noticed the change in her voice.

"Yes, sure, so stop whining!" Laughed Ina and Céline asked if she could engage Viviana for an evening so she could tell her stepbrother what she really thought of him.

"Just stop talking about that idiot!" said Viviana gruffly, and Céline's eyes widened in disbelief. Sophia feared the whole thing would get out of hand. Which, of course, it already did.

"You're in a leading position in your family's business, dealing with funds worth millions, talking to businessmen and aristocrats, so don't be such a baby and tell him to run! But you don't want to!" exclaimed Viviana and Céline only replied, "What?"

"Why don't you just admit it?", Ina joined in. "You love him and that's why you didn't tell your parents."

"Excuse me?" Céline looked shocked but Sophia knew it was the look of being caught and her cheeks glowed a bright red against her pale skin. Ina had struck a nerve and Sophia also believed that this was the real reason why Céline could not get involved with another man.

"You talk about him all the time, even more than Vivi talks about Jérôme or Pia talks about her boss lover."

"He's not my lover." Sophia defended herself tiredly, she had long since given up telling them that she hated this abbreviation of her name and was also aware that her protest fell on deaf ears. Her stomach cramped at the chaos that was unfolding before her eyes and for which she was to blame. If only she had kept her mouth shut!

"We know you would never have the courage to have an affair with him." said Ina in a mean tone and a nasty look in her direction and Viviana remarked dryly. "Pia is a prude, yes, but it's better than having a new one every week!"

"What are you saying?" cried Ina, standing up.

"Vivi is right, you are ... quite flexible when it comes to men," Céline explained, her eyes boring into Ina's.

Sophia's head was pounding from the yelling and screaming of her friends and all the things they were throwing at each other! Things you might have secretly thought about or wondered about, but things you should never throw at each other. Not even talk about them with the others. She knew it was her fault for not keeping quiet. She had to fix it, like she always did, but she had to think about what she could do, but that wasn't possible with this level of noise. The three of them were now standing around Viviana's coffee table arguing, throwing nasty things around and pointing their manicured fingers at each other. Céline had red marks on her flawless face and décolleté, Viviana was tugging at her hair and Ina drank her glass all at once, which she usually never did.

"Enough!" cried Sophia, and as it never happened before, the young women immediately fell silent and looked at her.

"I'm sorry, it's my fault," she began, but the others continued to vent their anger and ignored her. Sophia knew she was the reason, because this time she had not played the role she had obviously been meant to play. The role of the guardian, the caretaker who always smoothed the waters before a storm could even arise.

"Please let me finish for a moment."

The others sat down and looked at her expectantly.

"I understand your distress."

There was a loud puff, a sigh and a little "Really?" but Sophia didn't let that stop her from talking.

"I know you think just because I haven't had a boyfriend in a while I have no idea, but I do."

A raised eyebrow, a mouth twisted in mockery, a deep breath

rang out at her in reply.

"Ana, you and Jérôme are getting married soon!" Sophia smiled with joy, and Viviana couldn't help smiling either. "Be happy about that! It wasn't easy, and yes, you were right to remind him to do something good. He's with this organisation now and it's great. He's helping people who haven't been as lucky as others. You should be proud of him and show him that and not cry all the time that he's not here."

Viviana wiped away a tear.

"We'll all help you organise the wedding!" Céline told her.

"And if he doesn't have an opinion and leaves everything to you, that's his problem," Ina pointed out, squeezing Viviana's knee.

Sophia turned to Céline.

"Céline, you are beautiful and strong and many men would fall at your feet if you would only let them."

Céline lifted her chin and crossed her arms in front of her chest.

"Anton is charming and handsome, we would understand if you had a crush on him." Sophia looked helpfully at the others, but they only looked at Céline with concern.

"We don't judge, you've only been siblings for two years and not real ones, so ..." Viviana shrugged her shoulders.

"But he's an asshole!" remarked Ina, and then stammering confessed that she had almost had a one-night stand with him at Céline's last birthday party. For a moment Céline looked angrily at Ina, but then closed her eyes, shrugged her head and just said quietly, "I know."

"And what are you going to tell me?" Ina asked in a sarcastic tone as she turned to Sophia. She had a moist glint in her eye, probably thinking Sophia would see her consume of men the same way as the others. But Sophia didn't see it that way.

"I think you can do what you want if you're happy with it."

Ina lifted the refilled glass and took a generous sip.

"But you're not." Sophia squeezed her friend's arm. "You're looking for a new Sven, but this isn't one of them."

Sven had been Ina's great love back in university days, before he'd broken up with her because he'd accepted a scholarship in Australia. Since then, she tried to find a new Sven, but didn't have much success.

A silence spread and everyone hung on to their thoughts. Sophia filled her friends' glasses, got chocolate from Viviana's large stash and made everyone feel a little better after the argument when she asked about their families and their companies' plans for the Christmas parties.

"You really notice everything.", Viviana remarked after a while, cheering Sophia up as she massaged her aching temples. Ina rummaged in her bag and handed her a painkiller. Sophia thanked her and explained that she'd better get going home, as it would take her almost half an hour by bike.

"But we haven't talked about you yet," Ina smiled sweetly at Sophia.

"Oh, the last meeting regarding the Christmas party is tomorrow," she shrugged.

"And what about your *clichéd, stupid girl crush*?", Céline asked in a soft voice, and although Sophia knew she meant it kind of nicely, she just shook her head.

For a brief moment, she wondered if she should tell them about the encounter with Nick in the park or about his changed behaviour at work and how she felt about it. But she wasn't that stupid and wouldn't give them another reason to mock her. Not after what she had just caused. Sophia was sure they would still be angry with her and probably hurt her even more. No, her feelings for him were too special and the beginning of this ... friendship too fragile. She wouldn't share it with anyone.

She shook her head and laughed playfully. "You know there's nothing to talk about."

Although Sophia sensed that her friends were not entirely convinced, they left her alone. Her headache intensified and shortly afterwards she said goodbye. Although she had a bad feeling about leaving the three of them alone, as she was no longer there to settle their arguments, she simply couldn't take anymore. The last few days had been too intense.

Unlocking her bike, she tried not to think about the argument, but only about Nick, because the memory of his smile worked better than the tablet Ina had given her. The cold air and the fine spray that had just started blew into her heated face, but Sophia liked it and eventually even the tablet fogged her headache. She concentrated more on what he had said, what she would wear on Friday without him suspecting that she was dressing up for him. She hummed one of her favourite songs, a little annoyed that the battery of her mobile phone was dead, otherwise she would have been able to listen to it through her headphones. But since there was hardly anyone else on the street, she could sing out loud.

Just before she reached her neighbourhood, she thought about what his question *Shall I take you home?* had done to her. If only he knew that her desperate brain was twisting it into an ambiguous innuendo! And though she thought of what it would be like if he took her home, she had to laugh as she imagined how he would have reacted. His handsome face with his eyebrows drawn together and his beautiful mouth slightly open in shock. She laughed as she took the last turn and headed for the next traffic light. Oh, how she longed for her bed!

Nick was glad that not only his day had been such an up-and-down ride. After a stirring conversation with his siblings, he spontaneously met up with his buddies for a beer in a Mexican restaurant and discovered that they too had run from one heated conversation to the next as well.

"That's a day for the bucket!", Mark exclaimed and downed his tequila.

"Mad Monday.", Lucas groaned and told of a meeting with the management of an investment firm whose most beautiful member he had spontaneously fallen in love with, but who had immediately turned him down ice cold.

"It's your own fault! To blow off the deal and then ask her out." Laughed Mark and ordered another round.

"Not for me!", Nick exclaimed, after all he still had to drive.

While he listened to his friends and admired Lucas for his courage in asking the woman he desired for a date directly, his thoughts drifted back to Sophia and he wondered what exactly it was that he felt for her. He had an inkling, of course, but even admitting that to himself wasn't easy after everything that had happened back then. But he shook off the black hole of heartbreak and loneliness as he walked to his car and drove home, continuing to think about the feelings Sophia aroused in him.

At a red light he stopped and followed his thoughts. His strange behaviour, his insecurity, his accidentally ambiguous innuendos! Every time when he told himself that there was nothing from Sophia's side, the emptiness in his heart hurt much more than anything he could remember. What it was like to almost drown in heartbreak.

To distract himself, he scrolled through his playlist and paid no attention to the biker approaching the crossing. While listening to Bruno Mars singing exactly what he felt every time Sophia smiled at him.

Yes, his whole world stopped and froze for a while .... If only she would give him a sign! Just one little sign! He hummed along to the melody absent-mindedly, the traffic lights turned green.

He drove off and ....

Chapter 6

Sophia saw the red light in front of her. In the corner of her eye she sensed, paralysed, that a car was coming towards her, but before she could react properly, she heard car tyres squeaking. A skid as she braked. Sliding. A dull impact vibrated through her legs as she jumped off the seat, the steering wheel pressing uncomfortably into her stomach. The shrill screech of metal on metal. Shattering glass.

Oh crap, that was pretty close!

Everything happened so incredibly fast that Nick didn't even notice. Brake! Pull the steering wheel around! Damn it! Damn it! He jumped out of the car faster than he understood what he was doing, swearing more than he ever had before.

"Are you hurt?", he shouted before he reached the person on the bike. "I'm so sorry, shit, I wasn't ... are you hurt? Please... oh god!"

A scrunching sound under his shoes. Oh please, don't let the person be hurt! Just because he has to think about *her* all the time!

"Sophia!"

Taken aback, he stopped as he saw her face.

The cold rain became heavier and they stood frozen in that moment. Everything around them stopped, frozen. Even the air. Silence. Then suddenly he felt his heart pounding deeper, as if taking a deep breath before leaping into the water. Then it raced in his chest. Everything blurred into an unreal, ghostly dream. Like the darkest hour of the night. Sophia. Sophia! She looked terrified. Her eyes were huge and the shock on her face literally screamed at him. Before he realised what he was doing, he grabbed her by the upper arms, leaned down and sought her gaze.

"You ok?"

A small nod was all she was capable of. He had felt her flinch when he had grabbed her, so she was in pain!

"What's hurting you?"

"Nothing."

"But you flinched!", he shouted nervously and slowly palpated her arms.

Sophia could only stare at him. A small part of her brain knew that he was the driver, that he wanted to see if she was hurt, but all she could think about was that she had been thinking about him the whole time and now he was suddenly standing in front of her, looking at her worried. It was so surreal. Despite the quilted jacket she was wearing, she felt his big hands moving up and down her arms and she felt warm even though she was freezing at the same time. Her stomach tingled and so did her head. Her feet were probably standing in a puddle. Still, she was warm. His gaze was full of concern and his eyes shimmered from the raindrops that hit her face. She would have liked to put her hand on his cheek to reassure him, but she couldn't really feel her hands, she only saw that they were still clutching the steering wheel.

"Are you in pain?", he cried with desperation in his voice. "No."

"But you ... oh, you're cold!" He rubbed her shoulders and the next moment he pulled her into his arms and ....

Oh. That felt good.

For a little moment he tugged her a little closer, and then they stumbled over her bike, which crashed to the ground. One step and then another. Nick led Sophia to the passenger seat and pushed her in, then he was gone.

As he rummaged around in the boot, she took a deep breath to steady her heart. What had happened? Then she felt he was back. And so close. She could have counted every single stubble of his beard if he hadn't been moving so frantically. Then she heard a zipper open. He pushed the jacket off her shoulders, and the next moment she felt a cosy blanket around her. It smelled of freshly washed laundry and cold car. He tucked it around her and then looked into her eyes.

"Are you really okay?"

At last he stopped moving. But oh ... he was still so close and why did he smell so good? Somehow like damp wood. Sophia caught herself sinking deeper into the seat.

"I'm just cold." Was that really her voice?

"Yeah, sure. I..." He ran his fingers through his hair and closed his eyes.

Sophia saw that his eyelashes were not only long, but also very thick. And the deep furrow between his brows was so ... disturbing in his handsome face that she would have liked to wipe it away.

"I'm so sorry." He wanted to reach for her hand, but noticed that it was under the blanket, so he just squeezed her arm.

"It was red." Sophia confessed, suddenly realising that she really could have hurt herself badly if he hadn't reacted so quickly.

"But I was distracted..."

"I didn't stop and hit your car.", Sophia admitted softly. Her throat was tight and her eyes met his.

"Sorry about that."

He shook his head slightly, but she nodded.

"You are ... ", he took a deep breath and was about to say *stubborn*, but instead he smiled this crooked smile, and Sophia took

65

another deep breath, her heart swirling in her chest, and she felt a little dizzy.

"You're really not hurt?"

"No, I'm not." Sophia noticed how she smiled.

Her eyes were glued to his and Nick was about to wipe the stubborn strand of hair that stuck to her forehead from her face, but stopped when he reached out. Instead, he braced his hand against the doorframe and his brain suddenly went blank. Then he slowly began to realise that he had almost driven her over! He felt an urgent need to take her in his arms and press her against him, but instead he only clenched his jaw.

"Can you ...?" Her voice was soft, she seemed calm, as if the accident had not just happened.

"Anything you want." His head filled with images of what else his words could mean, and he was ashamed of it.

"... take me home?"

"Are you sure?"

She gave a silent nod as he stroked her arm again before taking the seat belt and wrapping it around her.

Heat reached her cheeks and they both held their breath, trying not to think about how close they were as he leaned over her. But Sophia's heart and eyes fluttered like a startled little bird when he was so close, and suddenly all she could think about was how she smelled. Luckily, she had chewed a piece of gum earlier, but she didn't know where it had gone. Wordlessly, Nick leaned away from her and closed the door without dropping his gaze from hers. Nick took a deep breath and his heart was beating even more calmly now, almost back to a normal rhythm as he pushed her bike into the boot. There was a cracking, scraping sound, but he didn't care. Nothing mattered. Only that she had to be all right!

"About your car..."

"Please, Sophia, it's really not important."

She looked at him as he started the car and drove off. Only a few moments later he parked in front of the apartment complex where she lived, came running around the car in a flash and helped her out. Sophia didn't know if the accident was still in her bones or if his nearness made her dizzy, but she staggered back a little and he grabbed her arms again. They both gasped for breath. They were so close, so close! Then, without a word, he pulled her with him. One arm wrapped lightly around her waist and Sophia would have liked to sink against him, but held herself upright like a stiff stick.

He asked where her key was and opened the front door when he found it in her jacket pocket. With whirling thoughts, they climbed the stairs and he unlocked her flat and pushed her inside. In her small hallway they faced each other and a certain heaviness suddenly settled on them. Sophia pulled the blanket tighter around her as his gaze seemed to see through her.

Nick nodded at her. "Dry off."

"Okay."

They looked at each other for another moment, then Sophia turned and went into the bathroom, opposite the front door. Nick stared after her. He heard a slight thud, she had probably dropped herself against the door. Then he heard clothes rustling and water running. After a while he heard the hiss of a hairdryer, he stood still for a moment longer before heading in search of the kitchen.

Sophia was shaking and her knees gave way as she suddenly realised what had just happened. A near-accident, was bad enough, but then she had to ride in his car? What was going on that they kept running into each other for the last two days? She shook her head and took off her soaked clothes. Under normal circumstances she would have taken a hot shower to warm herself up, but she couldn't do that with him running around in her apartment.

Oh God. Nick Falkner was in her home!

Suddenly, she felt warm again. Had she tidied up? Had she made her bed? After all, she had everything in one room, and he would see how she slept despite the bookshelf that served as a room divider. Not that he would be too interested, but ... she had better not leave him alone for too long. She quickly blow-dried her hair, which was curling like crazy, and thought about what to wear, after all, she couldn't run half-naked into the room he was in. Panic rose in her, but then she saw that luckily, she had her pyjamas hanging on the hook next to the door. She put it on and her bathrobe over it, and then she ran into the living room.

Nick was standing in the kitchenette preparing what looked and smelled like a cup of tea, and she had to smile because she liked the picture before her eyes. Not only the back of him, but also that he was standing in her kitchen.

"Sit down", he said, looking over his shoulder and pointing to her small sofa. Then he came with a hot, steaming, oversized cup, from which she always drank her latte in the morning, and handed it to her. "Here."

Sophia reached for it gratefully, for she was still cold. His eyes were so dark and she still recognised the worried look in them. Audibly she sucked in the air as she touched his fingers lightly. For that one small moment. Only then, and almost a little too slowly, did he release his fingers from the cup, it was almost as if he was caressing hers. Then he lowered his gaze and sat down opposite her on one of the colourful seat cushions. Her fingers tingled and a hot flash shot up her arm and into her chest. She almost dropped the cup, but instead she pressed it to her mouth and inhaled the hot steam. It all had to be a dream, it couldn't be true! But when she looked up again, Nick Falkner was still sitting opposite her.

"Are you hurt?", he asked again, he was very worried. Her fingers had still been quite cold when he had just touched them.

68

"No, I'm fine."

She lowered her eyes, why did she do that? Had she lied and had pain she wanted to hide from him? Or could she not look at him because he had almost driven her over?

"I can't tell you how sorry I am."

"Again, it was my fault, not yours."

Yes, he thought, not because she hadn't stopped at the red light, but because he was so completely lulled by the thought of her that he couldn't think straight. "But I was distracted..."

Sophia sighed and rubbed her forehead, apparently the effect of Ina's tablet was wearing off. Nick thought she was moaning because she was annoyed by his repeated confession of guilt.

"Okay", he then nodded and exhaled with a smile. "It's your fault."

"I know." She was incredibly tired.

"I didn't mean it like that."

"Hm?" She looked at him and his gaze was somehow so ... soft that she couldn't remember what they were talking about.

"Do you have a headache?" He was almost bursting with worry as he watched her continue to massage her forehead.

"I had it before."

"Is that the reason ... that you weren't paying attention?"

"Yes, that was one of the reasons."

Silently he looked at her and seemed to be waiting for more. Since she could hardly tell him she had been thinking about him, she told him about her friends.

"I was with Viviana and ... there was a fight and .... Yeah, it was pretty intense."

"I'm sorry."

"Don't be. I'm usually more of a referee, only this time it was different, they were very angry with each other."

That was all she wanted to tell him.

"Oh, well, yes, I know how hard it can be."

"Are you the referee in disputes too?"

Her heart lifted, thinking she had something in common with him, but he shook his head.

"I guess it's more Yvonne."

"I wouldn't have thought so." she said lost in thought and immediately bit her lip in a slight rising panic.

"What makes you think it's me?"

"Well, I thought you were the most sensible one of all."

Oh, no. She hadn't said that directly to his face, had she? Crap.

"The most sensible?" He laughed, but she could tell by the look on his face that he didn't quite agree. "What do you mean?"

"Well, I thought ... you always try to find another solution, whatever the problem." Sophia shrugged. "You try to keep costs down, try to keep things running for everyone, and ..."

Their eyes met again and that furrow between his brows irritated her. "Sorry," she nibbled at her hands.

He shook his head but was unable to say anything. Nick wondered why she saw him like that, although he was usually only called a killjoy by Jörn when he argued reasonably. And Ruben always accused him of not giving them the slightest pleasure. Which then usually led to them arguing, and Ruben rubbing in his face that he was so unfair and reminding him of his not exactly reasonable past, which Nick himself was reluctant to remember.

"It's been a crazy day." said Sophia in an apologetic tone.

"Are you sure you are okay?"

"Yes, Nick, I'm fine," she said and smiled, but her smile froze on her face when she saw the look on his face. After all, she had called him by his first name! That had really been the first time, until now she had always avoided addressing him directly.

"I'm just tired." She added stiffly and he took the hint and rose to his feet. Sophia stood up too, and he gestured her to remain seated. But she walked after him to the door anyway.

"Please call me if anything happens to you." He pointed to her head and his gaze was still full of concern, but she would never do that!

"It's all right."

Sophia smiled sheepishly, her emotions all mixed up. She didn't really want him to leave and on the other hand she couldn't wait to be alone.

"Alright." Still, Nick didn't move. He wanted to stay the night with her to see if she was really okay, and on the other hand, he just wanted to get away. He had to get away from her and her big eyes looking at him like that, or he might do something impulsive.

"Alright." she repeated like a soft echo.

"See you tomorrow then."

She nodded and Nick lifted his arm and stroked her shoulder and upper arm briefly, he just couldn't help it. A hot flash went through her and her breath caught, then he turned and pulled the door shut behind him.

He leaned heavily against it in the dark stairwell and reviewed what had happened. What a nightmare! Mixed with the most wonderful thing that could happen. She had called him by his first name and made him feel so warm! Only then did he realise that he was cold too. He turned around and raised his hand to knock, maybe he shouldn't go after all! But he decided not to, because she wanted to be alone. He had probably already crossed a line, for she had flinched every time he had touched her. Damn! But well, almost every time, not when he had stroked her fingers. He closed his eyes and put his hand on the door, as if he could somehow use it to pass on his feelings as a message to Sophia. Then he turned and left.

Sophia pressed her aching forehead against the cool surface of her apartment door and stroked it with her hand. She imagined it was him and closed her eyes. She really should go to sleep now, it was late and tomorrow would be another busy day.

Later she lay down wrapped in his blanket and tried to find his woody scent on it, but she fell asleep as soon as her head touched her pillow. Strangely, she only dreamt of his hands on her arms and the worried look in his eyes. Those soft dark blue eyes. Not for a second did she dream about the accident.

Quite the opposite of Nick, who tossed and turned in his sleep all night. He dreamt about the accident and her appearance on Halloween. It was horrible. At one point he woke up completely shaken and half-asleep he looked for his mobile phone and searched for her number. When he had already dialled it, he remembered what time it was and was convinced that she was probably already asleep. He decided to write her a message. But what should he write? Maybe that he would prefer to give her a lift every day instead of her continuing to go by bike, but he could hardly do that. Then he remembered that he still had it in his boot.

I'll pick you up tomorrow morning. Is 8 o'clock ok?

He lay back in the pillows and thought about their conversation. How that delightful blush lit up her pale face when she said he was the sensible one in his family.

Thank you, but I really enjoy going by bike.

Why was she awake? She was supposed to be asleep! Worry about her crept up his spine again. But he didn't want to upset her with his worry and simply wrote back.

Your bike's with me.

So now she had to react somehow. Either she would tell him to bring her bike back now or tomorrow morning, or he should take it to work. And that would make it clear that she wanted nothing more to do with him, and then he would finally know ...

You stole my bike?

Nick laughed, he hadn't thought she would write back in such a teasing way and thought about what to reply .... something funny, but before he could write, another message came from her.

What do I have to do to get it back?

Oh, she hadn't really written that, had she? Sophia's heart pumped harder when she realised it was clearly ambiguous and was about to delete the message when he replied.

Just come with me.

Nick would have had about a million other responses to her message, but that would have been a bit inappropriate, after all, they worked together and weren't buddies. Well, maybe they could become something like that. He groaned. What a load of rubbish! That would never work.

The next morning Sophia was already standing there when he came to pick her up and his heart pounded as she came closer. Then she stopped and stared at the damage on his car. He gestured her to get in and she immediately started talking about insurance and that she would fix it, and he just grinned and shook his head.

"It's really no problem, a friend will fix it for me."

"Really?", she asked contritely, and he was just glad to have her back again. In his car ... So safe and unharmed.

Sophia thought about what to say, after all, this night's events were now somehow between them, but he changed the subject and told her about his little acquisition trip and asked her opinion about his siblings' different ideas for the Christmas party.

The whole day was hectic again, but the meeting with the whole team was the highlight of the day, since Yvonne had announced some exciting news. But for Nick, all that mattered was that he could see Sophia without the disturbing plant between their offices being in his field of vision and blocking his view. He sat extra far away from her so he could watch her.

After a little welcome from Ruben, Jörn started with his proposal to hold the party in one of the hippest clubs in town. He had already spoken to the star DJ and set out some options. The idea didn't go down well, and Ruben of course upped the stakes with his idea that the company should not only have an internal party, but also a Christmas event to which all the photographers and clients would be invited and where something interesting and unexpected would happen. Nick rolled his eyes in annoyance as all he could think of was the unnecessary expense and met Sophia's smile, whereupon he thought the same and nodded at her. Yes, apparently, he really was the sensible brother.

Yvonne enthusiastically explained her idea to make it a team-building event and talked about the seminar she had attended. Then she tried to motivate the employees to share their own ideas with her and after the majority had nothing to say, Nick tried to end the meeting.

"Sophia had a good idea." He then explained and gestured for her to stay a moment longer. She never thought he would value her opinion so much, especially since they had only been spoken into the blue and in private. She thought for a moment about how best to put it and then explained.

"Maybe we could form individual teams to organise a certain part of the party after you have decided where exactly it should take place. That way everyone has something to contribute to the celebration and still gets surprised by each other's ideas."

"I like that!" exclaimed Jörn and Yvonne agreed.

"But what are we going to do with our clients?" asked Ruben in a tearful tone and Nick reminded him of the huge and very expensive summer party on Sylt they had given for their clients in August and that they would all have enough to do with their own Christmas parties.

"Yes, yes ... that's right."

"I will take care of the catering!", Jörn said and Yvonne told them how to put the teams together so that people would work together who would otherwise never do so. Sophia said goodbye and as she left, she could still hear Ruben shouting enthusiastically: "So, I will look for the location!"

And because Nick was afraid that Ruben might get the idea of moving the party to Dubai, he told him that the easiest place for it would be Pielsand. Since he hadn't been there for the big summer party on Sylt, he longed all the more to get back to the North Sea and especially back to their hometown on the coast. This way they could save money, as they not only owned parts of the biggest hotel there, which had once been their family's estate and where Nick had a flat, but also Ruben's holiday home. So, they could save even more money if they all stayed there.

Only about an hour later, Nick had to drive to the appointment with the South African production company and along with Sophia, got her bike out of his car.

"Please be careful this time." he said then and again the wind blew that stubborn curl in her face, but she just giggled briefly and held it in place.

"I promise."

Again that silence spread between them and Sophia wished him a good flight the next morning. But then she could think of nothing more to say. Having gone out in just her jumper, she was freezing and couldn't suppress a small shiver.

"Go in, it's cold."

"Yes, Daddy!" she laughed and he grinned as he replied.

"I'll see you on Friday then."

His voice was very dark, somehow almost promising. They both froze as Nick stroked her arm without thinking. His fingers tingled even though he hadn't even touched her skin yet.

He wondered what that would feel like as she said what would occupy his mind for the rest of the evening, or rather the whole week. And it was rather the way she said it. In a breathless whisper.

"Yes, Friday."

CHAPTER 7

Friday was still so far away and yet he could think of nothing else when he boarded the plane the next morning. Nick had to keep reminding himself that it was work and not a date. But he was happy all the same. They had never been to an evening event together, or any at all. They had never been on a production together since their first photoshoot, she managed that very well on her own. And if there was an invitation to an advertising agency or another party, he was either out of town or had arranged it so that he came with Ruben and spent the whole evening as a brother duo to acquire new clients.

When he thought of Ruben, he groaned heavily. Not only was the budget Ruben was prepared to spend on the over-the-top Christmas party or some other event heavy in his stomach, but also what he or the other two would think if they knew how he felt about Sophia. After all, he would be going against his own principles if he started anything with her. Apart from the fact that she probably didn't want him either. After all, he was one of her bosses!

Yet, he had not been able to get her out of his mind for a year! She had settled there, completely against his will. And not only that, as he now had to admit to himself. No, she was firmly anchored in his heart and difficult to get rid of. And God knows, he had tried! With ignorance, repression and escape. Even when he had ended up in bed with another woman, carefree and without feelings, he had a guilty conscience. As if he had cheated on Sophia!

Some women even asked him if he was involved with someone when he got up. He couldn't look at the woman next to him or himself in the mirror.

All he had wanted was to forget her, but that was not possible. No one could escape from someone who was always around. At some point, every thought led back to her. As if she were connected to him. By an invisible bond. And no matter how far he stretched it, in the end it tightened again like a rubber band and she stood before him again. Unexpectedly. With her kind eyes and sweet freckles. Her shy smile and that unruly strand of hair. And if that wasn't enough, for the past four days, the images of her incredible and unbelievably sensual figure had been added in. Those legs were insane, even when they were in bunny slippers. Not to think of what the tight shirt had presented him or the barely existent jeans shorts!

Yes, the last few days had been very interesting. Nick wondered if she still had that special attraction to him after several hours in a more casual atmosphere. Would she feel more secure and not be so shy and cautious around him anymore? But something had changed anyway. They talked more than they had in the whole year before, and she was funny, he often heard her laughing with her colleagues. He closed his eyes and saw her.

With her big, moss-green eyes, how she had stood freezing in the wind and laughed at her little joke when she had called him Daddy. How her mouth had split and the laughter had tugged at his heart strings. It was as if through a thick wall of fog, the sunlight suddenly shone through. She touched him. Deep inside.

So, Friday was also important for that very reason. Not only to spend a little more time with her, but also to find out if they got along as well as he thought. They only knew each other from work, and there was already this unspoken familiarity. The trust that the other already knew what he had to do. They complemented each other perfectly. He had never experienced anything like it. Not with

78

anyone at work or in real life. For that reason alone, he had to try to get to know her better. But was she even the person he saw in her? Or wished to see? Was she as real as she was at work? Thoughtful. A woman who kept her word? Or would she also rip out his heart and crush it in her hand like a raw egg and trample on it? He had to be sure before he would show her how he felt. Nick knew he had to think everything through carefully for he was afraid of the consequences. It would affect their work. Could he trust her to risk everything? Was she worth losing his heart again? Laughing, he stroked his face. That was nonsense to think about!

He knew he had already lost it.

Sophia felt a little lost. That was the stupid thing about standing in the underground with nothing to do but be alone with one's thoughts. Usually, she liked to ride her bike, so she could be alone with her thoughts, but not too much, as she had to watch out for the traffic. She smiled, since lately that wasn't working out too well either, as one could see on her bike, which she had taken to the bike shop only this morning. She sighed. As she was going home the night before, she had noticed not only that her light was broken, but also that the front wheel had completely warped. It was logical that something had happened to her bike and not just to his car in the crash. But neither of them had looked at it. No, stupid as she was, she only had eyes for him! She had stared at him ... But honestly, who could blame her? God, he was so handsome, it was almost unbearable! There had to be a flaw somewhere, after all, it wasn't normal for someone to be so damn good-looking, nice and worried ... about her! And somehow was so ... kind. Yes, she just didn't have another word for it. Whatever. She knew his weaknesses, after all. He was restless, always on the move and too much on the run, as if he were running away from something. *From life*, her inner voice said, but she didn't really believe that. Something was bothering him, but she couldn't quite put her finger on it. She hoped they would get to know each other a little better, so she would find out. Not that it would change anything about her feelings for him. Not even a dark, evil secret would cure her of her feelings.

Sophia smiled at the thought of him for a moment. How it had felt when he had briefly stroked her arm. It had been so warm. But what was even more amazing, it was as if it was something normal between them. As if it was allowed now, after he had done it after the accident. Did he know what he was doing? And did it have any meaning for him? She drifted off again, but that was actually good, after all she didn't want to wonder what she actually meant to her friends. When she thought about how she always dropped everything as soon as one of her friends called for help. But Viviana hadn't even called back after leaving a message on her voicemail to ask if she could come over, because her bike was broken. That should have alarmed her. She had never asked for help before!

Sophia shook her head and looked out of the window. On the other hand, she was glad that Viviana had had better things to do, otherwise she would have had to explain what exactly had happened, and she didn't really want that. She wanted to keep the thing with Nick to herself. It all seemed so ... fragile. But she would also like to tell someone about her feelings, to think about how she should act. Was there a way she could show him that she liked him? But what would happen and how would it affect their work together if he thought she was stupid? So, she needed to manage to talk to him on Friday so she could get to know him better in a more private setting.

She knew he did everything for the company, more than the other three, or so it seemed at least. He was more open and willing to talk and listen to suggestions for improvement. His door was open not only to her, but to all colleagues in all matters, unlike Jörn's and Yvonne's, who somehow always kept to themselves, even though they were so sociable on the other side. And Ruben, well, Ruben was like an island. Secluded. Far enough away from everyone else. The only one on the top floor from where he could look down on everyone else. The door always locked. And yet he sat in that glass box. It was supposed to suggest openness and visibility to everyone. As if he had nothing to hide, and yet there was something about him...

Her phone vibrated. For a moment she hoped it was a message from Nick, although she knew he was on a plane at the moment.

Hey, sweetie, what happened?

Wrote Viviana. Sophia was on the verge of not replying or ignoring the message. But she didn't want her friend to worry either.

Don't worry. I'll tell you later.

Okay, I'll be in court, call you during the break. xx

Sophia slid the phone back into her jacket pocket and looked out the window again as the train pulled into the station where she had to get off. Two days without him. It felt like an unreasonable situation, as if it had never happened before. She should be glad as she didn't have to keep looking in his direction and thinking about him. Okay, she would anyway, but it wouldn't be as embarrassing as the moments he was suddenly standing in front of her. She smiled at her twisted logic.

But she wasn't smiling when she drove back at half past eight in the evening. It had been a strange day. Somehow the whole day didn't feel as tense, but on the other hand, not as productive as usual either. She hardly had any energy.

Her two colleagues were back, and instead of sticking to the newly learned rules of dealing with each other, as one might expect after a team-building seminar with the boss, they kept to the newly learned rules for about ten minutes. About as long as it took Sophia to check her emails and make a quick phone call to a set builder. After that it was so unbearable that she had to get a coffee first to think about how she was going to get through the whole day with them. But she somehow managed, it was as if she had earplugs in her ears. Ignoring her nagging colleagues, she prepared all the upcoming productions, talked to her photographers and worked through the calculations so that hopefully she would get the cost approvals from Yvonne the next day so that she could start organising everything to be ready on Friday.

What annoyed her somehow, was that he hadn't written a message. Why should he even do that? He had never done it when he was on an acquisition trip. But she thought something had changed between them. Sophia shook her head. Maybe she had imagined all this. Yes, definitely! And the other thing that stung a bit was that Viviana hadn't called after all.

Nick lay in bed in the hotel room at ten thirty and looked expectantly at the display of his phone. He was quite happy that they were now at this point of communication. It was still a lot about work, but it was much more private than he could have imagined a week ago. He had written her a short note saying that everything had gone well in Vienna and that he had a request for a photo shooting, but he had also asked how she was doing. After she had told him that her bike was not doing so well, he shook his head that he had not looked at it when he had returned it to her. But then he understood that she hadn't either, and that gave him hope. Hope that it wasn't just in his head. The thing between them, whatever it was.

Of course, the conversation broke off at some point, but he dreamt a more pleasant dream about her that night than the last few nights, which had been marked by the accident and her Halloween costume. Her breathless *yes, Friday*, turned into a mere *yes!* And it was dark and warm, and he saw her smiling at him in front of an open fire.

The next morning, as he was on his way to his next appointment, he thought about how she had said those two words. As if she couldn't quite believe it. Maybe his imagination was running away with him, but he couldn't suppress the feeling that there was something there. Those encounters since last Saturday. Her gaze on him, which she lowered every time he caught it. The little smile that appeared on her face when she seemed to think he wasn't looking.

It was only a few more hours, but still Friday was *so* far away.

Tomorrow was Friday and Sophia couldn't really calm down or be happy about the fact that she was going out with him the next day. No, it was work! But more relaxed, at least there would be something to drink, a relaxed atmosphere, almost like meeting friends. Well, friends ... her friends hadn't been in touch. She had not heard from Viviana or the other two. Sophia had somehow suppressed the need to reach out to them. Even though she felt bad at the thought, at that moment it was the truth. On the one hand, she would have liked to ask them what she should wear, how she should do her hair, whether she should put on make-up? And above all, how should she behave towards him? But then the nasty remarks of the three came back to her mind and she was glad to be alone with her thoughts. One last time she stared into the wardrobe and thought about what she would wear if he wasn't there, and that's exactly what she laid out.

Since she had no reason to write him, she just stared at her phone for a few minutes. She would have liked to write to him that she was looking forward to the next day, but since she couldn't think of any harmless wording, she decided to switch off her phone.

After a relatively quiet morning and a stressful afternoon during which they were both glued to their phones, Nick knocked on her office door around ten past seven and indicated with a quick glance that it was time for them both to leave. Unfortunately, on the way home he was on the phone busy arguing with Ruben. Although he seemed to control himself, she could see the tension in his jaw and the white knuckles that stood out when he gripped the steering wheel too tightly.

"Ruben, I'll be home in a minute." Annoyed, Nick hung up and looked into her beautiful face, and strangely, a sense of calm immediately came over him. "I'm sorry."

"It's all right."

"I have to admit," he stroked his forehead briefly and looked ahead at the road, "I would rather have talked to you than argued with him." Then he let out a throaty laugh.

Sophia shrugged and before she could think about it, she muttered, "We still have all night."

Nick glanced quickly at her and caught her squinting her eyes before looking out into the evening. His heart beat faster and a certain unease gripped him. But not that exhausting, an annoying uneasiness, but that uneasiness seething with anticipation.

He cleared his throat and tried to suggest as calmly as possible a time when he would pick her up.

"That works for me, see you in a minute." she then called out and had jumped out of his car faster than he could pull into the small parking space.

The location where *Keith & July's* exhibition took place was in an old industrial area where many artists had their studios and there were also some bars and clubs. The car park was poorly lit, but they knew the way. After all, they had been here many times before, each of them alone, to support the photography team on productions. They went up the metal stairs to the top floor, as the freight lift was for years more something for adventurers. They went inside and took off their jackets before going to the brightly lit photo studio to find their hosts. July came to meet them, beaming with joy, and embraced them both enthusiastically.

"My God, you're so hot!" she exclaimed to Sophia, who shook her head, there was really no need to presume, since July said that to everyone, no matter what they looked like. But Nick agreed to the compliment in his head.

"Drink and have fun," July called over the music before disappearing to the door to greet some other guests.

Without saying anything, the two walked to the bar and both grabbed a small bottle of water.

"Don't you drink?"

"Not at work," she said, taking a sip.

So, it was just work for her. Nick clenched his jaw and stared at the people looking at the oversized photos.

"I knew it!" Sophia then moaned and he looked at her questioningly. Sophia pointed her chin towards the window where an older woman was standing, talking to Keith with an oversized glass of wine in one hand and a cigarette in the other, while she more or less poured the liquid of her glass over him.

"Oh no, she's so exhausting!" Nick also moaned after recognising Monique, the fashion director of one of the fashion magazines, who liked to drink too much at industry parties, and then argue about past jobs and their costs. She would even hit on young, good-looking photographers, models or other men who worked in the industry or even just happened to be guests at the event. Sophia grinned as she leaned closer to Nick's ear so he could hear her over the din of the music and the murmur of those present.

"Therefore, no alcohol until I am done with her."

"I understand." He turned with a smile and Sophia had to lean back as he was suddenly so close that she almost touched his face with her nose.

"She always makes you feel like a nobody," she explained, sipping her water to get some distance from his face and sucking in his scent for a little moment.

"I know, in her eyes everyone has absolutely no idea."

"Or you're money hungry and don't fit into the fashion scene at all," Sophia finished his sentence and they both laughed briefly.

"Yep, that fits!"

Sophia, who always felt a little out of place at such hip events, saw his unreadable look and hastily added, "Well, I mean me, not you."

"I don't like these kinds of events either."

Their eyes met again and both felt they had found an ally in the other.

"Are you saying you don't like going to your photographers' exhibitions?"

"Yes, I do. It's just all this fuss, this *we're all so fond of each other*, it's not really my thing."

Nick nodded and lost his gaze for a moment as he thought of someone who had always had the most fun at such events.

"I also prefer to let the photos sink in rather than talk about the latest gossip in the industry," she admitted, shrugging, "sometimes I think it's more important what rumours you know about someone than what you find fascinating about them."

She raised her arm and made a sweeping gesture. If only she knew how fascinating he found her, Nick thought. Sophia caught him looking at her and her eyebrows twitched briefly as if to ask him why he was staring at her like that. Nick smiled.

"And what do you find so fascinating?"

"About them as a team?"

He nodded.

"What's fascinating is that he's the technically skilled, trained photographer and takes July seriously, although as a make-up artist she wasn't taken seriously by many clients and colleagues at first. She has an amazing eye and with her lovely manner can give people so much confidence that they forget they are being photographed and ... Yes, I ramble. Sorry."

Sophia grinned sheepishly and Nick leaned closer. Her light lemon perfume mingled with the scent of her hair, and he suddenly felt fresh and somehow light, even though the harsh light and exhausting music had made him rather uncomfortable.

"I like that." He meant more than what he said, but he didn't want to push his luck.

Then Monique came up to them, greeted him with a brief teasing look and they both knew she would come back later to talk to him alone. Then she eyed Sophia from head to toe and spoke. "Not bad."

Then she pulled Sophia along with her and Nick greeted the client the photographer duo had worked with most recently. But he wasn't fully focused, he was looking at Sophia properly for the first time since she had got into his car.

Those tight black trousers and breakneck high heels made her legs look even longer and really showed off her back view too. She had casually tucked in the white blouse with the little black dots only on one side, and he loved the way she wore her hair. In soft, thick waves that he often imagined burying his hands in. He stroked his forehead to avert his gaze and pay attention to the art director who had joined him and the client.

Sophia didn't have time to really look at the photographs in the exhibition as she was talking to Monique who was telling her about her new, fifteen years younger lover, an aristocrat who would be joining them later. After talking to her, Sophia went around talking to some magazine editors, stylists and location managers, while her eyes wandered to Nick every few seconds. Just like her, he was pushed from one conversation to the next. Time and again their eyes met and both were pleased that the other seemed to be at least a little interested in what the other was doing. They nodded their heads. Or smiled. Or both.

After almost two hours, Keith and July gave a short speech and declared the party open. The lights were dimmed and the music turned up even louder. Sophia was glad that she had already seen the pictures of the exhibition, even if only as a PDF file, otherwise she wouldn't know what they were about at all. She hadn't had time to look at them in the bright light, and in the now dim red light they looked quite different, which was of course due to the effect the photographers wanted to achieve.

Again, she looked around for Nick, who by now was having what was obviously a difficult conversation with someone, because he looked rather annoyed, as if he wished he were somewhere else. That could only be Monique, Sophia thought, and she was right, of course, because she recognised her by her cocky gestures as she stood there with him on the other side of the studio, but of course much too close to him.

Sophia tried to find out if there was anything she could do to help him and slowly walked in his direction. Suddenly, his head jerked a little and then he looked at her with such a penetrating gaze that she felt warm all over. God, she wished he really meant her with *that* look, it made her all-tingly inside. It was as if he wanted to strip her down to her underwear with that look, or even more. As if he could read her most secret desires. But instead, it was most certainly just an angry look due to this annoying woman in front of him. Sophia turned around to collect herself and came face to face with none other than Kristina Schneider, the publisher and editor-in-chief of the best photo magazine in the world, if it were up to her.

For a few minutes she chatted with her, but all the time she had this certain feeling as if Nick was now coming closer and daring a glance at him. He seemed to finally be able to break away from Monique with his jaw clenched, but with a much more relaxed look than before, coming in her direction. Her heart began to pound violently, she had a very strange feeling in her stomach and could hardly listen to Kristina. She tried to resist the urge to look in his direction again after she felt he was looking at her too. But it was as if he was a magnet, and her eyes were forced to look at him as he fought his way through the crowd. Tall and with his broad shoulders and in the dark light, there was something ... she couldn't find the right word for how he seemed. But she liked the incredibly sexy way he kept stopping to talk to someone, but his eyes kept darting in her direction. Every time. With these little conversations he bought her a few more seconds to take a breath, being prevented from coming closer immediately.

Kristina followed Sophia's gaze and leaned in and in a conspiratorial way she said,

"God, how you can work with him is a mystery to me."

Something triggered these words in Sophia, something like protective instinct and she immediately tried to defend him.

"He's alright, really."

Kristina looked at her and grinned.

"I mean, he's often not around, but when he is ... I like working with him. And his view of things."

Sophia looked at Kristina questioningly, as she couldn't quite interpret her look. "What is it?"

"I couldn't concentrate around him."

Oh. Well, she never said she could.

"And the way he looks at you. Are you dating?"

"Oh God, no!" cried Sophia in horror, hoping she hadn't been staring at him so obviously that everyone knew what she was feeling.

"I wouldn't blame you." Kristina smiled knowingly.

"What?" puffed Sophia out laughing, knowing of course that she could hardly blame Kristina for her own stupidity in not hiding her feelings better.

"Well, the way you talk about him and ... It seems to me that you ... like him."

Oh, no! Such a bummer! What was she supposed to say to that?

"But don't worry, I won't tell anyone."

"There's nothing to tell," Sophia retorted annoyed, not because she got caught, but because it was sadly true.

"If you ever get tired of watching him from afar, you can come work for me." Then Kristina smiled kindly and suddenly changed the subject.

Sophia was about to deny the whole thing when she felt him approaching them. Kristina greeted Nick and watched every little look he gave Sophia. With a neutral face she explained to him "I was just telling your Sophia here, if she ever gets tired of..." here she paused dramatically and Sophia's eyes widened in shock, but she immediately relaxed as Kristina continued. "... working for your company, I'd love to hire her."

"Oh, I didn't know you were looking for a new job." Nick tilted his head and twisted his beautiful lips into that crooked smile, and Sophia could only barely audibly reply.

"I'm not."

"I was hoping you'd let me know if there was a problem."

"There's no problem." Except this one in front of me, she thought.

"I think we make a pretty good team." His voice was almost a little too soft as he nodded to her.

Silence.

Sophia's eyes fluttered for a moment, as somehow in her stupid heart that meant so much more than what he had obviously just said. The pause stretched and to get help from Kristina, she looked around, but she had disappeared. To buy time, she took her water bottle from the bar table next to her and took a sip. She hadn't even noticed that Kristina was gone.

Neither had Nick, who wished he could be anywhere else with Sophia. After catching her looking in his direction all evening, he was almost certain that she ... liked him at least a little, as a colleague. Now he just had to find out if there was something more. The dull thud of the bass and the black and red light in the studio evoked a certain heaviness in him, but somehow there was also something almost sensual about it. For the beat was like that of his heart, and he felt so close to her, as if they were alone in a small, dark room, even though there were so many people around them.

"Do you like it here?", actually he wanted to know if they could leave, he had an urgent need to be alone with her.

"Yes, very." Sophia was eager to stay, she didn't want him to leave and hoped he wouldn't say goodbye. "I like photography."

91

"I know."

He leaned closer, one hand on the table. And was that his other hand lightly touching her forearm? Warmth crept up her spine. Nick was relieved when this time she didn't flinch when he touched her and knew he should keep the conversation going, to avoid just kissing her.

"Are you photographing too?" He hoped they had something in common there too.

"Yes, sometimes."

"Will you show me?"

What was wrong with him today? Sophia couldn't believe that Nick Falkner was suddenly so interested in her and didn't know exactly what to make of it. It almost seemed as if he wanted to get to know her better. Maybe it was all in her head, but somehow, she liked it and leaned back towards him and at the same moment he leaned down towards her. Her mouth tingled as she said to him, "Only if you show me your things too."

Nick closed his eyes for a moment. If he was honest, there were many things he wanted to show her, but his photos were the last thing on his mind. Her breath tickled the spot under his ear and he wanted to put his arm around her so she couldn't move away again. There was that warmth in his chest, spreading. He sought her gaze as she leaned her head back. He gave her a quick nod as he almost drowned in her eyes. The dark atmosphere, heavy and somehow sexy, made him say, "I'd like to leave ..."

But her eyes moved and her face took on a different expression.

"What the hell?" she muttered and at that moment someone tapped him on the shoulder.

"Falkner!" The tall, handsome and obviously already slightly drunk man licked his lips and whispered smugly in Nick's ear, "Who's your little friend?" as he let his gaze wander over her.

Nick tried to somehow squeeze between Sophia and his old

acquaintance's gaze and clenched his jaw.

"Sophia Neuhaus, a colleague."

"Oooh. You're getting disloyal to your principles, huh?"

"Just go, Toni," Nick grumbled, trying to push him aside, but instead he leaned down to Sophia and revealed, while looking at her blatantly.

"His motto is *never fuck the company*' Ha!" Then he laughed out loud and gave Nick a friendly hug. He continued far too loudly, "Or in your case, never again."

Toni laughed again and Nick pulled him away, talking to him a few steps away and luckily the idiot didn't look at Sophia again and went back to his lover, Monique.

What a bummer! What would Sophia think of him now? Nick turned back to her and sought her gaze.

"I'm sorry, this is ..."

"Anton Michels."

"You know him?"

Nick leaned heavily on the cold metal table between them, it seemed as if the warmth had disappeared. Her voice sounded strange, so hollow somehow.

"That's the stepbrother of a friend of mine."

"Ah, but he didn't recognise you?"

Sophia curled her soft lips into a sarcastic smile and made a small twitching motion. "I'm usually overlooked." And she felt those words heavy in her chest.

Nick really couldn't imagine that and shook his head. Their eyes met for the length of a blink, but hers were no longer smiling, the sparkle was gone.

Sophia looked behind him at the Reichner sisters.

"I'm sorry, but I have to say hello to these two."

Next, she said the words he had hoped not to hear from her all evening, but he now knew for sure that she was trying to get away from him.

"You don't have to wait for me if you want to leave."

Then she looked at him. A look that said a thousand words and yet only silence reached him.

Chapter 8

Sophia greeted the Reichner sisters, models and influencers and asked over the loud music what they had been up to lately, knowing she would drown in their words. Apart from a few nods of the head and the occasional "Oh, really?", she was able to drift off with her thoughts and think about what had just happened. She thought about what Anton had said and about what it had done to her.

On the one hand, it confirmed her opinion of Anton. He was disgusting. And she understood even less why Céline pined for him. But of course, she also knew that you couldn't really choose who you liked and who you didn't. And about Nick … One of the things she admired about him was his steadfastness. His integrity. She had never noticed him allowing himself to be persuaded to do anything that went against his principles. Neither poaching a photographer from another agency, nor lowering costs into the red to steal clients from the competitors. He valued everyone's work and believed that one should be paid for it. She knew he was responsible for pay rises and commissions, even if on the other hand he was also the one who had to tell people they were being made redundant. She imagined that it was a deal he had made with Ruben. Some even had the evil thought that he liked to kick people out, but she didn't believe that.

Sophia imagined that she had got to know him well enough in that one year to know that he cared about the staff. That he listened to them and saw it as his duty to look after them. Yes, he did his duty and was true to himself.

Briefly she closed her eyes and tried to breathe calmly. She desperately needed to try and get her troubled emotions under control and drive home without bursting into tears. She brushed her hair back and looked at the young women in front of her, continuing to listen with half an ear. She dared a fleeting glance in Nick's direction.

He was standing at the table where she had left him. Upright, of course, his stony face looked proud. And in the dramatic light it looked like a painting. His gaze was lowered to the table, his hand seemed to be painting a pattern on it. He looked as if he had sprung from one of the photographs behind him. He was part of the whole room, belonged to them all, and yet it seemed to her that he was terribly alone. Her heart contracted painfully. For a moment, she thought of going back to him, but decided against it, probably he wanted a moment alone. Surely, he was thinking about what Anton had said. That was why she had told him he could go if he wanted, but she hoped he wouldn't. Sure, old wounds had been reopened, but she hoped it wasn't so painful anymore. It had to have been bad, what had happened then. She didn't pay attention to gossip and didn't participate in it, but every little bit of information about Nick she soaked up like a dried-up sponge. And just like that, she had absorbed his every look and word and stored them in her heart.

Apart from the fact that she had perhaps only imagined the whole thing that evening and that his approach was only due to the loud music, one thing was clear: contrary to what Anton had said, he would remain true to himself and his principles.

He would never get involved with a female colleague again after the story of nine years ago.

Sophia stroked her forehead and knew she had to be alone. With a quick wave of her finger in the direction of the toilets, she left the Reichner sisters and squeezed through the crowd. To be truly undisturbed, she went to the back washroom and wet her face with ice-cold water to clear her head. However, it was all in vain. Every look, touch and interest, imagined or not, led nowhere.

The mirror image of her face looked sadly back at her. But the closer she looked at herself, the more she thought her eyes looked tired rather than sad, and when she smiled, she saw a nice smile. That it was put on wouldn't really interest or be recognised by the people out there. Sophia came to a decision and left the washroom with quick steps.

Nick had watched Sophia talking to the two silly girls. It pricked his heart that she wanted to get away from him so quickly. But who wouldn't want that? After Toni's line, she probably thought he was the kind of bastard who would only try to get his female colleagues laid. Well, he'd been trying to scare Sophia away for twelve months, and now that he'd finally come to terms with the fact that he wasn't going to make it and had to somehow dare to show her his feelings, Bang! She ran away faster than he could think. And it hurt.

Hell, yes, it really hurt!

Not like back then. Of course, that had been different. He wiped his face, not wanting to go down that dark path of memory, ever again, but it was so unfair what Anton had said. He had had a relationship with her. Cora. A woman as beautiful as a bright spring morning, but just as cold and painfully shrill. His father, siblings and he agreed that they wouldn't tolerate relationships within the company, but since they'd been together since their school days and she worked in the accounting department, it was fine. She loved the parties of the scene, being looked at like you were special. Still, it had been a serious relationship. And yes, he had been stupid enough to ask her to marry him. So stupid that she had to think it over, since they were both so young, as she went skiing in Switzerland with her parents over Christmas. But then she came back, engaged to someone else! And as it turned out, she had also taken some company data and client files for her future husband, with whom she had been cheating on him for months. Later, they had also poached one or two photographers. It had been a difficult time, from which the company had recovered faster than he had.

Nick shook his head to push the thought away and stared at the table in front of him. He noticed how he tried to make out Sophia's face in the pattern that the red and black light conjured up on it. Her gaze as he had leaned closer. He had not been a child of sadness all these years. He'd had a few flings and even something like a relationship now and then, never serious enough to last more than a few weeks, and never with the kind of feelings Sophia evoked in him. He was well aware, even though Cora had played him and broken his heart, that certain physical reactions from another could not be ignored.

No, he hadn't imagined that Sophia's eyes had widened when he had leaned closer. She looked slightly nervous when he touched her arm, though he couldn't tell for sure if her cheeks were flushed in the light. Also, her quickening breath, which had tickled him a little as she spoke to him. He knew there was more. Only what exactly?

He lifted his eyes and looked over at her as she listened to the silly Reichner sisters with a smile on her face, but he knew her thoughts were elsewhere. He saw it in the little crease between her eyebrows. Sophia's gaze was fixed on a point in the distance. Her thumb drew small circles across her fingertips. The slightly unsteady twisting of her ankle gave him the certainty that she was about to run. All these little things he knew about her. And he wanted more. He wanted to know what was going on in her head, what she thought of him and about what Toni had said. Did she know about that time? Had she heard about it? Surely, she had heard about it, it was the best kept secret in the company and everyone knew about it. He groaned, rubbing his face, but nodded to himself.

Yes, he knew what he had to do.

Sophia walked out of the washroom with her back straight and let her eyes wander over the crowd, she couldn't see Nick anywhere and although she was disappointed that he had probably left, she told herself it was for the best. When she returned to the main room, the large photo studio, she saw the photographer duo finally standing together and she took the opportunity to thank them for a great evening and say goodbye. Luckily it wasn't too late and she might still catch one of the last buses heading in her direction. In the small room where they had deposited their jackets, she looked for hers and groaned when she felt the certainty that someone had probably taken her jacket by mistake. What wouldn't be so bad per se, the old thing was pretty thin anyway, but her house key was in its inside pocket. Grumbling, she turned and ran out of the dark alcove, just managing not to crash into a wall that wasn't a wall.

"Oh!", she moaned as she stumbled back a few steps.

"Hi."

"Hi."

Again there was that one too long moment of silence between them. Nick smiled slightly at her and her heart lifted with the curve of his lips.

"I was looking for you," he said simply and Sophia felt her heart tingle.

"I was looking for my jacket."

What kind of stupid answer was that? Even if it was the truth.

"Here," he handed her the jacket and explained without looking

99

at her, "I thought it's time to go."

"Oh, okay." Sophia nodded and put the jacket on. Her thoughts spun as if in a gigantic whirlpool, what was going on here? What was the meaning of this? Why had he done it? Did he just want to go home or did it have a deeper meaning?

Without another word, they walked silently side by side the few steps out into the corridor that led to the rickety freight lift and the stairs. As some people were about to leave, it was quite crowded and they were pushed from behind and prevented from going on from those in front. The grating of the metal stairs was not exactly heel-friendly and Sophia tried to find a way to the railing so she could get down the stairs without breaking her neck. It was barely moving forward and people were pressing up against her from behind. One very special person stood next to her like a protective wall. Nick had his hand behind hers on the railing and although he wasn't touching her, she felt his arm against her back. He was pressed against her left side and although she knew it was impossible, she still feared that he could feel her heart beating despite the thick jackets they wore. To distract herself from her thoughts, she tried to talk to him about the exhibition. But she soon realised that Nick didn't feel like talking. He only gave short, terse answers or nodded briefly at her before his gaze returned to the people in front of them.

Of course, Nick noticed that Sophia was talking more and faster than usual, so she was either nervous or uncomfortable with him. When they were finally downstairs, there was a general goodbye with the other guests who were about to leave. A few phrases were exchanged, little kisses on the cheeks, a few dates were made. A few more people went to one of the clubs nearby, but most headed for the buses or taxis. He was about to ask her if they wanted to go to one of the bars, but he didn't want to be disturbed by any kind of interruption. He tried to put himself in her place and had made a decision.

Sophia tried to talk to him again to cover her nervousness, but she could tell by the look on his face that she was somehow making it worse, and fell completely silent halfway to his car. They got in, and as they both buckled up at the same moment, his long fingers accidentally touched the back of her hand, and she quickly pulled her hand away. But pretended to look for something in her jacket pocket.

"I'm sorry."

"For what?", she asked somewhat breathlessly, inwardly scolding to herself for her obvious shortness of breath after that little innocent touch. Sophia could only hope that he wouldn't notice.

Nick pinched the root of his nose with his thumb and forefinger and squeezed his eyes shut for a moment. Sophia knew from previous observations that he usually did this in difficult negotiations, so although she was now even more prepared for something bad to happen, she hadn't expected what came next.

"About Toni."

"Oh." Her face twitched and then she looked out into the dark night. "It doesn't matter."

"What doesn't matter?"

"Well, that he didn't recognise me." She shrugged, hoping he wouldn't bring up the other subject.

"Would you have preferred him to recognise you?"

"No … I don't know." Sophia gave a short, embarrassed laugh. "It's probably better that way, or I would have given him a piece of my mind." She hoped to avoid the subject that somehow seemed to hover over them like a dark storm cloud.

"Really?"

"Of course," she glanced over at him briefly, "I think he's kind of greasy and there's something … I don't know, something really nasty about him."

"Ahh."

"And now you're telling me he's one of your closest friends?"

"No." Now it was Nick who laughed. "We attended school together, and we've had little contact over the years, but I don't think I've heard from him in two or three years."

"I don't think that's much of a loss." Again she looked over at him briefly, sensing that the matter was not over for him.

"You really don't like him, do you?"

"He makes Céline unhappy."

Nick looked over at her for a moment before looking back at the traffic.

"Other than that, I don't care about him." Hopefully, he understood the larger meaning behind her words without her actually having to say it.

But Nick preferred to be sure.

"So, you don't care what he says either?"

His voice was firm and his gaze fixed on the road ahead, but Sophia saw him clench his jaw.

"Yes, unless ..." Oh no, she really just wanted to say yes. What a bummer! She didn't want to, he would surely ask now, and no sooner had she finished the thought than he did.

"What?" He clenched his jaw even more.

"Well, unless he's talking shit about her."

"I see." His knuckles turned so white from gripping the steering wheel so tightly.

"Or about anyone else I care about."

Nick looked at her again and in the blackness of the night she couldn't quite make out what was written on his face. But she knew she had said more than she wanted to and hoped he understood anyway.

"He is someone who deliberately provokes, that's where he gets his energy from. He has always been like that." Unmoved, he threaded the car into another lane.

"Like I said, I don't care."

"I just don't want you to take it the wrong way."

There. Now he had said it. They both had to live with the truth that would come out of it. A quick glance at Sophia showed him that she seemed to be thinking about his words. She sucked her lips into her mouth and looked down at her hands. When she answered, her voice seemed rough.

"I did not." And that was the truth.

The choice of words had been disgusting, just as Sophia had assessed Anton after his initial charm had faded. But it didn't change the fact that she seemed to know Nick better than Anton. She just knew he would stay true to himself, his principles and his sense of duty. Looking out at the city lights, she realised they were almost home. Although she didn't want this tension between them to last and she desperately wanted to escape the car, she wanted just the opposite and to stay with him. To enjoy the last moments in his presence before running to her flat and giving in to her feelings.

"I dated Cora for a long time before we both started working at my father's agency." He parked the car and looked at her as she unbuckled her seatbelt.

"Really, you don't have to explain."

"But I want to."

Their eyes met and although the streetlight dimly illuminated the car, they couldn't quite make out the expression on each other's faces. Nick thought he was forcing a conversation on her, which she understandably didn't want to hear, but he wanted her to understand that she meant more to him than Toni had implied.

Sophia wasn't sure she could bear the story that would come out of his mouth. From what she knew of her colleagues, it had been a difficult time for him. There were rumours that alcohol and drugs had been involved and she was afraid she would start crying for him or have to pull him into her arms to comfort him.

"I'm sorry … I understand if you don't want to hear it …", Nick rowed back, gladly kicking himself for his stupidity. "It's just not how Toni made it look."

Sophia nodded with a slightly pursed mouth and turned her face to the side. What was she supposed to say now?

"I know."

Suspecting something or knowing it is different from having it confirmed. He wanted to be sure she knew he wasn't about to do what Anton had implied, that was clear with that statement. She felt a tingling behind her eyes and knew she had to get out of here. Sophia reached for the door handle, turned back to him and forced herself to smile. "Good night, Nick."

She got out, walked around the car and disappeared in the direction of her house. If Nick hadn't seen the movement, as if she'd wiped her face, he might wouldn't have got out, but he had the feeling that she was slipping away from him somehow, when he should have been holding her instead.

Sophia barely got three steps when it hit her like a hammer. What an outrageous person she was! He wanted to talk to her, tell her his side of things, and she had prevented him. Maybe he just needed a friend! She turned around and quickly walked back the few steps she had come.

"Sophia."

Suddenly, he was standing in front of her and she smiled tentatively as their eyes met for a brief moment and remained locked on each other for a moment longer. Why had he come after her? Her heart did a double beat and her stomach tingled again. Her throat was dry and she imagined she could tell by the look in his eyes that he didn't want to leave just yet.

"Hi."

"Hi."

He hadn't imagined that she had come back, had he? It was unexpected, but Nick knew she was on her way back to his car. He looked at her, searching for the right words. Say or leave it at that? Keep fiddling around or just straight out with it? Risk it then somehow coming between them or rely on how she had made him feel? He was literally lost, the look on her face only making his confusion worse. The expression on her face distracted him from thinking. Her big eyes and that look that could mean everything or nothing.

"I would like to … "

"I still have … "

Again they laughed and Nick made a gesture of prompting to make sure she would speak first.

"I still have your blanket." Said Sophia, and he saw her sucking on her lower lip after the words, she was nervous, though she tried to hide it. He found her so incredibly adorable at that moment that he involuntarily took a step towards her.

"And I would like to talk to you further."

"I'll listen, though I don't think I'm the right person for this kind of conversation."

Was there a moist glint in her eyes? He was eager to find out.

"I think you're the right person for any kind of conversation."

Sophia looked at him stunned. Could this really be? Was he serious? Did he want to get to know her better and had said it without actually saying it? And if so, did it mean what she wished it would mean? Did he like her? just as a friend or even … more?

"You're probably the only one," she tried to lighten the mood, but didn't succeed very well.

"I can't imagine that."

"When I think of Monique or …"

"Don't listen to those people. You're just right."

Sophia smiled that smile that made him feel warm inside and he smiled back, nodding. Before the two of them realised what they were doing, they climbed the stairs to her apartment side by side.

Chapter 9

It was only when Nick stood in her apartment door and waited for her to step aside so that he could enter that Sophia realised that it was the second time in five days that she had him in her flat. Once again, completely unexpected and unplanned. She felt warm and cold at the same time, not only because his broad shoulders seemed to barely fit in her small hallway and just the thought of it was so damn sexy, but also because for a moment she panicked and thought she hadn't cleaned up. And unlike Monday, when he'd come to her place after the accident and probably hadn't had an eye for it, maybe now he'd pay more attention to how her place looked. But she had no choice but to play it off.

"Would you like something to drink?" she hoped he wouldn't hear the nervousness in her voice.

"Yes, thank you."

She envied his completely calm response. For him, it seemed perfectly normal to go to a woman's flat with her, and although she knew it was perfectly fine, that nasty little sting of jealousy pricked her. She tried not to let her brain wander in that direction, but still thought of all the rumours that he only dated models and the stupid comments from her girls. So, she forced herself to quickly take off her shoes and disappear into the kitchen. Only then did it occur to her that it might not have been very polite not to take his jacket. But what did she know? She didn't get visits from the opposite sex that often. If she counted off the caretaker and the movers. The last man in her flat had been Jérôme when he was with Viviana at her housewarming party, and the guy Ina was dating at that time. She flitted through the kitchen and let her gaze wander briefly over her room. The bookshelf that stood as a screen in front of her bed, separating it from the rest of the room, was neatly tidied and the bed behind it was freshly made and not rumpled. There were no loose clothes lying around anywhere, and she had even washed her coffee cup in the morning because she had simply got up too early and had had enough time to do it. Sophia bent down to look in her sparsely filled fridge, which contained a few snacks and two bottles of mineral water, some leftover sparkling wine from Halloween and two small bottles of beer.

Slowly, Nick came sauntering into the room as if he were on holiday and walking on the beach. He seemed completely relaxed and Sophia realised that this was the way she liked him best. But at the same time, it made her quite sad because he rarely let this side of him come to the surface. Never around her until now either, or at least she thought he did. While he was apparently looking at the photos on her walls, Sophia kept her face in the fridge and rummaged around in it as if she had more than five things in it. On the one hand to buy time, on the other to cool her burning cheeks. She hoped he wouldn't notice that she was as red as a tomato.

Nick noticed a few things in the few minutes he was in her flat that he had apparently overlooked on his first visit or had not noticed out of sheer worry and fear for her. It was comfortably warm and there was a pleasant smell of vanilla. The walls in the hallway and in the room were painted a warm but not too dominant yellow, which made the photographs hanging on them stand out especially in the warm light created by many small fairy lights and lamps. He felt really comfortable and looked at the black and white photos with the trained eye of a photographer's agent and learned some more details about Sophia.

Apparently, she liked black and white photos, and instead of family photos or pictures of wild parties, she preferred various maritime shots. Grainy sand, seaweed, old boats eaten away by salt water. Smiling, he went into the living area and continued to look at the pictures she had hung on the wall in a loose pattern. Only when she asked him if he preferred the old sparkling wine or a small bottle of beer did he look over at her and let his eyes rest for a moment on her shapely, pretty butt before forcing himself to turn away again.

"A beer, please."

He heard her open two bottles and was glad that the working day was now over for her too. A quick glance over the shoulder showed him that she was hesitating, apparently considering whether to put the bottles on her small coffee table or bring them to him.

"Are these yours?" He pointed to the atmospheric photos on the wall.

"Yes." Her reply was curt, but the beauty of it was that her eyes lingered on his for a moment longer.

"Those are good."

"Yeah, sure." Giggling, she came over to him, just as he had wanted.

"No truly, they are! You have a good eye for detail and mood."

"Are you trying to contract me, Mr Falkner?" joked Sophia, and Nick liked that teasing side of her.

"I already have you."

His voice was so dark that it sent a shiver through her body. But he smiled that smile, unaware of the turmoil the truth in his words was causing in her. Sophia had to remind herself that this was really happening and not one of her very realistic dreams.

He was flirting with her.

Nick took his time looking at the photo in front of him, then reached for the bottle she held out to him and smiled gently at her. Her deep eyes slowly found their way back to his and only then did he let his gaze wander back to the image on the wall. Lightly he ran his fingers over the edge of the photo. It was a random pile of shells. The foaming water swam around them as if an invisible barrier prevented the spray from simply pulling the shells back into the sea. Suddenly, he felt as if he were looking through his own camera and standing with his feet in the cold water of the Northern Sea. When he lifted his head now in his memories, he looked directly at what used to be the family estate, which was now a hotel and where he had a flat. A strange heaviness came over him that he had not felt for so long, or rather had repressed for even longer. Sophia could tell from his changed facial expression that he was obviously struggling with a memory.

"What's wrong?" she asked anxiously before she could figure out what he might be thinking about.

"The picture reminds me of home."

Sophia said nothing and waited for him to continue. "Pielsand."

When he looked at her, she nodded silently at him, not wanting to interrupt him in case he wanted to tell her more.

"The atmosphere gives me a, I don't know, wistful feelings."

"I'm sorry about that."

"Don't be," he looked at her briefly again with that smile that made her knees go weak, and she gripped the bottle tighter, as if it would give her needed support. "Sometimes it's good to feel something like that, or .... longing."

Whether it was his words, or the gentleness with which he had said them, or his deep gaze, Sophia could not tell, but it made her avert her eyes as her heart pounded so violently in her chest.

Longing. Yes, she knew the feeling. But she tried to steer the conversation in another direction.

"Unfortunately, they all have a slight green tinge."

Astonished, Nick looked at the pictures even more closely and nodded, but his thoughts circled around the certainty that she also felt longing. He was quite sure he had seen it in her eyes.

"It's the paper," he said instead.

"I know," she agreed with a shrug, "but unfortunately there aren't that many photo labs that take pictures from negatives anymore."

"You photographed analogue?" Nick shook his head in admiration that she had made this dying art her hobby. "Then you'll have to enlarge them yourself."

Sophia laughed. "For the few pictures I take, the effort of building a darkroom would be a bit excessive." When she felt his gaze rest on her, she spoke on quickly. "There's no room for it in this flat."

Nick nodded knowingly, and the crease between his eyebrows deepened.

"And before you ask, I've asked all our photographers, but none of them have one."

"We have one."

Sophia fell silent and just looked at him. She found it strange and exciting at the same time and she felt her heart go back into that state of vibrating throbbing. Silently she waited for him to continue speaking.

"At home."

If that was an indirect invitation, Sophia didn't know how to respond. Flirting or whatever it was they were doing felt so strange. Not only had it been so long since she had last been interested in a man that she had forgotten how to do it - if she had ever known how to do it at all - but it felt so unreal with him. As if at any moment the illusion that he *could* feel the same would be over.

"I wish I knew how to do that," she only explained, expecting him to change the subject.

"I can show you."

His face was turned to the picture in front of him as if he wanted to avoid her rejection. But she couldn't, even if she had wanted to. Her curiosity and interest were greater than her insecurity towards him.

"Really?"

"Yes, sure." He gritted his teeth and Sophia was a little irritated by this observation, as he usually only did this when he was upset or very tense. "I can show you everything."

Then he looked at her. It was the same look he had given her earlier at the exhibition, when he had glided through the crowd after talking to Monique, looking at her. Penetrating. Sophia got all tingly and she felt her body begin to glow, not just her cheeks. Sophia had to swallow and took a sip of her much too cold beer and let it run slowly down her throat. Her imagination ran away with her as she directed his words to other aspects and she felt him looking at her.

"If you like."

Taking the urgency out of his words, Nick forced himself to smile softly, although he would have liked to grab her, she was just so adorable. With her insecurity written all over her beautiful face. Those deep green eyes, so dark and tender, asking questions she couldn't formulate with her mouth. Oh, yes, that beautiful mouth.

But he had to hold back, given that it had only been a week since they had begun to speak more than two words to each other. If he was right in his assumption that she also felt more than just work-related camaraderie for him, he should give her some more time to come to terms with his changed behaviour. After all, he knew how

112

she and others felt about this fact.

More often he had heard one or the other saying from co-workers or even his sister. Expressing their opinion that he was the only one who didn't get along with Sophia. Since he only spoke to her in such a curt and unfriendly manner and avoided any contact with her. If people knew that he had been falling more and more in love with her over the last twelve months or so, they would all think he was crazy. Puffing, he laughed out loud.

"I'd have to make sure the chemicals and paper were still good first." He chuckled briefly as he inhaled, "it's been a while."

Again Sophia noticed that sad look in his eyes and hoped not to offend him when she asked him why he had stopped. She feared that he would now talk about his horrible experience with his ex, but she was not prepared for what he told her instead.

"I used to do that with my father."

For a moment he looked over at her and she saw the glitter of tears in his eyes. She knew her bosses' parents were dead, but that was all she knew.

"We took photos all year and in the time before Christmas we enlarged the best five pictures of each and bound them into a homemade book." He smiled as he thought of how much he had loved working with his father.

"What a lovely idea."

"It was. During that time, my father took extra time for each of us," his gaze seemed to wander off into the distance, "each of us had him all to ourselves for once."

Sophia would have liked to take him in her arms. She had the feeling that, as big and strong as he always seemed, he was just a boy who missed his parents terribly. She felt the prickling of tears behind her eyelids.

Before she knew what she was doing, she stroked his arm. "I'm so sorry you lost your parents."

Although he had suppressed these feelings of loss for so long, and when the subject was discussed with his siblings, he was always the strong one who tried to keep a cool head and not give in completely to his emotions like the other three, he felt strangely light. The warmth emanating from her gentle and sincere compassion and the slender hand on his upper arm slowly seeped into his heart. This moment was so precious that he just wanted to enjoy it silently. Never before had he felt he could open up completely to someone without running the risk of exposing himself in an uncomfortable way. Of course, it had not been his intention to talk to her about how painfully he missed his parents, not on this evening when they were slowly becoming closer in some way, but at this moment it just felt right.

"I miss them." He nodded and turned his head slightly in her direction. "Especially at this time of year, but ... well, I haven't... let myself have those feelings in a long time."

Nick thought she understood what he was trying to tell her as their eyes locked on each other in silence. She felt for him. Slowly, very slowly, she also seemed to understand what he had just confessed to her. That he felt so comfortable with her, revealing himself to her in this way.

"Thank you for reminding me."

Only when he turned a little more towards her, did she notice that her hand was still on his upper arm and blushing, she let it drop. Sophia was at a bit of a loss as to how to act now and tried to cope with all the emotions that were stirring. For a moment they stood there in silence, but it was that pleasant kind of silence where they didn't feel the urge to say anything. They both realised independently that the other was the only one they could be comfortable with in silence.

Sophia would have liked to remain standing, but she urgently needed to go to the toilet and the brief interruption from so much emotion did her good. Again, she tried to calm down by splashing cold water on her face and thought about how she could get him to tell her more about himself. She could listen to him forever, painful as it was. His voice was like the soft warmth of a cosy blanket.

As Nick walked restlessly through her room, he couldn't help but stop at her bookshelf and take a closer look at the novels and photo books. He smiled when he found a book, he owned himself or that his sister had once forced him to read. He straightened up to inspect the books on the upper shelves as well, when something caught his eye through the gap between two thick photo books by Helmut Newton and Peter Lindbergh that made his heart stop for a brief moment. Stunned, he looked at the neatly made bed behind the shelf. His eyes prickled and his heart did a very strange double beat, as if it had just woken up, before quietly continuing to pound. Nick smiled broadly and forced himself not to read too much into it, but he absolutely failed. When he heard the bathroom door open and her feet on the wooden floor, quietly approaching, he took another breath and then tried to control his smile. He looked at her only briefly as she re-entered the room, went to the fridge to get out a bottle of water. After she had fetched two glasses from the cupboard and placed them on the small coffee table, he slowly joined her at the small sitting area. But he did not sit down yet, but thanked her in a soft voice and sought her gaze.

However, she seemed to have made it her business now to avoid his gaze, for she fiddled with one of the cushions as she sat on the couch. He was fine with that though and tried to change the subject a little to learn more about her.

"What about your parents?"

"They live on their farm and always come to me at the beginning of December to buy the Christmas presents."

"Do they stay with you then?" Nick turned around and looked at the room again.

"It's a pull-out couch, but I can only spend two days with them at most. Then I spend the rest of their visit with one of my friends."

"How long are they staying?"

"Since my little siblings are old enough now, usually a whole week."

Though Sophia smiled, he felt there was more, but he wouldn't ask unless she was ready to tell him. Their eyes met briefly, then she shrugged and explained as if she had heard his thoughts.

"We get on well, but they are also exhausting."

"May I ask in what way?"

"Sure."

Pulling her legs under her body, she put as much distance between them as possible after he had just sat down on the couch as well, almost right next to her. It was not his physical closeness that made her nervous at that moment, well ... not only, but his concerned and interested look. It also reminded her that neither her friends nor her parents seemed to have any real interest in her life.

"They weren't so pleased that I didn't want to stay on the farm or in my village."

Nick took a sip of water and waited for more.

"According to them, I should take over the farm with my brother at some point."

Sophia rolled her eyes and explained to him exactly how big the farm was, how many animals they had and what vegetables and fruit they grew. "But you know, I've always had the urge to leave."

Nick nodded and smiled at her as she told him that she had dreamed of living by the sea since she was a little girl and had always wanted to do something with photography, but that her parents had had very different plans for her.

"They're still angry with me."

116

"For leaving?"

She nodded and took a sip of her water. "You know, they just never listen."

Sophia got up and searched her cupboards for something to snack and then filled some peanuts into a bowl which she put on the table. But she didn't sit down again, instead she paced up and down the room.

"They have certain ideas and they don't understand that I want something completely different."

And they both knew he knew the feeling well, it was exactly the same with Ruben.

"Is that what you meant by your statement, that you usually get overlooked?"

Embarrassed, she pulled a face, barely able to tell him that she had also meant that for men in general and him in particular.

"Yes, too."

Frowning, Nick waited for more, and although she hadn't even hinted at it, he knew instinctively that this statement had to do with a man. Of course, it was completely absurd to be jealous of someone from her past, yet he couldn't fight this rising feeling that burned up his throat like hot flames.

Sophia stroked her face lightly, she definitely didn't want to think about any idiots. Especially not about her own personal break-up nightmare, but of course it was nothing like Nick's, and she tried to explain to him, without the awkward subject of past relationships, what she meant.

"I have many siblings, five to be exact, and..." she took another sip to steady herself, "I was the only one whose dream was not in my village."

Nick looked at her encouragingly and she went on about her dreams and the arguments with her parents, and finally she told him what she had been trying to avoid.

117

"Well, we were celebrating my leaving, and yes, I was also standing in the kitchen when I caught my boyfriend snogging someone else ..." She shrugged and closed her eyes for a moment. Happy that it didn't hurt anymore, happy that she had banished this guy from her life and was over it. But it hurt her to see the same pain in Nick's face.

"You caught him?"

"He had overlooked me, which of course doesn't make it any better, but he claimed that it was over for him when I decided to go to Hamburg." She nodded, hoping he wasn't thinking too hard about his own painful experiences. "He wasn't exactly a loss," she shrugged, "but she was. My best friend."

Nick lowered his eyes and clenched his jaw. "Damn."

He ran a hand through his hair, searching for the right words, but what could he say? It just sucked.

"I'm not so lucky either way," Sophia explained casually, though she wondered why she had told him that.

Nick, on the other hand, would have liked to tell her that he was completely different, that he would never hurt her, but after less than a week of getting closer, he found that somehow inappropriate.

"I don't think so, everyone likes you," he tried to cheer her up.

Sophia laughed briefly and then, like a popping balloon, told him how her three closest friends sometimes behaved towards her without even bringing up the subject of last week.

"I don't know, just cos I'm not whining about something all the time, I feel like I'm not an equal in our clique."

"Sophia."

"No, it's just that they ... I always run to them when they need me and when I have grief, I ..."

"Grief?"

Their eyes met and Sophia was sure that he had seen through
118

her at that moment. That she was completely blank in front of him, that he knew everything, with just that one look. She got goosebumps all over her body and was unable to answer. Weak as she was, she sat down in one of the seat cushions. The silence between them stretched again, but it was not uncomfortable. It was like slowly turning a page in a book that you read slowly on purpose to savour it even more.

"Anyway," Sophia said quietly and kind of cheerfully, "sometimes I think they don't really *want* to know me."

"I *want* to know you." Nick quietly returned, and was very pleased when her whole face began to smile. It seemed she just couldn't suppress it.

After another moment of silence passed between them, he cleared his throat.

"I um ... I'm going to leave now."

Then he took another sip of water to give her time to reply. Over the rim of his glass, he watched her face and was pleased to see her slightly disappointed look and also her emerging honest smile. She was probably glad to be able to think about the evening and the whole last week, for as he knew her, she would analyse every single word and think about every little gesture until her head almost burst.

On wobbly legs, Sophia brought him to the door. Her stomach tingled and her throat was dry from the constant swallowing, her fingers felt cold once again. How would they say goodbye? Would he do something, and if so, like what she wanted most? And if he did, would she survive it? She wasn't quite sure, for her heart was beating so wildly and her breathing was so rapid that she feared she would faint in his arms.

Nick put on his shoes and jacket and only turned back to her at the doorstep. As it was already well past midnight, it was already

Saturday and it had been exactly one week since their chance encounter on Halloween in this very stairwell. He smiled at the memory of seeing her and all that had happened that week, or rather, all that he had *allowed* to happen. Just as he had allowed her to make him fall even more in love with her.

How incredibly adorable she looked at him with her deep, big eyes. He could sink into her gaze, like into a dark mountain lake, and yet he decided to make sure first. The fact that his blanket was in her bed could simply have practical reasons. Maybe she was just too cold at night and didn't have another one. Nevertheless, he hoped that she wanted the blanket to lie next to her in bed for another reason. Then he looked deeply into her eyes once more. Leaning closer, he dared a slow glance at her lips, which seemed to be slightly open and incredibly seductive calling for his. Lifting his gaze, Nick sank back into her eyes. He tilted his head. Sophia's breath tickled the skin of his cheek. Once more his gaze sought hers and he watched her eyes flutter shut as if she could not help closing them.

The warm, soft skin under his lips felt so right. Although for a moment they glowed as much as if they were on fire. It was just too glorious. Nick let his lips linger a moment longer than he usually would with a kiss on the cheek, but he wanted to show her that it was a promise.

A promise of more.

Chapter 10

As he slowly detached from her, his gaze caressed her face and his heart beat wildly in his chest. His lips tingled. For a moment he thought about doing it right, but he was enjoying the sight of her too much, soaking up her emotions reflected on her face. The answer to his silent question, lingered in her eyes.

Over his face, which was in shadow, an expression of astonishment hovered almost imperceptibly. A small twitch of the eyebrows. Sophia simply could not suppress the slight smile when she saw it. Her heart beat deeply and violently, she was in a kind of breathless wonder. She had to admit to herself that she had been right. If a kiss on the cheek caused this physical reaction, perhaps she really could have fainted from a kiss on the mouth. What power did this man have over her? She could barely feel her legs and she could only guess that her fingers were still there as she ran her thumb over her fingertips.

"Good night, Sophia", he said hoarsely and in that brief moment she was almost certain he was as flustered as she was.

"Night" was all she was capable of to return.

Only after he had turned to her once more on the stairs did Sophia return to her flat, closed the door and leaned her back against it. She could still feel the light pressure of his soft lips on her cheek and how wonderful it felt in contrast to his shaggy stubble.

Sophia stared at the wall in her hallway and reviewed the

evening. The statements that seemed to be important for him to make her understand that he was in a serious relationship with his ex. Not a little fling or just sex, as Anton had tried to imply. Why had it been so important to him that she was aware of this? Why had he opened up to her and told her something as intimate as that about his parents? He had been so vulnerable. She had felt how much the memory hurt him, but also that it was somehow okay for him to let her see him like that. A very small part of her, deep down in the secret corner of her heart, gave in to the thought that he must have felt comfortable around her to do it. That he trusted her. That he subconsciously wanted her to know about him what he normally tried to hide. That was quite a lot. A pretty big explanation for something she couldn't allow herself to believe.

Suddenly, everything pressed down on her. The pining for him for almost a year, the heartache, the statements of her friends, the self-doubt. His eyes. That concern for her after the accident. His gentle look when she told him of her grief. Nick had said everyone liked her, did he mean himself as well? Could that really be? He wanted to get to know her, he had said. And then that gentle goodbye. Her stomach tingled at the memory. He must have realised that she would have let him kiss her, right? He could have seduced her if he'd wanted to, but he'd only kissed her gently on the cheek. Not in a friendship kind of way. It had not been short enough for that. Sophia did not know why, but tears came to her eyes. They ran down her cheeks unhindered as she slowly stood up and went into her room. Her throat seemed constricted. Could this really be? Really? She closed her eyes, threw herself on the bed and reached absent-mindedly for his blanket. The way he had looked at her in the shadows of the stairs. So dark and with that silent promise. Was it possible that her heart rose and slid into her stomach? The warmth on her cheek glowed for another moment, then she opened her eyes again. In her head she heard the sarcastic voices of her friends and their questions as to why he hadn't kissed her properly. And although she would hardly admit that she didn't want to tell them about their gradual approach in the first place, she knew what the answer was: Nick was holding back. Maybe not necessarily for her sake, after all, he couldn't know that she would surely drop dead if he kissed her properly. Sophia chuckled briefly and was now quite sure what he was. *Careful.* To open up and ... was she even allowed to think that? At least for a little moment she could dare to believe it. Secretly and alone in the deepest place of her heart. He was careful ... to fall in love. Sophia made a strange noise as she gasped for air. Her tears continued to stream down her face. But not out of sorrow or sadness. Instead, it was out of the indescribable feeling that it was possible. That Nick could feel something for her too. Now she just had to show him somehow that it was okay.

After Nick had come home and stared at the ceiling of his room for a while, he knew that the evening could have gone very differently. He had wanted to end up in her place and the fact that it had really happened was incredible enough and yet so special as it had been very different from how he had imagined it. He was happy about it. Somehow it was perverse too, but he liked this tingling tension between them. This cautious approach. This vibration that was in the air between them. But he was also a little angry with himself for not grabbing and just kissing her. Yet, he was incredibly glad he hadn't.

He wanted to scratch at her protective wall until her true self, her true feelings, would also come out. Sophia didn't know how long he had been attracted to her. Nick was sure that she would relax more and more if he could control his desire. At least for a little longer. It had been nice to open up to her unintentionally. To reveal this side of him that not even his siblings knew. After all, he was the sensible one who mourned their parents in silence, in secret, just for himself. Without her being aware of it, Sophia tugged at this façade. Helped him push it aside and carefully peel it away without him feeling uncomfortably exposed. It was very strange and yet it felt completely natural.

Oh, her tenderness! With a sigh, he took a deep breath. For a moment he imagined what it would be like to kiss her. And although he was sure that she could also be wild and would strongly shake his restraint, he believed that her tenderness would be his downfall. If she triggered so many feelings in him now, what would it be like when the time came? Maybe he should withdraw again and go to New York like Ruben expected him to. Maybe it hadn't been such a good idea after all to approach her, to get involved with her.

Laughing at this absurd thought, he turned on his side and stared into the night. Nick wanted to see her again, preferably right away. Wanted her next to him, even if they would do nothing but talk. That tugging in his stomach. Or rather, his heart seemed to twitch in one direction. He turned on his back again. When would he see her again? When? They hadn't agreed on anything. Could he call her? Now? No. Then maybe not until Monday? No! He *needed* to see her before then, yes, he had to find a way to meet her! Somehow, he had to get her to meet him. Maybe he could get her to come over under the pretence of preparing the darkroom?

Oh, how was he going to get through the night?

As Sophia stood in the shower the next morning, she ran through several scenarios of how she could meet him again. How she would approach him in the office on Monday and then set up a date with him. But then her colleagues would also find out and his siblings, who of course were against it, which was perfectly clear and .... but before she could drift back into the cave of rationality and what others might want, she shook off the thought and got out of the shower. Yes, an idea was forming in her head, now she just had to find a way to tell him. Somehow. As she hardly had anything to eat at home, she got dressed, blew-dried her hair and then went around the corner to her favourite café. She hoped it was already open at this time of day, but wasn't quite sure, as she usually went there later or not until the afternoon. She was hungry, or her empty stomach thought it was hunger, but it was actually just longing for a certain person.

Relieved that it was already open, she entered the café with its small alcoves and colourful tables, chairs and shelves on the walls displaying smaller treasures. Between cups, bowls and handicrafts that you could buy for a few euros, you could also borrow old and new books or change them for ones one brought along. Today she didn't have a book to exchange, although she usually found one, she wanted to read, she held back this morning. Sophia just wanted to eat a hearty meal to be ready for the day. And prepare herself for the phone call she was about to make.

Since she was the first guest today, as the owner explained to her, she could spread out on her favourite place. Right by the corner window, with the cushioned window sills. She put her green notebook on the table that she had taken with her to write down a few more ideas that came to her mind for Viviana's wedding. But instead of thinking of Viviana and her wishes and preferences, she tried to draw a face on one of the back pages, or rather his eyes. Their expression was still in her mind, but she could not manage to draw it. Only when the sumptuous Turkish breakfast arrived, which she had ordered, did she put pen and book aside and began to eat. Only now did Sophia notice the other guests in the small café and the few people who had only come for a small snack or a coffee-to-go. Nevertheless, it was still empty enough to stay a little longer. In her head, she formed sentences she could say or write to tell him about her idea. Twice she even took out her mobile phone, wrote a message, but deleted it again before she could bring herself to send it. Then she scrolled through the pictures Viviana had sent her of flower arrangements, cakes and dresses for the bridesmaids, but somehow, she couldn't think of anything on that subject either. As the murmur of other people's voices in the café, the soft music and the ringing of the little doorbell faded in the background, she looked out of the window. Her teacup forgotten in her hand, she remembered the previous evening with a slight smile on her face. As she thought of the sweet farewell, the tingling in her stomach intensified and crept up her throat as well. She had that strange feeling again and turned to the counter, having to take a deep breath in surprise.

Even though he was only standing there with his back to her and not wearing his everyday clothes, she knew it was Nick who was getting a coffee at the counter. The shape of his head, the line of his short-cropped hair at the nape of his neck. As if he could sense her gaze, he looked over his shoulder and his face lit up with this incredibly beautiful smile on seeing her. He was about to go to her when he was reminded to pay for his coffee first, and having done so, he came and sat at her table.

"Hey."

"Hello Nick."

"Are you alone here?" He turned around as if expecting someone to push him from his seat any moment.

"Yes, I haven't had anything to eat at home." Sophia smiled slyly at him and drank to hide it.

"I always come here for a coffee after my run," he explained, unzipping his hoodie a little.

Sophia could not prevent her gaze from slipping very briefly to his neck, which he had just bared. The spot underneath had caught her attention and she closed her eyes to lift her gaze to his face again. Into his heated face, where damp hair clung to his forehead, which he brushed back the next moment. Even though he was slightly sweaty, Sophia had quite inappropriate thoughts. Because to her, he was the most beautiful man she had ever seen and the memory of his lips on her skin made her imagination run away with her for a brief moment.

"I've never seen you here before." He remarked.

"Hmm"

"So early." He looked at his watch. "It's not even nine yet."

"I couldn't sleep anymore."

"Oh, I'm sorry." he said dryly, and yet they both smiled as if it was so obvious what had kept them from sleeping. After a short pause he said casually, "So you're not normally an early riser?"

"I am, but I usually like to spend more time snuggling in bed." Sophia said this innocently, but Nick looked at her again with that penetrating gaze, and she thought that somehow, he didn't seem to like what she was saying.

But before she could ask, the images flooded into her head as well. The two of them snuggling in her bed and she noticed how she blushed again. It was so embarrassing! Why didn't she have better control over her physical reactions when she was around him?

"I'm sorry, I didn't give you your blanket back." She bit her lip and waited for his reply, hoping he would say something like *I'll pick it up later*, but instead replied with just the opposite.

"Never mind. Keep it."

Well, that didn't work out as she had hoped and once again, she realised that she simply had no idea how to make a man come over again.

"Until the next time I come over."

Their eyes met as he said this and Sophia was about to reply that she was thinking exactly the same thing when he continued.

"So, ... I mean, if you invite me again ..."

"Well," she giggled, "I didn't actually invite you."

They both grinned.

Then they talked a little about the delicious food in the café where they were sitting, the cosy atmosphere. And if the alarm clock on Sophia's mobile hadn't gone off at some point, the two of them would have found even more topics of conversation. Sophia was annoyed that they had been interrupted, even if it didn't mean anything, and instead thought about how she could tell him what she had been thinking about that morning. She didn't think she would have the courage to ask him directly and tried to play out the course of the conversation in her head, but it went completely differently than planned.

"Well, I have to go too," Nick smiled and stood up.

"You don't have to, that was just my alarm clock, I forgot to turn it off."

"Oh, well..."

"So what else are you doing today?" asked Sophia, hoping he wasn't somehow annoyed by her direct question, because the corner of his mouth twitched briefly.

"First of all, I'm going to take a shower."

"Speaking of showers, when I was in the shower earlier, I thought we could ..."

"You were thinking about me when you were in the shower?" his gaze was intense and made the heat jump to her cheeks, but luckily his teasing smile claimed her attention and she tried to explain herself as he sat back down.

"Uh, no, I just had an idea. I mean ..."

"I always get my best ideas in the shower, too."

Sophia tried not to think about what he might mean by that and then blurted out her request.

"So, I was thinking, if you don't mind, I'd like to ... copy the photo book idea."

"Okay."

His look told her he was waiting for more information, but in fact that one unruly strand of hair that fell in her face distracted him yet again. Nick was already raising his hand as she continued.

"With the pictures you will enlarge with me."

There. Now it was out. She felt her cheeks grow even warmer, but maybe he wouldn't notice. Slowly her eyes sought his and she nervously sucked her lips into her mouth. He just looked at her and she tried to pull away, as much as she could when sitting at a table together. "If the offer still stands..."

"It does. Absolutely." Nick nodded eagerly, finding it just too enchanting the way she sat in front of him sipping her tea, which was surely cold by now. He must have actually intimidated her quite a bit with his grumpy manner, because he had never seen this reserved and shy Sophia like this at work. There she was self-confident and had firm convictions, didn't beat around the bush like that, but took things into her own hands. The conviction that this proposal, or much more the memory of his own proposal the night before, had cost her some effort made it all the more precious for him.

"Well, I thought you might also want to ..."

"Yes," he replied before she had even finished speaking.

"You don't even know what I was going to suggest." She laughed.

"Yes, that's true, but I'm ready for anything."

Why Sophia was at loss for words for a moment was obvious, but she didn't try to let her imagination take over, she could do that when she was alone with her thoughts.

"Well, I was going on a photo tour, and yes, I ..." Sophia brushed the strand from her face before he could dare reach for it,

129

and took another breath before saying the rest. "I thought maybe you'd like to come with me."

Nick's heart gave a little hop as she pronounced the last word more like a question and she slid back in her seat. Sophia looked over her shoulder out of the window, as if suddenly observing something interesting there, and he also saw her nervously playing with the fringes of her scarf, which was lying on the bench next to her.

"I'd love to." He replied seriously and that brought the desired response.

Her face shot around to him as if she really hadn't expected that answer and he could not help that knowing grin which he immediately tried to suppress. Sophia seemed relieved and suddenly much more relaxed than two minutes before.

"Okay, I just have to go home really quick and ..." he explained with a flowing hand movement over his body and added hastily. "I'll pick you up then!"

"All right."

"And erm ... where are we going then?"

Sophia was somehow too exhausted to think about it at that moment and pointed at him. "I'll leave that up to you."

"Fine," he nodded and then said goodbye.

Yet, Nick's cheerful mood changed abruptly when it started to rain as soon as he got home. He was glad that the rest of the family had just visited Tea's mother in Hanover and did not have to witness his outburst.

He immediately went into the shower and thought about what he could suggest instead, now that she had finally found the courage to ask him. What a mess! Still, like so often, the best ideas came while he was in the shower, and as soon as he had wrapped the towel around his hips, he wrote her a short message.

Sophia wondered what his siblings would think of her sudden appearance. Her caution annoyed her, but there was still the small doubt as to whether everything was as she hoped. Her emotions were in turmoil and she would have loved to jump for joy and the insecure part of her would have loved to make up an excuse not to come over. All those thoughts, however, were instantly dispelled when Nick opened the door with a big grin and just looked so unbelievably good doing it that she forgot everything else anyway, and pulled her into the house without further ado. He took the umbrella and jacket from her and offered her something to drink after she followed him into the kitchen. Of course, he noticed her searching looks.

"The others aren't here, in case you were wondering." He had said it in a neutral tone, but Sophia thought she heard a slightly ironic undertone. "And when you're ready, I'll show you the darkroom."

"Yes, fine."

Nick ran ahead of her down the stairs to the basement, telling her that he had cleaned and prepared everything before she came, and led her down a narrow corridor to a black-painted door. He opened it and pulled aside a heavy black curtain so Sophia could enter, then looked for the hidden light switch above the door.

The dim red light made everything seem so unreal, just as Sophia felt when she was near him. Like in a dream made of red Jell-O. Then she heard another click and the room was bathed in dazzling light. Only now did she recognise everything that was in the small room. The walls were painted black, the cellar windows were covered with black foil. On a long table against the long wall were several large rectangular basins and on the table in the corner was a device from which Nick now pulled off the cover and made a presenting gesture. He explained to her that it was the enlarger and she went to him to have the device explained to her. Interested, she listened to him, although she only understood half of what he told her about contrast filters, emulsions and different enlarging frames.

Much more fascinating she found how his rather casual fitting T-shirt stretched across his chest as he turned the enlarger to show her different settings. Afterwards, he explained the different stages of the development of the photos and in which basin what happened, but she couldn't remember all that at all. His smile simply distracted her too much. His enthusiasm was intoxicating and he suddenly seemed like an excited little boy. At some point he had explained to her that he had only found one pack of usable paper and that he wasn't sure if the chemistry for the individual baths was still okay, but that maybe they should just try it out.

After he had closed the door and switched off the bright light, the room sank back into the unreal redness. At first it was still quite cool in the cramped room, but after a while Sophia had to take off her pullover. Whether it was because the light from the enlarger warmed up the room or the fact that Nick was always standing so close to her, she couldn't say for sure. But it could also have been due that the two of them kept touching each other. Accidentally, she guessed, but wasn't quite sure. His arm touched hers, his hand touched her back. His face was so close as he explained to her how to adjust the focus on the lens, even though it seemed unnecessary to her. Nick smelled so good, and the warmth emanating from him gave her the strange goosebumps she sometimes got when she slipped into bath water that was too hot.

Eventually, she relaxed enough to enjoy it, though, and a sense of pride flooded through her as she slid the first sheet of photo paper into the developer tray and watched the image appear on it as if by magic.

After a minute had passed, she couldn't get it out of the

developer and Nick took the tongs from her, grazing her fingers ever so lightly. Although neither wanted to show it, they froze for a brief moment before Nick let the photo slide into the next basin.

He was well aware of her proximity. The apple scent of her hair masked the smell of chemicals on the table in front of him if he stood close enough. Her curls tickled his arm as soon as he pushed past her to get something from across the small room.

In the light he couldn't tell if her cheeks were so beautifully flushed again, but her eyes looked even bigger and darker in the ghostly light. His heart beat quietly, except for that one moment when their fingers had touched and the urge to just grab her and pull her into his arms became almost unbearable. But he certainly wouldn't be tempted to kiss her in the darkroom, surrounded by smelly chemical fluids. Yet, he knew he would have to do it eventually. Well ... soon.

As she hung the last motif, she had enlarged with his help to dry on the line above them, Nick caught a glimpse of her belly as her shirt slid up and was still staring at her when he automatically switched on the light. They looked at each other for a moment and it was that silence again that spread between them. Instead of feeling strange about it, they just smiled and left the room. They had another drink in the kitchen and then went upstairs to the terrace to get some fresh air. She had forgotten her pullover down in the basement, so he gave her a blanket, which she threw around her shoulders like a poncho before making herself comfortable on one of the wide sofas.

They talked again quite calmly, but kept slipping into that certain silence. It was that comfortable silence where no one expected the other to say anything. After a while, Nick explained that he still had to dispose of the chemicals but that she could stay up there. Sophia then made herself more comfortable, lay down and stared up at the now rain-free evening sky.

Nick was quite happy to get away from her for a moment and indulge his thoughts. While he put everything away and pulled the cover back over the enlarger, he thought that it would be best if they went out for dinner after they had finished their work, and in his head, he played through various scenarios of what would happen afterwards. Smiling, he collected the dried pictures and climbed the stairs to the terrace, noticing before he reached her that she had apparently fallen into a light sleep.

She lay there, covered with the blanket, and her head was turned away from him. Nick approached her, thought for a moment and then sat down on the edge of the couch. Before he knew what he was doing, he reached for the edge of the blanket and tugged it a little higher. She flinched briefly at that moment, as unintentionally his fingertips touched her collarbone. It felt so smooth and there was really nothing he could do about it as his fingers reached out and lightly caressed the tender skin.

"Sophia."

She made a noise as if she did not want to be woken and with a smile, he leaned closer.

"Sophia."

His fingers slid over her neck and settled very lightly under her cheek. Gently, he turned her face to his and continued to whisper her name. He was so close that he could feel the cool skin of her cheek against his nose. Stroking her cheek with his thumb, he continued to try to wake her up. Apparently, however though, she didn't want to open her eyes. Nick couldn't help himself and leaned a little closer to her and then gently pressed his lips to her cheek as he had done the night before.

As he slowly tried to pull away from her, somehow embarrassed by his action, she stretched her face towards him.

Her lips touched his very lightly. Very shortly. Just a gentle whiff.

Nick froze.

"Wake up." He was a little louder now, but snorted in an amused tone when she replied with a protesting sound.

"Hey Sophia, wake up."

Then finally her eyes fluttered open. At first her look was gentle, a slight smile on her face, then she looked surprised and that little crease between her brows twitched a little.

"Nick?"

"Yes."

Their eyes met.

He searched for an answer in her eyes as he leaned closer. His fingers cupped her cheek. It rustled in his head. She moved her face a little closer. A very tiny movement.

He gasped for breath. And then ...

Chapter 11

Sophia had felt she could breathe properly again when she had left the darkroom and climbed the stairs with Nick at her side. She sank, slightly tired, into the first chair she could find in the kitchen and Nick chuckled softly as he made them a coffee. It had been quite exhausting standing for hours. But Sophia knew that she also felt so worn out because of his closeness.

Every step he took evoked a matching one from her, and so they had either moved towards or around each other as if following a secret choreography that only their bodies seemed to know. That was also the reason why she had gone to the balustrade as soon as they had reached the terrace, ostensibly to have a look at the surroundings, but actually she just wanted to see where he would sit so that she could choose the seat furthest away from him. Not because she wanted to leave his side, but she needed a few minutes to get her thoughts and feelings under control so that she wouldn't push him away at some point or pounce on him the next moment. Well, she would never dare do that, of course, but she wished she had the courage. His shoulders were so broad and his arms looked so strong that she would surely feel completely safe in his embrace.

They then talked about their work and he explained the difference to a special paper his family had always used for their books. Sophia felt an excited uneasiness when he promised that he would order this special paper for her new photos. This would mean that they would once again enlarge pictures together, and before that he would accompany her on one of her photo tours to take photos together. At that moment she had been so happy that she would have liked to hug him if he hadn't been sitting so far away.

She laughed briefly at her illogical thoughts and watched his hands as he spoke. Sophia was sure that it would feel incredibly good if he put his hands over hers. They were so big and Sophia's imagination went crazy as she briefly thought that other things could fit perfectly in his hands as well. She shook her head at her thoughts and felt the blush shoot into her cheeks and his eyes on her. With him sitting just a few steps away, she really shouldn't have thought that!

Her cheeks glowed even more and she closed her eyes for a moment longer to block out the images, but instead she saw them both in her mind. Together. His hands on her and ... Oh, God! When she looked up again, Sophia caught him looking at her with that intense gaze once more, and his smile was so irresistible that her heart slipped into her stomach. Nick then explained that he had to clean up the darkroom and when he saw that she wanted to get up, he just waved her off.

"You can stay here." He nodded briefly and disappeared very quickly.

But Sophia didn't mind. She stretched out on the couch, wrapped the blanket around herself and looked up at the darkening sky. She had the feeling that her thoughts and her heart could now calm down for the first time after hours of tension. Which was not entirely true, of course, for she had been relaxed with him even when she was working in the darkroom. But only after she had become used to his closeness and this unreal light. His eyes had become even darker and his gaze even more intense. Trying to recapture in her mind that one moment when he had looked at her, she pulled the blanket tighter against her.

Nick had been so close to her that she could have counted his stubbles if she hadn't been too distracted by his eyes.

First, he had looked through the lens to focus on the motif, then she had looked through it and it was almost as if he was touching her back with his chest. Yet, he wasn't, it was just his closeness and warmth that made her think so. Just thinking about those moments gave her goosebumps, and actually she wanted to think about how the evening could go on, but she didn't really care. She just hoped that maybe he would accompany her home and that maybe he would come back upstairs with her. She closed her eyes and remembered his kiss. So warm and soft on her cheek. Then she tried to imagine what it would have been like if she had pulled him back into her apartment.

One moment later, everything that had really happened that evening blurred into a mixture of situations that could have led to a kiss, but they had both always turned away too soon. In her fantasy, Sophia allowed herself to be cheeky and push him against the wall, and in the process one of her pictures would have fallen off the wall. Oh, what would it be like to be kissed by him? Then all she saw were his darkening eyes. Suddenly, she was no longer alone in her bed, holding his blanket in her hands, but him in her arms and his gaze was the same like at the exhibition and then he was under her and she stripped down to her underwear and then she leaned closer and ...

"Sophia."

His lips didn't move, so the voice came from somewhere else, but no one would stop her from dreaming of his lips on hers now.

"Sophia."

No! No way would she stop now, she was dreaming of him touching her on her collarbone and oh ... her neck. It felt so real.

"Sophia."

Oh, he had kissed her on the cheek again. He was about to pull away. No, no! Don't go away. Don't go away! Pleading, she turned to him in her dream. Touched his lips. But the dark voice grew louder.

"Wake up."

138

"No!" She moaned and leaned closer, his scent and warmth ... but why did she suddenly open her eyes? Oh, what ...?

Suddenly, he was no longer lying under her in her bed, but hovering above her. Oh, and he was so handsome in the golden light of the terrace. Sophia felt herself smiling and also felt warmth on her cheek, like the touch of long fingers. The cool air of the coming night, rustling in her hair. The lightly scratching blanket she felt on her bare arm made her realise that this was not a dream.

What? It was real. Why was he so close?

"Nick?"

"Yes."

Their eyes met. Sophia searched for an answer when he leaned forward. His fingers cupped her cheek. A certain weight came closer. So did his face. Everything smelled like it was real! Was it real? It felt real. Did he want to ...? But suddenly he stopped in his movement. His eyes broke away from hers, they lowered to her lips and a breath later he sought her gaze again.

Remembering that he was careful, she realised that she had to show him that she wanted it too. Bravely, she jerked a little more in his direction. Oh God! Oh God! It was real! Sophia felt her lips tingle when he breathed her name one more time. She felt it more than she heard it. Should she answer? Gasp for air or for more?

Then finally that invisible bond tugged her closer and then ....

Oh.

Her lips melted into his. She felt nothing more, only a tingling. Everywhere.

They didn't move for quite a while, the moment stretched and extended, and Sophia felt everything at once. The light breeze, the clammy fabric of the couch beneath her. His fingers stretching out on her cheek. His cold nose on her skin. She softened the touch of her lips slightly, only to inhale his again immediately. So soft. So warm. Her lips opened a little and she kissed his gently. Slowly explored his lower one. Ever so gently, she pressed her lips to every millimetre until she reached the corner of his mouth. She felt his breath catch at her mouth. The next moment she let her lips brush over his upper one before he pressed his mouth a little harder on hers. It was still light and soft, but different.

Nick did the same to her, carefully and slowly exploring her mouth with his lips. Her breath mingled with his. Until she couldn't take it anymore, it just wasn't possible! Sophia pressed herself tighter against him, lifted her head a little and his fingers slid into her hair. She felt the pressure of his fingers on her scalp, a violent shiver ran through her and Sophia sank back. But she did not lose his lips, they remained on hers as if they were glued together, their lips melted. They were one!

Oh, her heart wanted to burst!

Fading into the background, she heard his heavy breathing through his nose, it tickled her skin and Sophia couldn't think straight, was this real? Was it real?

Oh, no.

He tried to lean away. No! He couldn't. He had to stay!

Nick heard her tiny little whimper as he tried to pull away from her. His heart twitched and then a burning jolt went through his body. Somehow, he was losing his strength. But she held him. Grounded him. Not only did he feel her cold hand on his forearm and on his back, but her lips clung to his as if they were her last hold. As if he was the air she needed to breathe. He could not believe it. He had to move away to see if she was real.

With great effort, Nick managed to lift his head, but he didn't get far. It was as if his lips needed the connection with hers. Slowly they stroked hers to better memorise them. Oh, he was sure, yes so sure. He had to tell her! Otherwise he would burst. Nick heard her suck in a sharp breath as he paused at the corner of her mouth. They lingered like that, not moving, as if they had forgotten how to do it and how to breathe.

Only at that moment did he realise that he was holding her face with both hands. His upper body hovered over hers. Her hands were very cold and were suddenly on his chest and on the heated skin of his neck. Was she trying to push him away? Although he couldn't quite remove his lips from hers, he tried to straighten up, but just as slowly her fingers clawed into his pullover. She wanted him to stay where he was! It was so indescribable.

She made him burst with happiness and he couldn't help but smile. He kissed her lovingly on the cheek. Her breath quickened. Nick felt the shaky sound. And it intensified as he pressed another kiss to her cheek. She glowed so hot, but so pleasant against the cool of the night. Nick had forgotten how to form words, and his lips touched every bit of skin beneath them. The pressure of her face against his as she leaned closer. He felt her lips graze his stubble as he pressed his lips to her heated skin. The dimple of her chin beneath his lips. Her breath came in waves.

Could he dare? No, he preferred to hold back a little and pushed his mouth back up. Her smooth lips took him back again. Gently, but full of pleasure.

Never before had Sophia been kissed so gently and tenderly. It was more than she had ever imagined. Her whole face was tingling. Although the cool wind brushed over her, reminding her of reality, it all felt like a dream. His stubble stung, but when she ran her fingertips over it, they felt soft. She drew an unfamiliar pattern on his jaw as he lifted away from her a little. Their lips touched anyway. Caressing each other with that wonderfully light contact. Neither of them wanted to risk taking a step further, and so they stayed a little longer in this silent agreement to be so close. Behind Sophia's eyes it tingled, overwhelmed by the wave of emotions that threatened to sweep her away. She gasped shakily, it almost sounded like a little sob, and exhaled puffingly when he kissed her again, laughing softly. She felt his forehead against hers, first lightly tickling and then pleasantly heavy. Just like all the other feelings inside her. The physical desire and intense feelings ran down her spine and exploded in her belly. Sophia felt so happy and overwhelmed. Speechless. That he felt it too ... for a brief moment her eyes fluttered open and she saw that his were still closed. As the night before, tears sprang to her eyes and she expelled the air with a smile, at the same moment he did the same. As if by magic, her fingers, which were resting on his cheek, slid back to his neck. There she felt his goosebumps. The other hand slid gently from his collar a little higher and her fingertips touched his neck. It vibrated as he hummed his approval and it made her fingers tingle.   Nick felt weak at the knees when she touched him. She tugged gently, telling him not to go anywhere, and he surrendered to his fate. Sliding his nose over her face, he tried to hold back. Hovering over her lips, he wanted to tell her all the feelings that were swirling around inside him. He inhaled, but she didn't seem to want to wait and claimed his mouth with loving pressure. It was gentle and soft as before, but also more intense. Not just the kiss, but the storm of emotions that raged within him. But just as he had feared, she overwhelmed him with her tenderness.

It was as if she was drawing poetry on his lips.

He had expected her to kiss him gentle and although he had imagined it, nothing in his mind could cope with how carefully she caressed his lips with hers. Such a soft touch. It was almost unbearable. But he was enjoying it too much, and for nothing in the world would he destroy this moment by letting his passion take over. If he was so in love with her before, how could he even try to

142

put his heavy feelings into words now? Nick was no longer able to think of anything so encompassing, or anything at all, when he heard her sigh and felt her trembling.

"Sophia?"

Was that his voice he heard from afar, or did he just think her name? He couldn't remember.

"You're totally frozen."

Those words in a hoarse voice gave her even more goosebumps and she shivered again. But she also shook her head and held him tight, not wanting it to be over.

"Let's go in." The vibration of his dark voice tugged at all her nerves. And that place in her stomach tingled. What would he want to do if they went inside? A small jolt of panic ran through her and her thoughts went completely wild. When she sought his gaze and he smiled that special smile, she knew she was so much more in love with him than before he had left the terrace. Sophia took a slow, deep breath as she thought about what else was about to happen as he continued.

"And maybe you would have dinner with me?"

The slight look of panic in her eyes had already disappeared and her whole face smiled as she nodded. Even if he didn't want to stop, he knew he had to stop at some point, otherwise he would try to convince her to go one step further too. And the way she had moved under him, she was not entirely averse to it. But he was a selfish man, he wanted to torture them both a little longer. Sophia had felt so perfect under him, he was afraid he would destroy their connection if he wanted too much at once. Besides, he felt too much for her that he didn't want to try anything she wasn't willing to give. How he felt their connection growing with all his senses!

He lost himself in her deep fir-dark eyes and was only distracted when the breeze blew her silky hair into her face. He pushed the unruly strand of hair out of her face, admitting that he had wanted to do this so many times.

"What exactly," she paused for a second with a look he could only describe as sensual. "Mr. Falkner?"

Her voice was husky, and the way she breathed his name made him reconsider his previous reticence. He cleared his throat.

Push away that one curl." He smiled, and seeing hers, he confessed, "and ... um ... yes, kiss you."

Sophia's smile was so beautiful it made his heart beat faster and when he saw the tiny nod of her head, he thought he was the luckiest man on earth. Nick leaned down again to give her another small, slow kiss and they both sighed as their lips touched. They were thirsty for each other. Moaning softly, they kissed a little longer and Sophia curled her fingernails into his short hair at the nape of his neck.

He took a deep breath, fearing he wouldn't be able to stop if he dared to kiss her any longer, and pushed himself up, another jerk jolting through him as he heard a protesting sound. "Come on, or you'll freeze to death." he said after a little while, standing up and pulling her to her feet, she swayed for a brief moment.

Sophia felt his arm around her waist and as that invisible bond pulled him even closer, she leaned against him and they both felt safer than they had ever felt before.

Of course, it was even harder to think of anything else now that they had left the terrace, and the two quickly returned to that pleasant silence. As if it were a matter of course, he held out his hand to her after she had put on her pullover, they walked wordlessly down the stairs and looked at the photos they had enlarged.

At some point Sophia had found her voice again and suggested they go to a small Asian restaurant nearby for something to eat.

When the nice lady behind the counter asked if they wanted to eat it in her shop or take it away, they looked at each other and spoke at the same moment. "We can eat here ..." "To go."

They twisted their mouths into meaningful grins, and then Nick happily agreed.

In vibrant silence they went straight to her place and Nick helped Sophia pour the curry into bowls as if he knew his way around her kitchen. Sophia felt very comfortable and light at that thought. Of course, she didn't know how he really felt about her, but what his kisses had told her was that it was definitely *more*. With more feeling than she would ever have allowed herself to dream of.

They talked little over the meal and when they did, it was only about general things and a few ideas she had in mind for this photo book she wanted to create.

There was that certain tension between them again as they got up and put the dishes on her kitchen counter. Hundreds of questions were buzzing around in Sophia's head and she was trying to get a clear thought while she was in the process of cleaning the dishes. Nick snuggled up to her from behind and rested his chin on her shoulder. His arms wrapped loosely around her waist.

Sophia closed her eyes too, drew the feelings in. As she slid her hands over his arms, she felt the twitch of his muscles underneath the warm skin and his embrace became tighter as she pressed her face to his.

Their breaths melted together and their hearts formed the knot in the invisible bond between them.

Chapter 12

Nick closed his eyes and nestled against her face. He felt as if he was holding the greatest treasure in his arms. It was a sublime feeling and he felt a tingle in his chest. He clasped his arms around her a little tighter to show her that he would not let her go. At least, if he had his way. And from the way she had reacted to him, he believed she wanted the same. They would have to talk about what to do next. After all, they would meet at the office on Monday, and it was the company code not to get involved with each other. So on the one hand he had to discuss with her how they should behave there, and on the other hand he also had to talk to his siblings. But that could wait. Nothing would stop him now from holding her in his arms without talking. Sophia was one of the few people he could be silent with. That was a great relief, but simply far too rare to find.

Nick smiled until she suddenly moved. He lifted his head from her shoulder and sought her gaze. It seemed kind of misty when she just leaned closer and pressed her nose against his. Their lips touched very light and gentle. Only very briefly, before they both took a shaky breath and seemed to inhale at the same time. When she tried to pull away again, he only managed to open his lips a little and then capture her mouth again. As he loosened his grip, he turned her in his arms and felt her arm slide around his middle and her other hand settled burning on his forearm as he sought hold of her face. As Nick pressed a hand into her back, he continued to kiss her as lovingly as he was able to. At some point he listened to his mind and pressed his forehead to hers once more. There was such a tugging all over, and he knew that if he didn't stop now, he would kiss her. Kiss her so hard that he would lose his mind. He didn't want to risk that. Sophia and these feelings she seemed to share were too precious to him, as to destroy it with desire. Nick cleared his throat and knew what he had to do. He spoke quietly.

"If you don't mind, I'd like to ..."

Sophia's brain was working at full speed. *Please*, she thought, *ask if you can stay!* Only to hope in the next millisecond that he wouldn't, since what was she supposed to do then? Say *yes*, of course. Then he would think she was that kind of girl and she didn't want that. Of course, they didn't have to do anything, but they would, if he kissed her so gently again, she wouldn't be able to hold back, she was already on the verge of losing her self-control. She wanted to show him who she really was and that she loved him.

Oh, had she just thought that? It was all good as long as she didn't say it out loud! So not yet. What would his face look like when she said those words to him? Would he look the way she felt at the thought alone? Would he say it then too? No, of course he wouldn't. They had only just come together, after all. They were together, weren't they? Or was he saying that that was it, that he didn't want to be with her? That it was that he couldn't be with her because of his family? Due to the company code? Oh no! No! Panic coursed through her body and she stiffened almost imperceptibly until he finally continued.

"... come back with breakfast."

Relief and a surge of warmth flowed through her. No one had ever said that to her before, and in the husky tone in which he had said it, it felt like a declaration of love. Nick looked deep into her eyes. Sophia was sure she would never get used to it. Just having

147

him look at her like that made her all tingly. Just that look made her head spin.

"I don't mind." She gasped and was glad when he pulled her to him once more, leaned in as if in slow motion and kissed her terribly slowly and Sophia could finally sink against him. Their mouths sucked tightly together. Her lips simply followed his.

The next time they caught their breath, he asked in a hoarse voice. "What do you like?"

Sophia had to swallow a few times, for she had very different things on her mind than what she wanted to eat in the morning.

"Everything." By that she meant the food and ... yes, even the things she was imagining in her brain, which had been fogged by him.

"Alright." But he wouldn't let go of her, and she wouldn't let go of him, and so they stood there for a while. Until finally he managed to lift his face from hers and smile at her.

"I'm going to leave now."

Sophia nodded, but at the same time her fingers clawed into his pullover. Of course, he felt it, and Nick nodded too, stroking her cheek so terribly gentle that she realised every millimetre of her skin was glowing as if it was on fire. Nick felt her lean into his hand and he wondered why he had even suggested leaving, but now he should better do it. He didn't want her to feel pressured in any way since he couldn't bring himself to go. No, he wouldn't risk that one more time.

As if it were a matter of course, their fingers intertwined and he gently pulled her with him until he had dressed and was standing outside her flat door as he had the night before. But this time he didn't lean down quite so slowly, yet he kissed her again just on the cheek as a goodbye, and it felt like a little inside joke between them.

Sophia briefly toyed with the idea of pulling him down and kissing him properly, but she also found it kind of exciting not to.

Nick held her hand and took two steps backwards. Only when he was far enough away did he let go of her hand and turned towards the stairs.

"We'll see each other later."

"Yes, later."

Sighing, Sophia stood still until he had disappeared, and again she leaned heavily against the door when she was back in her flat and closed her eyes. This time she did not sink to the floor, but immediately ran into the bathroom and looked at herself in the mirror. Sophia gasped. How she looked! Her lips were slightly swollen, although they had only kissed very tenderly. The skin on her chin and cheek was a little red from his stubble. That wasn't so bad, though. Her eyes had the expression of deepest contentment. But her hair! Yes, her hair was completely tousled, one could even say completely destroyed. It stood out wildly in all directions. Giggling, she tried to smooth it down with her hands and then finally gave free rein to all her feelings and grinned happily to herself.

Although she realised after a glance at the clock that it would be at least six hours before he would return, the tender ache of separation set in only briefly. It wasn't a real pain either, more like her stomach was completely knotted in her belly. It was the prickly, knowing feeling that he felt similar to her and would be back in a few hours. Until then, she should try to get some sleep, even if she didn't think it was possible, as flustered as she was, she soon lay down in her bed. Although she lay in it alone, she didn't feel lonely for the first time in a long time.

When Nick arrived at the bottom of the stairs, he thought about running back upstairs immediately. He wanted to change, after all, his clothes still smelled like a photo developer and he wanted to get his mobile phone and come back later with a delicious breakfast from their café. He wanted to do everything right. Slowly, slowly as his father had always said. On the one hand, he had wished she would ask him to stay, but he hadn't expected her to. Sophia seemed quite shy, which was no wonder given how he had behaved towards her. Besides, it had only been a week since that knot between them seemed to have burst. It hadn't really burst, but the knot had loosened very gentle and slow. Nick wondered what she would have done if he had said he wanted to stay? Just the thought that she had stiffened about *that* gave him an uneasy feeling. He immediately suppressed it with the memory that she had looked slightly disappointed when he said he was leaving.

Nick felt so light and happy when he thought about the way her fingers had clawed into his pullover. Yes, he was sure. Pretty sure she hadn't really wanted him to leave. The way she had kissed him. He touched his lips very carefully, as if not wanting to destroy the taste that was still on them. It had been so beautiful, so indescribably beautiful. Nick knew for sure that it would be hard not to be able to kiss her and control himself not to touch her. He was downright relieved that November was always filled with meetings, small celebrations and the last elaborate photo shootings of the year. Then his siblings and he had to go through the final changes for the new company logo, although he would have preferred to keep the original one created by his father. He was the only one who was sentimental about it. The others got caught up in Ruben's idea and enthusiasm that everything had to be more and more modern, and so he was silenced. Well, and then there was their own Christmas party, including overnight stays in Pielsand. He had to be very careful there too. Pielsand in winter was incredibly beautiful and, as his sister and Tea always pointed out, incredibly romantic. That's why he hoped the snow would wait a while longer, otherwise he might even embrace Sophia in front of the entire staff if the mood called for it. His body was already in that mood. Nick should create as much distraction as possible and throw himself into work. Yes, that was a good idea. It would stop them both from giving in to their feelings within the four walls of the company. They really had to be careful. The floor-talk was always well-informed, and he wanted to keep Sophia out of any kind of gossip. So later, at breakfast, they would have to talk about how to do it so that no one would notice. At least not yet. For one thing, he really wanted to be sure that she was being honest with him. His heart tightened painfully for a moment at the thought. Nick would have to be very wrong about Sophia if she was going to hurt him, he was quite sure of that.

His mood dropped, however, when he tried to leave the house a few hours later and found his nieces' and nephews' clothes in the hallway. With that, it was clear that the rest of the family was back and he couldn't bring Sophia here again. Of course, he had known that he didn't have the whole day at his disposal, as he had a few things to discuss with his siblings in the afternoon, but the fact that they had come back so early didn't bode well. Perhaps one of the children had fallen ill.

Quietly he slipped out of the house, went to the café, this time he was the first guest, drank a coffee while waiting for the order and thought about how to bring up the delicate subject. When he stood in front of Sophia's door, his heart beat as excitedly as if it was the first time he was at a woman's home.

When Sophia opened the door, she just stood there looking so incredibly beautiful that he could only shake his head slightly. She looked nervous, but in a happy way he hadn't seen her in a long time. Nick would have liked to know if her often unhappy appearance had anything to do with him.

Sophia took the bag of breakfast from him, disappeared into the room and came rushing back to him as soon as he had stepped into the room. One moment she seemed unsure of what to do, and the next her lips were already on his. Unable to help himself otherwise, he wrapped both arms around her small waist. There was this longing in him to pull her against him and the feeling as if they hadn't seen each other for weeks. He felt her hands on his chest and her warmth seeped into his heart. She made him feel safe. The most beautiful thing was when she leaned against him and seemed to sink completely into the kiss.

As Nick's hand travelled up her back and into her hair, Sophia panted. It tingled all the way up her spine and the heat in her belly seemed to pulse. They kissed as gently as they had the night before and Sophia's brain shut down. There was only one thought and one question left in her mind. What would it be like when he stopped holding back? Breathing heavily, he broke away from her and rested his forehead on hers again, it seemed even more intimate to Sophia than the kiss itself. The feelings inside her boiled up and poured out of her. *I love you!* Screamed her body and soul, even if her mouth remained silent. The only thing that betrayed her were her fingers, which once again could not let go of him. As they looked into each other's eyes, smiling, she realised that if the bad experience in his past had not made him completely blind, he had to see it.

Eventually they managed to eat the delicious breakfast. She had set the small kitchen counter and even lit candles, because it was a dark morning.

Nick was sure that this was exactly the feeling he would probably always have with her. It was warm and cosy. He became deeply aware that he had found his place. He felt more at home here with her than in his two rooms in his family's house, which anyway more or less belonged only to Ruben and his family and where he always felt only tolerated.

152

They ate in silence, each absorbed in his own thoughts, until he took her hand and stroked it.

"We need to talk."

A brief cold shiver ran through Sophia at those words. They never promised anything good and usually meant the beginning of the end. At least in most cases. She also realised that he simply wanted to discuss the inevitable with her, what they should do from the next day at work. Instead of sitting passively by until he went on talking, she tried to let him know that she realised it wasn't going to be easy.

"I know."

The deep crease between his eyebrows remained where it was, but his lips formed into a gentle smile.

"Please don't get me wrong," he began, "I um ... I'd like to tell everyone right away."

Her heart lifted at those words.

"But we've only just ... got together." He searched her face as if waiting for a statement to the contrary, but Sophia couldn't help it, she smiled impishly at him and placed her other hand on his.

Nodding, she said, "I also like it better when ..." She took another deep breath and looked at his large hand under which hers was completely hidden. She stroked that one prominent tendon and continued to speak excitedly. "... if it's just ...well," she bit her lip and Nick touched her face to show her that it was all right with him, no matter what she said. "If it's just ... us."

The air he had unconsciously been holding, he exhaled with a throaty laugh. He pulled her hand towards him, kissed the back of it and then laid it against his cheek. He wanted so much to say the three words, but he clenched his jaw to keep from doing it. It was too soon. Way too soon! Of course, it was. But he did. He was almost sure she did too.

The impact of this realisation Nick still felt hours later as he sat with his siblings in Ruben's study looking at the latest designs of the modernised company logo. Normally, alarm bells would still be ringing in his ears and the immense cost would give him a stomach ache, but he accepted it all without a word. For one thing, it had already been decided anyway and some of the bills had already been paid. The folders of the new photographers would be delivered in the next few weeks and would then have to be filled with their material before the Christmas party so that the surprise for the staff was then guaranteed.

"We'll put the stuff in the conference room, nobody uses it anyway," Jörn explained his decision, and Nick had to stifle a grin as his younger brother had once again made a subtle criticism of Ruben without him noticing.

"But we're running out of time," Yvonne whined, "I'm at the printers all week."

"I'll do the portfolios," Nick said, and in his mind, he didn't see himself alone in the conference room re-stocking the photographers' portfolios.

"But there are too many for you to do on your own," Yvonne remarked, looking at Ruben, who didn't understand or ignored her request, since such work was far below his level.

"Get someone you trust to do it."

"I will." Nick pretended to have to think, but of course he knew exactly who he would ask.

Then they talked about the final preparations for the Christmas party and what was coming up in the next two weeks. Yet, Nick's thoughts were completely elsewhere. He was thinking about what Sophia was doing right now and whether she also longed to be with him at her place as well. Tightly embraced at the kitchen table, lying in each other's arms, her warm lips on his skin…

Sophia smiled to herself as she thought of how hard it had been for both of them to part. Nick had to go to a meeting with his siblings and she had to go with Viviana and the others to the first fitting of her wedding dress, which a friend of Ina's had made especially for Viviana. This incredibly talented woman was a costume designer and her time was limited. Although the date for the wedding had not yet been set, Viviana was already busy planning everything. She hated being late and missing out. So they sat in the studio waiting for Viviana to finally come out of the dressing room with the first design. Sophia thought of Nick. His warm big hands on her back and face, his soft lips on hers. But she also thought about the fact that while they had discussed what they could and could not do at work, they had not set a time when they would see each other again. That fact made her giggle since, after all, they both spent a lot of their work time arranging appointments and doing everything they could to keep them.

"What are you laughing about?" asked Ina, and Céline also looked up from her phone and listened to what Sophia had to say.

"I just thought of something funny," she shrugged, trying not to elaborate on the subject.

"There's more to it than that!" exclaimed Ina and Céline remarked annoyed, "Oh, probably her boss smiled at her."

Both women laughed and Sophia was once again shocked by this rudeness, as if she were a silly little girl.

"Weren't you at an exhibition together?" asked Ina with interest, leaning towards Céline. "He probably spoke full three sentences to her instead of his usual two."

The two giggled again and Sophia could already feel the tears prickling behind her eyelids, why were they being so mean?

"Have you seen Toni, he was invited there too, he wanted me to come but I said no." Céline took a sip of the sparkling rosé Ina had brought and Sophia was surprised at her own words.

155

"Yes, but he didn't recognise me. He was there with his girlfriend Monique."

Céline choked on her drink and stared at Sophia in bewilderment.

"Monique Faigret, the fashion director of ..."

"I know who that is!"

Céline's voice and gaze were icy cold and under normal circumstances Sophia would have been surprised or maybe even startled, but she wasn't. Somehow, she had expected this reaction and for the first time in a while she realized that she was simply not willing to continue being the doormat and victim of her stupid and nasty remarks. Nor was she in the least sorry that she had told Céline so. Ina looked back and forth between the two and then asked Céline about Anton's circumstances. Sophia was glad that the two of them were engrossed in a conversation in no time about him and his much older girlfriend, about whom they made bitterly nasty comments, although Sophia was sure that neither of them knew Monique personally. Still, she was glad that the two of them left her alone with their stupid chatter. Sophia was so tired of always being the nice one who let them get away with everything. If necessary, she would do the same again if any stupid remark came from her friends.

Then finally Viviana came out of the changing room and all three of them were now fully engaged in admiring Viviana or expressing their opinions in some way.

Sophia sincerely felt that Viviana could wear anything, but being a modern woman, modern cuts suited her personality best. She looked simply amazing. Sophia then took photos of Viviana in the rough fabric design with her phone so that Viviana could look at it more closely later and make any changes to send back to the designer. Céline and Ina sat there smiling, but Sophia realised for the first time properly that they were wrapping their compliments in little jibes, which Viviana countered without seeming offended. Although none of them ever once simply told Viviana how stunningly beautiful she was, Viviana seemed to take the compliments wrapped in insults as such.

Maybe it was her own fault after all, Sophia thought. Maybe she was just too stupid or too simple-minded to laugh away the jokes at her expense and hear exactly the opposite of what the women were saying. Still, she wondered why they couldn't just complement each other once in a while.

Later, when they were eating, Céline couldn't help herself and asked Sophia again about the previous Friday. But she only talked about the brief greeting between Anton and Nick, keeping all the other details to herself. Of course, the group kept asking and at some point, Sophia couldn't help but admit that she and Nick had gotten along great, even if she didn't say how much, her friends could see it in her face.

"Oh God, don't tell me you're seeing him?" Viviana asked annoyed, as if the very idea was horrifying.

Sophia noticed how her cheeks glowed, but this time not out of shame at having exposed herself, but out of anger. She revealed nothing to them, only admitting, "I really like him." She brushed her hair back from her face and continued calmly and with conviction, "And he likes me too."

"You shouldn't get cocky and start imagining things just because he was nice to you for once," Céline instructed her.

"He probably only did it because he had no other choice," Ina laughed.

"Is it actually that hard to imagine that he could like me?" asked Sophia angrily, but didn't wait for an answer. "You don't know him at all, and you don't seem to know me either."

"Don't be so sensitive!" exclaimed Viviana, her face contorting

157

mockingly as if Sophia had done something wrong.

"Well, I am." Sophia admitted quietly, looking each of the three in turn in the face. "It's not just a crush because he's good looking. I've been in love with him for ages. All the sides of him I've known so far."

A startled, uncomfortable silence followed.

"And I know he likes me too. Really likes me."

Sophia was sure of this fact, and glad that she had finally told them, and hoped that they would now apologise.

But there was only silence for a few minutes and after a while the three of them talked about the changes Viviana was going to make to her dress just as if nothing had happened.

Yes, Sophia knew it was hard to apologise, but at least she was the one who always apologised when it was necessary. She was the one who always took care of everyone. Was it her own fault? Was she not good enough for these wonderful women she loved so much individually, but who together were like a pack of hungry wolves, ready to rip everything to pieces?

When she was back home, it still hurt that her friends could not or would not be happy for her. The questions sounded more like pure sensationalism than genuine interest. But she was actually quite happy about it. This way she didn't have to share Nick and what they both had and could keep it all to herself and enjoy everything that was to come.

But at first, not much really happened. The week began stressfully and was packed with work and appointments. Nick was hardly ever at his desk and when he was, he was always on the phone. Just like Sophia, who seemed glued to her desk and never once managed to go into his office. Apart from a penetrating glance and a brief nod, they hardly communicated. The one time she needed a signature from him and he was on the phone with someone, she went to his office as she did back then and put the papers on his desk. Unlike then, he put his hand on hers and their eyes met.

"Yes, yes, I'm still here." He laughed into the phone and then signed the estimate without checking it, staring instead at Sophia, who only managed to break away after a long while and pulled her hand more slowly out from under his.

Later, he texted her on her mobile and watched her from across the corridor while pretending to listen to another customer on the phone. Nick saw her look at her display, her face light up with her prettiest smile and then she looked over at him, nodding until he smiled too, lowered his gaze to the floor and disappeared from her sight.

When he came over late in the evening, Sophia dragged him unceremoniously into the flat and he leaned down to kiss her while still walking in. They both knew it was the only evening he could come over, as they both had evening appointments the rest of the week. Their photographers' little Christmas parties, studios or meetings with model agencies, set builders or clients were always quite cosy, but in hindsight more than exhausting. The next weekend Nick would be accompanying a client's photo shoot on Mallorca and would not return until the following week on Tuesday. So they both tried to make the most of their time together. They ate very little and spoke almost nothing, although their mouths were very busy. Just not with eating or talking.

At some point, as they sat nestled together on her couch, they both knew that soon the time would come for him to leave. Not because either of them wanted to, but because it was a really busy time and well past midnight. Nick cleared his throat, leaned over to her once more and stroked her face tenderly.

"I'm afraid I have to go."

"Stay.", Sophia blurted out, feeling her cheeks burn.

"I mean ... just a bit longer." She added quickly, searching his face for an answer.

His expression was unreadable and his eyebrows drawn together. She knew he was struggling and felt ashamed that she had taken the risk of asking him. Now he knew what she wanted. Whatever he said or did now would determine what would happen between them.

"You're really not making it easy for me, Sophia."

Just the way he breathed her name made her tremble slightly and she desperately hoped he hadn't noticed. What had he meant by that? To give the mood a lighter tone than she felt, she asked teasingly. "To stay?"

"Yes." He clenched his jaw and looked at their interlocked hands between them. Then he looked at her again, realising that he would have to be clearer if she was to understand what he meant.

Nick locked his eyes with hers, leaned closer, dropped his gaze to her lips and sought her gaze again. He tilted his head and kissed her. Tenderly. He let one hand slide to the back of her head and leaned heavier against her until she sank against the back of the sofa. Again she took a shaky breath as he paused at the corner of her mouth and then very slowly let his lips move over her cheek. At her jaw, he waited a moment until he thought her breathing had calmed and then gently pressed his hot lips to the sensitive spot below her ear. Sophia gasped loudly, her head sank to the side and her hands clawed into his pullover at his back as he tried desperately to be gentle with the tender skin, she offered him. He inhaled the scent of her neck and let his lips travel down to her collarbone.

Sophia's body tingled with overwhelming intensity in places

that had been awake but not alive only moments ago. It burned everywhere his lips touched her. She wriggled towards him and they both knew it was about to get even harder to separate, but neither of them cared.

Nick lost control at first, when her soft lips touched his forehead and one of her hands ran through his hair at the back of his head. In the blink of an eye, his lips were on hers again. First, they pressed firmly against hers before they became soft and tender again. But neither of them could really control themselves any longer. Slowly they opened their lips. Very carefully, the smooth tips of their tongues touched and they both gasped loudly at the burning sensation that found its way through their bodies.

They paused. Until Sophia dared and very lightly ran the tip of her tongue over his lower lip. In the background she heard him moaning quietly. Or was it her? A hot glow ran through her as he did the same to her and she dug her fingernails into what she could grasp of him as he let his tongue sink into her mouth for a moment and touched hers lightly. The tips touched. Fondly. Carefully and gently. No hurry. No frantic passion. Slow caressing, feeling and sensing.

Their lips were still touching lightly as they recovered from the force of that little kiss, both so full of emotion that they thought they would burst if they didn't finally tell the other how they felt. Sophia was unable to do more than let her fingertips fly over the stubble of his beard. She enjoyed feeling the muscles harden under her touch until her hand slid back down his neck. They sank silently into each other's arms. Together they felt the weight of their feelings and the certainty that they belonged together.

Chapter 13

It was the hardest week Sophia had ever had in the job she loved so much. Not because of the work, nor due to the knowledge that Nick and she couldn't see each other in the evenings and that he had to go to Mallorca for the coming weekend. It wasn't hard to avoid looking in the direction of his office every now and then either. The hardest part was seeing him but not being able to touch him. Now that she knew what it felt like. The smooth skin under her fingertips as she had very slowly stroked his beautiful face. The length of his lashes that tickled her fingers when he closed his eyes during the caress. The light scratching of his beard as he slowly stroked her cheek with his chin. The sound her fingernails made as she combed over his stubble. His fingers carefully tracing the contours of her face as if she were a fragile sculpture. The incredible tenderness with which he held her cheeks so that the touch could only be felt very lightly. The look in his soul-deep eyes, as if she were the most precious thing he had ever seen.

Sophia wondered how it was possible that he looked at her like that. Each time she fell deeper in love with him and feared that a simple *"I love you"*, would no longer be enough to describe her feelings for him, if she would ever be able to tell him. Her mind told her it was too soon, but she would love to scream those words at him. So far, he had only touched her face, her neck and her arms, and she felt as if she were already united with him. Not just physically. It was intense. She had never felt so deeply for anyone

162

before. It also scared her a little. Her logical-practical side warned her to be careful. Not to reveal so much of herself at once. This hesitant side also felt that a short break was necessary. As intense as the last ten days had been, after almost a year of longing. Sophia still didn't know how long he had felt something for her, she would like to know when and how it had finally come to that.

They both tried hard to act like they usually did. Like before. Hardly talking, never smiling. Above all, avoiding any physical contact so that no one would notice what was really going on. But they were like two magnets that kept moving towards each other.

On Tuesday morning, when Ruben was giving a little speech from the gallery and all the colleagues had gathered down in the hall, Sophia saw Nick leaning against the door to his office. A few breaths later, her whole back tingled. She didn't dare turn around, knowing full well that it was him standing behind her. The warmth crept up her spine and she wished she could just look at him for a second, but Annie, the biggest blabbermouth in the company, was standing next to her, so she preferred not to. The urge to touch him was so great that she clenched her hands into fists and was so busy trying to breathe calmly that she didn't even notice what Ruben was actually saying. She was glad that Nick was behind her and not next to her. She didn't want to be exposed to temptation. However, Nick still managed to touch her lightly. As he squeezed through the employees in front of him to get to his siblings, he stroked her arm with his long fingers, and that brief touch retained its effect for hours.

While they were separately at different parties that evening, they texted each other or even spoke briefly on the phone. Of course with the claim on their lips that it was about another job, without giving the client or the photographer the feeling that there could be other, more important people for them.

On Wednesday afternoon, as Sophia came down the stairs after getting a cup of coffee, Nick came towards her to join Jörn in his office. They looked at each other, smiled slyly and passed each other like normal colleagues. Only, as if they had made a secret agreement to do so, they both turned their palms outwards and touched each other lightly on the fingertips as they passed each other. In a flash, Sophia put her hand to her mouth and gasped out loud at the sensation. It was inexplicable. This electricity between them. She could feel it and even minutes later she felt as if she had received a small electric shock. Breathing heavily, she sat down at her desk and ran her hands through her hair. Her colleagues thought it was from the stressful day and looked at her with pity before each of them went back to their own work. She couldn't really enjoy the silence between her colleagues, who usually only argued, for the thing with Nick was already robbing her of her sanity after two days. And the control over her body. It seemed as if it had a mind of its own, she felt the urge to throw herself at him and kiss him mercilessly until they both lost their minds. This desire was something she had never felt so strongly before. It was a deep, heavy pull towards him, as if there was a strong bond between them. Or rather an inseparable wire rope.

After she had calmed down enough a short, or not so short, time later, she dared a glance in the direction of his office. He was back and a strange sight awaited her. Nick was sitting at his desk, on the far left, so that she could see him completely. He had both hands clenched into fists on the table in front of him. The tension made his upper arms look even stronger, and Sophia thought of how safe she felt in his embrace. How strong he was and what it would be like if he could lift her up and she could rest her face against his broad shoulder. Sophia tried to bring herself back under control, to breathe evenly. It seemed to her that since the first kiss, all her most secret fantasies spilled to the surface just by looking at him. But it wasn't just the sight of him, or his beautiful body. The most intense feeling she had was when she discovered his gaze.

Previously, she had always believed that he was angry with her when he looked at her like that, but now she believed that at that moment he really had a great desire to kiss her. Or to do even more. And yes, she wanted it too. So badly. Sophia craved his lips so much that she let her fingers slide over hers without consciously knowing what she was doing. She needed that light pressure and closed her eyes to calm herself, but it only got worse when she opened them again. She realised that if anyone saw him like that, they would know immediately what was really going on. It was that look that made her feel as if she was standing naked in front of him. She felt her breathing quicken, but she couldn't get enough of that intense look in his eyes. That he longed for her as much as she longed for him was so unimaginable that part of her brain was still searching for another explanation. But there was none. Nick had looked at her this way every time he had actually wanted to stay and then reluctantly said goodbye. Sophia closed her eyes again and tried to think of something else. Of the stress, of the upcoming shootings she had to attend, but his face and the look had burned into her brain.

"Sophia!", her colleague shouted, snapping her out of her daydream, only then noticing that her phone was ringing incessantly. She picked it up, but wondered how to answer it, as she had really forgotten at short notice. The blush shot to her cheeks as she uttered a soft, rasping

"Yes" and the voice on the other end rumbled harshly in her ear.

"Come here right now!"

Oh.

That tone in his voice shot another electric impulse through her.

165

The idea sounded tempting. But no. She couldn't . No, she couldn't do that. Everyone would notice, and if not immediately, then definitely *afterwards*, everyone would notice what was going on. Her cheeks would glow even more and her face would be covered with the scratches of his stubble.

"It's not a good time."

So that she couldn't see Nick anymore and he couldn't see her either, she leaned back in her chair and tried to breathe evenly again. One more look from him and she would run into his office as if by remote control, she was sure of it. Puffing breaths. Silence. Waiting.

"Yes, yes, you're right."

Silence again.

"What time is your appointment?"

"At eight."

"How on time do you have to be?"

Sophia bit her lip to keep from cheering, since there was this certain desperation in his voice that she sensed as well. It was such a beautiful feeling that he felt the same way she did.

"Ruben and I are leaving here at just before eight."

Again she closed her eyes as she heard Nick grumble.

"I see."

Then he hung up without another word. Sophia knew it couldn't go on like this for long, for either of them.

After they had been writing to each other the whole evening again, even though she was at the Christmas party of an advertising agency with Ruben and she had to be careful that he didn't notice, and even later in the evening when she was already in bed, it was even worse the next day. The tension was so great that they avoided all

166

eye contact and Sophia always put the estimates for which she needed a signature on his desk when he was not in the room. In between, he even left the company for a lunch date and the tension subsided. Nevertheless, Sophia continued to work without interruption, hoping to squeeze out a small window of time to meet him or at least have a few moments alone with him when most of her colleagues had already left the office. At some point she went to the kitchen to get a cup of coffee. But since none of her colleagues seemed to be able to refill the coffee beans or the water in the coffee maker, it was a slow process. After refilling everything and somehow relaxing as she watched the coffee slowly flow into her cup, she became aware of his presence. Her breath quickened immediately as he stepped closer. Glancing over her shoulder, she saw him twitch his jaw.

"Sophia."

"Mr Falkner." She had to call him that to keep the distance and turned back to her coffee, counting the last drops that trickled down as if in slow motion.

Suddenly, he stood very close to her, reached over her to the shelf to take down a cup, and murmured softly in her ear. "I thought I wouldn't catch you alone today, not even once."

Nick then gently ran a hand down her back and her very obvious physical reaction made Sophia step aside. He placed his cup next to hers and touched her little finger with his. Sophia turned around nervously to see if no one else was around. No colleague, and Ruben had fortunately just left his transparent glass cube to attend an appointment. Nevertheless, her heart was beating wildly.

Nick noticed her nervousness, followed her gaze to the door and smiled, God, how he would have loved to kiss her at that moment! But not here. On the other hand, no one was there right now. Could he dare? He had a huge desire to kiss her. It was like a human need, like breathing or drinking. The feeling of really the *need* to do it filled him completely. Without thinking any further about it, he grabbed her by the arm and swung her around to face that need. But instead of kissing her, he just looked at her again with that all-penetrating gaze.

Sophia stared at his lips, bit hers, closed her eyes and was a little surprised when he let go of her, and turned back to the coffee machine. A moment later Annie came rushing in, but luckily didn't notice Sophia's flushed cheeks as she left the room, nor the grim expression on Nick's face as he covered his frustration by accusing the coffee machine of causing trouble again.

Nick believed that it could not get any worse, but Friday was the worst day of all. Sophia was on a photo shooting followed by a dinner with the client and crew and wouldn't be back to the office all day, and would also spend the evening with other people instead of with him. He was supposed to go to the photo studio under the excuse of meeting the client, but then didn't make it because of his own appointments. The whole day was overcrowded with unnecessary extra interruptions. Yvonne had a problem with the printing company, Jörn got the news that his beloved DJ, whom he had asked for the Christmas party, had got a better offer and had already accepted it. Then there was a spontaneous crisis appointment with the company's tax advisor, which had reached Nick completely unexpectedly. The appointments went on until late in the evening and he had to catch an early flight to Mallorca the next morning. He groaned and ran his hand over his eyes in frustration. Somehow, he had to manage to see her or he would go mad. At that very moment, when she called, he had an idea.

"Hey, how are you?" he asked and Sophia was a little irritated by his good mood. She had the feeling that she could hear him smiling.

"Everything's fine here, how about you?"

"Hopefully, I'll be done with everything by eleven." He groaned, and Sophia knew it was no difference for her.

"I hope so too."

She waited, hoping he would say something more about whether they could still meet, but he only asked where they would have dinner later. Before they had to hang up, Sophia gathered all her courage and simply asked him. "Can we still see each other, at least for a little while?"

Relieved Nick smiled, glad that she wanted to see him as much as he wanted to see her. He could hear it in her trembling voice.

"I'll come over, but I can't say when exactly." He promised and then told her that he had to take the Art Buyer to the airport the next morning and leave quite early. Actually, rather in the middle of the night.

The rest of the day and evening dragged on like a lump of chewing gum, and although they sent each other a message now and then, they both had the uneasy feeling that things were not going to work out the way they had imagined. When Sophia got home around eleven, she tried staying awake for another hour by watching TV and reading, but she eventually gave up. She brushed her teeth, put on her sleeping clothes and lay down to sleep. But there was nothing she could do except toss and turn, so she stared at the ceiling for a while. She tried not to look at her mobile phone to protect herself from the pain of finding a message there that he wasn't coming after all. Which was actually already clear, but she still didn't want to give up hope completely. It was completely pointless and she knew it wasn't his fault, but still this little pain set in that she could just ease with dark chocolate instead of him. So she got up once more, put on a soft cardigan, went to the cupboard where she kept her sweets and broke off two pieces of the dark chocolate.

While she considered writing to him one more time, even though it was almost half past one, she ate a third piece and sat back down on her bed. She picked up the phone, which vibrated at that very moment and displayed a message.

Are you still awake?

yes

She wrote back immediately and then looked expectantly at the display to see what he would write next. But instead, the doorbell rang. Her heart gave a huge jump at the sound and she ran to open it for him. Even if she had wanted to, she couldn't have suppressed the happy smile when he finally came running up the stairs with an equally wide grin. In three long strides he was with her, clasping her face with both hands and pressing his lips so tightly to hers that the force made her dizzy. They stumbled into her apartment and she pushed the door shut before wrapping her arms around his neck.

One hand stayed on her face, but Nick wrapped his other arm around her body and pressed his hand into her back, forcing her to take another step closer. Nick's only thought was how good she tasted, and when their tongues finally touched, the thought of why of all things she tasted like chocolate popped into his head. But not the far too sweet one, but the sensual bitter one that lingered on his tongue. He kissed her even more gently now, as if he wanted to savour her taste for as long as possible. A shiver ran through him as her hands slid to the collar of his jacket and pushed it off his shoulders, causing it to land on the floor with an almost too loud thud.

Immediately his hands found their way back to her warm body, this time without the disturbing woollen jacket between them.

Nick felt her flinch for a second and realised he had never held her like this before.

The thin fabric of the pyjama top only covered her skin lightly and he held her at arm's length to look at her. He wanted to memorise Sophia for the few days he was away. That hair that lay in soft waves on her shoulders, those seductive full lips that called out for his. Those big eyes that looked at him brightly, as if he was something very special. Her whole face beamed at him. Nick wanted to hold that beautiful face. With his eyes fixed on hers, his hands gently stroked up her waist, embraced her ribs. Sophia's breathing quickened the higher his fingers went. As he leaned closer to kiss her again, he understood why.

She wasn't wearing a bra.

Oh damn! His thumbs were about to move to a certain spot. He really couldn't help it. It was as if his fingers had a life of their own. The tips of his thumbs could already sense the soft curves moving rapidly up and down. His fingers gripped hard into the fabric of her top to stop himself from doing what he wanted the most. Oh, how he longed to touch her! But he wanted to enjoy her. Yes, enjoy her, enjoy every millimetre of her when it came to it, and not have to look at the clock when he had to leave. That was why he really should hold back. But how difficult that was!

He broke away from her lips for a moment, but she was as hungry as he was and immediately caught his mouth once more. At the last moment he came to his senses and let his hands slide terribly slowly down her back. There the next seductive curve was already waiting for him. He simply had to caress her there for a very brief moment. Who could blame him? She was simply perfect. At the same moment, their kiss became more intense. Her tongue caressed his tenderly and he pressed himself more firmly against her, pushing her closer to the wall in the hallway. One hand slid back up her back and slipped under the collar of her cardigan into her hair. With the other, he pulled her body closer to him as he pressed her head against the wall in a fierce kiss until they both moaned. His lips moved back to her neck, but this time he couldn't be careful and kissed greedily down to her collarbone.

Sophia gasped, but held his head there so that he could not slip away. Her hand found its way under his pullover and also under the shirt he was wearing underneath. He twitched as she pressed her cool fingers to the heated skin of his back. They both held still. It was the first real touch of skin on skin on a part of his body that was usually hidden under clothes.

Good God! How intense it all was.

At the same time he noticed many other things. The apple scent of her hair. The soft skin under his lips. The vibrant pulsation underneath. The taste of bittersweet chocolate that was still on his tongue. The strong pull of her fingers on his hair. Her lips that desired his just as much, but still wanted to hold back. He felt so hot. Thinking he was going to burn up, he tore himself away from her and pulled off his pullover in one swift movement. The shirt slid up with it, and he gasped as Sophia's fingers found their way back underneath. She caressed his belly so damn tenderly that he tensed his muscles to protect himself and somehow suppress the vibration she was causing. He watched her and could not quite comprehend what he was seeing.

Her eyes lay fascinated on his face as her fingers continued to explore his belly and sides in a slow and soft rhythm. Wincing once more, he felt her trace the muscle at his side and at the same time press her lip between her teeth. He couldn't wait any longer and captured her mouth again, pressing her tighter against him.

Surprised by the fierceness, she clawed her fingernails into his skin. Groaning, he let his hand slide to her face and tried

172

desperately to slow the kiss. His lips found their way to the other side of her neck. Finally, he managed to kiss her all calm and soft again. Nevertheless, they both found it difficult to breathe.

Sophia felt his lips chasing an alternating bath of goosebumps and hot, short bursts of electricity through her body, so that she no longer knew exactly whether they were still standing in the hallway or were already in her room. Everything was spinning.

As Nick caressed her graceful neck, he felt her delicate body parts awaken dangerously seductive and pulled Sophia even closer to him. He could feel her. The delicate tips of her soft curves pressed against his chest. He took a step back. Grabbed her woollen jacket and was torn between tearing it off her body and buttoning it up. The sparks in her eyes literally jumped out at him and they both remembered that his flight would be leaving in a couple of hours and that neither of them wanted to take a step in that direction only to be disturbed by a clock or some kind of interruption. Of waking up together. To his surprise, Sophia took his face in both hands, pressed a small kiss to his lips and then cradled his neck as she snuggled heavily against him.

"Stay." She whispered and Nick shuddered as she pressed her soft lips to the hot skin of his neck.

"Sophia."

"To sleep."

"I know."

"But if you don't ..."

"I want to."

"But I don't want to rush things."

"Neither do I."

For a moment the two looked at each other before Sophia leaned back against him.

173

A current of happiness flashed through her as he lifted her, as she had so often dreamed of in her secret dreams and imagined in so many sleepless hours, and carried her to her bed.

Chapter 14

Even the third espresso didn't help to get that fuzzy feeling out of his head that always came over him when he had slept too little or not at all. As bad as this feeling was, Nick wouldn't change the past night for the world. Well, except for the fact that he would prefer to still be lying next to her. He smiled at the thought of Sophia. How she had clawed at his neck when he had lifted her up and carried her to her bed. There he had very slowly lowered her back down, but she had not moved an inch from him. Nick believed that she was either too overwhelmed by her own proposal and wondering what to do now, or that she was simply enjoying it too much in his arms. In any case, at some point, as if in slow motion, she let her hands slip from his neck, looked at him once more, then turned and crawled onto the bed.

Only then did he notice the many books and candles on the windowsill next to the bed. When he looked towards the end of the bed, he also discovered her television and saw himself spending one or two movie nights here, before he lay down next to her, on his side, to face her. Neither of them said a word. They just looked at each other. Sophia reached behind her and pulled out his blanket. Then she had slipped her hand under his and smiled at him. A very calm feeling spread through his chest, the kind that comes with being with just the right person at just the right moment. Nick had then leaned closer and seen her close her eyes, probably in anticipation of a kiss, but he had only rested his forehead against hers. Nick knew it was complete nonsense, but in that magical moment he had really believed that he was only communicating with her in her mind. Because in his, he had told her everything. The whole truth. How long he had felt something for her and how happy he was now and how much he wished he didn't have to pick up the Art Buyer two hours later.

Sophia had answered him. Nick was sure he had felt her nod. Only then had she turned her hand and slipped her fingers between his. Nick had no idea why, but this light caress of her slender fingers triggered something in him. Maybe it was the unexpected or the palpable tension between them, but he had lifted his hand, delaying the moment of contact even further. His fingers had tingled. When her fingernails had touched the thin skin between his fingers, it had prickled. In order for him to bear the sensation, he had to slide his fingers more firmly between hers. Sophia's breathing had quickened and he knew it would be a mistake, but he just couldn't suppress it. His lips found hers and this kiss was as gentle and careful as their very first. The tension had increased even more as he would have loved to roll on top of her, but at any moment his alarm would go off and then this magical moment would have been over and he just didn't want that.

Groaning, he had let reason prevail and abruptly turned onto his back. He had taken her hand in his and unconsciously pressed it to his chest until she released hers from his grip, came a little closer and slowly began to caress his face.

Fatigue and exhaustion had then struck mercilessly as he relaxed completely under her touch after this strenuous week, longingly taking in her closeness and warmth. He had noticed that he had smiled when he was still half awake, and the same smile he had now. He took out his mobile and wrote a message to her, intending to send it as soon as he landed. Then he put it away and just managed to stifle a yawn, but Jens, the Art Buyer sitting next to him, noticed anyway and asked amusedly.

"Busy night?"

"No," Nick replied shaking his head, "the night was just too short, unfortunately."

"I see." Jens murmured, then added mischievously, "too much work or too much woman?"

Nick gritted his teeth annoyed to suppress what was on the tip of his tongue and said only, "Just too less sleep."

Then he tried to change the subject and talked about the job until the end of the flight. As soon as they got off the plane, he switched on his phone and made sure the message went out to Sophia, only then could he concentrate on his work.

Sophia woke up in the late morning and, as she had never been one of those people who could sleep for long, she was numb for the rest of the day. This reinforced the feeling that it had all been a dream, but the scent of his aftershave still on her pillow reminded her that it really was true. How wonderful it had felt when he had put his arm around her and pulled her a little closer to him. Although he had tried to stay awake, he had had no chance against her caresses and had fallen asleep. It was only a light slumber, for as soon as she had stopped, his face had jerked in her direction or his hand, which was at her waist, had tightened its grip. Even she had been overcome by sleep and when his alarm clock had rung, it had taken her a few minutes to realise where she was and that he was really lying next to her. Or rather under her, for Sophia had been lying more on top of him than next to him. She had then woken him up and almost sunk into the sight of him. A sleepy Nick was somehow even a bit sexier than he already was.

His long lashes made it difficult for him to open his eyes, his hair was tousled and he smiled softly at her until he lifted his hand and brushed the wild curls out of her face. Then his gaze changed, and the crease between his eyebrows was visible for a moment. Then he had leaned closer, kissed her on the forehead and stood up. While he freshened up in the bathroom, she had made him a cup of coffee. Then, about twenty minutes later, they were at the door to say goodbye, and they were in each other's arms as if he were going away for months, not just four days.

"Sleep a bit more." He ordered in a soft voice, stroking with his thumb the dimple on her chin. Later, when she had woken up again, a message was already waiting for her.

Hope you got some more sleep.

Then she had first written him a longer reply about how much she had enjoyed having him by her side and how much she wished he was still there. But instead she had only answered him briefly and asked him to bring the sun with him when he came back.

Sophia spent the whole day doing everything that had been left undone. Paying bills, cleaning, tidying up and a quick phone call to her parents. She kept checking her mobile phone to see if another message had arrived, but he hadn't been in touch since the short message in the morning, which he must have written right after landing. But that was also quite normal, the first day was spent mainly with the photographer, checking out the locations and organising one or two relevant details for the shooting of the next two days. He made sure that the client and the Art Buyer of the advertising agency got everything they wanted and that the ordered things were there so they could do the job without delays. It wasn't until late afternoon, when she had just made herself a cup of tea, that her mobile phone showed a message, but it was from Ina and Sophia ignored it because she just didn't feel like letting anyone or anything spoil her good mood.

At some point she couldn't stand it anymore and messaged him to send a picture of the beach and was happy when he finally sent a picture of the setting sun and wrote.

Even more beautiful in real life.

Meanie!
I wish you could see it.

Sophia's heart skipped a beat. Had he perhaps said with these simple words that he missed her? Or was she just imagining it as her brain was completely overtired? In any case, she was satisfied with her answer and hoped that, despite her neutral tone, he had understood how she meant it.

I wish that too.

Nick already knew, of course, that he wasn't much of a talker and that Sophia was also someone who was rather reserved with her words. That would make it harder to talk about feelings, but this little back and forth between them made him realise that they missed each other. Even though she said she wished he would send the sun by and that she needed a few more degrees and couldn't wait until Tuesday, it showed him that she actually meant him. He would have liked to spend more time wondering what would happen on Tuesday, but first he had to go to dinner with the crew.

Since it would be an early start the next morning, fortunately everyone went to their rooms as soon as dinner was over. Nick couldn't run to his hotel room fast enough to call Sophia. As they spoke, the line echoed and he heard it burbling. When she finally answered his repeated question that she was in the bathtub, he closed his eyes and imagined her.

Of course, he had not forgotten the sight of her from the previous night and how wonderfully her sensual curves had nestled

179

against his body.

Nick knew that they were only at the very beginning, but also that he desperately wanted to be alone with her when he returned. Not just a few hours in the evening, he wanted to be with her for longer. He wanted to get to know her better and also her body. It was somehow inevitable.

Usually, Sophia loved Sundays. She mostly spent them in bed all day in her pyjamas, watching TV, reading a lot and talking on the phone. Of course, when the weather was nice, she always went out or met up with her friends. They seemed so strange to her since the last two weeks that she didn't feel like talking to them. Besides, they were going to meet the next evening anyway, and since she had resolved not to tell them anything more about Nick, she took her computer and prepared the pictures for Viviana. The pictures for the dress she had already sent her so that she could discuss any further changes of the dress directly with Ina and her friend. But now she made some collages for the flower arrangements, locations and a few small things according to the list the four of them had created. That way they would have enough to talk about without Sophia having to listen to any nonsense from them.

Of course, Sophia also knew that she was only postponing it this way. At some point she would have to discuss the subject with the girls. Not her relationship with Nick, but why they were acting like pouty teenagers and being so mean to her. But having friends and telling them honestly what was hurting you was a difficult thing. Sophia was afraid she might alienate the three of them and, in the worst case, even lose them. Since she hadn't been so lucky with friends so far, she tried to avoid that at all costs. It had worked out well so far and she had overlooked one thing or another. The thing with Nick, however, was too important for her not to be taken seriously by the three of them.

Nevertheless, Sophia decided to wait and worked at the computer for several hours, then copied everything onto an USB stick and was pleased when every now and then a small report about the shooting came in from Nick.

He sent pictures of the locations and a few silly ones of the crew, which she looked at excitedly. One of the next pictures that arrived made her heart jump once more, as he had sent her a selfie. Sophia had to swallow for he was shirtless and his muscles looked stunning in the golden light that shone on him. Behind him was the sea. How could he be so damn beautiful?

Nick wrote that it was no longer so warm, but he had still been in the water shortly, which she had already seen from his wet hair and damp shining face. Somehow it didn't matter what he wrote. Just the sight of him made her long to touch him and have him with her, and she was overcome by a feeling she hadn't felt in a long time. This pain in her chest, this tugging in her stomach. This mixture of pain like homesickness and anticipation of seeing him again soon. She knew they were still at the very beginning of their relationship, but she felt his absence as if he was already a part of her. Perhaps he was. Despite the fact that she was afraid of not being enough for him, that he might be disappointed in what he would get to see, she hoped she would dare. Would dare to show him next time that she longed for him all along.

For his touch. His kisses.

Monday was packed full of work for Sophia as usual and although she missed him and the pain of loss throbbed quietly in the background, she was able to throw herself into work and thus somehow endure his absence. They only sent a few messages back and forth in a flirty tone, and between phone calls to clients and organising other jobs, Sophia sent a message that sent a hot shiver down her spine as she honestly admitted that she was looking forward to seeing him again.

The evening with her friends was strangely quiet. Maybe it was because Viviana had talked to Jérôme on the phone for a long time and had finally discussed a few dates with him. Céline told them about a high-society event she was organising and Ina that she had met a new man. Sophia had briefly feared that she too would be questioned one more time, but fortunately that was not the case. She was glad that she was kept out of the gushing about the man and didn't have to say anything, even though she was so happy about how she felt about and with Nick.

Everyone had so much on their plate in the next few weeks before Christmas that they said goodbye relatively early and Sophia talked all the way home on the phone with Nick, who was already in his room telling her all the little and bigger events of the day.

Sophia knew, of course, when his plane was landing and when he would be back in the office, so she stared at the clock every few minutes from four o'clock the next day. When she finally *sensed* his arrival about an hour later, she almost jumped up and ran to meet him. But she kept control and sat tensely in her chair, reading through an email from a modelling agency for the tenth time and trying to stop herself from staring at him as he walked past her door. She looked up as he went into his office, and no sooner had he disappeared there than he called her and asked her to come into his office. Sophia almost ran over to him immediately, but she had packed some more papers first so that everyone could see that she was only there for work. As soon as she stood in the doorway, he got up and came towards her. Her heart was pounding deep in her chest and it seemed to be reaching for his. She felt so strongly drawn to him that she automatically stepped closer, as if she had no control over her body.

Nick reached for the door without taking his eyes off hers, but instead of closing it as she had expected, his brother rushed into the office and closed the door behind him instead.

"The portfolios arrived!"

"Hello Jörn." Grumbled Nick, looking at Sophia for a moment, annoyed.

"Yeah, sorry." Jörn hugged him and then glanced briefly over at Sophia, who was standing next to the door and making moves to leave again. "Oh hi. Didn't see you there. Do you have something to talk about?"

"I was just telling Sophia about the portfolio thing when you came in," Nick explained through clenched teeth, then asked his brother to leave.

Sophia's heart lifted in excitement and then continued to beat in anticipation, knowing what would happen as soon as they were alone in a closed room.

"Or even better, you both come with me right now!" shouted Jörn and then pushed Sophia out of the room.

Disappointment and frustration piled up in Nick's chest and he just couldn't stop himself from giving short, annoyed answers to everything Jörn said. The three of them went upstairs to the conference room and Jörn first closed the door and then started unpacking the photographers' new portfolios from the boxes that had been delivered. He showed them to Sophia, explained the new logo and that only she should know about it so that she could help Nick fill the folders secretly until the Christmas party in less than two weeks.

"We should do this when no one is left in the office, otherwise people will find out," Nick suggested in a neutral tone, and Jörn was pleased at his level-headedness. Sophia, on the other hand, tried to look as little as possible in Nick's direction and helped the two of them unpack the books and sort them according to the photographers' names.

Nick would have liked to throw his brother out of the room. But on the other hand, he was quite glad that he was standing between them, for who knows what he would have done otherwise.

Sophia was somehow even more beautiful than he remembered her. Her hair was tied in a shaggy knot at the back of her head, and a few small curls broke their way down her neck. That long, graceful neck, the line of which he wanted to run his fingers and lips over. He stood at the other end of the long table and watched her every move. Those slender but strong hands that placed the heavy black leather folders on the table. After putting on white cotton gloves, she carefully stroked the smooth, plastic-coated, shiny pages.

The truth dawned on him when he looked into her face. She avoided all eye contact, as she had always done in the past when she was near him. He became more and more aware that she must also have felt something for him for a long time, as he knew that expression on her face. He even allowed the absurd thought that he had known the expression from the beginning. An urgent desire to talk to her about it spread through his chest, it almost hurt and he had to take a deep breath. Even more that he wanted to know how long she had liked him, he wanted to be alone with her, even though he knew he would not be able to kiss her here, with all the people around. At some point he still couldn't take it anymore and asked Jörn in a harsh tone whether he wanted to fill the photo books with Sophia or whether they should do it the way it was actually planned. Then he added something that he knew Jörn would react to by fleeing.

"It's quite a lot of work, after all, and if you take over, I can do my stuff and maybe even leave a bit early."

"Oh no Nick, go ahead, you are a team after all." Jörn grinned at Sophia. "But you should really only do it in the evening when no one else is around."

After a few more words that it should definitely remain a secret, Jörn left the room. Unfortunately he had left the door open, Nick followed him with quick steps to close it. When he turned around, Sophia just looked at him but did not move. They were both aware that they had to control themselves, after all, Ruben's office was next door and someone could walk in at any time. So Nick decided to just say what he felt to relieve the palpable tension between them.

"I would like to be alone with you."

Sophia's heart lifted and she nodded wordlessly at him.

"I've been putting off all my appointments." he admitted, and though he would have liked to walk over to her, he stayed where he was.

"Me too." Her voice was quite breathless, but she smiled.

Nick didn't smile, he really thought he would burst at any moment. He had to say what was on his mind, or pull her into his arms and kiss her. It was obvious to him that it had to be now, they couldn't leave this room without him saying something.

"You know, I'm not so good with words."

"Yes, you are."

She thought of his last messages, which were clearly more than flirting, and grinned at him. But Nick couldn't think of anything immediately and he looked around, somehow trying to find the right words.

"You know, I erm ... I felt like those photo books when I was away." He pointed to the table where the portfolios were piled up and Sophia closed the open book, she had in front of her. She took off the white cotton gloves, since she needed the photographers'

185

photos first anyway in order to get on with the work. Sensing his discomfort, she chuckled slightly and remarked.

"Leathery, heavy and bulky?"

Nodding, Nick smiled and added simply, "And empty."

Sophia's heart beat even more wildly in her chest and she was aware that he was just making a declaration of love to her. She kept silent and looked at him and was glad that he was standing at the other end of the room, otherwise she would have hugged him and most likely kissed him too. Since he said nothing more but looked as if he was waiting for anything from her, she asked in a low voice.

"Do you still feel empty now?"

He just shook his head and took a few steps closer when the half-closed door was yanked open and Ruben rushed in with his head all red.

"Ah Nick, there you are, I need you urgently!"

"Ruben, we're in the middle of ..."

"That can wait, I have New York on the line."

Sophia saw Nick's face, which had just been full of warmth and gentleness, harden and without another word, just a scowl at her and a quick nod, he left the room. She knew about the rumours that the company would soon open an office in New York, but she didn't know anything more specific. In any case, it was probably something that got on Nick's nerves quite a bit, because from the looks of him, it wasn't exactly a pet project of his.

Since she had nothing to fill the new photographer's books and didn't want to start lugging the old, worn-out portfolios upstairs now, when the office was still full of colleagues, she left the room shortly afterwards, locked the door behind her and was on her way back to her office. As she passed Ruben's glass office cube, Nick glanced briefly in her direction and she tried to cheer him up with a small smile. He just had that grim look on his face that she had always despaired of in the past and, clenching his teeth, turned back to Ruben, who had apparently put the caller on speakerphone.

Sophia spent the rest of the day doing her work and continuing to put things on Nick's desk, who hadn't come out of Ruben's office for an hour and a half. She kept looking up at the glass office and saw him gesticulating wildly, putting his hands on his hips and staring at the ceiling in annoyance. Actually, she was ready to go home, but she wasn't sure whether she shouldn't wait for him and maybe start on the photobooks already and asked Jörn what she should do.

"Oh Sophia you ahem..." Jörn also looked up at Ruben's office and then told her she'd better go home. "I think it's best if we do this at the end of the week."

He smiled amiably down at her, but she couldn't quite shake the feeling that Jörn just wanted her to leave. He probably also sensed the underlying vibration of the whirlwind that was brewing up there on the first floor between his two older brothers.

"Alright."With one last look up, she went back, gathered her things, picked up her bike shortly afterwards and rode home.

When she got there, she immediately checked to see if Nick had written a message, but she still hadn't heard from him after another hour. She knew Ruben's long, unannounced meetings only too well, but they had never had such an effect on her before. Often, they had been long evenings in his office, with and without photographers, alone or with other colleagues, and often enough they had all witnessed the heated discussions between the siblings afterwards or before, or rather watched from below. Even though Ruben's office was made of glass, if you weren't standing in the kitchen or the conference room next door, you couldn't hear a word, not even if it was shouted.

Once, some of her colleagues had made a joke of it and put words into the mouths of the arguing bosses as if they were dubbing actors in a foreign language film. Although it had been quite funny,

Sophia had not joined in, but had wondered why they had to have these heated conversations and arguments in Ruben's office, where every employee could see it, and not in another office whose walls and doors were not made of glass.

Around half past nine, Nick called and she could still hear the tension in his voice. She wanted to see him so badly, but braced herself for the fact that he couldn't come because he might have to argue with Ruben some more or was just too tired.

"Can I still come?" He asked curtly.

"Of course."

After that, she ran around her home excitedly, lit all the candles she could find, turned on the oven to bake him a pizza, and then looked at herself in the mirror. Combed her hair again, mascaraed her eyelashes and applied some lip gloss. She didn't want to look too obviously styled up, she never was, but she wanted to be beautiful for him. Still with his interrupted explanation in her head, she yanked the door open full of energy when he finally rang the bell.

Unlike Friday, he did not come running up the stairs, but walked normally. He looked tired and exhausted, and a slight tug in her heart told her that something was wrong. Nick stopped in front of her and she pulled him into her apartment, slipping her arms around his middle and pressing herself tightly against him. He relaxed noticeably in her arms and his embrace tightened its hold on her.

He was quite agitated. Not only due to the gruelling conversation with Ruben, his plans for New York and the resulting problems. He was also not so clear about when he should finally talk to Sophia about it. The fact that his little spontaneous

188

declaration of love earlier in the office had been complete nonsense didn't make it any better.

"Sophia, I ...", he began softly as he broke away from her, but then he lost all thought of talking, he just couldn't help himself and kissed her. Briefly and still with that worried look on the face, but Sophia reacted quite differently than he had expected.

She took a step back, looked him in the eye and asked if he was hungry, but he could not answer. There was only one thing that could satisfy his hunger, and by the look she gave him and the delicate colouring of her cheeks, he knew she knew the answer. Before he could form another thought, he tore off his jacket. Sophia turned and ran into her kitchen. He saw her turn off the stove as he followed her. When she straightened up again, he was already standing by her and grabbed her by the shoulder to pull her into his arms. At the same time Sophia embraced his face and kissed him. Insistently. All the thoughts and frustrations he had felt only moments ago were abruptly gone. She stood on her tiptoes and pressed herself so tightly against him that he stumbled back a few steps.

They both had to gasp for air after their tongues engaged in a wild dance and then he finally pressed his face into her neck. A little calmer, Sophia stroked his back, sensing that he wanted to say something and she wanted him to know that whatever it was, she would listen.

"What's wrong?"

Nick stroked her face lovingly. His look was full of concern and something else she couldn't quite interpret. He could tell from her look that she sensed something was on his mind, but he couldn't find the courage to talk about it now. Pressing his forehead against hers, they both took deep breaths. He just wanted to be here with her, he didn't want to waste a thought on anything or anyone else. The only thing that stopped him from telling her was that she was standing right in front of him, looking at him like *that*. He needed her.

"I just don't want to talk right now."

Sophia caressed his face in response until he looked at her, then leaned closer and kissed him as gently as she could, wrapping both arms around his neck. And as she might have expected, he came towards her immediately and kissed her back just as passionately in that slow rhythm.

At some point he could no longer remain standing and pulled her onto her sofa with him. She slid on top of him. He caressed her back and sides and he heard her sigh quietly as he grazed her bra.

She kissed him lovingly, pressed herself more firmly against him and when she gave in to her feelings a little more, she slid one leg between his. The opportunity, as Nick gasped for a moment in response, she immediately seized and kissed tenderly up his neck. She held his face with both hands and found her way back to his lips as he pressed one hand firmly on her lower back and shoved the other hand into her hair. It was all so overwhelming. Warm and soft, until at some point Sophia lost her grip and somehow slipped sideways off him.

Now he took the opportunity and rolled on top of her, as he had wanted to do on Friday night. Her whole body was tingling and it was so warm that Sophia hoped he would finally take off one of her clothes, but instead he only propped himself up for a moment and took off his pullover. Just like Friday, she immediately let her hands slide under his shirt and caressed his firm body. A hot shiver ran through her body as he lay a little heavier on top of her and she put her leg up so he could come even closer. Finally, he kissed down her neck and sucked very tenderly on the soft spot between her shoulder and neck until she moaned and shivered so violently that he propped up on his arms and just looked at her.

"Sophia." Just the way he breathed her name made her do

190

everything he asked and she could only tighten her grip on his shirt.

"I ..." he stroked her face with his thumb, "I want to leave."

Her face immediately lost its colour and cheerful expression, and he was annoyed at his stupid choice of words.

"With you."

Astonished, she looked at him and there was this magical little wrinkle between her eyebrows and he tried to wipe it away with his thumb as they looked into each other's eyes. A thousand questions and possible answers ran through his mind that she could give him, but Sophia only nodded.

"When?"

His smile was the most beautiful one he had given her so far. He kissed her on the cheek before lying down beside her and slipping his arms around her waist.

"Friday."

Sophia waited for him to tell her more and he nodded to her as he said, "I just want to spend as much time with you as possible without any interruptions or work the next morning."

"Yes, me too."

She snuggled against him, her heart pounding up to her throat as he let his hand wander from her back to her side. The heat spread all over her body in the form of goosebumps once more and she wished he would take off her top, but his hand remained like a hot stone on her ribs. He didn't move, though Sophia could sense that he was as eager as she was for him to slide his hand further up. After another breath, she let herself tilt back a little so that he understood what she wanted. Her breathing quickened, it had been so long since she last been touched there. Her insides were in a state of complete turmoil of anticipation and desire. Trembling, she looked at him. She was simply not capable of more.

"We can wait." The sound of his voice sent a shiver through her. "Sometimes that's the best part of it."

He smirked, but the desire to touch her literally jumped out of his eyes.

"You being so thoughtful is the best part of it." She whispered and she felt tears prickling behind her lids. She closed her eyes and breathed harder as he let his fingers glide in a cruelly slow way to her beautiful curves.

"Only when I'm with you,..." he pressed a soft kiss to her lips as his hand caressed her tenderly, finally touching her where she desperately needed to feel his hand. "I am the best part of me."

Chapter 15

Once again, Friday was still far away and Sophia thought she would break out in a fever from all the tension and heated feelings. Ever since he had touched her for the first time on very sensitive parts of her body on Tuesday evening, she could think of nothing else. It had been so intoxicating, even though he hadn't even slipped his hand under her shirt. The arousal she had already felt was like nothing she had ever felt before. She almost couldn't bear the thought of what it would be like when he stroked her with no clothes on.

She buried her face in her hands and tried to focus her thoughts on the here and now, which really wasn't easy after the sight of him kept filling her head.

For he had been just as sensitive to her caress and at one point had lifted himself off her to free himself from his T-shirt. Sophia then embarrassingly couldn't suppress a moan when she had him shirtless and so close in front of her for the first time. Ever so gently, she had touched him, tracing every line and little valley between his abs and following the line of dark hair on his chest. And yes, it had filled her with pride that she caused that twitching of his muscles and his heavy breathing.

At some point he had grabbed her hands, intertwined their fingers and held her arms firmly above her head. Then he had lowered down heavily onto her and kissed her so torturously slow that she had thought her heart would burst from all the love she felt.

Later, at some point, the kisses had become wilder again, his hands wandering over her body in a restless and greedy frenzy until they both left each other gasping for air. After a much more tender and less wild moment, he had suddenly jumped up and stood beside the sofa for a few breaths, and she had watched in fascination the movement of his back muscles as they moved in shades of gold and orange in the light of the candles while he ran his hands through his hair several times.

Then Nick wordlessly went to the fridge, took out a bottle of water and returned with it and two glasses. He sat down on the sofa at the level of her knees and poured them both a glass of water and had almost dropped his when Sophia sat up and began to spread little kisses over his back. His muscles twitched under the touch of her lips, but best of all, when she slipped her arms around him, he leaned into the embrace and pressed her hand to his heart. She loved him all the more for not being pushy with her in any way, even though at more than one point she would have been ready for anything. She really had fallen completely in love with him, and she held on to the small hope that he felt the same way. After all, the way he had looked at her and touched her was much more than any man had ever done. It was deeper. The caresses, gentle as they had been, had burned deep into her heart.

His every touch was tattooed on her senses.

Sophia ran her hands over her face again and took a sip of water. She really should get a grip, if she walked around with red cheeks all day, everyone would know before the end of the week. They both tried to keep their encounters during working hours to a minimum, but it was even harder than when they had tried to avoid each other for months. Sophia also didn't think she would survive it if they started putting the photographers' portfolios together in the conference room over the next few days. She really wasn't sure if that was such a good idea, and wondered if they couldn't somehow postpone it until next week, as she knew he had appointments on at least two evenings, and then she could finish the portfolios alone and not run the risk of jumping him in the conference room. She should really only do *that* when they were alone.

Giggling at her own joke, she remembered that they would be alone for the next few evenings. But she also believed that he would wait for *that* until they didn't have to get out of bed the next morning. Just the thought of it made her body tingle with anticipation, even though she didn't know what exactly he had planned, she was so extremely looking forward to the weekend. But of course there was also the worry that either something would come up and disrupt their time together, or that she wouldn't be able to give him what he expected. After all, he had been with many women and had much more experience and certainly certain expectations of the woman who climbed into bed with him.

On the other hand, Sophia didn't really believe that was all that important to him. It was something quite different what connected them both and she was sure that he felt it too. Could it really be that it was the magical wonder of love?

Despite the fact that they both had jobs and had to go to one appointment or another, they managed to meet at her place every evening around ten or eleven. On Thursday, however, it almost looked like it wasn't going to work, since the siblings had another huge argument in Ruben's office when Sophia left at eight. Nick still came afterwards and that evening Sophia had the feeling that his thoughts were completely elsewhere and he didn't want her to be a part of it. Although she would have liked to help him with the problem he seemed to have at work and with Ruben, she didn't push him and tried to change the subject by asking him about their little trip. As if she had flipped a switch, he was immediately in a better mood.

"I hope you've prepared your photo material as there are some great subjects to photograph for your book."

"Oh really? "

He nodded, took her hand and kissed her knuckles.

"What else do you want me to pack?" The question was innocently spoken and meant, but she could tell from his darkening eyes that his thoughts were not quite so innocent.

"Not much." His voice was quite low and his lips softened as he ran them over the back of her hand to her wrist.

The hairs on the back of Sophia's neck stood up as he twisted her arm and pressed his mouth to her pulse, and of course they both knew he could feel it throbbing fiercely beneath his lips. Nick opened his mouth and sucked on the tender skin without taking his eyes off hers. Her breathing quickened as he carefully let his teeth travel up her arm to the crook of her elbow. There he became gentle again, but Sophia withdrew her arm, barely able to stand the tingling, and wrapped it around his head as she leaned against him and kissed him not-so-shyly.

It wasn't long before he pulled her more firmly onto his lap and pressed his hand under her shirt against her lower back. He had done the same the previous night and Sophia was so impatient that she leaned back and tried to pull her shirt off when he took her hands, wrapped them back around his neck and held them there.

"You need to pack."

She looked at him questioningly and pulled back a hand to stroke his face.

"We're leaving right after work tomorrow." He smiled and Sophia bit her lip to suppress a grin, which she only just managed.

A moment later he left, giving her enough time to pack her bag.

Still, she couldn't help but send him at least three messages begging for more information. But he only wrote back mysteriously that they were going somewhere cold and that he wanted to take her out to dinner one evening.

Friday seemed to fly by as if Nick were on a fast-moving train. The attraction Sophia had for him was becoming more and more palpable, and he kept noticing colleagues or his brother Jörn looking questioningly from one to the other as soon as they were less than a metre apart. But unlike Sophia, he was able to cover up his feelings with a neutral expression on his face as long as they didn't look him in the eye or feel his pulse. However, her cheeks, which always blushed so charming, and her gaze, which she always lowered very quickly, showed her tension around him. But fortunately he had always behaved so taciturnly and harshly towards her in the past that at least Jörn believed it was the exact opposite of the truth.

"Nick, you really need to talk to Sophia."

"Why?"

"She really is a great lady and you make such a good team, you just need to be a little nicer to her."

Nick struggled to suppress a laugh and made a noise that sounded to his brother like a grumble.

"You complement each other better than you think," Jörn said, and the images in Nick's head reflected exactly how well they complemented each other.

His head came to rest right in the curve between her smooth shoulder and graceful neck, as if it had been made to lie right there. Her slender fingers could follow the line of his muscles without interruption. The curve of her hips matched his exactly, as if they were two parts of a whole, and his hands were the right size to exactly cup her beautiful bosom. Even if he had only ever done so while she was still wearing a T-shirt. And her lips! Oh yes, her lips complemented his so well that he wished he never had to take another breath and could kiss her undisturbed until they drifted off into a shared sleep.

"What do you say?" Jörn tore Nick out of his memories. He stared questioningly at his brother.

"There's not much going on today, you can finish the portfolios next week and maybe you can send her home early and gain some plus points." Jörn nudged him lightly on the shoulder and Nick bit his cheek to keep from blurting out what he had already planned to earn plus points and just nodded.

Sophia waited impatiently in her office for Nick to pick her up, thinking about all the things she had packed. Since she only had two dresses suitable for a date, she had chosen the dark green one in sixties style, as the little black one that Ina had once forced her to buy just seemed too obviously sexy. Once again, she checked her photo bag to make sure she had packed enough material and to distract herself from thoughts of what would happen after dinner.

"Ah, are you going on a photo tour again?" Her colleague asked as he put on his coat and Sophia could only nod as she was already thinking of answers to questions that fortunately did not come. Her colleague said goodbye shortly afterwards and Sophia stared at the clock, wondering when Nick would finally join her so they could leave.

A few minutes later, Nick was walking towards her office when her eyes met his. He nodded to her as they walked silently out of the empty office and he took the bag from her and put it in his boot.

Of course, he could tell she was quite nervous since she didn't immediately fasten her seatbelt, kept talking and asking where they were going until he leaned in and just kissed her. Although they were still in the company car park, neither of them was afraid of being caught.

Just as her presence reassured him, he seemed to have a similar effect on her, for she was breathing much more calmly now and kept her eyes closed for a moment longer as he had long since settled back into his seat and driven out of the car park. If she had known how nervous he was as well, she would probably have calmed down even more, even if he had another reason to.

Of course, he was also tense, wondering if and how it would be when they finally did what they both seemed to long for. He hoped very much that he could make her happy and take away any inhibitions and doubts she still had. He didn't want her to feel insecure or question his feelings for her. He loved her and wanted to show it in every moment they spent together. But he was also afraid that somehow, he was pushing her too hard after all. Not with the fact that he wanted her, but with what he was putting her through, with where they were going. And with himself.

Since Cora he had not taken a woman home, apart from the brief affair in the mourning period after the break-up with the waitress from the noble fish restaurant, it was his safe place, his *safe place* that could bear witness to his inner turmoil and grief, to all the pain he had ever felt. Everywhere there was a place of memory. All of them he wanted to show Sophia when she wanted to see them, to give her everything of him and tell her what she wanted to know. He had never felt as safe with anyone as he did with her, and he hoped he could make her feel the same way. Make sure she could trust him.

Sophia's nervousness subsided the longer they drove, and at some point, she had a little idea where they were going. Her heart began to beat more wildly a second time. Not because of what lay ahead of them, but because of what it *meant*. She pretended not to notice and waited for him to say something, but he said nothing

199

until they passed the obvious shield. He looked over at her briefly and she could tell from his expression and the tense position of his hands on the steering wheel that he was probably a little nervous too.

"Pielsand?" She just couldn't wait any longer.

"Is that all right?"

"Of course!"

Nick was filled with that warm feeling he actually had every time he was with her, but which had been somewhat cooled down due to the trouble with Ruben, the many expectations and the fear he would scare her away if he took her home. But when he looked over at her and saw her honest smile and the anticipation shining from her eyes, he knew it was right. That he had done it right.

"I look forward to seeing where you grew up."

Again he smiled at her, although his thoughts briefly drifted to another person who had had no desire at all to travel to this small, barren village, but which meant so much to him.

When they were only a few kilometres away from Pielsand, Sophia had the feeling that Nick was much more relaxed. He told her who owned the estates they were driving past, even though of course in the darkness of the evening she couldn't make out that much, except that the first snow had already fallen. After a few more minutes they pulled into the car park next to a huge building, obviously a hotel, above the sandy cliffs. Sophia wondered if this was the former family estate she had always heard about. She was amazed at how big and beautiful it was. They got out of the car and the wild sea breeze caught them unexpectedly, but not unwelcome. He shouted something apologetic about the weather, but Sophia took a few steps away from the car, closer to the cliffs, spread her arms and let the wind really blow through her and whirl her hair around her nose. She loved the wind and the sea and licked the salty air from her lips.

"Do you like it?" he asked as he came closer.

Smiling, she nodded as he wrapped his arms around her and she leaned against him, closing her eyes and enjoying the cool wind on her face and the warmth radiating from him.

"Shall we go in?"

Sophia turned in his arms, gave him a little kiss and then followed him back to the car where he took the bags out of the boot and she took her camera bag.

"As you can see it's a hotel," he explained, pointing his chin upwards, "but that's where I live."

Sophia immediately felt confirmed in her suspicion that he was more at home here than in his two rooms in the family home in the city when she entered the apartment on the upper floor. It smelled like him, even though he said he hadn't been there in months.

"The good thing about living in a hotel is that you don't have to clean it yourself," he joked, adding, "they've already turned up the heat and the fireplace, too."

He led her into the living room, which looked eerily cosy and where she immediately felt at home. Warm wooden floors and a comfortable-looking wide couch stood in front of the fireplace, where the fire burned with a small flame and the wood in it crackled softly. Above it was a huge television and in front of it a soft-looking carpet, and obvious images formed in Sophia's mind. She thought of what a beautiful place this was, or *could be*, for some special moments, that heat immediately rose in her cheeks.

"Come here." Nick pointed to the huge window at the far end of the room that looked down on the cliffs and the sea, and although it was already dark and the path to the beach was not visible, the lights of the house glittered on the water of the wildly foaming sea. Sophia could have just stood there mesmerised if he hadn't kept talking.

"The view is just stunning," and Nick was referring not only to the view of the sea, but to her as well.

Sophia felt his gaze rest on her even before she saw his reflection in the window and turned to him, but instead of kissing her, he took her hand and pulled her into the next room. A bed built of grey-coloured flotsam was the only piece of furniture next to a small bedside table, and Sophia's breath quickened a little as she realised what might soon happen there.

"Here is the wardrobe." He explained further as he pointed to a small hallway, which he entered and opened another door to reveal a bathroom behind it.

Then he looked at her briefly with his ocean blue eyes, checked his watch and explained that he had booked a table at one of the restaurants on the cliffs so they would have plenty of time to change. But before he could talk further, she was already standing in front of him and gave him a light kiss that turned into more within another moment.

Having taken off her jacket in the living room, she was now wearing only her thin jumper, which slid up a little as she wrapped her arms around his neck and his hands immediately found their way underneath. He stroked her back and pulled her closer to and Sophia somehow couldn't wait any longer, she wanted to show him that she wanted him too. Leaning back, she simply removed the disturbing garment. He looked at her with a glowing gaze, stroking her face, neck and collarbones with light fingers.

"So beautiful." He whispered into her skin as he followed the path of his fingers with his lips, and as he kissed the soft spot below her neck, he tenderly enclosed her curves hidden under silk.

Sophia took a shaky breath and bent her head for another kiss. Her hands wandered to his hair, ruffling it as he took a few steps and stumbled with her to the bed. There he paused, laid her down and looked at her for a moment as if she were the most precious thing in the world, before he too took off his jumper and sank into her waiting arms. They kissed and caressed, and Nick pulled her leg over his hip and pressed himself so tightly against her that she had to gasp. His hungry mouth wandered over her flat, warm belly and his hands caressed every bit of skin not covered by fabric. Sophia grabbed his hair and arched her back to be even closer to him. She wanted to be touched by him, it was an urgent need. With one hand she reached behind her and unclasped her bra, and when Nick kissed up her arm and over her smooth shoulder, pushing the strap down a little, she simply removed it without a second thought.

He took a deep breath, touched her with his gaze. Opened his mouth as if he wanted to say something, but then only looked wordlessly into her eyes. When their lips met again, he let his agile fingers fly gently over the newly exposed skin. The feelings that his tenderness coupled with the almost rough touches of desire triggered in Sophia were so wonderful and almost frighteningly strange that she could no longer think straight.

Nick was taken with the feeling of Sophia moving so beautifully under and beside him that he almost forgot himself as his lips followed his fingers over her heated body. Still, he tried to hold back, remaining slow and tender. When one hand came to rest on her lower belly and his fingertips were already grazing the button of her jeans as he traced small patterns on her skin with his tongue, her sigh turned into a pant and she tightened her grip in his hair. Slowly he had undone the button, but he sensed that she was not ready even before she touched his arm.

He was worried about what was holding her back, but he didn't want her to feel uncomfortable either, so he let his hands wander over her soft skin again and caressed her belly with his chin. Her body was on fire, she had seductive goosebumps all over her body and responded to his caresses with passion. Her fingers were equally full of desire, yet he kissed her more slowly now and after caressing the most sensitive parts once more, he rolled them both to the side so they could look at each other.

"Are you alright?" He smiled gently at her.

Sophia nodded, but he saw tears begin to form in her eyes, which she tried to hide by closing her eyes.

"Hey, what's wrong?" A cold rod bored into his chest, had he hurt her somehow or had he been too brash?

"I've been ... been in a situation like this before." She explained meekly after a while, opening her eyes again at the exact moment he clenched his jaw, embarrassed that she saw it.

"I'm sure you were." But of course he didn't want to think about it, instead he tried to show her that she could tell him anything too, and kissed her hand.

"But I always blocked it off because ... because it felt wrong."

Nick closed his eyes for a moment, the thought that she thought it was wrong shook him to the core, but he didn't want to show her. Damn it, what had he done? Had he pushed her too hard? But she had taken off her jumper ... and her bra, she had wanted it too! Or had she simply been overwhelmed by what her body was asking for, but her mind, or worse, her *heart,* had not wanted it at all? Should he have taken it slower?

Sophia knew she had to explain, she had to say something. She didn't want to take the next step before he knew! He should know and she tried to find the right words.

"But with you," she said softly, stroking his three-day beard with her fingernails, which made that soft scratching sound over his stubble. His gentle gaze gave her the courage to continue.

"You made it feel right from the start." Her voice trembled slightly, and to lighten the mood, Nick tried a little joke.

"So you mean we could have done it already?"

Unimpressed by his little grin, she continued to speak as she slid a little closer.

"It feels so right, I don't even know why I'm so .... reserved."

"Hey, it's okay."

Nick gave her a little kiss, he could wait. Of course he would if that was what she needed. She should get everything she wanted, even if she didn't know exactly for herself what that was. He was aware that he was falling a little more in love with her at that moment, and he touched her forehead with his as she began to whisper.

"I think," she closed her eyes and put her fingers to his lips so he wouldn't interrupt her in this moment when she could finally say what had been weighing so heavily on her soul for so long.

"I'm scared ..." She took one last breath and then finally said it, "of the intensity of my feelings for you."

His heart, which had been hammering wildly in his chest, seemed to stop beating for a moment, his breath quickened, for no one had ever said anything so incredibly beautiful to him before. Knowing that Sophia was very careful with her words touched his heart all the more. He pulled her close, rested his temple against hers and spoke softly, but in a firm voice.

"Don't be." He pressed a light kiss to her ear and admitted. "It's not just you."

They lay like that for a long time, caressing each other in a soothing rhythm. Their hearts beat in unison and Sophia felt so safe in his arms that she could have stayed like that forever.

"Shall we go to dinner now?" He asked after a while and she nodded.

Nick was amazed when Sophia came into his living room a few minutes after him, and it wasn't necessarily because of the dark green swinging dress or her legs, which looked incredibly long and sexy in the high heels she was wearing. No, it was because of the glow that emanated from her. It was as if a weight had been lifted from her shoulders and she had regained her light-heartedness. He was sure that what she had said had really meant a lot to her and that she was even more relaxed now. Smiling, he took her hand and they left the warmth of the hotel, walked to his car and drove down the wide hill to the village where they arrived a few minutes late for their reservation at the restaurant. There weren't many guests and during the meal they relaxed even more, eating little, talking a lot and looking dreamily down at the sea, wrapped up in thoughts of each other and what they both now knew. Only when Nick took her hand in his and asked if they wanted to leave did the little nervousness return.

They came back to his apartment and while Nick added some firewood to the fireplace, Sophia disappeared into the bathroom for a short moment. She tried once again to calm herself with cold water and when she came back into the living room, she just knew what she had to do. Nick was standing at the little bar next to the window, looking over his shoulder and asking what she wanted to drink, but she just wanted a water and slowly walked over to the sofa, took a couple of cushions and laid them on the soft rug in front of the fireplace along with the blanket she found. Nick looked over at her once more and noticed what she was doing and that she had taken off her stockings. He thought he knew what she was up to. His heart leapt. A few moments and steps later he was finally with her, and smiling down at her.

"I like Barry White." She explained simply with a nod to his stereo and he took the remote control and turned the music up a little louder.

He didn't know that she had compared his voice to the sound of one of those songs, but Sophia was sure it was a sign somehow and walked slowly towards him. She put her head against his shoulder, slipped her arms around his middle and was glad when he understood that she wanted to dance with him. They moved very slowly, slower than the beat of the music and yet it was exactly the rhythm they needed. One warm, large hand was on her back and the other was slowly stroking her hair off her shoulder. Nick let the silky strands glide through his fingers. The feelings inside him were dark and heavy. He felt himself sinking deeper into the feeling that the music and her closeness were causing in him. He gently stroked her cheek with his chin, knowing she liked the slight scratch of his stubble on her skin, and kissed her slowly on the cheek.

Sophia let her hands slide to his chest before she stretched her face towards him and concentrated entirely on the softness of his lips. To show him that she desired him too, she let her fingers slide slowly to the top button of his shirt. She opened it and carefully slipped her fingers inside, stroking all the way to his neck and placing her fingers on the hollow beneath. When she felt his Adam's apple bob, she released her lips from his and let them trail down over his chin and throat.

Nick tilted his head back and moaned slightly as she kissed his neck so terribly soft. Then she laid a burning path down to his chest, which she had freed from his shirt. His heart was beating fast, she could feel it as she pressed a kiss to the smooth skin of his chest. Her fingers tickled him as she stripped his shirt completely off and when their eyes met, she smiled happily at him.

Nick leaned down and kissed her tenderly, slipping his arms around her and deepening the kiss. His lips travelled down her cheek to her neck, slowly and intimately kissing the skin he could reach until she slowly turned and brushed her hair aside. The sound of the zipper as he unzipped it inch by inch gave Sophia goosebumps, and his long fingers gripped her shoulders as he kissed her neck and shoved the dress off her shoulders. He saw that her underwear was the same dark green as her dress and her eyes, crocheted soft lace, and he couldn't help it, he had to feel it! Cruelly slow, he ran his index finger down her spine, watching in fascination as her muscles danced under his touch, her breathing quickened. Only when he reached the fabric of her panties did he close his eyes. Terribly gentle, he ran his fingers forward over the hem of the fabric and then placed his hands on her belly. She was shaking. Nick pressed against her and caressed her shoulders with his lips while one hand remained on her stomach and the other slowly stroked upwards.   But before he reached what longed for his touch, he walked around her and took her face in both hands. Sophia's eyes were closed and her cheeks had a golden glow from the flickering fire in the fireplace. He kissed her, her lips seeming to melt into his. With her fingernails she gently scraped across his chest, over the mounds of his muscles and his ribs. She slid both arms around him and placed her hands on his shoulder blades like two hot burning logs. Nick wrapped one arm around her while the other hand lingered on her face. The kiss didn't speed up, but he deepened it, the slow rhythm he set was very similar to the tone of their hearts. At some point he broke away from her lips, kissed her neck, the valley between her bosoms and when he knelt down, he kissed her belly and hips. He stroked his fingers over her flawless skin and pulled her to her knees.

Sophia stroked his face with astonishment in her eyes and locked her eyes with his. She couldn't really comprehend what was happening, after a year of longing and secretly loving him. They were finally here, at this very moment. Lightly she stroked over his shoulders, down his arms to his hands. Taking one in hers, she brought it to her mouth and kissed the palm. The piercing sensation of desire flooded through her as he groaned and pulled her closer. His hand wandered to the clasp of her bra and undid it, and Sophia breathed heavily as she let go of his hand and allowed herself to be freed from the delicate piece of fabric. His eyes were dark and literally glowing in the golden light of the fire as he simply looked at her for quite a while, caressing her with his gaze. Then finally he reached out and embraced her with one arm as he slowly lowered himself backwards, pulling her on top of him.

The turmoil inside her was a combination of swirling whirlpool and a feeling of complete release, of relaxation. Sophia gently nestled against his lips and leaned on one arm so he could touch her where she wanted it the most. Her body ached with desire and as soon as he touched her soft curves with his hands, she moaned and pressed herself harder against him. Again one of her hands wandered over his beautiful body, stroking so terrible slowly over the line of dark hair that disappeared into his jeans that she only wished he would understand to finally take them off and bravely she undid the top button. She could feel him, but he wasn't close enough and she moved restlessly on top of him until he gripped her tighter and rolled her onto her back.

The feeling of being trapped between the soft blanket and pillows at her back and his firm, strong body was so overwhelming that Sophia couldn't help but linger a moment and look at him. He was so handsome. There was that crease between his eyebrows and she stroked it with light fingers. Nick kissed her palm and she gasped, the feeling of this intimate act jerking through her. He rose from her and slipped off his jeans as he continued to kiss her hand, her wrist, the tender skin of her arm. The tingling sensation kept Sophia from noticing anything around her. She only felt the warmth and him. Him. Nick. Nick!

Lovingly he caressed her, kissed her so gentle and then grabbed her firmer and seduced her tongue in a wild dance that made her all dizzy even before he peeled the last piece of clothing off her body. And it didn't stop as he let his hands and lips roam over her body, finding every curve and dimple and telling her with everything he could give her how much he desired and loved her. Although he didn't say it with words, Sophia understood and gave him her answer.

Nick paused for a moment to gaze into her face. How was this possible? He almost couldn't believe that it was finally happening. That he was about to fulfil his dream and love her with all his senses. The fiery heat of the fireplace settled on his back and her warmth embraced him. Her hands caressed him and her gaze told him how deep her feelings were. Sophia had never been so beautiful as she was at that moment. Her eyes were large and dark, and the sparkle of fire glittered in them. The blush of her cheeks flowed down her neck and between her soft hills, which he was allowed to touch. The entrancing sigh of her desire echoed in his ears as he finally gave in to the fierce suction of the invisible bond between them.

In an intoxicated state of surrender and love, Nick lost himself completely in her. *I love you, I love you!* It burned in his body, in his soul, and he had to tell her.

Tell her! Tell her!

Now.

His heart exploded and love squeezed the words out with a sigh. "Sophia, oh Sophia!"

CHAPTER 16

Her skin had the scent of fire and love. That was all he was aware of.

Nick was too stunned by the rush of emotions raging in his mind and body. His heart was pounding deep and strong in his chest, and it mingled with the sound of her voice under his ear. Her breathing was a little slower now, but her fingers were still firmly buried in his hair, as if to make sure the moment was not a dream. They had been looking into each other's eyes the whole time, even if it was hard at a certain point to hold the gaze. But it had to be. It was like a higher power forcing them to do it. Only when their lips met again, after whispering their names countless times, were they able to close their eyes again and it was as if they were both released from a spell.

It was not a dream they had experienced. It had really happened and they both couldn't believe they had waited so long. It seemed so simple. As if they had always been destined to end up right here. At this very moment. The feeling was almost too much, and Nick pressed his forehead against hers one last time before he let himself sink down onto her, exhausted, and rested his head on her chest. He had to let this feeling sink in, it was so disturbing and wonderful at the same time. He could never have imagined that he would ever have deep feelings for someone again, and it had been a very long lesson to learn that it was possible after all.

But now? Now he felt as if he were experiencing all these feelings for the first time. As if everything he had ever felt, everything that had been before, everything that had happened before Sophia, was a faded lie. An idea. Just a copy of the original. What was going on inside him scared him. It was so intense that he didn't know if he could tell her, if he could even put it into words, or if he should run away.

When Sophia had told him the day before that she was scared of the depth of her feelings, he had thought he knew what she was talking about. But he had been blind and deaf, for only now did he understand the full meaning of her words, which, stupid as he was, he had also declared to be his truth. But the truth overwhelmed him now. Now that he lay completely helpless in her arms. Firmly embraced by her warmth. There was no turning back. Never again.

And it was ... all right.

Nick knew deep inside he was ready for this. He never wanted be anywhere else ever again. Only with her. Surrounded by her light. He wanted to drown in her. All thoughts of the three famous words that had been on the tip of his tongue for days vanished into thin air. The words were just words. But now, now he felt them with every cell in his body.

Nick suddenly became aware of more things. His fingers felt her soft goosebumps. Her trembling had slowed and was now shaking her in longer rhythms. He felt her leg leaning against his side. It was cool against his heated skin. Reluctantly, he disengaged his fingers from hers, which had entwined in the force of their love, and reached for the blanket they were lying on, which was fortunately large enough to cover them both with it.

Sophia let go of his hair and reached for the end of the blanket on his back and wrapped it around him as well. Her other hand found its way to his face and gently stroked his stubble along his chin. Slowly he lifted his head and sought her gaze. Her eyes gleamed as if she had been crying and he stroked her flushed face, worried that perhaps he had been too wild in his rush of emotion and had hurt her.

212

"Sophia," he croaked, his voice hoarse from saying her name so many times, "did I hurt you?"

She shook her head and her smile caused this strange feeling, this tugging in his heart as if it would stop for a moment and then beat on twice as fast. Sophia pulled him close until his face was next to hers and then she wrapped both arms around his neck.

Nick could not relax. A thousand questions swirled in his head, what was going on, what was going on inside her? His throat was tight, so he could only ask her more quietly: "What's wrong?"

Instead of answering, she tightened her grip around his neck and he felt her breathing quicken again.

"Are you hurt or ..." He lifted his head once more, seeking her gaze with concern, and finally she ended his worry.

"I'm just happy."

Oh. Yes! He felt it too! Happiness!

Nick's smile was beautiful. The twinkle in his eyes showed Sophia that he was as overwhelmed as she was. They smiled at each other, then chuckled a bit silly like little children, burying their faces in each other's necks as they rolled around wrapped in the blanket, until finally they lay laughing next to each other, gazing into the dawn outside the big window.

"It's snowing!" Sophia got up and went to the window. Although he wasn't cold, he would have preferred if she had left the blanket with him. Nick got up too, went after her and pulled her into his arms as they both watched the snowflakes play.

"I'm afraid there won't be enough for a snowball fight." He murmured into the skin under her ear.

"Why do you want to throw snow at me?"

"You took my blanket."

"Like you need it." Sophia giggled light-heartedly and leaned even tighter against him.

"You think I don't need it because I'm so hot?" He teased, kissing the back of her neck.

"Also," she laughed, turning to hug him with the blanket, "and so cuddly."

"Cuddly? I'm not cuddly!"

He constricted his eyes to narrow slits and gave her a firm kiss that made her stumble back until her bare shoulders pressed against the glass of the window and she hissed, startled by the cold.

"Will you take it back?" He asked as he kissed her neck and she drew a shaky breath.

"No ... No." She stammered and pulled him closer.

"Then I guess I'll have to show you."

His voice was a rough whisper with which he warned her and Sophia's little giggle turned into a sigh when he put her leg around his hips. Their eyes met. The blanket pulled tighter around them both as he lifted her up and she wrapped her other leg around him. Her breathing quickened. The thought of what he might do now made her slightly uncomfortable and she glanced over her shoulder. She was glad it wasn't the car park below her, but the rough sea. But Nick was already on the move. He walked slowly towards the bedroom, where she let the blanket slide off her shoulders before he threw her onto the bed.

It was snowing a little harder when, after several attempts, they finally managed to leave his apartment and go down to the town. Sophia took a few photos of his childhood home above the cliffs, which still looked imposing in the bright daylight, but no longer so dominant. As if it were the most natural thing in the world, she put her arm around his middle and he had his hand on her shoulder, pulling her close enough that they could have shared a coat. On the way down the hill Sophia knelt on the frozen ground from time to time and took a few photos towards the sea through seaweed that was sprinkled with a few snow crystals. Enraptured, she stopped and looked at the pastel colours of the landscape.

"It's so beautiful here, I'm madly in love!" she exclaimed, taking a few more steps to take another photo.

Nick watched her smiling and his heart lifted with each delighted exclamation, for he was sure it was her way of confessing her feelings to him. He had completely succumbed to her and her enchanting smile that she kept throwing at him over her shoulder. He also took a few photos, but not of the landscape, for he wanted to capture these moments as well as possible, knowing how quickly everything could suddenly be over. But he didn't want to allow any heavy thoughts, just the happy lightness of the here and now.

More than once Sophia turned to face him with the camera in front of her face, but before she could take another photo of him, he playfully took the camera away from her and held it above his head. Sophia tried to get it back from him, but gave up after three attempts. Nick looked at her with a nasty grin, but she simply stepped closer, looked deep into his eyes and leaned in to kiss him. The kiss, which was gentle and tender at first, immediately became wilder and Nick wrapped both arms around her and pulled her closer. Her plan had worked, she could have easily taken the camera away from him at this point, but she had long forgotten about it when their lips touched. Yes, that was how it was with him. He rested his forehead against hers to steady himself and not immediately drag her all the way back home. He wanted to show her more than just his two rooms.

After they had a cup of tea in a small tea shop, they walked on and Sophia was thrilled by the beautiful view from the promenade down to the sea. She took a few more photos and then sat down on one of the benches on the small terrace there and waved him over. But Nick stopped a few steps away and got a strange look on his face.

"What's wrong?"

Nick looked at the other four empty benches on the terrace and wondered why she had chosen this one of all. He walked slowly towards her until she grabbed his hand and pulled him to her on the bench. She looked at him questioningly and shaking his head, he pointed to a plaque on the back of the bench.

"I have loved none but you."

Sophia carefully stroked the engraved letters and of course remembered the book they came from. She got goosebumps and a very strange feeling. The feeling of a truth that lay in those words.

"For Eileen, who used to sit here looking out at the ocean." She read aloud the text that was written underneath and looked at Nick, who had tears glistening in his eyes.

"My father gave this bench to my mother as a wedding present, it was her favourite place."

Sophia waited for more and only touched him empathetically on the arm. Again she had unconsciously done something that reminded him of his parents.

"She waited forever for the engraving, but he didn't do it until after she died."

Tears stung her eyes, it hurt her to see him so vulnerable, though it also made her incredibly happy that he trusted her so much to show her that side of him. Nick turned away and seemed lost in his thoughts. She saw him clench his jaw and look at a distant point on the horizon.

"It's from *Persuasion*." He explained quietly.

"Jane Austen, I know." Briefly he looked at her.

"Of course, you know."

He remembered seeing the book on her shelf.

"One of my favourite books."

She interlaced her fingers with his and pressed her face against his shoulders. Nick looked at her and seemed to be searching for something in her eyes. She didn't know if he had found it, but he leaned closer and kissed her lovingly. And of course it wasn't just a little kiss. She put her hand around his neck and he flinched as her cool fingers touched his warm skin under his collar. He pressed her

216

closer and deepened the kiss until they were both gasping for breath.

"We, um ... should probably keep walking," he suggested, a little embarrassed, and laughing, they stood up and walked down the path to the beach.

Cautiously, she asked him about his parents, and he was so grateful that she was interested without pushing him, and he tried to keep the mood light and not tell her the darkest stories, but told her funny childhood memories, from summer holidays and Christmas. And although he hadn't planned it at first, he also told her about the death of his parents, which happened shortly one after the other. Not much and not every single moment, but enough that he felt a little lighter when she squeezed his hand a little more.

Every now and then there were these pleasant silent pauses that made him watch her and take in her every movement. To look at her beautiful face for a long moment and caress it tenderly. To give her a sweet kiss from time to time, which he immediately broke off as soon as it threatened to become more. Then he tried to distract her and pointed to a shell or a wave pattern that the receding sea had conjured up, prompting Sophia to take a few more photos. Only in very shady places had the snow remained, in all other places there was nothing to indicate that it was still snowing. Nevertheless, Sophia found many beautiful motifs and also took photos of Nick without him fighting it.

At some point it became too much for him and he playfully chased after her on the beach, grabbing her and twirling her around until she promised not to take any more photos of him. They lay laughing in each other's arms, cuddled up to each other and ran along the beach until it turned into rocky cliffs.

"Look, this is where the Christmas party is to be held." Nick pointed upstairs to a classy looking restaurant with a wide terrace and a narrow staircase that merged with the natural staircase of the cliffs halfway to the beach.

"Oh, you've picked a nice place." She bit her lip and tried to imagine it with festive lighting. "You could light the path down to the beach with torches." Sophia closed her eyes and let her imagination run wild.

"Hmm, go on ..." Nick pulled her close and began to kiss her neck, he loved her fantasy and could listen to her for hours.

"And down here, maybe you could ... something ... with fire."

"Yes, fire is good." He mumbled something else into her hair, which Sophia couldn't understand, but sighed quietly as he slipped a hand under her coat.

"Nick ... we shouldn't." But her body, snuggled against him, said just the opposite.

"Yes, we should."

He turned her to him and captured her mouth, which almost made her forget that they were at the seaside on a cool November day. Sophia suddenly felt so hot that she would have liked to tear off all her clothes and pressed herself greedily against him. Nick sensed her and was on the verge of grabbing her and dragging her into the snow-covered dunes, but instead he tore free and pushed her away from him at arm's length. The two looked at each other with a mixture of annoyance and amusement, then he took her hand and pulled her up the stairs after him.

Although the snowfall was getting heavier, they climbed the steps past the restaurant and then found themselves at a point that offered an incredible view of the countryside, and Sophia could only remark quietly: "So beautiful!"

She put a new film in the camera and photographed the fading sun from every angle.

Until Nick couldn't stand it any longer and turned her around to face him with a wink in his eye.

"If you'd rather keep taking pictures, fine, but I'm going back to my warm apartment. Where the fireplace and a cosy blanket are waiting for me."

His gaze darkened so much that Sophia had to swallow and could only nod in silence. Then he grinned at her, turned and trudged further up the hill. Sophia let her gaze wander over the cliffs once more and saw a small pile of snow in front of her as she watched after him. Suddenly, she had a good idea. A little revenge for the fact that he had thrown her on the bed earlier and, instead of doing what she had been prepared to do, had just tickled her nastily. He had said something about a snowball fight, although she knew perfectly well that the snow was still too soft for that, she took a handful and ran after him.

Nick gasped as the cold snow slid into his collar. He turned and saw the glint in her eyes for a moment before she took off running. She dashed past him and he chased after her. Of course, he caught up with her, grabbed her and turned her around to look at him. Sure, he knew why she had done it, and he loved that little joke, but he also knew he didn't want to play any more games.   When his lips fell on hers, they both knew what was going on. He wanted her and she wanted him, and they couldn't run back to the hotel fast enough. They stumbled laughing into the waiting lift, and as Nick wrapped both arms around her shoulders to pull her close, Sophia couldn't help but tease him a little one last time, sliding her cold hands under his coat and pullover. He growled and the sound still vibrated through her body when he had already unlocked the door to his flat and pushed her inside.

They tugged at their clothes, clung to the other and literally devoured each other. Until Nick lifted her up and pressed her against the wall. Her restless hands caressed his body and now and then he still flinched under the touch of her cold fingers. Sophia giggled and pressed herself against him while he kissed her neck and tore her shirt off. She only stopped laughing when he took off her bra too and touched her so tenderly that her whole body was covered in heavy goosebumps and at the same time set on fire.

Nick gripped her tighter so that she wouldn't slip out of his arms and made his way to the bedroom, but she tugged at his hair and whispered in his ear what she would like better.

It was not the first time she had said what she wanted, but it was more or less the first time that the man she was with listened and then did exactly what she wished.

The gentle pressure of his fingers travelling from her hand up her arm left a pleasant line of warmth and the idea of goosebumps. Only at her shoulder did his fingers soften and then travel lightly like the touch of a feather down her back. Again and again he paused, painting enjoyable little patterns on her heated skin, which still seemed to glow in the dim light of the fireplace. But perhaps it was him.

Sophia slowly opened her eyes and looked at the curve of his shoulder. Immediately she touched it tenderly with her finger. She heard the pumping of his heart quicken as she moved lightly on top of him. Her lips pressed as if of their own accord on the spot where her ear had been a moment ago. She just couldn't stop kissing and caressing his beautiful body with both hands, and she slid up a little to kiss the smooth skin at the curve of his shoulder. As her lips made their slow journey to his neck, his grip on her back tightened and his gentle fingers lingered at her waist. They both enjoyed each other's warmth, the loving caress, and even though Sophia sensed that he was already ready for more, he didn't push her, but let himself settle completely into the rhythm of her touch.

The soft crackling of the almost burned down fire filled her thoughts. The flames had diminished, but the fire was not yet extinguished. It glowed softly and seemed to flare up again with every single touch. Nick's hands caressed her back and traced lines down her sides. Until finally she had worked her way to his mouth and kissed him so soft, he almost thought he had imagined it. He opened his eyes and when they met hers, a light burned in them that continued to glow in his heart. Once more they kissed so gentle and his hand slowly slid up from her waist.

Sophia turned to meet his fingers and her breathing sped up when he touched her again for the first time after her short nap. His thumb stroked the delicate skin so tenderly that her breath trembled. Her gaze locked with his as he continued to caress her, she could not move. No one said a word, their breathes the only sounds. Even when he pulled her closer and their lips touched only lightly, her gaze remained locked on his. The moment their tongues gently touched, they both inhaled and Sophia held onto his face with both hands.

Nick let his hand rest on her back as he slid the other between them, moaning a little as he reached his destination. Sophia deepened the kiss as she sank heavier on top of him, and they both closed their eyes briefly from the ferocity of their feelings sloshing around inside them. Nick pulled the blanket up to her shoulders and cradled her face until their eyes met again. They never lost their gaze as they, wrapped in warmth, made love in front of the fireplace one more time.

Chapter 17

Even though they tried to delay the goodbye and savour every moment of their closeness until then, the parting came so painfully that Sophia almost cried. It hurt. It hurt to let him go, and that tugging inside her, in her heart, ached. It was complete nonsense. They would see each other again, after all; it was only goodbye for a few hours. Still, it felt deeper. Perhaps because they were aware that they had spent this weekend in a bubble. Far away from real life. Maybe it was the everyday life that awaited them, with all its little and bigger problems, or maybe it was the knowledge that soon they would no longer be able to keep it a secret and the intolerability of having to continue to pretend that they meant nothing to each other.

Nick stood at the door, shaking his head at how much he missed her already, even though he hadn't even taken a step out of her apartment. When she looked up at him with that look in her eyes that said everything her mouth couldn't, he just couldn't resist. He grabbed her face, kissed her hard and pushed her back into her flat. With his foot he pushed the door shut and tugged at her and she at him without his lips leaving hers. Once he heard her whisper his name, but she didn't really seem to want him to stop. It wasn't until they both felt each other's warm skin under their fingers that they took time to breathe and relaxed as they pressed their foreheads against each other. They both wanted to stay together, and although their longing for each other's closeness was so strong, they also did not want to prevent the beauty of their feelings from growing by giving in to their passion repeatedly or too quickly.

Sometimes it was necessary to be reasonable. For a moment realism took over. Sophia knew he had to go, he had conversations with his siblings that seemed important, because his brother Jörn had written to him several times and even Ruben had called twice. It was also a good training to get a grip on their longing. After all, they would continue to work side by side without anyone knowing what was really going on between them, at least until Nick had discussed it with his siblings.

On the other hand, they both knew that the week would be filled with work and a few meetings in the evening and that they would probably hardly see each other. This back and forth of feelings almost felt like the time when she had only dreamed of being with him. That unreal longing for something that would never be. But she shook off that dark thought as quickly as it came and leaned against him. Pressed herself even closer and then let her lips melt into his once more before they both broke away from each other, their eyes heavy.

"I really need to go over there, there are things we need to sort out."

She nodded her understanding and squeezed his hands.

"I'm not sure if I can come over later."

"Please, don't stress," she looked at him and smiled, "of course I want you to come back, but if you can't ..."

"I'd love to explain everything in detail, but it's .... it's just ..." he grimaced as if in pain and she stroked his thickening three-day beard lovingly.

"When you're ready."

Nick stroked his thumb over the dimple on her chin, the words heavy on his tongue once more at that moment, to collect himself he looked at her lips. Sophia opened them slightly under the touch of his thumb, and when she kissed it, he grabbed her chin and kissed her with such fierce desire that he thought he would never be able to leave her, and certainly not at that moment. But as so often, she was the sensible one and shoved him away, breathing heavily.

"Go and solve the problem."

"I don't know if I can do that." He groaned, meaning not only the things he had to sort out with his siblings, but also leaving Sophia.

"I think you can handle it."

He nodded confidently then, kissed her forehead and stroked her face tenderly once more before turning and leaving her apartment wordlessly.

Sophia was so full of emotion that she felt like she had to burst so she could keep breathing. She was so happy and kept giggling, throwing herself on her bed and closing her eyes to think of the things she had experienced that weekend. Not only did she think Pielsand was a beautiful place, that she shared her favourite book with Nick's mum and that Nick was still very affected by the death of his parents. But also that Nick was an incredibly thoughtful man. With a tenderness she would never have thought possible. She was not only thinking of the physical tenderness, but of his tender, vulnerable nature. Which he had hidden behind his expressionless face and his sometimes arrogant or rude behaviour towards her.

That he allowed her to see this side of him had such great meaning, it was simply more than she could put into words. When her thoughts wandered to him as he really was, his playful humour, his cheerfulness and hearty laughter, her heart rumbled loudly in her chest. And all the feelings he had triggered in her body! He had found the most sensitive parts that she had not even known existed.

Sophia had never liked that part in a relationship so much, but with Nick she had engaged all her senses. With his reaction to every touch or kiss, he had encouraged her to dare, and it had been so wonderful. So wonderful that it ached in her whole body.

Not of pain, but of longing for him. With every fibre. The scent of his skin on hers. The touch of his fingers and the gentle scratching of his beard. His lips from which her name fell as if it were a declaration of love. A poem. The poetry of the love he gave her with his whole body. His kisses. Oh, she had never been kissed like that before! Or she just couldn't remember.

His lips wiped away any memory of what had once been. He pushed away every other thought. There was only him now. Nick.

As expected, the evening was getting longer and longer and Nick wasn't sure if he would be able to return to Sophia after hours of talking to his siblings. There was nothing he would have liked better than to snuggle in her arms, but he was so restless that he feared he would not be able to give her what they both craved. But he just couldn't stand it at home any more. He had to get out of the house, put on his jogging clothes, grabbed his keys and started running to clear his head, even though it was almost two in the morning.

No sooner had he cleared his mind of everything that had come out of the conversation with his siblings than he was standing in front of her door. Strangely enough, it seemed as if his body had made its way to her before he had even consciously realised it. Or his heart had simply flown to her, he thought with a shake of his head at his strangely sentimental thoughts. The front door was unlocked, he immediately ran up to her apartment and rang the bell. He had left his mobile phone at home, so he hadn't been able to call and ask if she was still awake, and just when he feared she was fast asleep and he would have to go home, he heard her turn the key and unlock the door.

"Hey." She was surprised and tired, her eyes small and sleepy, but of course she opened the door for him and waited until he entered.

"I'm sorry I woke you up."

"It's okay." She smiled that smile that melted his heart and snuggled up to him. "I'm glad you're here."

"Me too." He kissed her softly and Sophia took his hand and was about to pull him into the room when he held her and said he wanted to jump in the shower first.

"Sure."

Nick briefly considered asking her to join him, but she looked so tired that he let her go.

With only a towel around his hips, he came into her room a little later and his heart pounded in his chest when he saw her lying on the bed. Sophia had made room for him, wrapped in his blanket, her hair spread out around her head like a fan. She had closed her eyes and was breathing quietly. He looked at her sleeping peacefully and the sight of her alone touched him deeply. Her face shimmered in the light of the candles, which flickered as he dropped the towel on the floor and joined her under the covers. He had no intention of seducing her, he just needed her warmth to pass over to him. No sooner had he put his arm around her than she snuggled closer and pressed her face to his bare chest without opening her eyes. Her even breath tickled him. Lovingly, he stroked her hair. Sleepily, Sophia put her hand around his middle and pressed a kiss to the spot above his heart, nestling so close that he automatically breathed in the same rhythm.

Nick had spent the last few days thinking that her smile and laugh were the most beautiful things, and kissing her and making love to her was the most wonderful thing he had ever done. But there was something so fulfilling about holding her in his arms while she slept and he pressed his face into her silky hair that he couldn't hold it back any longer and finally whispered into the still

226

of the night what he had known for so long.

"I love you."

A few hours later they woke up to the blare of her wake-up call. Nick jumped up so quickly that Sophia didn't even notice his naked body next to her and gasped loudly as he walked as God had created him, towards the bathroom. She had to admit that she was a little disappointed that he didn't let her discover this until he had almost disappeared into the bathroom. But maybe it was better that way, otherwise they would be late for work. She giggled briefly and stood up as well. Back in his jogging clothes, Nick hurriedly left the house so he could get ready at home.

They arrived at work at different times and each focused on their work all morning. They didn't even have time to give in to the nagging desire to steal at least one little kiss. Of course, that tug and urge to go over to the other remained all day. However, Nick seemed at ease as he looked forward to the evening. He had a meeting with Ruben with a photographer who was not yet under contract, but he hoped he could spend the night with Sophia. But of course that was not the reason for his almost palpable cheerfulness, rather that he had said what she had not heard, but had perhaps sensed. For she had trembled slightly and he had simply held her a little tighter.

Throughout the day he had tried to avoid looking in Sophia's direction, and was rather proud of himself for keeping it up. It wasn't until many of the colleagues had left that he looked after her as she walked up the stairs carrying the photographers' portfolios, and knew he had to follow her, and entered the conference room shortly after she did. Cause he was holding so many photographers' portfolios in his arms, she came to his rescue and took some from him. As she did so, she brushed his arm and they both froze in their movement. Sophia stood on her tiptoes and pressed a gentle kiss to

227

his mouth, but since they were both holding the large portfolios in their arms, unfortunately it didn't last very long. Smiling, she turned away from him and sorted the books by the photographers' names.

Wordlessly they worked side by side and Sophia sensed that Nick was in a good mood and she kept looking over at him. Then he casually asked if she could remember the last conversation they had had in this room.

"You're like one of those portfolios." She grinned and then continued, amused, "Big, heavy and bulky."

He chuckled and Sophia added, "Oh yeah, and empty."

"Yes." He looked to her and their eyes met across the length of the room.

"Do you still feel empty?" She asked cheerfully, but when she spotted the crease between his eyebrows, she knew this was going to be a serious conversation.

"No."

"How then?" Sophia's voice was just a hoarse whisper as she took a few steps closer, still holding the picture she was about to slide into one of the portfolios.

"New." He nodded and twisted his mouth into that smile that made her knees go weak.

Not wanting to lose control, she broke eye contact, slipped the photo into the next sheath and then reached for the next picture as he continued to speak.

"That's you." He pointed to the photograph in her hand.

"An old fisherman in front of a blue boat?" She asked with a serious expression and he laughed out loud.

"No, colourful." Again he sought her gaze, and Sophia was struck right in the heart as she saw tears glistening in his eyes. "Colourful pictures that fulfil me."

Oh.

Sophia gasped, she didn't know what to say. Her breathing and heartbeat quickened as she automatically moved towards him. Had Nick just made her a declaration of love? Astonished and stunned, she looked at him, how could a conversation of this kind turn into something so magical?

"Nick." The way she breathed his name gave him the courage to go on, and the tears in her eyes gave him the certainty that she too was filled with emotion.

"I know this isn't the right place, but I really must tell you ..."

Her smile was irresistible.

"Sophia, I..."

"Nick!" Ruben came running into the room and they both wordlessly turned to the table and pretended to be busy. "We have to go!"

Nick didn't reply, just clenched his jaw so tightly that Sophia could hear his teeth grinding.

"Next time you should lock the door or someone will discover it!" shouted Ruben, of course completely oblivious to the looks the two were giving each other as to what his words meant to them both. "Need a lift?" asked Ruben, reaching for one of the newly stocked portfolios and flicking through it.

Inwardly Sophia rolled her eyes as Nick and she had donned cotton gloves to avoid staining the shiny new sleeves with fingerprints while Ruben carelessly spread his greasy prints on each of the new pages.

"No thanks, I'm meeting a friend who lives nearby."

"Oh come on, we'll take you there!" Ruben patted his brother on the chest, "Right?"

"Yeah, sure." Nick's reply was so curt and brusque that anyone who overheard would have thought he was utterly annoyed by this extra task.

"Good, good!" Ruben ran out of the room to his office and grabbed his coat.

"Text me and I'll pick you up there." Nick murmured to Sophia as they left the room and the two looked into each other's eyes briefly before she nodded.

"It seems like you guys are really getting on better now!" said Ruben later when he was alone in the car with Nick.

"What do you mean?"

"Well, you and Sophia. Ha! What a close working relationship can do sometimes." Ruben acted as if he could take credit for that and Nick bit his lip to stifle a laugh.

Sophia didn't feel like laughing, but she plastered a fake smile on her face one more time, which none of her friends seemed to notice. They sat on Viviana's sofa with chocolate and wine, looking at the final changes to her wedding dress and the presentation Sophia had prepared and copied onto a USB stick for her. Céline had proudly announced that her family would allow Viviana to hold the wedding celebrations at their estate. Viviana had then excitedly told them that Jérôme would soon be coming home after promising not to prolong his stay abroad. That had been the cue, since then everything was about men all over again. Ina and Céline literally outdid themselves with their stories about their latest successes in getting a man. Everything was reported in great detail, the first dinner, the first kiss and of course the respective first time.

Sophia didn't want to hear all that in detail, nor did she want to tell them those details. For that, everything with Nick meant far too much to her and was far too precious, but still it pained her that her friends didn't even ask her how she was doing in terms of love. She had believed that if she avoided the subject of Nick, it would work out with them somehow again. But this lack of interest just hurt, and it almost seemed as if they were deliberately avoiding her.

Every time she uttered even a little "Yes!" to agree with the description of a particular feeling, there was no counter-question.

However, there were also no stupid and hurtful remarks about her not knowing what it was all about or that her feelings were just a *silly girly crush*. Then, when the group broke up and said goodbye to Viviana, Sophia deliberately dawdled so they wouldn't get to see Nick when he came to pick her up. She was the last to leave and was glad to see his car parked on the opposite corner of the street. Stupidly, Ina and Céline were still standing together on the sidewalk talking, and Sophia was overcome with a completely pointless feeling of guilt. Almost as if she had lied to them and to Viviana.

The two looked at her with raised eyebrows and Ina asked with a grin, "Is that car waiting for you?"

"Yes." admitted Sophia, then said goodbye to the two and was about to cross the street when she heard Céline's question. "Who's that?"

Sophia stopped, her heart hammering in her chest as if she were uncovering a rather dark secret.

"That's my boyfriend." She shrugged, as if it was no big deal.

"You didn't tell us that." Céline seemed rather annoyed and Sophia had never noticed before how ugly her friend could look when that arrogant expression appeared on her otherwise flawlessly beautiful face.

"You didn't ask." Replied Sophia with a smile, and looked at them waiting.

"What's his name and where did you pick him up?" Ina was still looking at the car in disbelief, as if it really was just too unimaginable.

"At work." Confessed Sophia, making moves to leave.

"But ..." Sophia saw Céline grasp, "but that's Nick Falkner!"

"Yes."

"Are you dating?" Céline seemed unable to believe that, and the tone in her voice, dripping with disbelief, hurt Sophia even more than the piqued expression on her face.

Why did they have to make her feel this was such a strange event? "Yes."

"But ..." Ina then began and Sophia became angry.

"Nothing but. We are together. Full stop."

"But Pia ..."

"Nothing *but Pia*." Sophia brushed her hair back and collected herself for a moment for the question that had been burning under her nails for a while. "Do you think I'm not good enough for him?"

"That's not at all what I meant." Céline returned her gaze briefly and then continued to stare at the car.

"Then what? Cause I really don't get it. Why is it that you two can have new men all the time and when I have a boyfriend you can't accept it?"

"That's not the point." Ina said, falling silent as Sophia fired off another question.

"Then what is the point?" Sophia looked from one to the other and shook her head.

"We're just worried." Ina then explained.

"About what exactly?"

"Well, it's because of *Nick Falkner*."

"You're acting like I'm way beneath him, am I that ugly and not worthy of him or what are you actually trying to tell me?"

"He's only ever dated models." Bluffed Céline at her rather nastily and then bit her lip as she only now seemed to realise what she had just implied.

"So, I'm not pretty enough?"

Céline opened her mouth to say something more, but then fell silent.

"Well then, thank you." Sophia exhaled loudly to hold back her tears.

"That's not what Céline meant," Ina explained, trying to calm their tempers.

"To be honest, I don't really care what you mean," Sophia confessed, looking them in the face and gesturing with her arm towards the car. "He has a completely different opinion on that."

"Yes, yes we believe you."

Ina screwed her face up as if she was completely surprised at the turn this conversation had taken, and somehow only made things worse with her defensive hand gesture. For whatever she was trying to say, it would not mean anything good for Sophia.

"But?" Sophia glanced at the car and saw that Nick had a questioning expression on his face, she smiled at him and indicated that she would be right there.

"But, well ... it's kind of ..."

"Unrealistic? Weird?" Sophia's sarcastic tone, made the other two take notice.

"Pia, no I mean ..."

"We fell in love, is that really so strange?"

"No, but ..."

"No!" Sophia nodded at them both and then continued speaking quietly. "We are together. End of story."

"Is it official?" asked Céline, boring her gaze into Sophia's.

"Not yet, but ..."

Céline made a throwing away hand gesture as if to say, *I told you so*, but Sophia didn't feel like talking to them anymore and shrugged.

"I love him."

Their faces dropped and Sophia smiled at them.

"You should be happy for me."

The two mumbled something unintelligible and Sophia just left them there, turned to walk to his car and froze.

In the middle of the road, not five steps away, stood Nick.

Chapter 18

The feeling that overcame Sophia at that moment was that of being caught. As if she had said or done something bad and he had caught her in the very act. That particular spot on her forehead stung painfully and a cold shiver ran through her as if she had shoved too much ice cream into her mouth at once.

How long had he stood there? What had he heard of their conversation? Had he heard the last things she had said? The expression on his face told her nothing, or rather, she was too confused to interpret it. Only his eyes bored into hers and everything else blurred.

Nick couldn't even name what he felt. It was a strange feeling that filled his insides. It was as if he were on a ship, looking over the railing into the water. Unimagined depths stretched below him, but he was ready. Ready to jump in and dive for the treasure that hid beneath the surface. The leap required strength and confidence in his abilities. The air whizzed past him and he felt free. So incredibly free. As he dived into the water, he was weightless and felt so immensely light. Maybe that was why he was suddenly standing in front of her without having felt the steps he had taken to get there.

Her eyes glistened. In the sparse light of the street lamps, he saw tears shimmering in her eyes. Had he seen fear there? She really shouldn't have any doubts after what he had said to her earlier and what magic they felt as soon as they were together. But after the strange conversation with those women, maybe she was doubting herself or their relationship. She must not. That he could not allow!

A blink later, he put his arm around her shoulders and buried a hand in her hair. His lips pressed to hers and the kiss said more than anything he could say with words. Passionate and at the same moment with that tenderness with which they always kissed, it was quite soft and yet firm.

Her fingers clawed at his sides and she sank into his embrace. He needed her even closer. Closer! He felt as if he needed to breathe her in, he needed her so much that it ached in his chest. His strong arms pulled her even tighter and they seemed to melt into one. There was nothing more. They were no longer aware of anything or anyone. Not that they were being watched by their cynical friends, who watched wordlessly as the connection became visible before their eyes. That they were standing in the middle of the road and that a car passed them with an approving honk and the driver of another one angrily sped past them. They didn't notice that it had started to drizzle and that they were cold when they separated and he pressed his forehead against hers.

Sophia wanted, no, *needed* to know if he had heard her, she almost couldn't stand it anymore and opened her mouth to ask him when he interrupted her with a breathless whisper.

"Please repeat what you said."

That look that melted her bones looked at her begging and Sophia's heart hammered in her throat and she tried to stall for time.

"You should be happy for me." It sounded like a question, and he made a sound of agreement, but then said a little more quietly.

"Before that."

Sophia swallowed and remained silent. Oh, he'd heard it and it was kind of hard to repeat it. Her breath caught as he continued.

"Cause that's exactly what I've been trying to tell you all day."

Sophia inhaled sharply.

"And said to you last night when you were sleeping in my arms."

Now she exhaled audibly and gripped his coat tighter. Just say it. Just say it!

Nick lifted his head and sought her gaze, smiling lightly, though his face had taken on a serious expression she'd only ever seen on him in a really difficult discussion with a client or Ruben. Her heart threatened to leap out of her chest, she felt slightly dizzy, which could also be because she was breathing way too fast and too shallow.

"Sophia.", he let his hands slide to her cheeks and nodded as if to encourage himself to speak. "I love you."

In a mixture of relief, joy and the urge to breathe, they hugged and Nick whispered in her ear. "For quite a while now."

She closed her eyes and pressed against him until he pulled her along. After a few steps, she felt the car at her back. He kissed her again, much more passionately than before, and if the rain hadn't been getting harder, he wouldn't have pulled open the door and pushed her inside, but so he did and ran around the car. Slipping behind the steering wheel, he pulled her hand in to his mouth to kiss it as he drove off, past the silent observers of their confessions who stared after them, stunned. But the two in the car didn't see it, they only had eyes for each other.

When they got home, the rain had become much heavier and they ran up the stairs and Sophia's hand was stiff from the cold and she couldn't open the door until Nick took the key from her. He opened the door and they pushed, pulled and shoved their way into the apartment, tore off their coats and laughing he took her face in both hands and kissed her and told her again.

"I love you."

Sophia literally tore off his pullover as he pulled back briefly, reaching into his hair as he spread kisses over her neck. With a thud, she pushed him against the wall and took off her shirt and he his. As if a switch had been flipped, she grabbed his head and kissed him almost roughly while he wrapped his arms around her and pulled her up so that she could only stand on her tiptoes. His warm big hands were firmly on her back and she knew she could rely on his strength. Sophia tugged at his jeans and sighed his name as he buried his face in the warm tender skin of her curves after ripping off her bra. They stumbled into the room, dropped onto the bed and let their feelings flow to each other in a passionate dance of their emotions.

A long time later they lay close together on the rumpled sheets. Finally, they could breathe easier and Nick stroked the no longer damp hair out of her face and kissed her forehead.

"What was that earlier?"

She looked at him with wide, questioning eyes, her head still a little foggy.

"Were you arguing with them ... about us?"

In fact, Sophia didn't want to let her mood be spoiled by the memory of her friends who were becoming strangers to her. It was as if she was betraying the wonderful moment they had just experienced and pressed herself even closer to Nick. As always, he didn't push her, but continued his gentle stroking of her hair and back.

Then she straightened up and looked at him for a long time before nodding. She lay down on his chest, which was pleasantly warm, and kissed the spot above his heart, which was still throbbing violently from their lovemaking. Sophia propped her chin on her hand and looked into his face. She knew that love was also made of courage and that she should not be ashamed of the fact that she had had feelings for him for a long time. He had confessed it to her too, even if she didn't know the exact moment yet, she believed she owed it to him to confess it.

238

"I've liked you quite a while too."

Nick grinned. "Oh yeah, how long?"

"Oh, it's not that important for now," Sophia tried to remain serious, but Nick didn't let up, running his finger over her bare shoulder.

"I think this is very important." He grinned, pulled himself up and kissed her gently.

"I can't talk if you distract me." Sophia explained to him with mock indignation in her voice but unimpressed he just continued kissing her neck.

"I can't think when *you* distract me!" whispered Nick into her skin.

"I didn't do anything." Her voice trembled as he ran his lips over her collarbones.

"You're lying naked on top of me!" pointed Nick out with a serious expression on his face, pulling the blanket aside and caressing her curves until Sophia leaned against him and kissed him softly. He wrapped both arms around her and rolled them both around.

"Are you going to tell me how long?" he asked with a cheeky grin, burying his face in the soft parts of her body.

"If you ..." she stammered, "go on like this ..."

"Hmm, yes I intend to." He emphasised his words by caressing particularly sensitive parts of her with his lips. Breathing heavily, Sophia squeezed out her not really serious threat.

"Will you never ... oh ... um ... know."

Feigning shock, he raised his head, narrowed his eyes and pretended to think.

"It seems you don't want to tell me anyway .... ", he shrugged and then continued his caress where he had left off a moment before, but after she tugged at his shoulders, he lay down beside her

239

and looked into her eyes, he just knew she was now ready to tell him.

"I told them about my feelings for you and they made fun of it."

Nick clenched his jaw. He hated it when people made fun of other people's feelings.

"Now they're acting like they care about me."

"Because I was such an ass, I guess."

"No, ... yeah that too, basically they've been telling me all along, directly or indirectly, that I'm not good enough. For you."

Sophia released her gaze from his eyes. Nick lifted her chin so that she had to look back at him and shook his head. "Sophia." he said her name in that particular tone. "You don't believe that!"

He was honestly angry and couldn't believe she really thought that! What an ass he must have been to make her doubt herself. His grip on her arm tightened. Silently she looked at him, and the puckering of her mouth gave him the answer.

"Don't doubt yourself. Really, you're ..."

"Good enough for you?" She grinned mischievously.

Nick shook his head. "So much more than anyone else."

He stroked her face. "Strange how we had the same doubts, except I told myself that and didn't need friends to do it."

"Nick," Sophia gave him a kiss, "don't doubt yourself." She smiled, took a deep breath and then finally told him, "I love you."

And those were the last words she said for the rest of the night, except for sighing his name every now and then.

The next morning they got up a little earlier to have breakfast together. Nick smiled at her before mentioning what he planned to do that day.

240

"I'm talking to my siblings today."

"But you don't have to, just because my girls know doesn't mean you have to tell them ..."

"Yes, I do." He grinned, "But not because of them, it's cos I want everyone to know."

Sophia was still searching for words when he continued.

"If that's all right with you."

Sophia nodded and smiled at him.

"I've wanted to do it for a long time, but we've had some problems." He clenched his jaw and continued to explain. "You know, the rumours about New York are true."

Sophia looked at him and quietly asked him to continue.

"Ruben thinks we would have more success in the US market if we had an office there and not just a few American photographers in the portfolio." He took a sip of coffee and told her more. "We argued about the cost, it's not cheap and you know Ruben." He paused artificially and grimaced, "Nothing but the best for Ruben Falkner." Nick rolled his eyes. "The plan was for me to take over the office there." He took a deep breath and Sophia looked at him anxiously. "But since end of October I have decided against it."

Sophia's heart warmed, had he changed those plans because of her? Nick smiled. He could tell by the look on her face that she was thinking about what that meant, but before she could say anything he took her hand.

"That's why I had a little too much wine on Halloween before I came down your street with the kids."

"Oh, good," she gasped in relief, "I was afraid it was my fault."

"No." He said mischievously, though he nodded, "Well, in a way it was. I must say I was very confused. I wanted to leave, because I didn't think it would work," he made a hand gesture that applied to them both. "But on the other hand, I didn't want to be chased away either."

"Chased away by me." Sophia bit her lip, the guilty conscience literally screaming from her face. Nick stroked with his thumb over the lip she was maltreating and sought her gaze before continuing with a tone lower.

"And look where we are now."

The tension at work was easier to bear that Tuesday. Strangely, they could even talk about several jobs without feeling the urgent need to fall into each other's arms. Maybe it was the fact that they now knew what the other was feeling. Or maybe it was in the sense that they were sure they would have a lot to do with each other all day and that they would have to finish the photo portfolios side by side in the evening. At least a large part of them, because Yvonne wanted to have them ready by Thursday morning so that she could then go to Pielsand with Jörn to put the finishing touches to the celebration.

Sophia and Nick had not yet discussed how it would go in Pielsand, as they wanted to wait for Nick's talk with his siblings, but of course they would not celebrate their love in front of the entire staff. Still, Sophia hoped it wouldn't be too weird. She also had to admit that she was afraid of what some people, especially the defamers, would say about it. Maybe they should keep it a secret from their colleagues a little longer.

Since Ruben was out of the house most of the day, Nick told her that it might not be possible to talk to him until the next day. At some point, however, he had holed up with Yvonne and Jörn in their office and came out of the conversation with a broad grin and bright eyes. As he passed Sophia's office, he winked at her before disappearing into his. In the coffee kitchen, Jörn had also winked at her, it seemed rather conspiratorial, but he hadn't said anything or implied anything because gossip Annie was also in the room.

Sophia didn't have time to look at her phone and check some messages and calls until around six in the evening. The first call was from her mother who wanted to go over the details of her visit. Another was from her sister Sara who wanted to talk to her about Christmas presents for the family. Then Sophia opened the messages. The first was from Ina, who apologised for her behaviour in a rather long *WhatsApp* message.

I hope I didn't hurt you too much. I'm really sorry. You know I had some bad experiences with my boss myself and that's why I said stupid things ... I got carried away and I was mean. To be honest, I was jealous that you, as inexperienced as you are (please don't be mad!), still believed it might work out with him. I am happy for you. XX

Sophia was so surprised by Ina's confession that she did not know what to think or how to react. Of course, she was pleased that she had written to her, but a certain doubt remained. Not whether Ina had really meant it, she thought she did, but if she would ever tell her or the others about her relationship with Nick. Somehow it was a rather strange explanation. To be jealous, because one believed in oneself or in love? Even though Sophia had doubted herself from time to time and especially that he could ever feel the same. But the next message was even stranger. Céline wrote her a much shorter one and even though it was somehow apologetic, it drove a dull feeling through Sophia's body.

I saw you yesterday and it looked really serious. I have no beef with him, but that it's a secret. Hugs

What was she trying to tell her? Was Céline not concerned for Sophia and her feelings, but the secret? If so, she wouldn't have made fun of the *clichéd girl crush* when she found out about it, right? She had been mean, just like the other two, before she even knew they were together. And if the secret was fine with Sophia, surely it should be fine with Céline too. Sophia couldn't figure out this strange message and somehow, she didn't want to. Was Céline just being mean for not having a real relationship with Anton? Wasn't he with Monique anyway? Was Céline perhaps angry that a relationship with the boss was more accepted by society than a relationship between step-siblings?

Sophia didn't feel like thinking about it any further and put the phone away. She tried to ignore the whole thing. She was so far done with her work, however, and since she had nothing else to do at the moment, she slipped into the conference room and, after locking the door, began to fill the portfolios with the photographers' pictures.

At some point there was a knock and she let Nick in, who turned around to make sure they hadn't been seen, and then closed the door behind him. The two stared at each other for a long moment. After all, they had agreed not to do anything during work that might give away their secret, even if his siblings accepted it, they sure wouldn't approve of them making out during work. Still, a closed door (a *locked* door) and the spontaneous privacy, was quite tempting.

"Just one.", she said seriously and the last thing she saw was Nick's grin before he grabbed her face and kissed her so slow and tender that she was completely dizzy afterwards.

Sophia couldn't catch her breath for what felt like ten minutes. After that they looked at each other with much more desire in their eyes, until he cleared his throat, turned around and did his work. Sophia envied that he could do that, but she had to sit down on one of the chairs for a moment to collect herself.

"We can do the rest tomorrow before we go to the party," Nick said in a casual tone, and immediately Sophia jumped up and nodded vigorously.

"Yes please, let's go."

Later, as they were talking about the strange messages from her friends during dinner, which this time they ate with their legs knotted at her coffee table, and he was talking about the successful conversation with Yvonne and Jörn, who were happy for them both, a message came from Viviana. Nick saw Sophia's features distort.

"What's wrong?"

"Oh, nothing." Sophia waved it off and, knowing he wouldn't press her to tell him though, she switched off her phone so as not to think about what Viviana's message meant. Still, she couldn't relax completely for the rest of the evening, even though Nick did his best to distract her from everything.

Finally, they lay down in bed arm in arm. Nick's chest nestled comfortingly warm against her back, as if it was made for just that. He had slid his arm under her neck and she stroked the smooth skin of his forearm until she heard him breathing in a steady rhythm. His other arm was wrapped around her body and their fingers were loosely intertwined. It was a great feeling to be in his arms. Sophia felt safe. Still, the news from Viviana had been somehow unsettling and had given her a strange sense of ominous foreboding. Even if it turned out to be harmless, the result of jealousy or some kind of envy, Sophia had already let it into her head and reacted to it. She hadn't shown Nick the message or asked him what Viviana's words might mean. She had kept it to herself. Sophia felt like she had betrayed him by hiding the message and not giving him a chance to explain. If there was anything to explain at all. But the words and her behaviour now somehow stood between them.

Even on the following day, Sophia could think of nothing else.

I wouldn't believe a word he says.

Why did Viviana write something like that? What did it mean? Did it mean that Viviana couldn't believe he was serious, that he wanted to tell his family or even ... that he didn't love her? Why did Viviana think that? What did she know about him that Sophia didn't? Sophia remembered a conversation about a year ago when she had started her job at the company and talked about the Falkners. Apart from Céline, who knew a little about the family connections through Anton but had never mentioned Nick in particular, none of them seemed to know them or Nick in particular. Since Nick was often away from the office for weeks at a time back then, Sophia had hardly mentioned him. Of course, she had told them about work, and of course especially about Ruben for often behaving so strangely, but that this had caused special reactions or that one of her friends knew Nick personally had never been mentioned. Just the usual gossip that he was dating an upcoming model. She couldn't accept Viviana believing any nonsense either. Nick himself had told her that he hadn't behaved particularly well for a while, but that was perfectly fine if he wasn't in a serious relationship. Sophia hated to doubt, but somehow, she couldn't help it, nor did she want to accept that Viviana wanted to spoil her happiness. Maybe she should call her and ask, but she wouldn't do that until she had spoken to Nick. He was more important to her than anyone else, especially after the behaviour of her so-called friends.

So she somehow dragged on through the day. On the one hand she was glad that Nick was on a shooting, but on the other hand she also hoped that he would come back early and she could tell him about the message. She felt ashamed that she had allowed herself to think badly of him. In any case, she didn't want to call Viviana and ask her, as it would be like admitting that she believed her at least a little bit.

Since she didn't want to run into anyone, especially not the Falkners, she stayed in her office. Sophia suspected that they would immediately see what was wrong with her, that she was stupid and easily influenced, which Sophia usually was not. But the whole drama with her friends was more serious than she had thought. To take her mind off the subject altogether, she went upstairs after her work was done, locked the conference room and worked her way through the last few portfolios.

After more than an hour, she had finished stocking them all and was glad that she had managed to get everything done while clearing her head. With a glance at the time, she knew she still had enough time to get ready for the Christmas party of Kristina Schneider's photo magazine "Klick", to which they had been invited. Nick had already announced that he would be a little late, but it was clear that they would definitely attend the party together. The thought made her heart leap.

Sophia tried to think in a positive way and not let anything distract her from enjoying the evening and Nick. She left the room, locked up and walked past Ruben's glass cube, stopping for a moment frozen with worry. The glass walls of his office seemed to vibrate under Ruben's choleric shouting. His face was red and he paced behind his desk while Nick sat slumped in a chair opposite him, his head buried in his hands. Not as if in shame or pain, but rather in disbelief or completely annoyed. Suddenly, he jumped up, banged violently on the table between him and his brother, and said something, but Sophia couldn't understand it. Then Ruben saw Sophia standing in the semi-darkness of the hallway, obviously communicating this to Nick, who immediately turned to her. His look was tense and full of anger, but he smiled at her and nodded before opening the door and asked her to wait for him in her office so they could go to Kristina's Christmas party together.

Smiling, she nodded at him, and in the corner of her eye she saw Nick turn back to his brother and remark in a firm tone of voice: "We're done here."

Chapter 19

Nick had an unusual swing in his walk, for he ran down the stairs more than he walked at a normal pace. He grabbed his jacket and then ran to Sophia, took her hand and pulled her with him to his car. As soon as they were seated, he leaned over and kissed her urgently, as if he hadn't seen her in days. Almost startled, even though she would have liked to continue, she looked around the dark car park when he broke away after what felt like an eternity, but he reassured her.

"Don't worry, there's no one there."

Then he started the car and drove off. He was relieved that he had also spoken to Ruben, but he still wondered whether he should tell her the whole conversation or whether he should rather filter it so that she wouldn't worry. Nick thought about the conversation that had led from one to the other and had only confirmed his decision.

After he had come back from the photoshoot, where he had actually only wanted to shake a few hands and then leave, but which had turned into an hour-long crisis conversation, he had immediately run into Ruben's office. Nick had gone in, even though Ruben was on the phone and didn't like being watched at work at all. Nick had not wanted to wait in the hallway and let Ruben shoo him away with an annoying wave of his hand.

Unmoved, he had sat down on the chair opposite Ruben and waited until he had finished his phone call. Yet, of course, Ruben took his time.

The whole day so far had not gone as Nick had imagined, despite waking up with Sophia in his arms had been so promising. When he thought of it, his heart lifted and a thousand little fires tingled over his skin at the memory of her gentle fingers stroking his shoulders. He had cleared his throat to remind himself that he now had to have a serious conversation with his brother, who acted as boss, in spite of the fact that the four siblings were equal business partners.

After what felt like an eternity, Ruben had finally said goodbye to his telephone partner in the slimy tone he always used with people from whom he had asked a favour or whom he had to put off for some reason.

"Why are you bursting in here like this?" Ruben had been visibly annoyed and pointed to the pile of papers in front of him to show how busy he was, even though everyone knew he spent most of his time in his office just looking for photographers to "steal" from other agents. Even if that was against the unspoken code of honour.

"I need to talk to you and I didn't want to wait any longer for you to give me a few minutes of your precious time." However, Nick's jibes rolled off Ruben mercilessly, as Ruben didn't even seem to notice the irony in them. Nick leaned back in his chair to stretch out his long legs and waited.

Nick leaned back in his chair to stretch out his long legs and waited.

"What do you want?" Ruben's face hardened, for he knew exactly what was coming now.

"Several things."

"I don't have time for that."

"Then you must take the time!" Nick had clenched his teeth to keep from saying something else that was on the tip of his tongue, but made no move to be shooed away. In his typical exaggerated way, Ruben had looked at his watch to show what an important man he was and was about to give Nick a time limit when he interrupted him.

"The less you cry about how little time you have, the shorter it will take ..."

"What's it about?" "About work and something private. And, well, something that involves both."

Ruben then leaned back in his chair as well and waited.

"I know there are some problems with the finances, in case you've forgotten the other three of us can see them too."

"But I ..."

"You don't have to talk your way out of this, Ruben, I know the bills haven't been paid yet!" Now he had leaned forward and looked Ruben firmly in the eye. "At the photoshoot this morning, I was called out on it in a not-so-gentle way. In front of the client's very eyes and ears!"

"By whom?"

"From the stylist and Pets, the make-up artist." He nodded to make it clear he knew more. "It was hard to convince them that it was probably a booking error, for what else could it be if they still haven't been paid for the jobs, they had eight months ago?"

"That's up to their agencies then," Ruben mewled innocently.

"You know Rafael only works with freelancers." Nick had snorted at Ruben's carelessness and stroked his forehead. "Listen, I've sorted everything out, the payments will go out today, but before Yvonne and I look at the rest, I want to know if there's anything else you'd rather tell us *beforehand*."

"We've already discussed all that." Of course, Nick remembered the last arguments about it, but even then, Ruben had assured him there was nothing more to confess.

"Anyway, I spoke to the other two yesterday and since the

Christmas party is on Friday, we'll give you until Monday."

"For what?" Ruben had gone pale and was breathing a little harder.

"To commission the payment orders for all outstanding invoices." Nick crossed that item off his mental to-do list and leaned back in. "The other thing is New York."

As Nick left the car park, he wanted to start telling Sophia all of that, as far as the length of the drive allowed, but when he started, she asked in a voice that dripped with uncertainty: "May I ask you something?"

"Sure."

"What would you do if someone warns you of me?"

"What?" He puffed in amusement and looked at her briefly before turning his attention back to the traffic.

"Well, I mean ... if a friend told you not to believe what I say."

Again Nick looked over at her and waited, but she was silent and then he asked his counter questions. "Who would do that? And why should I care?" He turned smoothly into another lane.

"You wouldn't care?" Sophia looked at him sceptically and saw that he was thinking about it.

"Sophia, I don't know what that means."

Was he angry? Why was he angry?

"Are you angry?"

"No, but you know I was with Ruben and I just don't have any energy left for weird questions," he squeezed her hand, "just tell me what it's about."

She pursed her lips and looked out the window.

"Tell me, I won't bite." He chuckled, and Sophia gave a short laugh too.

"That's not really true."

Was she blushing? He loved it when she blushed.

Nick's thoughts briefly drifted to the previous evening, when he had tried every trick in the book to distract her from her cloudy thoughts, which surely had something to do with that ominous message she had received but not told him. A gentle bite on the back of her neck had worked wonders and led to a long and wild kissing session, with brief interruptions by laughter. The memory of her laughter had made his whole day sweeter, even though it had been such an annoying and exhausting day.

"Do you know Viviana?" Her voice was so shaky she almost couldn't get the name out. Nick glanced at her one more time before turning left.

"Your friend?"

"Yes."

"No, what makes you think that?"

"I ... well. I got this message from her."

"What message?"

This talking around was starting to get on his nerves and he hoped Sophia would finally get to the point, he didn't like it when she seemed so insecure, as if she was still intimidated by him like she was weeks ago when they hadn't found each other yet.

"I'm not supposed to believe you."

"Excuse me?" Nick was taken aback by this impertinence from a woman he didn't know and had no idea what to make of it. "What does she mean by that?"

"I don't know, that's why I'm asking you."

"Well, I'm the wrong person to answer that for you, I don't know."

"Of course." Sophia returned a little flippantly, more for being angry with herself for bringing it up at all, as she had the uneasy feeling that Nick was quite annoyed.

"Listen, I don't know any Viviana or Ana, as you sometimes call her. I don't know what she means by that, best you ask her."

Was he angry? Oh yes, he looked angry, he was angry. Yes, definitely! Sophia could see him clenching his jaw and staring ahead.

"I'm sorry."

"For what?"

Again he looked over at her and saw her sitting there slumped over, and he assured her that everything was all right.

"I just thought ... I don't know, what I thought."

"Oh, you." He stroked her cheek briefly and then invited her to say what she was thinking.

"I was going to ask her, but then I thought, I don't want this to come between us somehow, and .... Well, I'd rather hear from you than her ... that there was once something between you two." Sophia turned and looked out into the gathering night.

"I can assure you, even if your *friends*," he emphasised the word in a sarcastic undertone, "think they know me and that I'm a really crap guy, that I know exactly who I used to have a thing with." So now he was definitely angry and Sophia made a face. This conversation with him was not going at all as she had imagined, oh, she should have just kept her mouth shut! Why had she said anything at all?

"If you want, I can name all the women I've been with after Cora, and I can also name the girls I chased at school." His voice was hard.   "

Don't be like that."

The voice in which she said these words almost hurt him, he closed his eyes and took a quick breath. "I'm sorry ... honestly!" He definitely didn't want to argue with her. "I'm just so tired of people trying to sabotage our relationship."

It also hurt him that some people thought he was a male slut just because he had a few affairs in the last few years and was occasionally photographed at events with pretty women. Sophia said nothing more, but Nick saw her trying to secretly wipe away a tear. This really wasn't how he had imagined the evening to go and he asked again.

"What else did she say?"

"Nothing."

"Then you'll have to ask her, Sophia. I don't know." And after a short pause: "By the way, I think it's nice that you wanted to ask me first instead of just believing her."

Their gazes lingered on each other and it seemed as if they were communicating silently, but nothing was said aloud.

A few minutes later, they had arrived at the magnificent townhouse from the founding period, that was the office of the photo magazine. It looked like a photo set itself, with all the lights decorating the windows. He turned off the engine and faced her and Sophia looked at him and curled her mouth into a smile, but it didn't really work. Nick wanted to kiss her so badly. He was already leaning over to her, but then a few other party guests passed by the car and he sat up again. After clearing his throat, he had a proposal to make.

"What do you say we go in, say hello, enjoy the delicious food and then leave as soon as we can?"

"To do what?" A fleeting hint of a grin appeared on her face.

"Whatever you want." his voice had taken on that deep Barry White tone so Sophia nodded in agreement.

"Talk and play Sherlock Holmes?" She hoped he would forget all the nonsense from earlier and help her to know what Viviana meant by her statement.

"I'm good at playing Sherlock Holmes." He stroked her hand lightly with his thumb.

Sophia was sure that he would come up with some excuse to check her body for fingerprints, and just the thought of it sent heat to her cheeks and stomach. Laughing, they then got out, and though this dark cloud somehow hovered over them, it seemed much smaller now than before, and perhaps it would disappear altogether in the course of the evening.

She had that sparkle in her big eyes that he loved so much as they walked towards the house. The light was almost magical and her skin glowed. Nick felt an urgent need to take her hand, but of course he did not. He looked at her for a tiny moment longer and smiled as they climbed the stairs. He was so in love with her! And nothing could change that, not even that she didn't really seem to believe him, but they would sort that out later.

Collecting himself, he shook his head and they stepped into the large entrance hall with its chessboard tiled floor. They came into the room that was normally the open-plan office, but which had been cleared of all tables and chairs for the party tonight. As they had arrived a little late, the official part was already over and the guests strolled through the impressive room to sophisticated classical music. Sophia stared more at the ceiling and the ornate decorations on the walls and did not see Nick take a glass of champagne from one of the waiters walking around and hand it to her.

"Oh, thank you."

"We should say hello to Kristina."

He slowly stroked her finger as he handed her the glass, but Sophia looked at him in alarm. It would be even more shitty if they provided fodder for gossip to those present before their colleagues found out. Or her parents. Not that they would find out in any way, but well, it was kind of a matter by principle.

On their way to meet Kristina, who caught everyone's eye in a bright green designer dress, they met photographers they knew, had once worked with or would never work with. Colleagues from other production and photo agencies and of course Kristina's co-workers.

"Hello, you two!" Kristina called from a distance and greeted them with a single kiss on the cheek, which was roughly equivalent to an accolade in the industry, at least that's how many felt.

"I hear you're opening an office in New York?"

Nick, only gave her a tiny smile and remained rather vague in his explanation. Yes, they were planning to open one there, but it wouldn't be that easy. Sophia wondered why he was holding back so much, but blamed it on their little argument, if you could call it that, and felt guilty. He seemed to have been in a good mood when he had come into her office earlier, but now he seemed a little distant. Kristina, who didn't really seem interested in the rumours anyway, told Nick what goodies were on the buffet and more or less sent him off to get something to eat, since he looked so hungry. Nick took the hint with a grin and excused himself with a quick glance at Sophia, who was determined to talk to him again later and better explain her worries about what hadn't gone so well in the car.

"So?" Asked Kristina as soon as Nick was on his way through the crowd to the buffet. "Does he know?"

Surprised by this open question, Sophia did not know how to react at first and took a big sip of her champagne.

"So yes." Kristina looked over at Nick, who was standing at the buffet talking to another photographer's agent. Sophia struggled for words, but Kristina smiled in compassion as she took Sophia's arm and pulled her along.

"With their company policy it might be difficult."

Of course Sophia knew what Kristina meant, but pretended not to and took another sip to consider an answer.

"My offer still stands.", Kristina then explained with a grin and Sophia was glad to change the subject.

Nick was also glad that Sophia was again smiling. It gave him hope that the evening had not been spoiled by that little question and answer game in the car. Though the little sexual innuendos always helped to put a smile on her face, that couldn't be the solution. He hoped they could drive home in an hour at the latest to talk in peace. He knew nothing about her friend and thought it was terribly unfair that these women were trying to manipulate Sophia and talk her out of him. What was that all about? Why were they doing this? The evening could only get better, after the exhausting conversations all day, and Ruben's impossible behaviour.

"Are you trying to tell me you're in *love*?" Ruben had said this word as if it were a disgusting disease that Nick had contracted through his own fault and would fall ill with.

"With Sophia Neuhaus?"

After this outcry, Nick was surprised that the whole office had not heard it, but he remained calm, even though it pained him that his brother had reacted in such a way. In a very calm voice, he had explained to him that it was not a little love affair, but that he had deep, serious feelings for Sophia that he had not felt for ages, or rather, never had. He reminded Ruben that he had also met Tea at work, but Ruben would not allow the comparison.

"Tea was not a permanent employee, just a temp."

"Still." Nick had insisted, trying really hard to remain calm.

"She is the love of my life and the mother of my children. I adore her. I'm going to grow old with her, and you're comparing that to *this* Sophia Neuhaus?"

Of course, Nick couldn't stay calm any longer after that comment and had argued with Ruben so much that he was just glad the table was between them, otherwise he probably would have grabbed him. He may even have pushed or punched him, but he couldn't say for sure. Ruben wouldn't stop and even demanded that one of them leave the company. Since Sophia was doing a good job, Nick - despite his reluctance - should move to New York. Although he had already ruled that out for himself in their last arguments and even had a good solution ready. But Ruben didn't want to hear about that either. Ruben only knew that Nick should set up the new office in no time and that his many contacts in New York would soon bring them success. Nick was aware that Ruben knew perfectly well that he would control him more than the gullible - and also somewhat lazy - Yvonne and Jörn during a permanent stay in Hamburg. Their responsibility was limited anyway and as much in need of harmony as the two of them were, Ruben would not have to expect much headwind from them.

A remnant from their childhood. Ruben's behaviour also reminded him of it, as if he could still treat Nick like the stupid boy he had once been. His big brother had sat there endlessly annoyed and listened to the words, but that only caused exactly what he actually wanted to avoid.

"I hate to say it, Nick, but you have to make a choice."

"I already have."

"Fine, New York it is."

It wasn't a question for Ruben and it wasn't for Nick either. He slammed down on the table so forcefully that his hand still felt a little thick.

"As you say, Sophia is good and ready for more and I think she's a good choice to replace you."

"Ruben!" Nick's good mood shattered into a thousand shards when his brother started the subject all over again, but when he went to defend his opinion, he saw Ruben's face freeze. "What's wrong?" Briefly he had feared Ruben would have a heart attack, he had witnessed one before and a cold shiver ran through him, but Ruben only said. "Sophia."

After Nick had freed himself from his memory, like from an annoying nightmare that had been haunting him all day, he let his eyes wander over the people at the party. Looking at Sophia always had a calming effect on him and he watched her smiling as she was still talking to Kristina and a photographer. To join in the conversation and be near her, he slowly strolled over to them.

"Oh interesting.", Kristina whispered to Sophia at that moment. Whether this referred to the photographer, whom they had almost convinced that he really needed an agent, or to the fact that Nick was coming towards them with a plate full of delicious-looking food, another glass of champagne and a captivating smile, Sophia couldn't tell. Her heart immediately beat a little faster as the look on his face told her he wanted to get out of here quickly. Instinctively, she licked her lips, but first she should definitely try some of the delicacies, since the champagne on an empty stomach was already getting a little to her head. Actually, she wasn't hungry. At least not for food. She looked at his lips and remembered his kiss from earlier ...

Kristina nudged her lightly and gestured discreetly towards the entrance. Sophia followed her gaze, as did almost everyone in the room, and what they saw seemed intimidating and ridiculously staged at the same time. There was an appearance. A diva straight out of an old Hollywood movie. A classic beautiful face, a lush fur coat casually draped around the shoulders, a tight dress and killer high heels. She floated into the room like a model and as if this was a Dior fashion show and not a nice little Christmas party.

"Wow!" Sophia almost gasped and was amazed at the ethereal being, as was almost everyone else in the room.

"That's Cora Bergmann." Kristina explained, waiting for

Sophia's reaction, which of course confirmed what she had suspected all along. "But she's not as perfect as she seems."

Sophia's eyes darted back to Nick, who continued to fight his way back through the crowd to her, still looking at her as if she were the most wonderful person in the room. Without saying goodbye, Sophia walked towards him. She had to warn him! How bad it would be for him to meet Cora here, after all this time! It would certainly be painful or perhaps even embarrassing for him in some way. She reached him and he wordlessly handed her the glass, which Sophia gratefully accepted and took another generous sip, thinking for a moment how to tell him.

"Are you ok?"

She nodded drinking and then hastily told him that Cora had arrived and waited for his reaction. Strangely, he smiled down at her and just shrugged unconcerned. Was this all? Sophia was a little irritated, after all, this woman had lied to him, stolen from him, cheated on him and, worst of all of course, broken him. How could he remain so calm? Sophia knew she couldn't stay in the same room if her ex-boyfriend or ex-best friend showed up.

"Aren't you kind of ... surprised?"

"No, it's an event to which other agents are invited. You can't avoid meeting people." He was still looking at her face with a smile.

"Do you see each other?" Confused, Sophia looked at him, did that mean that he had been in contact with her all along but hadn't told her? It stung deep and nasty in her heart and to avoid showing it, she took another sip of champagne.

"You make it sound like I'm secretly seeing her," he remarked dryly, trying to sound amused but it hurt him that Sophia didn't seem to trust him. "I haven't spoken a word to her since she left. Not even a hello, if that makes you feel any better."

Oh, crap! Now Sophia felt caught being the jealous little girlfriend. Actually, she had to admit that she was, after all, this woman was gorgeous and she was just ... Sophia.

Nick could tell by the look on Sophia's face that he had caught her being jealous. But who could blame her after what her ex-boyfriend had done to her? Trust is a sensitive matter and he certainly didn't want to make her feel bad, especially not after the nonsense earlier in the car. Leaning down to her, he suggested a change of the location. Apart from wanting to be alone with her, he didn't want to run into Cora or watch her eyeing Sophia and making a nasty crack. Knowing Cora, he was sure that she would be the one to start a rumour just to stop him from taking on a certain photographer under contract or acquire a client that her agency was also interested in.

Sophia wanted to say goodbye to Kristina, who was deep in conversation with someone else, but just as they reached the two, Cora approached Kristina as well.

"Hello Niklas ...."

"Kristina, we were just leaving. Thank you so much for the invitation." Nick spoke as if Cora wasn't even there and shook Kristina's hand, but unfortunately, she didn't play along as he had hoped and pulled Sophia to her side.

"But you'll stay a little longer my dear, won't you?"

Turning to Cora, Kristina confessed. "I'm desperate to free Miss Neuhaus from the clutches of the Falkners, but I haven't managed to convince her yet."

With a slight panic, Sophia realised how beautiful Cora was up close, and smiled intimidated.

"Well, some girls take longer and want to be begged, others are quicker to convince."

Her laughter was clear as a bell and yet it caused a certain nausea in Sophia's stomach. She looked up at Nick, who had a strange expression on his face. Somehow, she had expected him to clench his jaw or look angry. Also, she would have understood if he had just left, but he just stood there with a very slight smile on his face that Sophia was too tired to interpret. Slowly, a lot of questions swirled around in her head.

"Aren't there enough interns with you?" Cora then turned with her head held high to Sophia, who almost choked, but she caught herself and simply gave an honest answer.

"I'm not an intern, I'm a full-fledged employee..."

"Quit university, tss." Interrupted this creature from old Hollywood in a reproachful tone, as if it were really an absolute impertinence not to study.

"What's that?" Cora leaned closer so that Sophia threatened to suffocate in a gush of her intrusive perfume. Disdainfully, Cora eyed her, then laughed artificial and declared snidely into the round

"Freckles."

As if anyone would be interested in that. Sophia already dismissed it as nonsense, but then she heard the rest of the sentence.

"Can't you put make-up on?"

Suddenly, Sophia felt taken back to her school days. When she had been teased for her many freckles and moles, which her mother called beauty spots. The other children, however, called them *shit spots*.

"I would also endeavour for Sophia if she was *only* a *trainee*, why not?", Kristina asked with interest, completely ignoring the rest. She wanted to have a little fun parading Cora Bergmann and her arrogance.

"Ah, I just wanted to say that she looks... young." It didn't sound like any kind of compliment to Sophia's young appearance at all, more like a disapproval, as Cora gave Sophia a disdainful look before continuing bored, "Almost still like a child. You can also tell she's uncomfortable in the company of adults."

Again she giggled in that clear bell tone, as if her ramblings made any sense or were at least funny.

"You're right, Mrs Bergmann", Sophia said in a remarkable firm voice, "I look younger than I am." Then she finished her glass and added. "And I'm certainly not comfortable in this company. Bye."

She pressed the glass to Nick's stomach before pushing past him and hurrying away, almost crying. What was that? What a stupid ... bit... woman! Why had she done this? What had Sophia done to her to talk to her like that? Who gave her the right to do that, and why in God's name had Nick stood there silently and said *nothing*? Nothing at all? Did she mean so little to him that he had not even found it necessary to jump to her side?

Only when she had reached the entrance did she turn back to him. It seemed as if he wanted to hurry after her, but someone had stopped him. Not just someone. The ethereal, beautiful creature from old Hollywood. Cora. With whom he supposedly had not spoken for years. She saw that this woman had her slender fingers around his upper arm and was looking up at him, and what was even more painful was that he still had that slight smile on his face. Now he leaned down and seemed to whisper something in this horrible woman's ear. This horrible but beautiful, successful woman, this woman he had once loved. So much so that it almost destroyed him when she had dumped him. His first love!

Sophia felt sick. Really sick. She put her hand over her mouth and ran out.

Chapter 20

It was as if Nick was on an Express train where someone had forgotten to close the doors. Everything was happening so fast and so many things at once that he didn't know if it was all really happening at that moment or if he was just imagining it. That uncomfortable chill - the kind that gets into your bones when it was so unpleasantly wet and cold outside - gripped him when he noticed Cora next to him. Nick, however, completely blanked her out and said goodbye to Kristina. Inwardly, he was relieved that they could leave. But Kristina Schneider had her own plan. She didn't like Cora much, he knew that from earlier hints, but the fact that she was now using Sophia to trap Cora made him freak out inside. He clenched his fists and stared at Sophia's shoulder, trying not to push the bitch who had cost him so many years of his life out of the way and give Kristina a spiteful look. He just stood there paralysed as he heard the *toxic syringe*, as he called her in his mind, speak in that sweet purring voice as if she couldn't hurt a fly. For a minimum of seconds, he was back to everyday life with her.

The constant nagging. The belittling in this way, so that in the end *he* had always felt guilty and had crawled back like a puppy to get her to forgive him, even though sometimes he hadn't really understood what exactly it was all about. It was only clear that he was to blame for everything. He had overreacted, was paranoid and acted like a defiant little child. His reasons and resulting actions were always immature, wrong and absolutely ridiculous in her eyes.

In any case, he had to be glad that she was with him, the complete loser. Cora had constantly suggested to him that he was nothing without *her*, and the worst thing was that this subliminal manipulation had worked. For years.

Also with others, men as well as women, she had successfully used this method to make them feel insecure as soon as she had seen them as competition. Whether professionally or privately, with some of them even the smallest remark about their looks, their intelligence, their abilities were usually enough. These devaluations worked, especially when one was insecure or not quite as stable, caused by other worries.

That's why it had worked with Sophia as well.

It made his heart burst into a thousand splinters. Yet, he had remained silent. It was as if his voice had been stolen, he had so many words in his head but could get nothing out. Nothing! But Sophia needed him! *Do something*! he screamed in his head, but was trapped inside himself and could not react. Long ago he had sworn never to be a victim of Cora again, never to let her win again, and in doing so he had also sworn never to speak to her ever again.

Boris the biggest gossip in the business was also standing in their little circle. What could be the consequences if he were to say something? *Damn it, do something!* he shouted to himself. *Think, think!* What had his therapist advised him to do? *Stay calm.* Yes, but he needed to stop her hurting Sophia!

"I'm certainly not comfortable in this company. Bye."

Sophia said at that moment, and he was so proud of her that she could speak in such a strong voice and then just walk away as if she had more important things to do right now. But what now, what now? He had to go after her. What a mess! He loved her all the more for standing up to that bitch, which he never seemed to be able to do! Until now.

"Neither do I, considering that Mrs Bergmann made it her business to humiliate people and built her success on stealing data and photographers from others. I wish you all a nice evening."

Although he couldn't quite grasp all these feelings inside him, boundless anger at himself, fear for Sophia, pride and infinite warmth just thinking of her - and everything happening so quickly, he suddenly saw clearly. Felt all the details. The thick air, the murmur of the people, the lulling sounds of the music, the whispers of Kristina and Boris. His movements were as if in slow motion, as if his feet were sticking to the ground or he was wading through silt.

As Cora's fingers wrapped around his arm, he felt a tiny flash back to when he was a boy and Ruben had put a crab on his arm after feeding him all the horror scenarios of what it could do to him. Disgust and fear of the pain, coldness and a primal instinct to push the beast off his arm took hold of him. The voice of his therapist became Sophia's.

Stay calm! Don't make the scene she wants to provoke! No scene! Stay calm!

Outwardly unmoved, but with a cutting voice, the *toxic syringe* confirmed what he had already been thinking in his cotton-filled head.

"I knew I'd make you talk if I offended that sweet little thing. I saw you before ... nice girl."

"That *girl*," Nick growled between clenched teeth with such a menacing tone that Cora's eyes widened in shock. "Is more woman than you will ever be."

Before he could turn away completely, though, he got carried away and quietly hurled a blatant and really dirty insult in her ear.

Sophia immediately felt a little better as soon as she stood outside in the cutting cold air and automatically ran towards the car before disappearing into the bushes for a moment. Her heart was hammering in her head and she looked around in worry to see if anyone had been watching her. Luckily, she was alone out here and it was so dark that she had remained undetected even by the smokers on the terrace. At least she hoped so. Her stomach felt a little better now, she was downright relieved. But it was so cold. She had left her jacket and bag in the car earlier. She wished she had everything with her so she could just leave this place, but then she scolded herself for thinking that. That really would be downright immature behaviour. Like Nick's. He acted like he didn't mind seeing his ex and then he stood there like a complete idiot and said nothing. Nothing!

Even though all these reflections formed within a few moments, Sophia decided to remember her own thoughts. The ones from *before*. Otherwise she would be nothing more than a hypocrite. *It would certainly be painful or maybe even kind of embarrassing for him.* Yes, and apparently it was.

Nick had told her what had happened at the end of their relationship, but never any details about the time they had been together. He had appeared to be thrown off his feet before. Frozen. The only question now was, frozen with fond memories and awe of this beautiful woman or for the exact opposite reason. And although it pained Sophia that this ... woman had hurt him so much that he had sworn off love - at least for a long time, she fervently hoped it was the latter. Closing her eyes briefly, she made a deal with herself before stepping out of the bushes. If he didn't come after her in the next few minutes, then ...

"Sophia!"

The next moment she was already pressed against his rock-hard chest. His scent soothed her immediately, though she could also smell the tension he was in, but as soon as she put her arms around his middle, he somehow got *softer*.

"I am so sorry. Forgive me, please forgive me!"

Feelings, thoughts and so many words swirled around in Nick's head that he didn't know what he was thinking and what he actually wanted to say. He was relieved when she sank into his embrace. As he felt her crying, for his shirt got wet where her face was, he wanted so much to hit someone, or better even, give a right hook. Most of all, himself of course. It was only when she started shaking violently that he realised she was cold. Or exhausted from all the shit. Of course, both was possible, and without saying a word, he opened the car door and pushed her inside. Sophia didn't look at him as she got in and put on her jacket and scarf.

He knew that he deserved the punishment she would inflict on him. He would do everything, absolutely *everything* she wanted, to make her forgive him. The deadly thought that she now loathed him because he had done nothing to help her, and saw him as the worthless wretch he had seen himself as for years - thanks to the *toxic syringe* - was nothing compared to the evil fear that tore him apart. The possibility that Sophia might leave him. It was a pain so sharp, piercing, that he could not move. His lungs tightened violently and slowly and cruelly began to pulverise his heart. Sophia was not only the air he desperately needed, but also the engine that made his lungs gasp for her. In that moment, one thing that had been hovering over him in the distance since their first kiss, became quite clear to him. He didn't need to fool himself, he *knew* he was incapable of living without her. Sophia ... he heard himself taking a deep breath, it sounded more like a sob, and then he moved so fast he didn't realise what he was doing, and yet suddenly he sat next to her in the car. He looked at her.

"Sophia." His voice was a rough whisper and Sophia also seemed to wake up from her rigidity at that moment, gasping greedy for air as if her head had been under water for too long. Her gaze was fixed forward and as he reached for her, a begging *please!* slipped from his mouth.

"Can we go home?", she asked at the same moment in a small voice that brought tears to his eyes. Immediately he started the car and drove out of the car park so fast that for a brief second, he wondered why he hadn't knocked anyone down. *Say something! Say something, you stupid ass!*, he roared in his overflowing, booming head and hit the steering wheel hard. Sophia didn't even flinch. Was she so indifferent because she was done with him? Or did she know that he didn't mean her, but would rather punch himself? But stop! Suddenly, her words hit him like a bomb. Home. Not to *my home*, but *home*. Did that mean it was *their* home, even if it was only Sophia's home? Meant as *our* home? That would mean there was still an *us*.

A small pinch of hope crawled slowly into his crumpled heart and, soft as an air pump, blew some relief into it.

He looked at her. She was pale. In the unreal lights of the city at night that flashed over her, she could have been a ghost. But her expression also showed strength. She was thinking. The small crease between her brows revealed this. Two more times Nick tried to start a conversation, but Sophia turned to the window and leaned her forehead against the cool window.

"Do you feel sick?"

"Yes." Finally an answer.

"We'll right there." Nick didn't dare say *home*, lest she realise that it was actually just *her* home and she didn't want him there anymore.

270

While parking, she jumped out of the car so fast that he could hardly follow and had to run to keep up with her. He ran up the stairs behind her and fear almost consumed him. In his mind's eye he could see himself camped outside her locked door for the next few days, hopeless and lost forever. But the door was wide open when he got up there. Obviously, she was in the bathroom, he heard water splashing and her electric toothbrush buzzing. Cautiously he knocked on the door and asked if she needed anything, but she made it clear that she could manage everything on her own.

Yes, he knew and feared that in equal measure.

Sophia was shaking like a leaf on a stormy autumn day, but still couldn't walk any faster into the warm room. She saw Nick working in the kitchen and she smiled at the sight of him, even if it would not have shown on her expressionless face. With trembling hands, she wrapped the cosy blanket that had once been his around her shoulders. Exhausted, she then plopped down on the sofa, her eyes fixed on the edge of the table, feeling infinitely tired. Nick turned as soon as he noticed her and placed whatever edibles he could find on the table. Salty pretzels, wasabi peanuts, a few chips that had already lost their flavour, and cheese that he had cut into generous pieces. Plus a bottle of water.

Her stomach was empty and cold. She should eat something, but she no longer knew how to do it.

"Tea is almost ready." In a neutral tone, he waited to see if she would yell at him or question him in an icy tone. But there came nothing. Not a single word and not a single movement, except that she trembled slightly and was occasionally seized by a larger shake.

"Sophia..." Nothing. "Do you want me to shut up?"

"Like before?"

Bang! Yes, he deserved that. Even if her voice hurt more. Not because it was sharp or piercing, cutting or hurting him, no, it was so paper-thin that it peeled the flesh from his bones and pierced his

271

heart with a thin but deadly tip.

"I'm so sorry."

He took her hand and as she did not move, he knelt on the floor in front of her and tried to capture her gaze. It was an urgent need for him to tell her everything, to explain it all, to reveal himself completely. His feelings and thoughts, his past, his manipulated dependence on this woman who had hurt her today and given her the rest. But it wasn't about what he wanted. It was about her.

"How are you feeling?"

"I'm cold."

He rubbed her arms briefly, remembering a similar situation after he had almost driven her over.

"I'll just get the other blanket..."

Nick stood up quickly, but Sophia held his hand tightly. Fear overwhelmed him. His breath hitched, his heart hammered in his chest, the seconds ticked by, waiting, as if in an exam. The most important exam of all. Tick-tock. Tick *go away*, tock *leave me alone*, tick *just go*. The sweat on his forehead was cold, he had so much to explain. Please give me this chance!

Tick-tock. Please! Tick... *I*... ...tick... ...*love*... ...tick... *you*... ...tick... *so*!

"Don't go."

Sophia was sure that she had only thought those words, but he seemed to have heard them anyway. Suddenly, she was sitting on his lap and he held her so tightly in his arms that she suddenly felt warm. Even her stomach, as if she had already drunk the tea that was still standing steaming on the kitchen counter.

"Never."

Oh.

That was huge. Did he mean it seriously? That was a really huge statement, that she couldn't really think about it now. Well, somehow, she did. *Never.* She felt her fingers digging into the cosy blanket and she sank closer to him as if she belonged right there. That bond just pulled her towards him. Yet, he had to say something, explain it to her. And that's exactly what he did.

"It's a gift to hit someone right where it hurts."
"Sophia."
Gritting his teeth, he carefully touched her fingers, not wanting her to keep thinking about the *toxic syringe* or letting her words drag her down.
"How did she know about the university? I mean, I could have if I'd chosen agricultural science or veterinary medicine. My parents were flexible about that." She laughed sarcastically and didn't listen when Nick tried to explain that it was pure coincidence that Cora had hit a sore spot.
Tiredly, she ran her hand over her face and pulled down the sleeve of her blouse, which had ridden up and exposed the pale freckles on her arm.
"Well, and people bitching about my freckles is nothing new."
"I love every single one of them.", declared Nick seriously, promising her something to provoke a small smile, which came, but didn't last long.
"I was that insecure, ugly little girl again, and I'm so angry at myself that she managed to do that."
"You're not a little girl!" Nick stroked the hand that was in her lap. "And you're so beautiful."
"She is beautiful." Sophia objected, turning her face away so he couldn't see her tears. She had never cared much about her appearance, but this person had managed to make her feel small and ugly. Like her friends. It's as if everyone was shouting at her

that she didn't fit in with the handsome man next to her.

"Sophia", his voice had taken on a dark tone, but not that Barry White tone of emotion and longing, but the *I'm starting to get pissed* -tone. He took her face in his hands and slowly shook his head. "For me, you are the most beautiful woman I have ever met. From the outside, as from the inside!" His voice softened a little. "Don't let anyone tell you otherwise. And she's a nobody. On the outside, she may be pretty, but inside she's ugly, rotten to the core and full of maggots."

Even without the serious tone of his voice, she would have believed what he said, for the expression on his face allowed no protest and absolutely no doubt. Eager to kiss him, she lowered her gaze to his lips, but lifted it again to read once more in his eyes the truth they both knew.

"How can anyone be like that?" asked Sophia wearily, though it was a rhetorical question and Nick could only shake his head. "Tell me what you whispered in her ear."

"That's too horrible to repeat."

"We said no more secrets and no more *I'm not telling you because I want to protect you.* Come on, tell me."

Sophia tried to strike a teasing tone, but didn't really succeed. Still, Nick appreciated her efforts. Trying not to make him feel like a total loser, even though he had cried like one. Sophia had said she didn't see it that way, and he believed her.

"I said she was a..."

Sophia opened her eyes and didn't know whether to be shocked or happy, for even though she would never have said it out loud, that was also her opinion of this bitch ... woman.

"... and that she will choke on her wickedness at some point."

Nick made a disgusted face and Sophia asked dryly, "You feel better now?"

She tried desperately to suppress a laugh, but the overtiredness, the alcohol, his confession about the terrible relationship with that woman and all the crap her friends had done to her in recent days had made her go crazy. She burst out laughing when he replied just as dryly. "Yes."

The laughter shook her, but she couldn't stop. Nick joined in and she slid closer to him. Before it turned into a fit of laughter, they suddenly became serious again and looked firmly into each other's eyes.

"I love you." His voice was hoarse and although he didn't let on, he just wanted to let her know, to reassure her that she was the one. Sophia couldn't help but answer him. The kiss was light. She lingered at the touch of their lips and then pressed her forehead to his.

"And I you."

It tickled tenderly against his lips as he pulled her tighter into his arms in relief.

"I know it's late and we have to be back at work in a few hours, but I'd like to tell you a few things about Ruben."

"Of course."

Sophia leaned back on the couch and rested her head against his shoulder. Although Nick tried to only touch on the story and give her the basic facts, he realised after only a few sentences that Sophia had almost fallen asleep. For a moment he rested his face against hers before getting up and gently carrying her to bed.

"What are we doing about Viviana?" she asked softly against his chest. With a firm look in her eyes, he promised her, "We'll take care of that tomorrow."

Chapter 21

No sooner had Nick parted from Sophia at the entrance to the company than he went straight into his sister's office.

"Oh good, you're here, I've already seen that the portfolios are ready, so I'll be leaving soon."

"That's not why I'm here," he explained, then asked, "do you know a lawyer called Viviana Brecht?"

Yvonne thought for a moment, but then shook her head. Nick ran his hand through his hair, lost in thought, and sat down in Jörn's chair, who was not yet in the office.

"What's wrong?" Yvonne wanted to know and looked at her brother sceptically. "Who is Viviana Brecht?"

"A so-called friend of Sophia's."

"Okay, and why would I know her?"

"You're always doing all this lawyer stuff." Nick shrugged. "I thought maybe there was something with a photographer or a client that she ..."

"What? You're talking in riddles!" she laughed shortly.

"She sent Sophia a message and told her not to believe what I am saying."

"You?" Yvonne was surprised, "you're the most honest person I know."

"Thank you."

"A bit grumpy, but honest." She smiled. "What did she mean?"

"I don't know."

Nick stood up and was already heading for the door when Yvonne asked why Sophia hadn't asked, and trusting Yvonne, he told her a little more.

"These women don't sound like they're real friends."

Nick agreed with his sister and was about to open the door when Yvonne had an idea.

"Which law firm does this Viviana work at?"

Nick took the piece of paper from his pocket on which Sophia had written the name. "Reibold & Partner."

"Ahh." Yvonne turned to one of the filing cabinets and rummaged around in it, then handed him a thick folder and explained: "Helmko's law firm was bought out by them a few years ago."

Nick stared at the folder in his hands. Mr Helmko had been the lawyer they had hired to make Cora pay for the data theft. The matter had been off the table for a long time, as it was a delicate matter that was difficult to prove. Why Yvonne had kept it in her office all these years, he didn't know, but he didn't care. Briefly, he thought about returning the folder to her, after all, what would he find in it? Except that Helmko negotiated with the other side's lawyer and the matter was never really settled, because Cora had of course denied everything. He couldn't remember exactly how it had turned out, he wasn't doing so well at the time for understandable reasons, and well, his siblings thought it would be better if he travelled abroad and accompanied the productions.

Yvonne then shooed him out, for she still had some things to do, so he went to his office with the folder under his arm. He would have preferred to discuss the matter directly with Sophia, but she had a lot to do before the office closed early the next day for the Christmas party. He glanced at her as he passed her room, realised she was having a tense conversation and was already looking forward to how he could help her relax in the evening.

After he had retired to his office, he opened the folder. It was all neatly filed by date, probably by Yvonne herself. Although he did not think he would find anything in it that could have prompted Viviana to write to Sophia what she did, he set about the arduous task of looking for the solution in it.

No sooner had Sophia finished the phone call with a very demanding client than the next one called. Everyone acted as if the company was closing for good at twelve o'clock the next day, and not just the one time for the annual Christmas party. Sophia thought the clients knew the time was a lie anyway. But that was the official time, so everyone could relax a little and work through the last things in peace. A few colleagues would definitely also take the opportunity to go home for another hour or two before they had to be back in time for the departure of the two minibuses that would take them to Pielsand. Sophia was curious to see what it would be like when she returned to Pielsand.

The impressions of her first time there were still so present that she closed her eyes for a moment and surrendered to the memory. How incredibly beautiful it had been! Yes, and she meant everything, not only the small town and the sea, but also the romantic dinner, Nick and their love, which they had physically shared there for the first time ... Nick was so wonderfully attentive, gentle and passionate. So eager to please her, and not selfish at all.

Suddenly, she had an urgent need to be close to him, and without thinking any further about it, she got up, took some papers and went into his office.

"Hey, what's up?" He asked, seeing her flushed cheeks and a look that resembled her look when they both ...

"I need... erm, yes... so I ... um." Sophia turned back towards the door, and although no one came by, she still couldn't do what she really wanted to do right now, and stood a little lost half in and half outside his office.

Nick was worried that there was some kind of problem. He saw that she was holding the papers so tightly in her hand that they were already crumpled. The next moment he stood up, pulled her into the office and pushed the door a little shut.

"Is there a problem?", he asked worried.

Sophia felt stupid and didn't know what to say, she looked back at him and then stared at her feet.

"Tell me." His voice was rough. Suddenly, he was standing so close that Sophia really didn't know what she was doing there, and looked up at him. "No secrets!" he reminded her of their mutual promise and smiled.

"Okay." She nodded, cleared her throat, then stared back down at her feet. "I was thinking about Pielsand."

"Do you worry about..."

"No."

"But what were you thinking about?"

Again she raised her eyes.

"Oh."

Indeed. He realised and a feeling of understanding and unspeakable desire shot through his body. Given everything that had happened in the last few days, it seemed like an eternity since they had last been close. Despite the fact that they had woken up this morning tightly entwined.

"Sophia, I ..."

"I know ..." she said quickly, it was a bit embarrassing to tell the boyfriend that she was pining for him while they were both trying to work.

So she turned and was half a step away when he grabbed her by the arm and spun her around. His arms wrapped around her body and his lips were hot and longing on hers, she barely understood what was happening. It was so hot where they touched that they literally melted into each other. The next moment he had already broken away and taken two steps back from her, as if he had burnt himself, all before Sophia could open her eyes.

"Yes, well ... I ..." she stammered, and he seemed as confused as she.

"I know."

Their eyes remained fixed on each other for a moment as they both searched for words to describe what was going on inside them.

"This wasn't such a good idea." he said sourly, stroking his face.

A brief stab of rejection pricked at her heart and Sophia took a deep breath so she would be strong enough to finally leave his office when he added quietly. "Now I want you even more."

Oh. Yes, that was exactly what she felt too, nodding she let out the breath she had been holding.

"I ... erm ... better go." It sounded like a question.

"Yes, I also don't want us to..." Nick made a hand gesture that could have meant the office or the whole company, and although she knew it was a stupid idea to have come here in the first place, she couldn't regret it. She would never regret kissing him. Nor the failure to suppress a smile at the sight of his desperate expression, since she probably looked very much like him.

They stared at each other until Sophia recognised a change in his expression, and she tensed in electrifying anticipation as he came towards her a second time. They really shouldn't, but oh, how she longed for him! Her arms lifted as if by magic to embrace him when Jörn came in.

"Oh, hello you two."

He grinned and closed the door behind him.

Frozen in their movements, the two looked at Jörn and Sophia slowly lowered her arms, feeling herself turning bright red.

"I hope I haven't disturbed you."

"What makes you think that?" Nick bluffed at him, a little annoyed, and walked back behind his desk with his jaw clenched.

"Oh, I wouldn't have a problem with it." Jörn said with a smile and Sophia smiled back kindly, or at least she tried to. "I mean, a little kiss without anyone noticing should be allowed, right?" Jörn laughed out. When neither of them answered, it dawned on him that that was exactly the point.

"Oh, well. It's a good thing it was me then ..." Once more he laughed, he really didn't seem to mind.

"Yes." Nick said more harshly than he had intended, but he didn't want his brother to play down the subject. After all, it physically hurt him not to be able to hold Sophia in his arms anymore, and judging by the expression on her face, she felt exactly the same.

"Ahh well, then ... um. I just wanted to get to the safe."

Nick nodded to his brother and went to the cupboard where the safe was kept. When the numbers he entered made beeping noises, Sophia finally woke up from her stupor, said a quick goodbye and ran out of the office.

Luckily no one else had noticed, as that was exactly what they wanted to avoid. She really wasn't sure how to continue working under the same roof with this tension between them. Being close to him and yet not close enough and not being allowed to touch him ... They could make as many rules as they wanted, at some point they wouldn't be able to stand it anymore, like just now, and they would get carried away with a kiss and someone would catch them sooner or later. It wasn't so much that someone knew, she just didn't want their relationship to become a problem between Nick and his siblings.

However, before she could think about it further, the phone

rang yet again, it was a set builder with questions about a shooting next week, so she postponed the subject until later. While listening to the next caller, she went through her to-do list and remembered that she still had to wrap the rest of the portfolios for Yvonne. After she had finished the call, she ran out of her room and briefly looked into Nick's office. The door was closed, which either meant he wasn't there or didn't want to be disturbed. She ran up the stairs and met Jörn in the conference room, who tucked a box of photographers' portfolios under his arm and gave her a friendly nod before leaving the room.

Sophia grabbed another box, filled it with portfolios and closed it just as the door slid shut behind her. As she turned in joyful anticipation, the smile on her face died when she realised it was not the Falkner brother she had hoped for.

Nick struggled through the folder and felt ... well, he didn't know exactly how he felt. He felt empty, uninvolved, like he was reading something that had nothing to do with him personally. Yes, he read his name in more than one email or lawyer's letter, but none of the statements were his own words, and so there was a certain distance. He shook his head, it wasn't much and there wasn't even a settlement since they hadn't been able to prove that Cora had stolen data. She could have got all the information from the internet, as she had claimed. Nick made copies of some papers and looked for a statement Viviana might have meant, but he didn't know for sure and would discuss it with Sophia. She had already told him what she was going to do and he was glad that she finally dared to confront her friends directly.

He went out of the office to see if he could talk to her, but she was not at her desk. Instead Jörn came up to him and pressed a heavy box into his arms.

"Come."

"I think you can do this quite well on your own."

"Nick, I'm doing you a favour, you're doing me a favour. Simple."

Together they went out to the car park and loaded the boxes into Jörn's car, which contained a few other things Yvonne had organised for the Christmas party.

"Torches?" Nick remembered what Sophia had said on the beach at Pielsand and was pleased that her idea had been taken up.

"Yes, lighting the way to the beach was your sweetheart's idea."

Nick looked at his brother, waiting for more, for Jörn had broached the subject for a reason.

"I like her, don't screw up!" He then said seriously and Nick shook his head.

"I don't intend to."

"Ruben will warm up too ..."

"What's he getting on about? Him and Tea ..."

"Yes, it annoys him that you make that comparison."

"Why is that?" Nick flipped the boot lid shut and looked angrily at Jörn as if they were his words.

"I think Ruben has a problem with ..."

"What kind of problem?" Nick was starting to get angry, "that I'm finally happy?"

"No, I think he's happy when you're happy, but I don't know, either he's afraid it's not serious ..."

"It is serious." Nick's voice left no doubt.

"I know." Jörn grinned.

"You know?"

"Yeah, sure, Nick honestly ... you're so changed."

Nick rolled his eyes.

"She's ... oh I don't know, I can see that she's good for you and you're so thoughtful when it concerns her .... I feel that ... oh." Jörn turned away and Nick was taken aback by his brother's reaction.

"Are you crying?"

"It's with joy, you idiot."

"Jörn ..."

"I think ... ah, the way she looks at you ... it's exactly the same look. It's a gift." He nodded and wiped away his tears. "Such a ... you rarely get to see a connection like that."

Nick struggled a little to respond. He loved his brother, but talking to him about feelings was even more difficult than doing it with Sophia, even though they had such an intimate connection. Nevertheless, he searched for words here in the cold of the company car park, but they did not cross his lips.

"I'm happy for you and I'm on your side, just like Yvonne," Jörn said in a conspiratorial tone. "And as soon as you bring her home, Tea will join our club too." He winked at Nick and the two laughed before going back inside.

Sophia couldn't quite understand what had just happened, especially though Nick had already prepared her for the fact that Ruben didn't approve of their relationship. The fact that he spoke to her so bluntly and almost threatening scared her involuntarily. Nevertheless, she would tell Nick even against Ruben's will, but so much was happening at once that she had to gather herself first.

She took one of the boxes and left the conference room without glancing at Ruben in his glass office. Probably he thought now that he had intimidated her enough to get exactly what he wanted. At the bottom of the stairs she met Nick, he took the box from her wordlessly but with a gentle smile and that special light in his eyes, and it seemed to her at that moment that he was also taking away the pressure Ruben had just put on her. Sophia never wanted to be pressured, neither by Ruben nor anyone else, yet she often didn't know how to react to something like that.

So, a few hours later she stood in front of the mirror in her bathroom and practised the words she wanted to say to Viviana. She wanted to confront her so that she, and the others too, would finally tell her why they were behaving like this and why they couldn't be happy for her. An exciting tingling had taken possession of her, as if she had another job interview, and that alone made her realise that this was not the feeling one should have towards a friend. Once again, she went through her prepared text, knowing full well that she would certainly be no match for Viviana's retort if she used legal jargon on her. Or perhaps she would forget her planned sentences altogether and do exactly what Nick had advised her to do.

Stay the way you are, don't doubt yourself, tell her ... tell them how much they have hurt you.

While she continued to encourage herself, the doorbell rang and she went to open it and let Viviana in. The greeting was rather subdued, even though they gave each other a little kiss on the cheek, even a blind man would have seen that something was wrong between them.

"It's cold, isn't it?" remarked Viviana, and Sophia couldn't believe they had sunk so low as to exchange pleasantries about the weather.

"What exactly did you mean by that?" Sophia blurted out as she took the damp coat from Viviana.

"It's cold." Viviana bluffed at her with a raised eyebrow, as if she doubted Sophia's sanity, knowing exactly what Sophia had meant by her question. But attack was the best defence.

"You know I mean your message." Wow. Sophia surprised herself that she managed to say it without her voice shaking.

Viviana straightened up after taking off her boots, looked at Sophia piercingly and gave her the expected answer in a snippy tone. "Exactly what I said."

"But you don't even know each other."

Viviana rolled her eyes and took a deep breath, as if she were dealing with a really stupid person.

"A person doesn't have to know someone personally to make a judgement about them." She raised both eyebrows now that they almost disappeared into her hairline and Sophia understood why some of her clients flinched under her gaze.

"Tell me why you think that, since I trust him and what he says...."

Viviana probably realised that she would not have it easy this time, groaned in annoyance and pointed to the door leading into the room, as if to say that she would rather sit down. But Sophia crossed her arms and looked at her, waiting.

"Okay. I found something in a colleague's office who was sorting through his files."

"What?"

Viviana licked her lips and then said in her typical *I told you so* tone. "Evidence that he still loves his ex, Cora Bergmann, and they do business together."

Now followed the *so, there you go* look and Viviana pushed past Sophia into the room, but stopped abruptly halfway to the sofa.

"What the ...?"

"Hi, I'm Nick." Nick held out his hand to her with a friendly smile and gestured her to sit down nevertheless. He was a born host and pretended not be aware of their conversation in the hallway. He placed a glass of wine on the table in front of Viviana, who accepted it gratefully and immediately took a greedy sip. Sophia and Nick glanced at each other and then Sophia sat down next to Viviana on the sofa.

"Nick hasn't been in contact with Cora for years."

Viviana said nothing, but took another sip.

"It was about data theft, but we could never prove it, or rather my siblings, since I was abroad at the time.", explained Nick with a smile and there was not the slightest emotion on his face as he handed the folder to Viviana. She looked up at him in question and then at Sophia.

"It's all in there, maybe you'll read it ..."

"I don't need to read it," Viviana grumbled, shaking her head. "I remember exactly what it said. Namely, that he still loves her after all this time, even though he's had major personal problems with the break-up and a nice little girlfriend here and there."

Viviana jumped up, but Sophia wasn't going to let her off that easily. "Sit down."

And amazingly, Viviana did just that.

"Read the date!", Sophia ordered in a stern tone that surprised everyone present and Nick had to admit that he liked the way she insisted that Viviana realise her mistake.

"Yes, well," Viviana got that arrogant look on her face that Sophia didn't like so much about her, and read aloud in a smug tone, "3rd October." She raised an eyebrow and looked at Sophia mockingly.

"What year?" Sophia asked and Viviana read it silently, glancing briefly at her and back at the paper.

"2008." she then read slowly and flipped through the whole

folder in a panic, looking at the date on each page. She had been so sure that this guy was playing games with Sophia, naive as she was, she was an easy victim after all. Especially for such a cunning guy as he was, judging by what she had heard about him from Céline.

Just at that moment, the doorbell rang and Nick hurried into the hallway to open it for the other two.

"Oh, hi." Ina was the first to compose and took Nick's hand, introduced herself and then stripped off her jacket, which Nick took from her and hung up. Céline, on the other hand, stared at him as if she was quite surprised to meet him here, and it was obvious from her expression that she didn't like this meeting at all. Annoyed, she went to the others and sat down on one of the comfortable cushions.

"What's all this about?" she asked bluntly, glaring at Sophia.

"Well, I thought if you all claim to know so much about my boyfriend, it wouldn't hurt to meet him for once."

"What's the point?" Céline asked annoyed, looking with narrowed eyebrows at Viviana who was still staring at the papers in her lap, searching for words.

Sophia saw Ina poke her in the ribs, but Céline ignored her and sought the gaze of Nick, who was leaning against the kitchen counter, his eyes fixed on Sophia. She had asked him to stay quiet, that this thing was something she had to deal with alone, albeit she wanted him there at least briefly too, to show the others that he really was her boyfriend and that they were getting through this *together*. But Sophia also knew that it could probably be awkward for the others, and so she had also discussed with him that he would have to leave at some point so that the women could talk freely.

"Can you explain this nonsense to me?" cried Céline "what's the point?"

"I'm asking you the same thing," Sophia stated calmly and sat up straighter. "You've been talking about him from the beginning as if you knew him, but neither of you do."

Ina nodded and looked down at her knees in dismay.

"Viviana read something in some old file that doesn't show who Nick really is."

Sophia waited in vain for Viviana to say something back, but she seemed to have lost her voice and said nothing. She continued to stare at the papers in front of her, then picked up her wine glass and emptied the contents in one gulp. The silence stretched on, an uncomfortable, dragging silence. Everyone looked furtively at Nick, but he only had eyes for Sophia and looked waiting at her with a gentle smile. Finally, she nodded at him and he went to her and gave her a sweet kiss on the cheek.

"I'll see you later." He stroked her face in that tender way he always did, turned to the others and said only a simple "Bye."

As soon as he was out the door, Sophia continued.

"Céline, you talked about him and then later dismissed it as if it only bothered you that we wanted to keep it a secret for a while." But Céline remained true to her stubborn attitude and answered nothing.

"It sucks how we acted.", admitted Ina, nodding and smiling sheepishly, but the other two remained silent.

Sophia looked at Ina and waited for more, but she was probably also searching for words or waiting for support from the other two. Then Sophia brought out her original self-doubt again and explained to them, whether they wanted to hear it or not, what was going on inside her. "Do you know how much you hurt me?"

Céline finally made a move. Her left eye twitched before she stared at the table between them.

"You made me feel immature because I fell in love with him and doubted I could ever have a chance!" Sophia breathed a sigh of relief. "You called it a *clichéd, stupid girl crush*!"

And it hurt the others to be reminded of how much they had hurt Sophia.

"Like I'm a stupid little girl."

"You're not stupid." Those were Viviana's first words, and Sophia could hardly take her eyes off her, for essentially, she had thus confirmed once again that she thought she was ugly.

"And like I'm ugly and not worthy of him," Sophia continued because of that.

"You're not ugly either." Were Céline's muttered words as she slowly gave up her defensive posture and slumped a little.

"I'm sorry," Ina said, looking at the others, "we're all sorry, ok?"

Sophia wanted more, needed more, to finally make peace. The two great speakers, one a self-confident lawyer whose reputation already now - at the beginning of her career - preceded her and who would certainly develop a huge career, and the other a chairwoman of the board of the foundation of a family dynasty worth millions, remained silent. They left it to Ina, who was visibly struggling and who also looked furtively at Sophia a few times, but of course could not expect any support from her, to put the whole thing into words.

"I don't know, it had taken on such a momentum," Ina said vaguely, but no one else said anything, so she had to keep talking. "First of all, it was so clichéd, the young innocent thing from the countryside falling in love with her boss, good-looking and not exactly someone who takes relationships that seriously."

Sophia gasped and then Viviana finally explained, "Yes, at least what we've heard about him," she cleared her throat embarrassed, it was awkward to have to say the whole thing out loud, but of course she understood why it was so important to Sophia.

"Anton bragged about knowing things about him whenever I mentioned his name," Céline said but didn't look at Sophia.

"It was so easy.", Ina sighed and everyone stared at her, dumbfounded, she stroked her hair, took a deep breath and then tried to explain what exactly. "To make you feel insecure, I mean ... at first it was meant as a joke, then you didn't talk about him for ages and we had already forgotten about it until Halloween ...", she paused for a moment and looked at Sophia, who nodded to tell Ina it was okay to keep talking. "You were so excited and nervous and ... I don't know, we just didn't think it was anything more and ..."

"Ina, you mean to tell me that you didn't take me seriously because I didn't tell you that much about him and as I did you dismissed it and talked bad about him to .... To do what?"

"To talk you out of him, because we thought he was an ass," and turning to Sophia she muttered a soft "Sorry."

"You believed what Céline heard from Anton, even though they have nothing to do with each other at all?"

"Yes, I just believed him." Céline admitted, gritting her teeth before continuing, "When you're in love, you just believe everything he says."

Sophia could say nothing more in reply and then asked her last question, which she had thought of a thousand times.

"And after you knew we were together and ..."

"Jeez, don't be so naïve!" interjected Céline, and everyone froze. "Jealousy. It's jealousy!"

"You're jealous that Nick wants me?" Sophia's voice was all hoarse, she didn't want to cry, but her throat tightened more and more.

"No, of course not!" Céline jumped up and walked around the room. "We were jealous because you're someone who wasn't out to get a man, and then you get him."

"So I'm not worth it..."

"No, not that, we were jealous due to the fact that we ..." Ina left the sentence unfinished.

"But Viviana is getting married and you both have boyfriends, why can't I have one too?"

Sophia no longer understood anything at all and stood up, she needed a moment for herself, but of course she wanted to hear it anyway so that she could finally put it to an end somehow.

"Yes, everything you do ends positively, you never have to do anything for it," Viviana explained as if it was no big deal.

"What makes you think that?" Sophia didn't know what they were talking about. After all, it had taken a year between Nick and her to develop, how many times had she cried herself to sleep knowing that he would just remain a dream forever!

"You're always cheerful, you find a solution to every problem, you always see something positive in everything and yes, you're unhappily in love ... that was the only thing where we were ..."

"That's where we were superior to you." Viviana interrupted Ina in a cold, stern voice and everyone sank into a kind of rigor mortis.

It couldn't be true! That her so-called friends were envious and jealous, because everything was *oh so great* for her, although it wasn't like that at all?

"But it's not all positive with me, I just don't cry about it as much!", Sophia yelped and because she was too shocked by this revelation, she didn't notice the tears streaming down her face.

"Like I said, we're sorry. It kind of took on this dynamic of its own," Ina explained again, standing up and approaching Sophia.

Did she really think Sophia would let herself be hugged by her or one of the others? That she would forgive them so quickly? Sophia took a step back and hurried back to the table, rinsing her voice with the sticky wine and wiping her tears. Viviana then stood up too, her hands already stretched out towards Sophia, but Sophia also took a few steps back from her, walked on wobbly knees back to the kitchenette and propped herself up on the kitchen counter, as if the piece of furniture could give her some of its stability.

"I'm really sorry, sweetie.", Viviana said and Céline also tried to speak in an ingratiating voice, but Sophia needed her privacy.

She had always believed that the others thought she was not good or beautiful enough for Nick, or that in their opinion he was not good to her. Then she had believed that it had all snowballed into something bigger and bigger through gossip and false assumptions. But that all this was also related to the fact that she had a positive attitude and whined so much less made her so sad that she couldn't say anything. She could barely hear what the girls were saying. Her friends. She couldn't really call them that anymore. They had become strangers.

"Shall we go?" asked Céline after a while of silence and Sophia just nodded. It all felt dull and unreal, like the heartbreak she had felt for Nick until a few weeks ago.

"Should we tell him?" Viviana looked at her questioningly from the doorway. Only tonelessly could Sophia answer.

"Nick, his name is Nick."

"Should we tell Nick?", Viviana tried again and closed her eyes.

The tears Sophia didn't see, she could only shake her head, she certainly wouldn't give them his number! She had to protect him from these women. When Sophia heard the door slam, she took her mobile phone out of her pocket and texted Nick.   Barely four minutes later he was there, taking her in his arms as soon as she opened the door. They stood in her hallway and Sophia told him everything before they were even back in the room.

"It hurts." she said tearfully and it hurt him that she was so hurt. I know."

He pulled her close and Sophia leaned against him and it was as if all the sadness, tension, frustration and pain were simply absorbed by him. She felt lighter and somehow liberated and she could feel the bond with him grow another fibre thicker, making their connection even stronger.

293

Chapter 22

The tension prickled on her skin the closer they got to Pielsand. The minibus pulled into the car park of the hotel and for a moment Sophia felt transported back to the first time she arrived here with Nick. How nervous she had been! She had panicked that he wouldn't like what he got to see, that she wouldn't be enough, but then it had been so indescribably beautiful that she wished it had never ended.

They checked into their rooms and Sophia was surprised but grateful that she was staying in the part that led more quickly to Nick's apartment and she made a mental note to thank Yvonne for it later. The hotel was busy and so no one noticed that she was the only one from the company staying in that part of the hotel.

She was glad that Ruben was staying with Jörn and Yvonne in his holiday residence. Sophia knew she wouldn't be able to relax if she had to live under the same roof as Ruben. Especially not after what he had said and how Nick had reacted when she had told him.

She was sure that if she hadn't been heartbroken about her friends, he would have gone home immediately to give Ruben a piece of his mind. But for her sake he had held back. The frustration had vanished from his face immediately when she had touched his cheek with her fingers. They had stopped talking, just looked at each other for a while.

"Come here.", he had whispered and then hugged her tightly, with his whole body. In the past, she used to find these tight hugs uncomfortable, she felt cornered and couldn't relax and sleep when someone had their arms wrapped around her too tightly and possessively. But with Nick it was as if it couldn't be tight enough. As if she wanted to crawl into him and he into her. Somehow, she still had to slide closer to him to sink into him.

She couldn't sleep well when he wasn't there. That night was the first time she had really noticed it. She had woken up when he was no longer beside her. The loss had startled her. But he had only been in the bathroom for a moment and had made himself more comfortable by taking off his jeans and pullover.

"Hey, why are you awake?" he asked as he snuggled back under the covers. Sophia had only answered after a while.

"You were gone."

In response, he had simply pulled her closer and planted a kiss on her hair, then they had both gone back to sleep.

Sophia thought about what it would be like if they were separated from each other for days and especially nights. She would then probably suffer from insomnia and run around like a zombie. All this went through her mind when she entered her cosy room and saw the king-size bed in front of her, where she would surely feel lost. Maybe coming here had not been such a good idea. The thought that he was sleeping nearby but separated from her by several floors, walls and, above all, observers, hit her. Sophia shook her head at this nonsense. It was perfectly fine and natural, after all, they didn't have to be glued to each other day and night! But she would like to, she admitted to herself.

During the day they would surely soon get a grip on this tension between them, but at night? How was she supposed to sleep without him? Oh, she had to deal with that. Soon, but not now, she decided.

At that moment, however, she was also glad to be alone. So much had happened in the last four weeks that she hadn't really had a chance to analyse everything in detail and think about it. It was good to have some peace and quiet before the party started. She brushed off her jacket and shoes before dropping onto the bed and immersing herself in the most intense weeks of her life.

The thought that she would ever break up with her friends had never crossed her mind. Her mother had always told her that friends were more important than any man, but she had probably forgotten how nasty some women could be to others. The betrayal of her former best friend had hurt her even more than the betrayal of her ex-boyfriend.

After last night, none of the girls had contacted her and Sophia had to admit that she didn't expect them to. What was there left to talk about? What they had said and what was left unsaid was so much and so hurtful that Sophia wasn't sure she could ever trust them again. Probably not. No matter what they would say, what she would confide in them or how she would act, it would depend on how they reacted. It would become a kind of cat and mouse game. A dance around the shadows of the past.

Sometimes Sophia would play a question-and-answer game in her head, and the question she would ask at that moment was: "When trust and respect are gone, what's left?" and the answer from her wounded heart was, "There is nothing left."

The girls didn't accept her as she was, or they just couldn't stand her any more. They were jealous of her positive attitude! That was the reason! Sophia herself was the reason why she had been treated like that. Only if she changed could she be sure that the girls would accept her. And even then, not really.

A saying her mother had once written in a poetry album came back to her mind.

"O do not break the bond of friendship in haste! Even if it is tied anew, one knot remains."

But that's exactly what they would do and that's exactly what it would be. It would always be between them, this knot. Every remark, every little joke would remind her that it had not been a joke in the past. Sophia knew she couldn't bear to be on guard every time they met. She took a deep breath and wiped away the one small tear that ran down her cheek from the corner of her eye. She felt ... she thought it was strange how she felt.

Her father used to say that the air was clearer after a thunderstorm. She saw more clearly now, and she saw no future with these women, at least for the moment. Where friends should support each other, help each other, be proud of each other and be there for each other, they had not taken her seriously. Had laughed at her and put her and her feelings down. Had made her self-doubt worse and betrayed the friendship and love she had felt for them. It was awful and mean. Nick had confirmed her deepest belief in herself by saying: "You deserve the best."

Yes. Sophia knew she should be treated better than this. The same way she treated others. With respect, support and sympathy. Even though she would naturally miss the old days when it was less about the personal dramas of them all and more about the big picture, she knew that sometimes it just had to be over. Even if it hurt. Sometimes you had to part with things and, unfortunately, with people. Like once a year she rummaged through her closet looking for things she could or should discard. Unnecessary things. Things she no longer wore, things that were too tight or worn out.

However. Sometimes it was necessary to clean up even among friends, no matter how terrible and painful it was. Sophia took a deep breath to keep from crying. In her mind she thought about what she liked most about the three of them as individuals and what had hurt her the most. The conclusion was that she didn't want to "keep" any of them as friends, at least not at the moment. Maybe she should think about it at another time, at the moment it was all still too fresh. It just still hurt too much. It was another distorting heartbreak.

Sophia thought about the last time she had felt like this and now knew that the pain of unrequited love had turned into the most wonderful thing she had ever experienced. That meant it could only get better. A smile appeared on her face and with these positive thoughts she got up, settled in the room, jumped in the shower and calmly got ready for the evening.

She wanted to dress the way she felt so as not to please anyone but herself, and, granted, Nick. But of course she also wanted to tease him a little. Even though it was cruel, she liked the desperate look on his face when he couldn't hug, touch or kiss her.

Sophia smiled at the thought and put on her lingerie, matching the dress she had bought for the special occasion.

Nick was standing in the lobby with Jörn and Yvonne, waiting for his colleagues to lead them all to the restaurant where the Christmas party was being held. Ruben, as usual, didn't feel like it and maybe it was better that way, because he was about to explode at the slightest thought of his older brother. It was only for the reason that Sophia had been so hurt by that stupid crap with those horrible women the night before, that he had remained calm. She was much more important to him than his brother, but because she meant so much to him, he would have loved to slap Ruben.

To distract his mind from thoughts of Ruben, he greeted his colleagues warmly as they gradually arrived in the lobby. He wished he was alone waiting for Sophia. He missed her, which was total nonsense, of course, but that was how he felt. Finally, he wanted to be alone with her once again, without all the things that had been keeping them so busy. Nick was looking forward to the moment when they would all climb on the bus and go home, and Sophia would stay with him until Sunday.

In his head he had some ideas of what he could do to make her relax and forget everything that had happened. The thought of locking them both up in his apartment for more than twenty-four hours and what they would then do most of the time made him smile. Only the voices of his colleagues prompted him to clear his throat and join the conversation next to him.

The few people who had already joined them were festively dressed, like his siblings and him. The men in dark suits with ties and the women in classically cut dresses, as far as he could tell under their thick coats. He tried to imagine what Sophia would be wearing to keep himself from staring in her direction with his tongue hanging out. Eagerly, he looked towards the lift, just like everyone else, as the last group of employees arrived in the lobby.

The expression on his face was treacherous, but only Jörn seemed to understand and patted him sympathetically on the shoulder as he leaned closer.

"It's going to be a tough night for you, my dear brother."

Jörn laughed and watched Nick's face, unable to hide his affection. He had that, *that's my girl* look and his whole posture seemed broader and strangely, somehow more open too. There was this little smile around his mouth that was barely noticeable and this glimmer of love in his eyes. Shaking his head, Jörn nudged his brother and Nick seemed to wake up from a magical spell. Feeling caught, he gave a short, embarrassed laugh and looked down at the floor to get a grip.

"You are totally lost."

Nick laughingly agreed with his brother and tried to shield his eyes from the sight of her. She was stunning. Her hair was blow-dried into soft waves that she wore over one shoulder. Beneath her open coat flashed a burgundy, straight-cut dress that hid her shoulders and collarbones under a thin fabric, probably mesh. It was neither obtrusive nor deliberately sexy. But precisely the fact that it underlined Sophia's character so much made him weak. It wasn't too tight either, and yet it showed off her curves so perfectly that Nick had trouble really averting his eyes.

Fortunately, they finally left and he deepened the conversation with one of the employees. But he couldn't help but give her a certain look, which she obviously understood, because he saw her cheeks change colour and her eyes take on a certain expression before they went out into the cool, snow-smelling air.

It was only when they arrived at the restaurant and they all lined up at the wardrobe to hand in their coats and jackets that he realised the full extent of what she had done. Between a small button at the nape of her neck and the zipper that started at shoulder blade level, there was a hole in the shape of a heart that literally cried out to have his lips pressed against the exposed, wonderfully tender skin.

Sophia felt his gaze on her all evening, even though he didn't look at her when she sought his gaze. He seemed tense, even though he talked to everyone, was friendly and charming as he made his rounds through the staff. He went up to everyone but her, and she thought of how unhappy she would be now if she didn't know that he just didn't want to show her he loved her in front of everyone. Apparently, he was afraid that everyone would notice as soon as he came near her. That was why she tried not to press him further. She had noticed the look on his face and even though she wanted to tease him a little, she didn't want to torture him unnecessarily. Sophia knew how he felt. She too felt that her body was hypersensitive and electrified. A heat surrounded her and a tingling sensation was under her skin that at some point she went out onto the terrace to cool down.

Outside, she joined some colleagues who were smoking a cigarette. Then she closed her eyes and enjoyed the cold air on her heated cheeks and the cool wind brushing through her hair. When they went back inside, one of their already somewhat drunk colleagues, Clemens, pressed past them. But before he could get even a little too close to Sophia, Nick pushed his way between them, as if he too were in a hurry to get out into the cool air.

It was the first time that evening that they were so close. Their gazes remained glued to each other as if they were completely alone in the world. Time stretched out. Their heartbeats slowed. Sophia felt how every millimetre of her body brushed against his as they passed, as if a thousand tiny fires had been lit.

Nick saw the sparkling glint in her eyes. His attention shifted to that little glimmer. He would almost have forgotten that they weren't alone if Clemens hadn't held a cigarette under his nose at that very moment as he leaned closer to Sophia. He stepped out into the cold and watched Sophia make her way to her seat in the festive light of the restaurant.

"Man, that girl is so hot!", Clemens said and Nick clenched his fists. "Do you think she has a boyfriend, or should I try my luck?"

Clemens was still staring into the restaurant, although Nick was sure he couldn't see her anymore either.

"I'm sure she's good ..."

"Shut up!"

Clemens looked at him, startled, and immediately sobered up. Only now did he realise he was talking to his boss, and he felt ashamed. "I'm sorry, I mean ... I didn't mean to ... well, I just think she's ... cute."

"Keep your hands off her!"

And if Clemens didn't know for sure that his boss and this cute colleague hated each other, he would have taken his counterpart's behaviour as jealousy. But so, of course, he only understood it as a reference to the company code, which he found rather outdated but nevertheless sensible.

Nick, on the other hand, did not think his behaviour made sense when he joined the others again a little later. He couldn't and didn't want to go on like this. He wanted everyone to know that Sophia and he were together, that he belonged with her. They would just have to see how his colleagues took it and find a solution. It couldn't be right that Sophia and he should pretend and lie that they didn't like each other. It was time to step out of the shadows and stand up for what meant the world to him. Possibly he was overreacting, but he didn't have enough to drink to ignore this injustice. They should both have the right to happiness without being punished for it or having to change their lives. He should talk to Ruben and, above all, threaten to beat him if he ever again talked to Sophia the way he had.

But before Nick had fought his way to him, Ruben began his speech. The speech took what felt like an eternity. He took his time presenting the new logo, as if he was being paid to waste time. All the colleagues were already groaning quietly when Yvonne finally stood up and held up one of the new photographers' portfolios.

Then her brothers distributed the portfolios on the tables and everyone could admire the new logo. The applause was rather subdued, but Nick couldn't tell if it was a result of everyone eagerly awaiting the next course in the menu or because they had simply liked the old logo better. However, he did find something that made him smile.

Just as Yvonne was praising the team that had put the portfolios together, his eyes met Sophia's and it was again as if they were alone in the room. He felt her touch, although she was sitting so far away that he couldn't even tell if she was drinking water or white wine. Only when Sophia got a strange, almost sad expression on her face and averted her eyes did he realise that Ruben was telling more news.

"New York, New York!" sang Ruben, and at last came the applause that was so important to him. "I am happy to announce that we will open the office there on the fifteenth of January!"

Some of the staff even cheered. "And it will be run by my beloved brother!"

The rest of the party was actually quite comfortable and when Yvonne announced that they were now all going down to the beach, everyone was quite happy to stretch their legs in the fresh air. Sophia's idea with the torches lining the way down to the beach went down well. Although she didn't take any credit for it, Nick saw that she was pleased. Not as it was her idea, but because it made people happy and got them in the mood for the festival of love.

Down on the beach there was a bonfire. Jörn, armed with his guitar, sang Christmas carols, whereupon everyone joined him, staring into the fire, clapping and toasting with the glasses they had brought.

Nick took advantage of the moment and took Sophia's hand. Very gentle and light, and no one who was looking at them noticed. It just looked like they just happened to be standing next to each other. But it was so much more. They both closed their eyes as the tension finally released. And when they looked into each other's eyes for a moment, they could see the flames glowing in them. They both knew that they just had to wait a little longer and then they could finally be together.

"Nick, could you stop teasing me..." sighed Sophia.

"I promised two days ago to kiss every freckle and there are so many ..."

"Not that many, you're just saying that."

"It depends on how you're lying there, if you're fidgeting all the time then they'll look different and I'll have to have another good look." He explained with a furrowed brow.

"Only you don't look, you *lick* .... ", she had trouble breathing. "Nick!"

"What?"

"Definitely I don't have any *there!*" She shouted in feigned shock.

"I promised to kiss every freckle and beauty mark, I didn't promise not to kiss the places in between as well." A smug grin played around his lips.

"You are incredible.", she giggled in release and ruffled his hair, finally needing to hold on to something.

Then he lifted his head from her belly, where three more little enchanting beauty spots, arranged in a crescent around her belly button, awaited his caress. In his dark velvet voice, which always sent a shiver down her spine, he admitted: "I know."

As he continued to scan her body agonisingly slowly with his lips, giving each freckle the attention it deserved, as promised, an idea formed in her mind. She wanted him to stop teasing her and finally do what she wanted him to do. Just as he propped himself up on his elbow and lifted her arm to his lips, Sophia couldn't take it any longer. She surprised him by pouncing on him and pinning him to the mattress.

"Hey, I wasn't done yet!" He complained with a grin. "You naughty little minx."

"I hadn't thought that, *I'll kiss your freckles forever,* would take forever." She explained dryly and buried her face in his neck.

Now Nick was the one who winced and sighed her name. "I love when you... take things... in hand."

Sophia giggled before kissing him in the same maddeningly slow way. However, Nick was far less patient than she, and after just another moment he pulled her back to eye level. Their gazes merged, as did their lips and finally their bodies.

Chapter 23

It was just as Nick had imagined. As soon as all the colleagues had left, tired from their hangovers and too blind to see that Sophia was not with them, Sophia relaxed even more. Less than an hour later she had moved into his apartment, and after a late breakfast they had relaxed together in the bathtub.

Sophia felt wonderful. It was all peaceful, calm and serene. Nick was so tender and caring, and she could feel the love growing. They washed each other's hair and splashed water and foam on each other. They laughed a lot and kissed even more. After he wrote a love message on her back, she wrote the answer on his thigh and shortly after they agreed to leave the bathtub. They settled down in their favourite spot in front of the fireplace and Nick was glad to be able to repeat the promise she had so shamelessly broken the night before.

"So you really meant forever." She laughed with a sigh as his lips began their journey over her body.

"Exactly ... forever."

They laughed and Sophia was so happy, but had no idea that he really meant what he said. Nick looked at her for a moment but kept his thoughts to himself. After all, it had only been a few weeks, although it felt like so much longer. He couldn't do that!

"What are you thinking about?"

"About the fact that I love you very much."

Sophia laughed, but of course she knew it was true.

"If you did," she teased him, "you wouldn't torture me like this."

"I don't find kissing you torturous."

"You know what I mean."

"Hmm, no." He laughed knowingly and kissed very slowly down her neck.

"Yes, you do."

"I don't know, just tell me." He let his lips wander over her shoulder and lingered quite a long time on a pretty beauty spot on the side of her left breast.

"You like it too much that I'm ..." she moaned, "will-less."

"You can't call it will-less, you tug at me, pull my hair and I do exactly what you want." Smirking, he shrugged his shoulders, but he didn't stop caressing her, pressing his lips elsewhere until she followed his words with action and pulled him closer.

Later, they ate by the large window in his living room and watched the snowflakes dance through the air.

"Do you want to go for a walk?"

"I'd love to," she said enthusiastically, smiling at him. "I was beginning to think you were serious about us not leaving your apartment all weekend." She grinned cheekily at him, and the look on her face told him she liked the idea too.

"I was serious, but a bit of fresh air will do us good, and I think there's enough snow now." He winked at her and she knew he was implying a snowball fight.

For now, they just walked along the magical snowy beach and Nick casually told her that the new chemistry and special paper he had ordered for further enlargements had arrived.

"When should we do it?"

Sophia was excited, but then the cruel thought occurred to her that they didn't have that much time left.

"I was thinking next weekend when your parents are coming."

"That's good, I'll be busy then and won't have to go Christmas shopping with them." She nodded and pressed her head against his shoulder, ignoring the burgeoning pain as she realised time was passing too quickly.

"Will you stay with me then?" asked Nick, pressing his nose into her hair.

Sophia looked up at him and detected a sign of insecurity. Heavens, how much she loved him! She didn't want to disappoint him and would gladly do so, but she had doubts.

"I'm not sure if ..."

"Because of Ruben?" It was a rhetorical question, for he knew the answer, even if Sophia remained silent.

While he had been able to control himself at work and at the Christmas party, at that moment he was almost unable to suppress his anger at how Ruben had threatened her!

"It's my house too." He growled and Sophia pressed even closer, hoping to calm him down. "And my company too!"

"I know."

"What he has done!" He stopped abruptly.

"He didn't do anything." Sophia tried to calm Nick down. Even though she had been startled by how close Ruben had come to her in the conference room, and since she had been standing at the table, she had not been able to back away.

"But he has!"

The fact that Ruben had cornered Sophia physically was unforgivable. Ruben had then also threatened her that she would lose her job if she didn't keep her hands off Nick. Nick would gladly do things to him in return that he hadn't done since they were out of their teens.

"I can't be in the same house after he said I would destroy the

308

company and your family." Sophia said these words with a sad expression on her face, but another reason was that she didn't want to share Nick with others, especially if Ruben tried to separate them. He wouldn't like to see her in his house, even if it was actually the whole family's house.

"I will tell him to leave."

"But..."

"No buts, Sophia." Nick stroked her cheek and kissed her on the tip of her nose. "If he doesn't leave on his own, I'll make him leave."

The fire in his eyes told her that Nick meant what he said, but then Ruben would be right that she was the cause of trouble and strife in the family. Sophia knew how much Nick loved his family. Under no circumstances did she want to cause a rift, and she also knew that she was the only one who could do something about it. Sophia leaned harder against him, because she desperately needed a kiss.

Although anger still burned in his eyes, his lips tenderly brushed hers and she sighed as she felt his warmth. The tingling in her stomach became a burning and she needed him closer. One hand curled into the collar of his coat and the other wrapped around his middle as if she would never let him go. That's what she tried to show him when she opened her lips and let his hungry tongue in. He held her face with both hands and it was as if they were one.

They stayed for a while until they just couldn't take it anymore and left the beach as fast as they could. They ran up the hill to the hotel and didn't even notice when they ran past Yvonne and Jörn who were eating cake in one of the cafés.

As is always the case with beautiful things, these too eventually pass and much later than planned, they left Pielsand on Sunday evening. Nick dropped her off at home and promised to come over.

"If it's too late though, I won't come, I don't want to wake you." He looked at the watch and groaned, but she touched his arm and handed him a small box with a smile.

"For you."

He looked at the box questioningly. For a moment his imagination ran away with him, but then he opened the box and stared at the gift.

"I was going to give it to you earlier, but well, I was a bit distracted." She grinned, but he didn't respond to the innuendo. "I thought it would be ok, because you ..." suddenly unsettled by his unreadable look, Sophia let the sentence hang unfinished in the air.

"Sophia." Nick breathed her name in that special way and she raised her eyes to meet his.

Only then did she notice that he was beaming all over, and although it was already dark, she felt as if the sun had risen. His smile was simply everything.

"Thank you." He leaned closer and stroked her face, genuinely touched. "I'll see you later then." he said in an amused voice to lighten the serious mood, holding up the key she had had made for him.

She laughed and gave him a pat on the arm before getting out to get her bag from the boot, but of course he jumped out too and didn't let her go until he had thanked her properly for the gift. And what a gift it was! A huge one, with a lot of meaning. Symbolically it was always a key to the heart, practically it was the key to her apartment, but he just knew it was the key to her life. Sophia had let him in, and he would nestle in there, never to leave.

Unfortunately, at the moment, he had to go and talk to Ruben, despite the fact that he would love to hit him, but of course didn't really plan to. But honestly, only ten minutes later he was already very tempted to do it.

When he came into the house, his siblings and Tea were sitting in the living room.

"Nick!" Tea greeted him kindly and hugged him, but when she asked him how the Christmas party was, he interrupted her and pointed at Ruben instead.

"I need to talk to you."

"What, why?" Ruben was innocence personified and actually Nick didn't want to do it in front of the others and asked him to come into the kitchen with him, but Ruben refused and replied like a patron, "I have nothing to hide!"

"Is that so?" Nick asked sarcastically and the softly murmured conversation between Yvonne and Tea immediately fell silent.

"No." Ruben laughed and seemed genuinely convinced that he had intimidated Sophia into not telling Nick, but fortunately there were no more secrets between them.

"Are you sure?", Nick asked again and gave Ruben a penetrating look, so that he became a little uneasy, but still acted as if he had nothing to blame himself for. He raised his hands and said gallantly, with a slight laugh.

"I didn't do anything."

"Nothing?" Nick roared, and everyone stared at him in shock. "Didn't you threaten Sophia that she would lose her job if she didn't keep her hands off me?" Nick deliberately chose the same words and Ruben's face fell.

"What?" Jörn slowly got up from the chair he had been sitting on, as he sensed that Nick was about to explode.

"That's not true!" Ruben tried to talk his way out of it. "I mean .. it was ... I ..."

"You cornered her. You said she was just a distraction for me, nothing more!" Nick was so angry that his voice was hoarse and his body completely tensed.

"Is that what she said? She's lying!"

"No." Nick had not the slightest doubt that it was just as Sophia had told him.

"I was just ... Trying to figure out what she wants from you." Ruben shrugged.

"What she wants from me?" Nick took a step forward and Ruben jumped up, stupidly holding his glass so that the rest of his red wine dripped onto the carpet.

"Yeah, what she wants!" he shouted, "she wants to take everything away from me! My photographers, my money and my company!"   "

Yours?" Yvonne rarely got angry, but you could tell by her big eyes, which slowly deformed into narrow slits. Everyone waited for Ruben's explanation.

"I mean ours, of course." Ruben said angrily, but the words hung in the air, as heavy as the dark red wine he had drunk.

He looked angrily at Nick, who just shrugged, after all he had warned him.

"But I know she's one of those," Ruben continued.

"Excuse me?"

Everyone looked at him as Nick rushed towards Ruben, but before he could say or do anything, Yvonne asked with horror in her voice.

"Is that why you pushed Nick to go to New York?" She looked from one brother to the other.

"To separate them!" Shouted Jörn, he knew how much Nick loved Sophia and stared at his eldest brother in disbelief and then back at Yvonne.

"She will destroy our family!" Ruben shouted in despair. "Look! It's starting already!"

"That's nonsense!" Nick's voice was a loud growl, like that of an angry lion. "You do it, only you!" He ran his fingers through his hair to calm himself, not wanting to wake the children.

"You're never here anymore!" scolded Ruben, as if Nick had to give him a report and as if that was what this argument was all about. "And you don't do what I want!" Ruben stamped his foot. "Because of her!"

"My decision about New York has nothing to do with her!" Nick replied, even if that was not entirely true.

Ruben ignored Nick's words and remarked in a low, nasty voice. "She'll string you along forever until she dumps you too! And she will after she gets everything, she stole from me!"

"She's my girlfriend, deal with it!" Nick tried to ignore the cruel implication behind Ruben's words.

"It's not your business alone, Ruben!" Shouted Jörn at the same time and Ruben replied, "You don't know anything!" as if Jörn was still a little boy.

"He's grown up." Tea said quietly to reassure everyone, and no one knew whether she meant Jörn or Nick. Then she touched Nick's arm. "Bring Sophia sometime, I'd love to meet her."

"I'd love to, on Friday for the weekend," he stared at Ruben again, "but as you can imagine, she doesn't want to come."

"Oh, is she scared? Is she going to sue me?" Shouted Ruben in a childishly disguised voice.

"She's not scared!" gasped Nick, "and you're lucky she loves me too much to sue you!" Although that would never have occurred to Sophia.

"You're going." said Jörn to Ruben.

"Yes!" Yvonne nodded in agreement.

"Now this… *girl* is driving me out of my house!" he was running red, so much he yelled that sentence.

"Except it's not just *your* house!" Tea shook her head at her husband and looked to Nick, trying to reassure him that Ruben would be leaving on Friday.

"Thank you!" Nick smiled.

Like a defiant child, Ruben pushed past the others and wanted to leave the room. But as he tried to get past Nick, the latter grabbed him by the collar.

"If you ever threaten Sophia again ..." Nick's voice was low and dangerous.

Ruben remembered the time Nick had beaten him up after holding Jörn under water for a dangerously long time to force him to swim. Nick had been fifteen then and skinny as a stick, but like a wild animal when someone hurt the ones, he loved the most. Ruben didn't want to feel his fists today or ever again. He grimaced, and if everyone looked closely, they saw his slight nod before he left the room.

"I'll talk to him." said Tea, and Nick smiled slightly at her. "What has gotten into him?"

Yes, the rest of the siblings were sure of it, this was the side of Ruben that Tea never got to see.

"He should be happy for you, right?" She gave Nick a kiss on the cheek and followed her husband up the stairs.

"I had no idea that was the reason for all the fights you had." Yvonne and shook her head. "I thought he only wanted you in New York because he didn't trust Jörn to do it!"

Yvonne had always found Ruben's behaviour towards Jörn so unfair, he always had to thwart him as if he was still a little child! Luckily the three of them had voted against him. "But that Sophia is the reason ..."

"She isn't. The reason is that Ruben wants to control everything and everyone." said Nick with his voice hoarse from yelling. "I think he was trying to drive a wedge between us so I would do what he wanted."

"Because you just watch him too closely.", Jörn explained, chuckling sarcastically, and Nick looked at him with pride. For years he had been sure that Jörn could develop better if he was far away from Ruben, who still considered him a little boy. The three of them were of the same opinion that Nick could take much better care of Ruben. But that was not easy for Ruben to accept.

"We should keep an eye on him." Yvonne looked anxiously up the stairs, "I'm worried about him."

All three nodded in agreement.

They talked a bit more until Nick went to get some things and then went back to Sophia's, sneaking into her apartment with his own key. It was a sublime feeling to lie down next to her, to feel her warmth and without her really waking up, she snuggled up to him. He knew that this was exactly what he wanted for the rest of his life. Yes, exactly that!

Every night after that they lay together, either him sneaking in or, even nicer, them lying down together. It was an intense week with a lot of work, but they enjoyed every moment they were together. On Thursday evening Sophia packed her bag so she could spend the weekend with Nick. He saw her stuffing all her lingerie into the bag and was curious what her excuse was.

"You have plans." He wrapped his arms around her, breathed his next words into her neck. "Tell me."

"No plans, just nothing my mum needs to find."

"No plans?" He lifted her up and spun her around. "I'll show you my plans."

He tickled her. Sophia laughed and his heart lifted at the sound and he watched her face and her eyes lit up as they locked with his. She and her laughter were so beautiful and he knew he would hear her laugh even if there was nothing else to hear.

It was seared into his soul.

On Friday, Sophia left the office a little early to meet her parents at her flat and then went to Nick's house. Yvonne was there and she smiled happily to have her there and pulled her into the kitchen. Jörn was mixing drinks and Nick was at the oven cooking. Ruben and his family were in Pielsand and Yvonne told Sophia that Tea was looking forward to meeting her.

"Are you going home to your parents for Christmas?", she asked, and Sophia told her that she was leaving two days early to help her mother with her younger siblings, who were of course always very excited before Christmas.

They told each other some funny Christmas stories from their childhood and every now and then Sophia learned some naughty and dangerous things Nick had done when he was younger. She looked at him with an expression on her face as if she wanted to scold him, but he just came around the table and kissed her lovingly.

When Sophia was in the bathroom for a moment, Yvonne patted Nick's arm and when he turned to her, she hugged him.

"You're so in love." She smiled broadly.

"I know." He replied with a laugh, but caught himself when he saw Yvonne's serious look.

"She's adorable."

"She is." Yes, he knew that too.

"I know you made your decision about New York before, but now it makes it even better."

Nick nodded and gave his sister a kiss on the cheek.

It was a very cosy evening and the four of them got on very well, until Yvonne became a little sad in view of the upcoming farewell in a few days. For her, it would be nicest if they all stayed together forever.

The next morning, Sophia and Nick got up early to have breakfast with her parents at the nice café around the corner. Sophia had told her parents about Nick and that he was one of her bosses, which of course they didn't approve of. So she was a little nervous, but that subsided as soon as they sat down. Her parents not only knew that Sophia did not fall in love easily, but they also saw with their own eyes how serious she was. As the men stood at the counter to get another round of coffee, her mother leaned in and hugged Sophia.

"He's ... well, he's ..."

"Wonderful." Sophia gave her mother an appropriate word and she nodded, pleased to see her daughter happy.

"It seems like you've been together for a while."

"Yeah, we get that feeling sometimes too." Sophia admitted, pleased that her parents seemed to have taken Nick to their hearts already.

"It looks like you two fit really well together."

"We do." Sophia confirmed confidently, smiling and nibbling on a strawberry that was lying on one of the plates as a decoration.

"We really do!" Nick confirmed when Sophia told him about it while they went into the darkroom to enlarge the photos Sophia had taken in Pielsand.

There was one of the pictures she liked best and she stared at it until Nick teased her that just staring at it wouldn't make it dry any faster.

"I love that picture," she admitted. It was the picture she'd taken of Nick on the beach just as it was starting to snow harder, and she'd been lucky enough to get a few snowflakes in the picture with him. If she had coloured it, it could have been mistaken for falling leaves in autumn.

317

"It reminds me of that picture of you."

"What picture of me?" she asked curiously.

"Here." Nick tapped his head and said that ever since they had first met, he had saved that picture of her under the tree with the falling leaves.

"The leaves were dancing around you."

He smiled at the memory and pulled her out of the darkroom, after all the pictures could dry without them.

"And you fell in love with me right then and there!" she joked, and he stopped abruptly on the stairs and turned to her with a serious face.

"Yes." He took her hand and kissed it. "I remember all the details, it was all like slow motion."

Sophia was speechless after this explanation. They both had feelings for each other since exactly the same time. It was unbelievable. Her heart lifted, fluttered around in her chest like an excited little bird, and then beat normally again, as if the little excited bird had finally settled down.

Then they climbed the stairs to his rooms and sat down on the terrace with thick blankets and talked for most of the rest of the day. Later, when they were looking at the photos, Sophia caught Nick staring at her with a slight smile and a sort of festive expression on his face, and she asked him what was going on.

"Oh, I just love having you with me." He was not yet ready to say everything that was going through his mind and smiled to assure her that he was absolutely happy.

"I also love having you with me." Sophia said it much more seriously and he felt the light-heartedness of the moment fade.

"Hey, don't think about it."

He reached for her and pulled her onto his lap. Sophia let her fingers run over his three-day beard and bent down to kiss him. When she broke away, he saw a small tear steal into her eye, but she blinked it away.

"I'm sorry", she shrugged, "I've known for so long, but now it hit me ... I suddenly realised you were leaving so soon."

"We still have a few days."

She nodded and kissed him so tenderly, in such a real way, that he felt she was giving him her soul. In return, he was ready to give her his as well and decided, before leaving for New York, to say the things that burned in his heart.

Although they knew he had to go, they tried - as best they could - to ignore the fact that their time together was running out. But finally the day came and they stood together in her hallway, holding each other close. Sophia could not suppress her feelings and tears ran down her face.

"I'm so sorry", she cried. "I didn't want to cry, I feel so stupid."

"I'll miss you too." But the word didn't come close to what it meant to leave her.

"It's complete nonsense," she sniffed, "but it's like it's forever."

"It's not, I'll be back sooner than you think."

"I know. It's just been so intense the last few weeks. It feels like we've been together forever." That word again.

"We will." he said in a strange voice. His breathing quickened as Sophia noticed between her sobs and looked up at him.

"Sophia."

His face took on a strange expression. Somehow again so festive, as if he was moved and overly nervous. There were just too many feelings in her to read everything.

"I am so happy I met you." He finally said with his wry smile, and Sophia smiled too, although her heart slipped into her pants. This was it, this was the goodbye.

"Me too." Her voice was just a whisper.

"I'll do everything to keep it that way."

Sophia pressed even more against him, she knew he would come back, but it hurt so much, as if a part of her had been amputated.

"I know it's so early, we haven't been together that long and I erm mean, I just wanted you to know that you are ... well, that you're *all* I've ever wanted, even though I didn't even know I wanted it... until I met you." It burst out of him in a gush.

With that little, magical crease between her eyebrows, Sophia looked at him. Her heart was hammering in her chest and the blood was rushing in her head. What was going on here?

"I love you, too." She simply said.

Nick's face looked as if he was about to cry, as if he was exhausted and broken and infinitely lost. Sophia was so touched by the fact that he felt the same way she did.

"I love you and ..." he cleared his throat, "I just want you."

Sophia could only nod, what did he want to tell her? *Talk! Talk!* She screamed in her head, but remained silent so as not to interrupt him. Her heart had an inkling of what he might say, but she didn't want to believe it, she couldn't believe it!

"Sophia..."

The doorbell rang. It was Jörn and Yvonne, who came to pick him up on the way to the airport. Nick gritted his teeth, pressed the intercom and growled that he would be right down.

"We will continue this conversation when I'm back." he muttered, annoyed that things had not gone as he had planned. Yet, he also didn't quite know whether what he had actually planned would have been right. It was all so confusing. He had wanted to delay saying goodbye and then tell her everything and ask her, and now it was too late.

"Tell me now!" her voice was a soft rasp and he tenderly caressed her face.

"Sophia."

"I can't wait. What if Jörn needs you longer?" No! He can't leave her without saying what he wanted to say, even if she had a small idea of what it was.

"He doesn't!"

"Please tell me what you wanted to say!", Sophia begged, clawing at his coat and looking at him so intensely as if she could suck the words out of his mouth with that look. The doorbell rang again and Nick shouted into the intercom that he would be right there.

"When I'm back."

"It'll be forever before you are back."

"Sweetie, it's only twelve days!" Chuckling, he tried to ease her worry.

"That's too long." Sophia pierced him with her gaze.

He sighed, as if it were so hard. In this case it was. When Sophia looked at him with her big, moss-green eyes, warm and tender, he couldn't resist. One last breath, then he gathered all his courage, leaned closer to her ear and asked the question she couldn't wait to answer.

Chapter 24

Sophia felt his breath tickle her skin as he said the words that instantly changed her life. It was so unbelievable. She could neither think about it nor stop thinking about it.

"Will you marry me?"

"Yes."

Silence. A heartbeat. The touch of the next words.

"Do you?"

"I do."

"You want to marry me?" He suddenly held her at arm's length, searching her eyes for the truth.

"Nick, I told you, I won't repeat it." She grinned, knowing he wanted her to say it.

"Please say it."

"I love you."

"The other thing." He was grinning now too.

"Yes, I'll marry you." Sophia couldn't see the tears in his eyes as hers robbed her of the sight of him.

"That sounds so good." He kissed her on the forehead.

"Yes, it does."

Their laughter was full of happiness and they lay in each other's arms. As he kissed her neck, Nick repeated the fact.

"You will marry me."

Then there was a knock at the door and Jörn called from outside that they really had to hurry. Sophia's heart clenched and she fought against it, but reason, her stupid, stupid reason prevailed and she opened the door for Jörn.

"We really need to ..."

"She will marry me." interrupted Nick, who beamed, kissed Sophia once more and wiped away her tears.

She cried silently with joy and longing and for the pain of the separation, even if it was only for a short time. The next moment Sophia felt herself pressed against Jörn, who gave her a loud smack on the cheek and at the same time pushed his somewhat silly grinning brother out of the apartment.

"I wish you'd done this sooner so we could have celebrated, but now we have to go!" cried Jörn, wiping his eyes.

"Aren't you happy for me?", Nick called out in a playfully annoyed voice, nothing could spoil his mood, his heart seemed to burst with happiness. Once again, he went to Sophia and hugged her until Jörn threatened to lose patience and push him down the stairs if he didn't go down immediately.

Sophia didn't want to make it any harder for them both, nodded, waved to Nick and took the one step back into the apartment and closed the door. She wanted to go to the window and watch after him, but she couldn't move for a while.

Had that really just happened? Were they about to be married? She thought about that fact, the truth throbbing in her heart with every beat, but her head didn't understand it until that moment.

Slowly she realised that she was the luckiest woman in the world. She held the door handle for what felt like an eternity until the ringing of her mobile phone woke her from her trance. Sophia hurried into the kitchen and answered her phone.

"Are you sure?" his voice was breathless.

"Yes, I am." And she was.

"We're getting married." he repeated, as if he couldn't quite yet believe it himself.

"Yes."

"You're really saying yes?"

Sophia giggled at his silliness. "Of course, silly."

"Why silly?"

"If you don't know that I've been yours for months, I don't know if I should marry you. You're silly ... and crazy." she joked, feeling a little lighter.

"Heavens, I love you." Nick sighed contentedly.

Silence. This pleasant silence once again filled the air.

"Sophia."

"Hmm?"

"And I'm yours."

"I know." Sophia laughed and shook her head, he really was just as crazy as she was.

Even hours later and during an annoying, tough negotiation with a client, Sophia couldn't suppress her grin. Repeatedly, she stroked the spot below her ear that Nick had touched with the words she had secretly wished for but had not dared to hope for. It was absolute madness! They had only been a couple for such a short time and so much had already happened. But because they had been secretly in love for so long, it seemed so right to them both. One question kept running through Sophia's mind: what would their families say? But then she remembered Jörn's reaction, how happy he was for them both, and the doubts disappeared.

A little later, as she and her colleagues were putting the new photographers' portfolios back in the cupboards, Yvonne asked her into her office. Sophia had hardly entered the room when Yvonne closed the door and hugged her.

"Honestly ..." Yvonne shook her head, "you two!" She took a handkerchief and wiped her eyes. "I'm so happy for him ... for you too, of course."

Yvonne laughed and gave Sophia another hug.

"Maybe you'd like to have dinner with me and Tea tomorrow or Friday?"

"Yes, very much!" Sophia was happy, since she recognised in Yvonne the honesty that also radiated from Jörn.

"But you'll wait to tell Ruben, won't you?" Yvonne suddenly looked a little worried.

"I'm not going to tell him." Sophia declared with a vigorous shake of her head that under no circumstances did she want to give him any more reasons to hate her.

"He doesn't hate you. It has nothing to do with you, it's ..." Yvonne shrugged. "This thing with Cora has taken its toll on all of us. Why do you think mostly men or married people work here? He doesn't trust Nick in making the right decision in matters of the heart."

It was clear to Sophia that Yvonne, as the most harmony-seeking of the siblings, always tried to justify everything the others did. She couldn't blame her for that, she had always tried to do the same with her friends.

"I think it's like Nick said: Ruben always wants to control everything so that something like that doesn't happen again."

Sophia said nothing, but of course knew about the conversation between the siblings.

"Only he should finally realise that Nick has also learned from the past. Of course, he has!"

Yvonne's gaze wandered out of the window, into a past Sophia knew only from rumours, until she heard Nick's version and read the lawyer's files. Now she heard Yvonne's version.

How hard it had been for the whole family. That Cora had treated Nick like that had been a shock to everyone. That the break-up and *how* it had happened had hit him so hard and that his siblings were standing by more or less helpless, as they didn't know what to do.

Yvonne and Jörn had not even been twenty. Ruben had had to manage everything on his own. He made sure that Nick got back on track. Till he stopped going to every party and getting drunk all the time. He had forced him to get a grip on himself. Sent him abroad, put him in charge of the shootings on location, which had been a big step for him. Handing over responsibility and trusting someone - even if it was his own brother - like that. It had worked, just like the company itself. Under his leadership and Nick's efforts to numb the pain of his broken heart with work in the future, the company had become more successful. They had been a good team, everything had worked out.

Until Nick suddenly no longer wanted to do what Ruben asked him to do and additionally took a closer look at the finances.

"Nick just wanted to finally be back with us, at home, you know?" Yvonne smiled at Sophia and then nodded. "That he had fallen in love, we didn't know." She shook her head with a grin. "Gosh, considering he's been wrestling with himself for almost a year!"

Yvonne wiped her eyes again and Sophia's heart lifted at these words. He really had been in love with her for as long as she had been in love with him. As crazy and improbable as that was!

"That's why Ruben has to realise that it's serious." Yvonne stroked Sophia's arm encouragingly, "You'll see, everything will be fine."

Even though Sophia wanted to believe Yvonne, she knew deep in her heart that things with Ruben were not that simple. Even if he eventually came to terms with the idea that they were a couple and wanted to marry - here her heart leapt again and that warmth crept into every part of her body - his behaviour towards her would not be so easily forgotten.

His choleric shouting would still have been forgivable, the harassment in the conference room not so easy. So close he had come to her that she could have counted every large pore in his face and the firm grip on her upper arm. The saliva that hung in the corner of his mouth like an angry dog.

No, that was something Sophia couldn't forgive, especially not if he didn't at least apologise for it in a believable manner. And she knew Nick couldn't do that either.

Jörn pushed his way through the crowds that flowed towards him and Nick as they rushed from one advertising agency to the next. Acquiring appointments face to face was in his blood. Nick watched him with amusement and was sure that he could sell even rusty nails to people, as charmingly as he wrapped everyone around his little finger. Only the very short times between the appointments did not seem to agree with the traffic and the oncoming stream of pedestrians. That was something Jörn urgently needed to work out.

"Oh!", Nick exclaimed and stopped abruptly in front of a shop window.

"What' s up?" his brother shouted and Nick pointed to a ring. "Don't tell me you proposed without a ring?" Jörn asked this in a tone as if it were the greatest human failing, he could imagine.

"Well, I um ... it wasn't quite thought through, I guess." Nick admitted contritely.

"No, I guess it wasn't." Jörn pulled a face and shook his head as if he really resented Nick for that.

"But it was important."

"Yes, I know." Jörn patted his brother on the shoulder and looked at his watch. "We have to."

"But that's her ring!" Nick was so sure, just as sure as the moment he asked her the question of all questions. Jörn smirked at his desperate face.

"You go in there and I'll go to our appointment." Jörn turned to go.

"Jörn!" Nick grabbed his brother's arm and tugged him back. "I can't do this alone."

"But you have to, we only have eight minutes ..."

"No, I mean ... I need *you* by my side ... be my ..." Nick smiled that warm happy smile and Jörn was touched and nodding already before Nick finished his sentence, "be my best man."

"I will be, whenever you want me to be." Jörn hugged Nick, patted him on the back, then turned and hurried away.

As the days went by, Sophia and Nick wrote each other messages and even spoke on the phone between appointments and in the evenings. While Sophia looked at the photo of him in Pielsand with the snowflake in front of the lens, they talked about their day until Sophia went to bed. When Sophia didn't think about him sleeping so many hours away in his hotel bed, but imagined that he was only a few minutes away from her in his family's house, it somehow made it more bearable for her. Every now and then, gloomy thoughts crept into her mind, but she immediately pushed them away. As soon as she got up in the morning, she crossed off the days on the calendar and immediately sent him a message with the most important information of the day.

Only 10 days left.

The days flew by and her date with Yvonne and Tea was the only thing that got Sophia through the rest of the week. She was happy to get to know them better and it was a lovely evening at the Mexican restaurant Nick had told her about. What she found particularly relaxing was that they didn't try to ask her about Nick or their relationship, but asked her questions about her, her family and her interests. A few things they already knew and she was pleased that Nick had told them about her passion for photography.

Tea told some nice little anecdotes about her children, what they had planned for Christmas, and Yvonne got a little sad again, because it was the first time in years that they wouldn't celebrate Christmas all together.

Sophia was glad they were going to her parents' house, she couldn't think of anything worse than spending the holidays with Ruben and his constant nagging and trying to persuade Nick to do what he wanted.

When she got home, she called Nick and told him about the evening. He was glad that she got on well with his sister and sister-in-law and hoped that Tea could convince Ruben to shut up and leave Sophia alone. After they had talked a little more, he was about to leave for his next appointment and they hung up with the words: "Not much longer!"

But the nights were long and lonely. Sophia missed him, although the sensible side of her said he would be back soon. She held to him as he did, and bonded together she dreamed of him almost every night. When she sent him her daily "good morning" message two days later at half past seven in the morning, he answered immediately.

I'm going to bed now and I'll dream about you.

Why are you up so late?

A few moments later he called her and told her about his day, the many appointments they had and that Jörn had got a room in an old friend's shared flat. It had been quite spontaneous and he had moved in immediately. Afterwards they had dinner and celebrated a bit.

"I can hear that," Sophia remarked, amused, and Nick claimed he hadn't drunk that much, but judging by his very soft pronunciation, it definitely had to have been more than one or two glasses of wine. She thought it was kind of cute when he tried to explain.

"Well, I was celebrating," he admitted, chuckling, "because I'm engaged."

"Really?"

Somehow it sounded so strange when she heard that word.

"To the most enchanting woman who ever lived."

Laughing, Sophia blamed his words on the alcohol, but he was serious and tried to convince her. They talked a little more until Sophia told him that she had to hurry to go to work and that he should get some sleep since the day included an appointment at the bank.

Sophia went to work with a happy smile. She thought of Nick all the time and imagined how he went to the appointments with Jörn and how the two of them charmed everyone. How he tried hard not to yawn during the boring appointment with the banker and how he also crossed off the day in the calendar in the evening. Still absorbed in her thoughts, she went into her office. As usual, her colleagues were not there yet, they always arrived at least half an hour after her, but she was startled when she saw someone sitting behind her desk.

"Are you *finally* here?"

She tried not to let that spoil her mood and replied with a smile. "Good morning, Ruben."

He just nodded and slowly got up, coming around the desk just as slowly. "Just because you get to call yourself his girlfriend for a few minutes doesn't mean you can come and go as you please."

Sophia stared at him in disbelief.

"He'll get tired of you anyway and stay in New York."

She just shook her head mutely.

"As long as *you're* here, he won't come back." He slowly moved closer and closer to her and lowered his head down to her, not as close as in the conference room, but uncomfortable nonetheless. "I assure you of that."

Sophia knew, of course, that what Ruben was saying was not the truth, but still tears pricked her eyes. She couldn't believe it, why was Ruben so mean? Nick's theory was that Ruben thought he could cause trouble between them that way and provoke a break-up so Nick would stay in New York. But was Ruben really that blind? Did he really think it would be so easy to turn them against each other?

"Did you know they share the office with Bergmann?"

Sophia felt a cold shiver run down her spine and apparently Ruben could tell, it was just as he had planned, for he grinned smugly and walked out.

After only a few clicks Sophia had found out who else was based in the building complex where Nick and Jörn had moved into the New York office. There was indeed a *"Bergmann Com"*, but that was a computer company and had nothing whatsoever to do with Cora Bergmann. Her company, or rather her husband's company, did not even have an office outside Germany.

While Sophia was thinking about what Ruben was really up to, her phone rang and the idea that had been forming in her head for some time took on even more concrete form.

For one thing was clear: Ruben would not stop trying to drive a wedge between them both.

"Still five days!" Nick groaned, stared out the window of the tiny office and watched the traffic below him without really seeing anything.

He wanted to go home. To Sophia. He missed her. So much. Her laugh, her scent, her soft skin and kisses. And her smile, her beautiful smile. Just talking on the phone was not enough. The photo book with the pictures of Pielsand that she had secretly stuffed in his bag only made it harder for him. He could not look at the pictures, they made him sad. He wanted to be close to her again. Undisturbed. The feeling of loss was terrible. Without her, he felt like he was missing a part of his body. It was almost a little ridiculous how he felt, but that was how it was. He needed to know she was near him, to feel her.

"Here!" Jörn handed him a sheet of paper with various departure dates and grinned.

"What shall I do with this?"

"Change your flight, fly back and surprise her." That was clear enough.

"But ... Jörn, I ..."

"I can manage on my own and Yvonne will be here soon."

"Are you sure?"

"Yes," with that Jörn went back to his desk. "And your whining is annoying."

Nick laughed and took his phone out of his pocket to change his flight.

"I look forward for you working for me!", Kristina Schneider said cheerfully and hugged Sophia. She knew that this young woman could be her deputy at some point. She had only heard positive things about her and was sure she had that special eye for spotting talented photographers and knew from shootings together that she was great at organising.

Although she believed the real reason for leaving the Falkner company was Ruben. He hated couples within the company and voiced his displeasure at every event if he thought something was brewing between colleagues.

Being part of the gossip was always exhausting and Kristina knew from experience how much it could strain the relationship. She was happy for Sophia that she had found love in Nick Falkner, but she was also absolutely sure that it would be better for him to look after his brother without worrying about his girlfriend all the time.

For Sophia it was a big step. She would be working for one of the biggest photo magazines, and she would no longer be a service provider but on the client side. It was exciting and scary at the same time, but neither Kristina nor Nick doubted that she could do it if she wanted to. Sophia wanted the change and firmly believed that it was better for everyone. She didn't want to be constantly used by Ruben as leverage against Nick. He couldn't protect her all the time and she couldn't protect him either. At some point she would probably interfere and tell Ruben what she really thought of him, and that in turn would lead to further tension between the brothers. Sophia only hoped that her rather spontaneous decision would not lead to tension between Nick and her. He knew she had thought about accepting Kristina's job offer, but she hadn't told him yet. She thought it was somehow inappropriate to do it over the phone, but decided to tell him in the evening anyway, after all she had to quit as soon as possible.

Oh, she missed Nick, she felt almost sick, unable to eat or do anything but think of him. How can you miss someone so much that it really hurt all over?

Sophia's rational side feared that she had caught a virus or that all the stress with Ruben and the girls beforehand had taken its toll. As she dragged herself home late that evening, she took a hot bath and tried to relax. That didn't work, though, since she kept looking at her phone and wondering why Nick wasn't answering her messages.

She knew they had a lot to do in New York. Their schedules were full and they already had two photo shoots to organise locally, but she still had such a terrible longing for him that she wished she could just beam him over.

She closed her eyes and dreamed of him lying in the bathtub with her. This cold emptiness tugged at her heart and she wrote him another message. It hurt. It wasn't as bad as her earlier heartbreak, but it was still similar. Or almost worse, because she now knew what it felt like to be loved by him. To have him with her. Why hadn't he answered her? Was he so stressed that he had switched off his phone? How could she help him? Did he miss her too or was he too busy with everything else? Was he regretting his decision not to take over the office after all?

The sensible side of her told her that it didn't mean anything and that she simply had no reception in the bathroom. After a while, she got out of the bath, wrapped herself in a towel, brushed her teeth, but no matter how long she stared at the phone, he didn't answer.

Disappointed, Sophia lay down in bed. Suddenly, she was infinitely exhausted. She didn't even care that her hair was still damp and she was only wearing her bathrobe. Nothing would make her leave the bed to put on her pyjamas. She never wanted to leave this warmth, and she pulled at the blanket that had once been his and buried her face in it. It smelled of her sandalwood-scented laundry soap and not at all of Nick, but still, with it in her arms, she felt closer to him.

Nick felt closer to Sophia as soon as the plane landed, but he forbade himself to call her. He wanted to surprise her and could only hope that she wouldn't be frightened if he suddenly stood by her bed while she slept. Less than an hour later, he quietly opened the door to her apartment and was as quiet as he could be. He showered quickly and brushed his teeth before slipping into the room and kneeling beside the bed. Softly he whispered her name, she turned to him and her hands blindly searched his face.

"Sophia?", his lips found hers and he lingered in that feeling of being home again as he felt her awaken.

"You're here." She whispered sleepily against his lips, tracing the outline with her fingers.

"Yes, I'm here."

"Really?" Her eyes fluttered open, probably thinking she was dreaming.

"Yes, I wanted to surprise you." Even though it was dark, he could see her smile for a moment before she pulled him close.

"Stay and never leave again," she murmured in mock frustration, pulling at him until he was finally beside her.

"Never again."

They both chuckled, happy to be reunited, and he gently stroked the hair from her face. His lips were soft as they touched her face, dripping down her neck and coming to rest beneath her throat.

Sophia let her hands slide tenderly over his chest and pulled his T-shirt over his head. Her bathrobe gaped open and Nick moaned softly when he was finally able to wrap his hands around her waiting

335

curves. His lips left a burning trail as he slowly explored her. The tips of her curves seemed to cry out for him and he took his time giving her what she wanted. Eagerly, yet agonisingly slowly. His fingers sent a tremor through her body and his skin burned too. Her fingers gently caressed the smooth skin of his back and then slowly slid to his boxers. Her lips found every sensitive spot and a shiver gripped him. It had been so long and yet they wanted to savour every little moment. His tenderness touched her and she thought she would dissolve when she finally took him in and their bodies melted into one single feeling.

Sophia permeated his whole being. Nick thought nothing and felt nothing but her. Sophia. Sophia. Incarnated love. It was so much more that he could never find the words for. This connection with her, it was as if they had once been one and years apart. There was nothing he could use to describe it better. She made him whole.

Shaken and completely connected to her and the same feelings, they were caught in this wave, fierce and intense and yet slow and calm. Their bond was never broken and yet it was tied stronger together once more. Nothing else mattered as long as they were together. They had no more words. They no longer needed words. They looked at each other, questioningly, and yet they knew. They knew it was special, this bond that connected them. It was precious and pure.

"Take the day off." He murmured sleepily into the smooth skin of her shoulder as the alarm clock rang the next morning and he pulled her closer. "I need you here in my arms."

"I'd love to, but I have an important appointment."

Sophia's heartbeat quickened, although he knew what she was

about to do, it was something else that she really wanted to do it now. As she remained silent, Nick lifted his head with difficulty, he was still a little groggy from the flight.

"What did he do?"

"I'll tell you later." She didn't want to talk about Ruben, especially not when she was holding a naked Nick in her arms.

"Are you sure?" he then asked, his voice taking on a strange tone.

"Are you angry?"

"No," he smiled slightly, "just sad. I like having you around, and ... well, you love this job." He clenched his jaw, Ruben taking that away from her was the next item on his list of reasons to slap his brother.

"But I love you more.", Sophia said and only her smile stopped Nick from jumping out of bed and running straight to Ruben.

"Only on one condition I'll let you go." He grinned and told her about his plan to give Ruben something to think about. Of course, he didn't say anything about his promise to him, otherwise Sophia would try to talk him out of it.

But he always kept his promises.

Chapter 25

With the resignation in her pocket and the right words in her head, Sophia felt well prepared for the more difficult part of giving her future a new direction. She also had the printout of her remaining holidays and also a list of her many overtime hours which she had received from Yvonne in her purse. The time until Christmas would still be packed to hand everything over to her colleagues, just like the week after her leave over the holidays - which she would spend with Nick and with her family. But when she thought about it, a tingling anticipation gripped her. She could hardly wait to inform the photographers and clients that she would be leaving the company in January.

Most of all, however, she was looking forward to seeing Ruben's reaction, because Nick and his sister were convinced that he was not expecting it. How simple-minded of him, Sophia thought, shaking her head. Did he really think he could treat his employee like that? Yelling, threatening and even getting physical without any consequences? Not to mention Nick's consequences. Sophia didn't know exactly what Nick was planning, but she had sensed that he wasn't going to let his brother get away with it. He could forgive him even less for his behaviour towards her than Sophia herself.

Interrupted by a call from an editor, she was distracted from her reflections and when she hung up twenty minutes later, one of her colleagues told her to go and see the boss.

"He sounded pretty pissed."

Sophia frowned to show that she had no idea what he meant, but she could guess that he knew about Nick's return by now. He would probably repeat his threat or insult them once more. She smiled, he would not expect her reaction to that.

"Good luck." Wished her colleague, and at that moment she noticed for the first time how all her colleagues flitted over the corridors like little scurrying mice. Always careful not to get caught when Ruben was the only Falkner around. She thought about this while she gathered her things and left her office to talk to Ruben. All the colleagues were most relaxed when Nick was in the house with them. It was as if he was the protective wall between them and Ruben, the buffer that gave everyone the security and calm they needed to do their job well. No one was in the mood for Ruben's choleric fits or far-fetched complaints that he made up to distract from other, much more serious problems. Or his own mistakes.

Sophia stopped in front of the stairs and looked up at the glass office for a moment. There sat Ruben. Floating above things, aloof, and everyone had to look up to him, even his siblings. And yet he also seemed like an animal in a terrarium. Shielded and isolated. A hairy spider, with watchful eyes on everyone down here. Looking to catch someone making a mistake so he could devour them in his glass box in front of everyone. Or, as in her case, stomp her down for all to see.

"You are finally here." It was not a question, but Ruben's greeting. He acted as if he had waited forever for her to appear, when less than two minutes had passed since she finished her phone call and knocked on his door.

"Sit down." he commanded gruffly, and Sophia had to refrain from commenting. Wordlessly, she sat down and waited until the busy man in front of her finally deigned to look at her.

"You know why you're here?"

Silently, she shook her head and looked at him, waiting. Ruben nodded with a small, Sophia would almost say nasty, grin and folded his hands in front of him, raised his eyebrows and sighed theatrically.

"Actually, I was always satisfied with your work." The emphasis was, of course, on *actually*. "But lately ... well."

Sophia expected him to say something to her now, like: *since you've been Nick's little girlfriend ....*

"Anyway, let's not go there." he said instead, eyeing her up and down and smiling smugly. "It's come to my attention that you've been acting like a boss."

"Excuse me?" Sophia was shocked, what was that about?

"You control the colleagues when they take their lunch break."

Sophia could not believe what she was hearing. She and her colleagues, with whom she shared the office, simply agreed on when who would take a break so that at least one would stay in the office to take incoming calls. That's exactly what she told Ruben, but he waved her off.

"I don't want to hear that shit."

Still amazed at what this was all about, Sophia immediately fell silent at once and was only able to stare at Ruben.

"Well, Sophia, Sophia." He stood up, went to his cupboard that was against the wall, pushed a few books back and forth and then turned back to her. "Unfortunately, that will add to it."

"To what?" Sophia did not know what Ruben was up to.

He sat back down, leaned back in his chair with a smug expression on his face and put his clasped hands to his mouth as if he was contemplating a difficult decision. However, his sardonic little smile gave him away.

"To the items on the list." he gave her another cryptic reply."I don't know which list you're talking about."

Ruben straightened up, reached into his desk drawer and put a sheet of paper in front of Sophia's nose, she could only make out one word, in thick letters at the top it said warning letter.

Dumbfounded, Sophia stared at the sheet in front of her and then back at Ruben's face, what was she going to get a warning letter for? She was always the first one in the office, rarely went to lunch and never went home on time. Neither clients nor photographers ever complained about her or her way of working. Not even when it was a somewhat difficult shoot or an unpleasant client, or the whole crew was stuck in a traffic jam.

But wait! She closed her eyes, took a deep breath and tried to calm down. That wasn't the point. It didn't matter what it said and that Ruben was trying to intimidate her with that. It was done. Still, she wanted an explanation. And she got one without having asked for it.

"I told you to keep your hands off him."

Sophia did not answer.

"And since you don't seem to want that, I'll have to find other ways."

There was something almost frightening about his smile. Slight madness could be read in it, but she was probably overreacting. Sophia closed her eyes once more, then nodded.

"You want to give me a warning letter for not leaving Nick?"

Ruben didn't say anything at first, but just rested his chin on his folded hands as if he were waiting to hear the rest of what she had to say. Sophia was so bewildered that she could only gasp.

"I told you what I expect you to do." he said in an icy tone and Ruben had never seemed so unbelievably disgusting to her as he did at that moment. "This all has to end."

This statement gave her a deep sting. How could he wish to do this to his brother?

"You're right."

His grin widened and Sophia was amazed at how firm her voice sounded as she continued to speak. "All of this has to end."

Her hands did not tremble a single bit when she took out the letter and presented it to Ruben. She didn't feel if she was smiling, but she felt disbelief take hold of her when he asked his question.

"Your demand?" he laughed, "Nick was convinced you weren't after my money, but well, well."

He opened the envelope, pulled out the sheet and paled. He really hadn't expected her resignation, he stared at her in silence as she stood up.

"Here is a copy from Yvonne listing my remaining holidays and overtime." She handed it to him and without another word she headed for the door.

"You can't do that."

"Yes, I can." She forced a smile.

"I knew it, you're just like that other bitch! You're going to work for the competitors and steal my photographers!", he didn't shout, he said it quietly.

"No I won't."

Sophia looked at Ruben. She was so disappointed. With him and his mistrust, but unfortunately, she could comprehend it, had understanding for it and against her will she also felt sorry for him. And Nick, of course, because the whole thing was a bigger crisis than any of them had ever admitted to themselves.

That Ruben would put up with hurting Nick left a bitter taste in her mouth and showed how little Nick meant to his brother. She briefly considered telling him that she was going to start working for Kristina Schneider, but she shook her head. It was none of his business and he would find out soon enough and probably suck up to her to book photographers for the shoots at *Falkner Production Company* as often as possible.

342

"Get out." Was the only thing he uttered before slumping down in his chair and staring incredulously at the sheet of paper on the desk in front of him, as if it had been written in blood.

A sarcastic thought sprouted in Sophia, after all, she had sweated blood and water often enough when Ruben had been in a fury. She had always been relieved when it wasn't her turn and when it was, it was much more harmless than with some of her colleagues.

She had imagined that Ruben liked her, her modest manner and her work, of course. The fact that she was now getting it worse like all the others before her was once again her own fault, similar to the situation with her friends. But just as in that point, she was glad to close this chapter. Sometimes things just weren't meant to be.

A deep breath later, she went into the kitchen, fetched a fresh coffee and did not look at Ruben once more as she walked past his terrarium to the stairs. With her head held high, she went down. And felt as if she had climbed a high tower, with countless steps, and had finally reached the top.

After exhausting efforts, finally in the fresh air, with a view of the horizon and a pastel-coloured future.

A few hours later, Nick walked past her office, his expression spoke volumes and she struggled to repress a laugh. But as they had planned, she got up with a worried look on her face, walked to the door and watched him as he climbed the stairs to Ruben's office.

Two more steps and she could see Ruben leaning against the banister, a nasty grin on his face. He seemed to really think that Sophia hadn't told Nick about her resignation. Perhaps hoping to drive a wedge between them and chase Nick to New York after the supposed loss of trust.

A few minutes later, the phone rang and Sophia's colleague told her that she was expected by the bosses. Ignoring the chatter and questions from her colleagues, she went up to the glass cube. Nick stood there with his back to her, hands on his hips. She knocked, waited for Ruben's nod and went inside.

"Ruben told me you were leaving?", Nick looked at her with a slight smile.

"Yes."

"Cause Ruben threatened you again?"

Ruben gasped and looked worriedly back and forth between them.

"He said he'd make sure you would stay in New York."

"And today?"

"He gave me a warning letter."

Nick puffed in disdain. "But you had already decided to leave."

"Yes."

"So you accepted Kristina's offer."

"Yes."

"But you love this job." His voice took on a rough tone, but his eyes sparkled.

"I love you more." She repeated her words from the morning.

A step later, Nick took her in his arms and kissed her, and one more time she forgot everything around her. That they were standing in Ruben's office, that Ruben and probably the whole company were watching them. She buried her hands in Nick's hair and he lifted her up a little. She heard him moan softly as they deepened the kiss. Only from a distance did she recognise Ruben's loud snort.

"Stop it!" he shouted.

"I'll kiss my fiancée as much as I can," Nick said, without looking at Ruben.

"What?" Ruben was absolutely shocked. Nick broke away from Sophia and took her hand to show his brother the ring he had given her the night before they had fallen asleep.

"Sophia. My fiancée. The woman I'm going to marry. Any questions?"

Ruben stared at Nick in disbelief, his face turning ashen.

"And I warned you!" growled Nick, before breaking away from Sophia and grabbing his brother by the collar.

Even Sophia's shrieking "No!", couldn't stop him from keeping his promise.

*

"You really hit him?" asked Sophia's father as they sat together after the Christmas dinner, which was once again far too sumptuous, in the Neuhaus family living room.

"Yes.", Nick admitted, embarrassed. He was glad they waited to tell that part of the story until Sophia's younger siblings were busy unwrapping presents. It was important to him that they didn't have to hear it.

Of course, he knew that violence was no solution, but Ruben had deserved it, even Tea had said so and refused to feel sorry for Ruben. Everyone hoped that after the holidays they could find a way to get back to normal with each other. Ruben had to understand what Sophia meant to Nick and not only that, but that it was finally time for him to also let go of the past. He had to learn again to trust others, not only co-workers, but especially his siblings. Together they would find a solution, also in the context of Ruben's money problems, which he has himself to blame for, but only if they were all honest with each other.

"You have truly earned your holiday!", Sophia's mother said and hugged her daughter. "After everything that happened!"

Fortunately, she left it at a meaningful glance, said nothing about the tragedy with the friends.

Even though Sophia was brave and looked to the future with courage to find new ones, Nick knew that she still had a lot to gnaw on. But apart from a few photos of Viviana's wedding dress that she had shared in the group chat, none of the three had contacted Sophia since the conversation, and that fact alone said it all.

Nick watched Sophia with her family and it was so nice to see how carefree and unaffected they were with each other. She was so lovely and sweet with her siblings and a fleeting thought, or rather an image of Sophia with a small child - their child - filled his mind. He bit his lips and shooed the thought away and focused on her parents. He could sense no displeasure that they still resented her decision not to take over the farm. Perhaps the photo book she had made for her parents helped with that. It was as if they were finally seeing, in black and white, where her passion lay.

His face was already hurting from smiling so much, for her family were a bunch of happy people, telling funny anecdotes from Sophia's childhood and their own, and laughing so heartily that his heart lifted every time. And since it happened so often, he almost felt a little giddy.

Nick was relieved when he was able to withdraw a bit with Sophia's father. At first, he was just glad to escape the commotion a little and find some peace in the kitchen, which was only separated from the rest of the dining and living area by a counter. He enjoyed watching Sophia from a distance. A free of all negative people Sophia, enchanted him just a little bit more. She was so detached and visibly happy. She seemed to be literally glowing.

He silently helped her father prepare the dessert, too caught up in how much he loved her. At that thought, she turned to him as if he had called her and she flung him that smile that blew him away every single moment.

"Thank you."

"Sure, no problem, Paul." Nick smiled at his father-in-law-to-be and was about to carry the dessert to the dining table when he held him back.

"Not for this," his gaze wandered to his daughter, "for that." He took a deep breath as if he had to brace himself for something. "At last she's so cheerful again, she's positively radiant."

Nick knew that Sophia's father, as witty and talkative as he was, was not a man of big words either and appreciated the compliment all the more. Even though he was still very sorry that he had been the cause of her grief for a long time.

"Yeah, she's like the light." He admitted, which earned him a knowing grin.

Then they went back to the others and while they ate the dessert, actually all of them already much too full for the ice cream cake, Nick dwelled on his thoughts. If he had his way, he would marry Sophia right away. He just didn't want to wait any longer, to finally be able to officially tell everyone that she was his wife and he, her husband. Pride filled him that she really belonged to him, that she wanted to tie this bond.

Again, Sophia looked at him at that very moment and her eyes seemed to say exactly the same thing. Their gazes lingered on each other for a moment. As if they were alone, everything else faded into the background.

The two of them did not notice how Sophia's parents exchanged a glance and were happy that the two of them had found each other. Even though it hadn't even been two months since Halloween, they saw this serious connection between them that the two of them probably didn't even realise. They watched them for the rest of the evening. Even though they were apart from one another in terms of space, they seemed to be one. Like the shadow that belonged indivisibly to a person.

Without the light, it could not exist.

Sophia and Nick talked about these words that her obviously moved mother had whispered to them before the rest of Sophia's family had gone to bed. They tidied up the mountains of gift-wrapping paper before dropping, exhausted but happy, onto the sofa where they would also sleep.

Sophia's back was pressed against his chest and they held their hands intertwined. Silently they looked at the ring on her finger, on which the glow of the candles in the room and the small lights from the Christmas tree drew a golden light.

Sophia felt exactly the same as Nick. It was her ring. No flourishes, no flashy diamonds. It was an intertwined bond, a symbol of attachment.

"It's old and beautiful." Sophia kissed Nick's fingers, which brushed over the ring. "Just like you." She teased him giggling, although the six-year age difference was of course in no way a problem. It was simply a little gag between them.

For he growled as expected as he pulled her tighter against him before whispering in her ear: "I'll show you what I do with young, naughty things like you ..."

That earned him a shiver before they became a little more serious and started playing around with the ring some more. The last few weeks had been so intense, so exhausting and also tragic, yet they had given each other strength and support. It was as if everything had passed by them in a wild frenzy, a whirlpool that had swept them both away, and yet the other was the anchor that held them steady.

Once again Nick had the image of their very first meeting in his mind's eye, how she stumbled into his arms in slow motion, the leaves dancing around her. It had started for them both then and here they were now.

Sophia turned to him at that very moment, her head and heart so full of words and feelings that she couldn't get any of them out. She just looked deep into his eyes, those ocean blue, soul-deep eyes. She caressed his face.

"The ring, this bond has no visible start and no visible end." Nick remarked in a hoarse voice and kissed her behind the ear.

"That's the way it should be, it can't come loose." Her voice was just a whisper.

Nick nodded before leaning down to kiss her gently.

"Yes."

His words tenderly brushed her lips before he looked firmly into her eyes to find exactly the words, they were both thinking.

"Just as this bond between us."

Notes

p. 63, Nick listens to the song "Just the way you are" by Bruno Mars from the album "Doo-Wops & Hooligans".

P. 76 ff, "Pielsand" is an invented town, the word *Pielsand* is Low German and means flying sand.

p. 219, the (incomplete) quotation from Jane Austen's *Persuasion*

p. 300, the poem is by Friedrich Rückert. Source: Rückert, Poems. "Wisdom of the Brahmans", 1836-1839

p. 306, Ruben sings the song "New York, New York" (exact song title: *Theme from New York, New York*), written by Fred Ebb and John Kander.

THANK YOU

I would like to thank some very special people for their immense help and support:

My beloved sister Anja,
my lovely friends Alina, Jenn & Nicola,
all the readers of my fanfictions who encouraged me to write
a novel.

Furthermore, I would like to thank all of you who gave this story of Sophia & Nick a chance.